BETWEEN HERE AND THE HORIZON

CALLIE HART

BETWEEN HERE AND THE HORIZON
Copyright © 2016 Callie Hart

All rights reserved.
No part of this publication may be reproduced, distributed, or transmitted in any form or by any means, including photocopying, recording, or other electronic or mechanical methods, without the prior written permission of the author, except in the case of brief quotations embodied in critical reviews and certain other noncommercial uses permitted by copyright law. For permission requests, write to the author, addressed "Attention: Permissions Coordinator," at callie@calliehart.com

This is a work of fiction. Any resemblance to peoples either living or deceased is purely coincidental. Names, places and characters are figments of the author's imagination, or, if real, used fictitiously. The author recognises the trademarks and copyrights of all registered products and works mentioned within this work.

Formatting by Max Effect
    www.formaxeffect.com

1. KEEP THE CHILDREN CALM.

2. KEEP THE CHILDREN SAFE.

CHAPTER ONE

AFGHANISTAN
2009

"*Get back, Fletcher! Get back! The tank's gonna blow!*"

I was running. Behind me, seven miles of desert stretched out toward Kabul city, glowing in places where burned out military trucks were being devoured by fire. Twisted metal rained down from the sky, on fire and sharper than a razor's edge, impacting in the dirt. *Thud. Thud, thud. Thud.* Shrapnel whistled through the air, striking the ground a few feet away from me as I weaved my way through the wreckage. Smoke was biting at my lungs, acrid and burning, making it hard to breath.

"*Fletcher! What the fuck, man!*"

Behind me, Specialist Crowe was losing his mind. Alternating between shouting into his radio and shouting at me, he couldn't seem to decide which course of action to take. I'd ordered him to follow, but I could understand why he hadn't. The situation was more than unsafe; charging headlong into the fire and destruction was a suicide mission, and I knew it. I also knew that my men were trapped inside the upturned vehicle still a hundred feet ahead of me, however, and I knew the truck was going to blow any second. They were going to burn to death if I didn't help them. I wasn't going to abandon them to that fate.

"*Captain! God, man, stop!*"

My heart was surging, my veins overflowing with adrenalin. My boots hit the dirt, *left, right, left, right, left, right,* my fists pumping back and forth as I sprinted toward the truck that was laying on its roof up ahead. Through the fractured windshield, I could see Hellaman and Wicks still strapped into the front seats of the vehicle, upside down and unmoving. They were either unconscious or dead. Hopefully they were just out for the count, but there was a lot of blood splattered on the inside of the glass. A lot of blood.

Black smoke curled upward from the underside of the truck, and I could already hear the hissing sound of fuel burning and sizzling somewhere. Groaning. I could hear groaning, too.

I reached the truck just as something inside the engine caught fire, and Hellaman came to. His eyes were wide with pain and fear as I dropped down onto my belly next to the driver's side window, which was smashed out, small cubes of safety glass scattered into the dirt.

"Captain? Captain Fletcher. Shit, I can't breathe. I can't...breathe." His face was deathly pale, and his hands shook violently as he tried to claw at the seatbelt that was digging into his chest.

"It's okay. It's okay, Private. We're gonna get you out of there, okay? Just hold on a moment." My bowie knife was in my hand. I took it and made quick work of slashing through the webbing holding Hellaman in place. There was nothing I could do to cushion his fall. Slamming into the roof of the truck, Hellaman groaned weakly, and then passed out again, either from pain or from the shock, I didn't know. I stowed my blade and grabbed him by the shoulders, then wrestled him free through the window. His face was cut; his arms were striped with blood and running rivers of crimson out onto the ground. No time to be gentle, though. No time to be safe. I hooked my hands under his arms and I quickly jogged backwards, dragging him away from the wreckage. Twenty feet was enough.

I ran back to the truck. Flames were visibly licking at the underside of the vehicle now, snaking upward toward the night sky. Wick was still out cold. I ran around to the back of the truck and tried to force the loading doors open, but they were jammed closed, bent and warped, refusing to budge.

"*Shit.*"

Clang.

Clang.

Clang.

There was someone alive inside. Running out of time. Almost no time left. I positioned myself by the truck's rear right window, thanking god the thing was already splintered. The bulletproof windows on military trucks were no joke. You could take a semi automatic to them and it would take longer than I had to smash them. The impact of rolling three times had obviously been enough to compromise the glass, though.

"Shield your faces," I hollered. "*Glass, glass, glass!*" Bracing, I spun around and smashed the sole of my boot against the window as hard as I possibly could. The glass groaned, fracturing some more, but it didn't shatter. I kicked again, and again, and again. Finally, the window exploded in a shower of bright shards, giving in under the force of my boot.

"Captain, there's fuel in here," someone inside yelled. "Get back!"

I ducked down and lay flat on my stomach again, crawling in through the now empty window frame. Inside the truck, gasoline hung heavy in the air, burning my nostrils and my eyes. Next to me, Roberts was dead, his head twisted at an odd angle, eyes staring, unseeing into the abyss.

On the other side of the truck Private Coleridge, Sam, a nineteen-year-old kid from Houston, was lying on his back on the roof, holding his rifle in both hands, his body convulsing wildly. His eyes swivelled to look at me, but his head remained locked in position, his teeth grinding together.

"What...what happened, Capt'n?" he asked. "We were drivin' along, and then...everything was...spinning."

"IED," I told him. "Desert's full of them. Come on, let's get you out of here."

"I can't...move. I can't feel...anything."

He wasn't paralyzed. If he were, he wouldn't be shaking the way he was right now. He was just in shock. A sharp slap to the face would probably go a long way to getting him moving, but there simply wasn't time for that kind of motivation. Grabbing him by the webbing stitched onto the strap of his pack, which was still on his back, I hauled him to me and then backed out through the window as quickly as I could. The fire was raging now. I dragged Sam back to where I'd left Hellaman and was about to run back to the truck when a loud metallic crack split the air apart, and then a ball of fire rocked the truck, a wall of heat and pressure slamming into my body, sending me reeling back into the dirt.

"*Oscar!*" Sam yelled. "Oscar's still alive in there!"

"*Fuck.*" I was up on my feet and running. The heat was intense—so intense that I had to shield my face as I grew closer to the wreck. The fire had consumed the underside of the truck, the tires blazing, the gas roaring as the fuel line was engulfed. And I could hear screaming. The kind of blood curdling, awful screaming of a man being burned alive.

My radio headset crackled with static, and then Colonel Whitlock's voice barked out through the speaker. "Fletcher, do *not* go back inside that vehicle. Do you hear me? Do not go back inside that vehicle."

Disobeying a direct order from a colonel was an offense worthy of court marshal. I ripped my headset from my ears and threw it to the ground, ignoring it. Ignoring the consequences. Another blood curdling scream reached me, and that was it. I was on my stomach, crawling into the mouth of hell.

My side pressed up against the frame of the window, and pain tore at me, sinking its teeth into my skin. Heat. The heat was overwhelming, so fierce and violent that there was no oxygen inside the truck. Only smoke and confusion. Only death.

"Oscar!" I called out, reaching with both hands, trying to find him. "Where are you, man?" The truck was only a six-guy transport, but the billowing, rolling clouds of black smoke hid everything. I went by touch until I heard him cry out again, weaker this time, voice riddled with agony. He was at the very rear of the truck. A few seconds was all

I had. Any longer and I would either suffocate or burn up myself. My head was pounding, my lungs begging for clean air, and I could feel myself start to drift.

The journey to the back of the truck took an eternity. One hand over the other, I pulled myself around an upturned transport box, and jammed my body in between the narrow gap at the right hand side of the vehicle, reaching out, groping, searching, until I found what I was looking for. A leg. A foot, to be precise. I grabbed hold of it and pulled. An agonised yell filled the truck.

"Ahh, my leg. My leg. It's fucked!"

"I know. I'm sorry, man. I can't get you any other way." I gritted my teeth, and I pulled. In any other situation it would have been a crime that I was handling an injured man this way. The clock was running down, though, and if causing more pain, causing even more damage meant the difference between one of my guys being injured or being dead, then I was going to do what I had to do.

I somehow managed to maneuverer myself so that I was over Oscar—I couldn't even see his face, the smoke was so thick—and then I started shoving. Six hard pushes and I managed to drive him through the gap in the window frame, out onto the desert floor. His body was ripped away, pulled free by someone else, and then he was gone. I was almost too tired to heave myself free, but I scrounged up my last scrap of energy and I crawled forward, determined to make it out before the entire vehicle was enveloped. Halfway out, my fingers clawing in the dirt, my body lit up with pain. Indescribable. Unbearable. A pain so sharp and breathtaking that I couldn't even cry out. It felt like something was ripping my body in two. I spun around and looked up to see a burning line of fuel pouring down on me, hitting my side, burning into me. I was on fire.

I kicked and jerked myself out of the truck, ripping at my jacket. Tearing at the material, trying to get it off. The fabric seemed to come away in my hands, and then I was shirtless in the cold, cold desert, rolling on the ground, trying to put the flames out.

The world went black. Someone threw something over me, and

then hands were beating at my body, slapping and trying to roll me. A strangled gasp worked its way out of my mouth, but that's all I could manage. The flames were out. The thick, heavy material that had been thrown over me was pulled back, and Crowe stood over me, face covered in soot and grease, eyes the size of dollar coins. I could barely see him properly. Barely hear the words coming out of his mouth.

Colonel Whitlock appeared next to him, and then the sky was filled with the beating thump of helicopter blades. They spoke for a second, and the thundering drum of the helo overhead dipped long enough for me to make out what Crowe said to Whitlock.

"He didn't stop, sir. He didn't stop until they were all out."

Whitlock scowled. "I can see that, Specialist. He disobeyed a direct order in doing so, too."

"He'll be reprimanded?" Crowe asked. He was speaking as if I was no longer present; both of them were.

"No," Whitlock said sternly. "Ironically, I think Captain Fletcher's more likely to be honored than punished in this particular instance. Now get him on the chopper before I change my mind. The crazy bastard's bleeding everywhere."

CHAPTER TWO

THE LAW OF ODDS

I had been waiting for disaster to strike all my life.

It had seemed, for want of a more intelligent, rational explanation, *inevitable*. Ever since I was old enough to read the paper or tune into the evening news, I had been bombarded with people losing their loved ones in terrorist attacks, cars crashing and burning, trains derailing, bank robberies turned horribly wrong. Every day, some natural disaster or terrifying violence splintered the world in two. Everywhere you looked someone's life was lying in ruins, irreparably damaged and unrecognizable.

I'd spent the last five years, since I moved out of my parents' house in Manhattan Beach, California, wondering when it would be my time. When would the bomb go off on *my* bus? When would *I* get held up at knifepoint for my fourth generation iPhone? When would *I* not look where I was going and step out in front of a Mac truck?

It was a matter of playing an odds game, after all, and no matter how hard I tried to avoid thinking that way, it seemed unreasonable to assume that tragedy wouldn't visit my doorstep at some point in my life. Until that time I was simply holding my breath, waiting. Perhaps it would happen tomorrow. More likely, it would happen today, as the plane I'd boarded to travel from one side of the country to another, all the way from L.A. to New York, crashed into the Hudson. It had already happened once in recent years. No reason why it wouldn't happen again.

My stomach tumbled over itself as the plane pitched to one side, swinging dramatically to the left, circling wide over New York. Out of the window next to me, the city sprawled in every direction for as far as the eye could see, only coming to an abrupt halt in the distance where steel colored water ate up the horizon.

I was being stupid. I knew the plane wasn't going to crash, but I couldn't seem to convince myself that I was perfectly safe when we were hurtling through the air toward so much concrete and glass and metal.

"Miss Lang?" The woman sitting next to me smiled, patting my hand reassuringly. "I just wanted to wish you luck again. I'm sure you'll do just fine, y'know. These things, these job interviews—" She waved her hand dismissively. "They're never as scary as you assume they're gonna be. And you being such a lovely, charming girl and all? I'm sure everything's going to work out just fine." She hadn't stopped talking the entire six-hour flight. I'd had the full rundown, gotten most of her life story in between the marginally unpleasant in-flight meal that came around somewhere over Colorado and the lone glass of gin and tonic I threw back somewhere closer to Indiana: her name was Margie Fenech, fifty-eight years old, and she had three grown sons, all of whom were now married, but boy if they weren't any one of them would have just loved to date me. She'd been patting my hand and touching my arm like we were old friends for hours now, and to be honest I hadn't minded. Not one bit. The contact, if anything, had been reassuring.

There were breaks in between her constant chattering, where she'd asked me questions about myself and I felt obliged to respond in kind. She'd easily managed to wheedle out of me my purpose for visiting New York in the middle of the week. She knew all about my parents' struggling restaurant back in the South Bay. I'd told her of the illusive Ronan Fletcher, about whom I knew a few sporadic facts: he was ex-military, the recipient of the Purple Heart, so obviously a bit of a badass. His wife had died last year, leaving him with two young children to care for. And his personal net worth was pretty up there, somewhere close to the billion-dollar mark. Margie also knew that I hated flying, and she knew that I had no stomach for turbulence; in her own way I supposed she was trying to distract me from the abrupt angle to the ground the plane had adopted now that it was coming in for its final approach to land.

"Yes. Yes, I'm sure it'll be okay. Has to be, right?" I said, flashing a brief, watery smile in her direction.

"Oh sure, sweetheart. If you take care of those little kiddies for six whole months, think about all the money you can save to help out your parents. You said it yourself. You won't have any expenses. And you won't know anyone in the city, so you won't be out wasting your money every night of the week like some youngsters are prone to do."

I objected to being called a "youngster" on a very deep level. I was twenty-eight years old, past the point in my life where I was out partying and frittering away my money every weekend. I'd been an elementary school teacher for the past five years, paying my bills, saving fifteen percent of my income religiously every paycheck, squirrelling away my funds in order to buy a house. I thought those were all very grownup things to have been doing for such a long time. I'd still have been doing them if the public school I'd been working for hadn't had to close down due to insufficient government funding, too. I lost my job along with the rest of the school faculty four months ago, around about the same time Mom and Dad pulled me aside and told me, embarrassedly, that the restaurant was going under. They hadn't asked for help, but I'd seen that they'd needed it. Needed it badly. So there went my savings. All of it. Now I had no more money saved to give them, and no job to make any more, which was how I found myself on this plane next to Margie, on my way to interview for a glorified babysitting job on the other side of the country.

I didn't know how it had come to this. I should have been able to find another teaching job, but it was the middle of the school year and all positions had been filled. Support teaching was fine, but it was also sporadic and unreliable and I needed a steady income to make sure I could keep Mom and Dad afloat. When the agency I signed up with called and told me about Ronan Fletcher and his two young children, I hadn't had much of a choice but agree to accept the all-expenses paid trip across the States to meet with this strange, wealthy individual and find out what he's looking for.

"How old are the children again?" Margie asked. My arm got a squeeze this time.

"I'm not sure. I think the file said five and seven."

Margie pulled an impressed face. "So young. And you say you don't have any children of your own yet?" I got the impression that she thought I was ill equipped to deal with the challenge of dealing with a five and a seven-year-old.

"No, I don't actually want children," I said. "I love taking care of the kids at school, but I don't plan on having my own."

"Oh, goodness, sweetie, why on earth not? Being a mother…it's the most miraculous thing. My life just wouldn't be the same without those boys of mine."

Over time, I'd learned that telling people I *couldn't* have children always made them uncomfortable. It was always better to lie. To make something up. *My lifestyle's too hectic for dependents. I'm just not a maternal person.* Anything was easier than explaining that I was married once, for a grand total of eighteen months, before I found out it was unlikely I was ever going to be able to conceive. My son of a bitch ex hadn't taken the news well. He *had* taken the cash sitting in our joint savings account—thank god it wasn't everything—and he *had* taken off with my best friend. Last I'd heard, they'd just had their first kid together, a little girl, and they were living up in San Francisco.

I smiled blankly at Margie, shrugging my shoulders. "I'm sure motherhood's wonderful. It's just not for me."

Margie's brow creased, as if she couldn't comprehend what could possibly be mentally wrong with me. "That's okay, sweetie," she said. "You'll probably change your mind, you know. One day you'll just wake up and all of a sudden—" She jostled into me as the plane's wheels touched down. Somewhere at the back of the plane, a lone person started clapping. Margie looked momentarily side tracked, while I did my best to wrestle my heart back into its rightful spot in my chest, out from where it had lodged itself high in my throat.

"There. That wasn't so bad, was it?" Margie asked. She seemed to have forgotten all about the sentence she was halfway through just now. I was glad for it, too. I'd heard the whole, *you'll wake up one morning and just need to have a baby*. The *it'll hit you like a wrecking ball, and you won't be able to deny your body* bit. The problem was that I'd already woken up and felt it, that call deep in my bones, but my body had denied *me*, and I'd been having to deal with that sorrowful reality ever since.

"*Attention all passengers. Please remain seated with your seatbelts fastened until the pilot has turned off the seatbelt sign. When opening overhead lockers, please proceed with caution, as items may have moved during the flight and are at risk of falling.*" Over the tinny loudspeakers, a pre-recorded message continued to loop, warning the passengers on the oversized Airbus A380—barely a quarter full—that increased security measures within the airport might mean extended waiting time for disembarkation and baggage collection. I was barely listening. I already felt too crowded, my throat swelling a little, tiny beads of sweat bursting through the pores of my skin, sending cold chills dancing over my stomach and down my arms.

"Do they still have a monument?" I asked abruptly. "You know, where the World Trade Center used to be."

Margie stopped rooting in her cracked black leather purse and looked at me sharply. She was somewhere between feeling intensely sorry for me and a little wary of me all of a sudden. "Why, of course they do, honey. Why on earth wouldn't they?"

I looked out of the window, away from her, not wanting to trade in strange expressions. "I don't know. It seems like such a long time ago now. People...they forget."

"Oh, no. No, that's not likely to *ever* happen. New York doesn't forget. We'll remember those poor people for generations. Until the city falls into the sea. Probably longer."

An hour and a half later, I was swearing under my breath, sweating, cursing myself out for not giving myself longer to get from the airport to the Fletcher building. West 23rd and 6th was a long old way from JFK, and I only had twelve minutes to spare as I hopped out of the cab and dashed inside the imposing, tall, spear-like glass structure that seemed to rocket up out of the sidewalk.

The lobby of the Fletcher building was modest and simple but spoke of money. The floors were cool, polished marble, and the seating area set back to the right was comprised of beautiful gray leather armchairs that looked like they cost more than my car back in L.A. I hurried to the reception desk, frantically patting down my hair, hoping against hope that I didn't look completely frazzled, which I undoubtedly did. The woman behind the desk glanced up at me and smiled.

"How may I help you?" she asked. Her voice was smooth and cool, but not unfriendly. Her bright blonde hair was swept back into a perfectly styled coiffeur that made me want to weep with jealousy.

"My name is Ophelia Lang. I have a four o'clock appointment with Mr. Fletcher."

"Ahh, yes. Miss Lang. One moment, please." She rolled back in her chair and opened a drawer at her side, from which she produced a small laminated name badge with my photograph on it. She slid the laminate across the counter toward me, smiling. "It's a good picture," she informed me. "Most of the time they look awful."

I glanced down at the photo and grimaced. It was more of a mug shot than an identification picture. I looked startled. My eyes, usually green, were tinged with red somehow, so I looked fairly demonic. The contrast on the image was way off, too, so that my long, light brown hair seemed almost black. My tan was non-existent, and my lips looked blood red. Basically, I looked like a vampire.

I gave the receptionist a polite, awkward smile anyway. "Thanks."

She leaned forward and placed a hand on my forearm, speaking very softly. "Don't look so worried. Mr. Fletcher can be a bit of a cold fish sometimes, but he's a decent guy. He's fair, and he's a good boss. Everything's going to be okay."

I had no idea why she felt the need to reassure me, but her words actually slowed my pulse from racing quite as fast, and that was something.

"You'd better head on up to the penthouse office now, though, Miss Lang." She pointed at a bank of elevators on the other side of the lobby. "While he may be a good boss, he also really does hate when people are late."

CHAPTER THREE

THE OFFER

A stern looking security guard escorted me up in the elevator to Fletcher's office.

I hadn't travelled much. A weekend in Arizona here. A trip to Vegas there. I'd only been out of the States once, when Dad stumped up for a ten-day trip to Canada for the family—a graduation present, back when the restaurant was doing much better and money was nowhere near as tight. As I stepped into Ronan Fletcher's private offices on the thirty-first floor, which also just so happened to be the very highest floor of the Fletcher Corporation building, I was accosted by the strangest, most wonderful sights, from countries I doubted I'd ever get to visit: African tribal face masks made out of intricately carved wood. Japanese silk fans, beautifully painted, perched on the walls like rare butterflies. Russian Faberge eggs the size of my fist, seated in gilded golden stands on walnut sideboards. A glass case ran along the entire length of the right-hand wall, where an array of golden necklaces and hammered copper earrings were arranged with delicate precision on top of rich, ruby red velvets. It looked more like a museum exhibition than an office. If it weren't for the huge, imposing desk, complete with a ginormous iMac that sat directly in front of the wall of floor to ceiling glass windows, overlooking the city, then I'd have thought I'd stepped into the Natural History Museum and not someone's place of work.

"Mr. Fletcher will be with you in a moment," the guard told me.

"Have a seat. And don't touch anything."

I wouldn't have touched anything anyway—everything looked like it cost more than my life was worth. I sat myself down on the other side of the desk and tried not to fidget. I checked my watch: Three fifty-nine. Four o'clock. Four oh-one. Four oh-two. Ronan Fletcher was officially late. Unbelievable, really, given what the receptionist had just told me. Two further minutes passed, and I began to think that maybe Fletcher had already left to attend to his children, but then a door to the right opened and in walked the man himself, pulling on the white cuffs of his sleeves as he hurried into the room.

I watched him, dumbstruck, as he seated himself opposite me. Not what I had been expecting at all. Ronan Fletcher wasn't some stuffy, overweight trader with an extended gut from too many late night, fat-loaded meals and beers at his desk. He was tall, over six feet; he would have dwarfed my five-foot-eight frame if we were to stand side-by-side. Dark hair, and dark eyes; he could easily have been of Italian descent by his coloring, but his skin was pale. His shoulders were broad, his arms muscular, straining at the expensive looking material of his button-down shirt. He didn't look up at me until he had himself settled into his chair.

When he lifted his head and finally pinned me in his gaze, I was stunned by the harsh angles and lines of his face. They were magnificent—a rough sketch in charcoal, torn out of Michelangelo's notebook, all sweeping, bold strokes. Strong jawline. High cheek bones. Perfectly straight nose. His bottom lip was fuller than the top, formed into a perfect Cupid's bow. There was no denying it: the man was a work of art, as rare and exquisite as any of the artifacts mounted on his walls.

"Hello, Miss Lang," he said coolly. "Thank you for taking the time to come out to New York. I know what an inconvenience it must have been." His voice was lilting, a subtle melody teasing at the cadence of his words. Such a strange accent. One I couldn't place.

"Not at all." From my breezy tone, it sounded like I really meant it, that the journey really wasn't a huge thing for me and I hadn't minded it at all. Fletcher's dark eyebrows dipped ever so slightly as he frowned.

"Some people don't enjoy flying," he said. "I'm glad to hear everything went smoothly for you, though, Miss Lang. Apologies that we couldn't meet in Los Angeles, however my schedule has been rather punishing recently. There have been a lot of loose ends that needed tying up."

I nod. "Of course. It's wasn't a problem."

"Well, thank you regardless. Your punctuality and professional appearance in the face of such a long journey is very impressive. Professionalism is paramount to me, Ophelia. May I call you Ophelia?"

"Yes, of course."

"Good. You'll call me Ronan, too. Especially if we're in front of the children." I didn't expect him to say that. I'd thought I would need to call him Mr. Fletcher or Sir or something. Addressing him by his first name seemed like an alien concept. Far too personal. Ronan must have seen the surprise flicker across my face. "The children don't need another strict, formal nanny, Ophelia. They don't need another of my ass-kissing employees hovering around them twenty-four seven. They need a friend. That's what I'm looking for in the successful candidate for this role."

"I see. I can do that," I said.

"Good. Now. Why don't we begin by you telling me about yourself and your experience as a teacher?"

I had always hated this part of interviews. Ronan must have already read my resume at length—he would never have paid to fly me out to New York if he hadn't read my credentials—so it was frustrating that companies and individuals alike always went through the tired process of having you run down your skill sets and capabilities. It seemed like such a waste of time. I could hardly tell him that, though, so I obliged him.

Degree in social sciences and photography. Master's in English literature and language. A diploma in statistical mathematics that I really only did for fun a couple of years ago. I explained about my time at Saint Augustus's, detailing the extra roles I took on within the school, providing tutoring after hours for students who wanted or needed it.

"And the children at your school were all well adjusted? Did you have to work with any...*problem* children?"

Oh, boy. That seemed like a leading question. Were his kids little terrors, disruptive, incapable of behaving themselves? If they were, it wasn't a big deal. I'd had to deal with plenty of spoiled shits back home, over privileged and entitled, who thought you were their servants, at their beck and call whenever the mood took them. "I've dealt with a number of kids who had difficulties, yes."

"Speak plainly, Ophelia. There's no room for political correctness here. When you say difficulties, what do you mean?" His voice had little to no inflection as he spoke. Everything about him was calm and devoid of emotion, though his dark eyes sparked with an intelligence that was more than a little intimidating.

"Problem" was always a dirty word at St. Augustus's. We were never allowed to make a student feel any less than anyone else in class, so we'd have to use words like *challenged*, or *high energy*. It seemed as though Ronan Fletcher wanted to get down to brass tacks, though. "Problems with authority. Issues with violence, and with aggression. Some of the kids refused to cooperate on any level. Some could be unresponsive. Physically and verbally abusive at times."

"Were you ever tempted to respond in kind? When you were attacked physically or verbally?" His words were said with complete and utter detachment, which was at odds with the reaction they inspired inside me. Rage fluttered in the pit of my belly, burning quickly outwards, flushing through my body.

"No! Absolutely not. Even if teachers were allowed to manhandle children, which we're obviously *not*, I would never physically discipline a student. It's not our place. And children can be hurtful to the people surrounding them at the best of times. If they're feeling vulnerable or threatened in any way by the situation they find themselves in, they lash out. It's my job to make them feel safe and comfortable, so they don't need to curse and swear, or say horrible things. It would be counterproductive for me to respond in any way to that kind of behavior." I knew he was testing me; he had to make sure I was a suitable role model to care for his children, but asking such a blatant, awful question was borderline offensive. Ronan remained impassive, hands stacked in his lap, leaning back in his chair, watching me.

"Okay. Let's discuss your availability. The agency I hired to fill this position said you weren't working at the moment. Why is that?"

"The school closed down. I wasn't fired, if that's what you're implying. All the staff at St. Augustus's were made redundant." I could feel myself growing pricklier by the second, but I couldn't seem to help myself. There was something infuriating about the way he was asking his questions that made me feel inferior and unqualified to essentially babysit his children. I didn't like it. I didn't like it one bit.

"*I see.*" In that small statement, Ronan Fletcher made me feel as though it were my fault that St. Augustus's had gone under. My fault that the funds couldn't be raised to keep the school going; My fault that the other faculty members had lost their jobs, too. In my head, I was reeling, all kinds of excuses and explanations dancing on the tip of my tongue, begging to be unleashed. I didn't utter a word, though. I just sat there, hollowed out and miserable, as Ronan seemed to consider his next move.

"So you would be available to start immediately?" he said finally.

"I would." I was surprised he was even bothering to check this information, given how clear it was that he didn't think me fit for the job.

"And do you get sea sick?

"I'm sorry?"

"Sea sick. There's a considerable amount of boat travel involved in this job."

I just stared at him blankly. "I would have to cross the river a lot?"

"Not the Hudson, no. I need someone to care for my children in my hometown, which just so happens to be on a remote island off the coast of Maine. There is a six-mile ferry journey between the mainland and The Causeway, and sometimes the waters can be pretty rough. The position is a six-month contract, as I'm sure the agency explained to you. You will have two days off a week, and the children's aunt will also be on hand to assist in their care. Ideally, the successful candidate for this role will take care of the children during the day, making them breakfast, taking them to school after the new year, once they're enrolled at the local elementary. Collecting them and helping them with any homework, playing with them in the evenings etc. Before they are able to go to the local school, both Connor and Amie would need to be home schooled.

"Rose, their aunt, will take care of them two days of the week, as well as some evenings, which she can work out with the successful candidate once they have arrived on The Causeway." He said *"The Causeway"* like it was difficult for him to form the words in his mouth.

"An *island*?" He wanted me to leave the mainland? He wanted me to travel to some remote speck of land out in the ocean with him and his children? I couldn't quite manage to make the information sink in. I'd been devastated by the idea of being a six hour flight away on the other side of the country, but Mom had talked me down. She'd reminded me how easy it would be to jump on a plane in New York and get back to L.A. whenever I wanted, and cheap enough too, if I was earning decent money, but an island? Off the coast of Maine? That was not a simple hop, skip and a jump away. That was far more complicated indeed.

Ronan seemed unsettled as he continued, which didn't reassure me at all. "I was born on The Causeway," he explained. "I haven't been home in some time. If you were selected for the role, you would need to commit to traveling to the island and staying for a full six-month period."

"I wouldn't be able to fly back to L.A. on the weekends?"

Ronan shook his head. "Unfortunately that wouldn't be practical. It would take more than a full day to travel in each direction, and I would like someone on hand in case of an emergency. You're more than welcome to spend your free time as you want on the island, but I would prefer if you have your cell phone with you at all times, so Rose can reach you should she need to. I'm going to be writing a book, and so I won't be available for much of the time. Once the six-month contract is at an end, I'm hoping I can arrange for another family member to take care of Connor and Amie in my absence."

"I see. This…isn't really what I was expecting. Are the children okay with such a huge change of scenery?"

Ronan's expression grew cold, turning his perfect features to smooth, flawless marble. "Ever since their mother died this time last year, Connor and Amie are still…" He frowned, lips slightly parted as he seemed to search for the right word. "*Adjusting* to the loss. A change of scenery is exactly what they need."

Shit. I'd overstepped. I shouldn't have suggested he didn't know what was best for his kids. And the second he'd mentioned his wife's death, something had altered in him. Ronan was a storm now. A perfectly dangerous storm. I could see the clouds forming over his head, twisting and turning as a darkness seemed to overtake him. "Yes, of course. I'm sorry." My words were weightless, inconsequential, but they were all I could manage. What I could possibly say to rewind the past few minutes and reset the interview. Nothing fitting came to mind.

"It's of no consequence," he said hurriedly. "If you're offered the job, you will be given a file containing information you should know about Connor and Amie. Their personalities, their issues and their specific needs."

"I still…I don't think I can move to a remote island for six months, Mr. Fletcher. I'm sorry. I just can't."

"I told you, call me Ronan. And I'm aware a six-month contract such as this is a lot to ask, which is why the pay is so generous. I assume the agency told you what the salary was?"

I shook my head. "Generally that's discussed once the job's been awarded."

"I'm offering a hundred-thousand-dollar payout upon completion of the six-month term. During the six months on the island, you would receive a stipend to cover any costs you might incur through your work with the children, or your own personal requirements. This monthly sum is outside of the final one-hundred-thousand-dollar payment. Perhaps you'd like to think about what your answer will be should you be offered the job, Ophelia."

A hundred thousand dollars? My salary at St. Augustus's was only fifty-five thousand, and that was for an entire year. A hundred grand could solve a lot of problems at the restaurant. It could literally turn everything around for Mom and Dad. I just couldn't envisage it, though. Another state? Another time zone? A tiny little island off the coast, in the middle of nowhere? God, it was all too much to take in.

"I suppose you're right," I said. "I'd at least *think* about it if I were offered the job," I said. "It's a very tempting offer."

Ronan scratched his clean-shaven jaw, giving me a tight smile. "Excellent. Thank you, Ophelia. Then I suppose we shall be in touch soon to let you know one way or another."

"That's it?" I'd barely been sitting in the chair for twenty minutes. They told us repeatedly at the agency that a good, successful interview generally lasted anywhere between thirty minutes and an hour. A paltry twenty-minute conversation definitely wasn't going to impress them when I gave them telephone feedback tomorrow. Damn it. Who knew how many more people he was going to interview, or how many people he'd already seen? There was no way my bumbling explanation of my capabilities, followed by my hostile reaction to his line of questioning had made anything but a bad impression.

"Yes, Ophelia. I've heard all I need to hear. Thank you for coming all this way to meet with me." Ronan got to his feet, his composure well and truly regained now. "Please return your security pass to Davey, the security guard who showed you up here on your way out."

What the hell did he think I was going to try and do, break in here later and try to steal his confidential files or something? Ridiculous. I arranged my face into what I hoped looked like professional gratitude, but on the inside I was burning with disappointment, alongside a splash of anger. Getting to my feet, I hoped he didn't notice the identical flushed, red spots coloring my cheeks.

"Thank you, Ronan. I'll make sure I do that." I didn't offer my hand out to shake his, even though I knew I should. It would be ill advised to leave the interview on an awkward or discordant note, and yet I couldn't get myself to toe the line.

I felt naked for a moment, then collected my purse that I'd sat at my feet. I felt foolish as I turned away from Ronan Fletcher and walked quickly to the same elevator I came out of only a short while ago.

I almost expected the man behind me to call out to me, wish me a safe flight back to Los Angeles or something equally as polite and measured, but he didn't. He didn't speak another word. As the elevator doors closed, his figure was silhouetted against the bright afternoon sun blazing through the high windows behind him, and I couldn't see his face. I would always remember it, though. I would never be able to forget.

CHAPTER FOUR

PATIENCE

"The Causeway? That doesn't sound in the least bit exotic at all. Sounds cold if you ask me." No one *had* asked my mother, but that never seemed to matter to her. She'd always been one to voice her opinion, solicited or otherwise, and woe betide the poor bastard who ever disagreed with her. In light of this, I nodded sagely from the bussing station at the entrance to the kitchen while Mom shouted to me from the meat section, where she was cooking a pair of steaks. Dad was nowhere to be seen, as usual.

"It's a part of Maine, Mom. I don't think it's ever particularly warm there."

"And this Fletcher guy was rude to you?" I'd mentioned that Ronan hadn't exactly been warm in welcoming me or making me feel at ease, and she hadn't been able to let the matter drop. For three days I'd been telling her the same story over and over again, and her outrage hadn't dissipated a single iota. "And after that ridiculously long flight, too. I tell you, these big business guys in big cities, they're all the same. They must be the absolute worst in New York, though. The height of arrogance. Never mind, baby. You'll find work closer to home. You'll be able to come back to the South Bay in the evenings. And your father and I will be just fine, don't worry about us."

I was worried, though. I'd been worrying non-stop for the past year and no amount of plotting and planning appeared to be helping the situation. I'd seen the stack of envelopes on the kitchen counter this morning, all marked with "Final Notice" or "Passed Due." Mom had swept them deftly into the cutlery drawer when she noticed me helping myself to cereal, but she wasn't that stealthy a woman. There had been at least four envelopes there.

"I know, Mom. It's not a big deal. I would never have cut it on a tiny island, anyway. I would have gone crazy, especially if I couldn't even call you guys whenever I wanted to. The time difference would have been awful." It was only three hours, but with their busy schedule and my own, I would have missed my opportunity to talk to them most of the time.

"Ophelia?" Mom called. "While it's quiet, would you mind running upstairs to the office and seeing if there's any word from Waylan's? We were supposed to get a delivery this morning and nothing's shown up yet."

"Sure thing." Aside from the couple sitting at the table by the window, the restaurant was empty and lunch service was over. I had a few minutes to leave the floor, so I did as she asked, jogging up the stairs to check the online bookings and listen to the messages on the answering machine. There were seven new messages waiting. I hit the play button, sitting myself down in front of the prehistoric computer my Dad refused to get rid of, and the entire time the machine clicked through the messages (a call center, wondering if we want to renew our home owner's insurance; Aunt Simone, wanting Mom to call her back when she had a second; croaky, hoarse sounding old Mr. Robson, confirming the table for tomorrow night that he and his wife always reserved on a Sunday) I was holding my breath, waiting to hear that cool, calm voice with the strange lilt to it, telling me in no uncertain terms that I hadn't gotten the job, and I needn't bother googling Causeway Island anymore.

The message never came, though. That was probably the most frustrating part. I *knew* I hadn't gotten the job, but it would have been nice to be put out of my misery. It seemed highly irregular that Ronan

Fletcher hadn't even had one of his receptionists call or even email to let me know that someone else had filled the position. I didn't care. I didn't. At least that's what I kept telling myself. If I didn't recite to myself constantly that I didn't need that *particular* job, then my heart rate kept accelerating at the prospect of earning a hundred thousand dollars in a short six-month period, and I was on the verge of weeping at the missed opportunity. There were no messages in the email from Waylan's about our missing delivery. While I was there, I checked my personal email account to see if I had actually received something from the Fletcher Corporation there, but my inbox was notably empty.

Well, shit.

Damn Ronan Fletcher. Damn him for tempting me with all that money. Somehow he'd made me want a job I'd never have even truly considered before. I hadn't been lying earlier; I really would go crazy on a tiny little island, and the distance between Maine and California would have been brutal, but it would only have been for six months. I could have done it. I could have, if I'd really tried.

• • • •

My car was in the shop and hadn't been ready to collect when I'd returned from New York, so Dad drove us all home in the dusty, beaten-up 4Runner he'd had since I was in high school. Admittedly, the thing was still running perfectly, so there was no reason for him to replace it. Still, Dad had a thing about new technology, new cars, new anything. If it meant he'd have to learn how to navigate his way around some new system or software, he wasn't having any part of it. Not unless he absolutely had to. I sat in the back behind Mom, traveling the memorized route back to the house—a route so familiar and rote to me that the houses and gardens we passed felt like they had probably been there since the dawn of time, nothing ever changing, nothing ever evolving or growing, and I felt suddenly cut adrift. This was the life I'd had fifteen years ago. Yes, the sound of Mom and Dad bickering affectionately every morning over breakfast made me feel safe and warm, but the ritual of it all, working at the restaurant, going to sleep in the twin bed Mom had bought me for my twelfth birthday, shopping at the Save & Weigh and taking Mrs. Freeman's newspaper up her drive to her every morning, as I had done ever since she'd had her hip replacement surgery back in 2003, it all felt needlessly crushing, to the point where I felt like I couldn't breathe.

I closed my eyes and tracked out the rest of the journey home in my head, knowing exactly when the car would tilt and shift either left or right. Knowing exactly when we would turn onto our street. When we would turn into our driveway.

"Look, George. We missed another package," Mom said, as she got out of the car. Sure enough, a UPS *"Sorry We Missed You"* sticker was stuck to the front door, the lower half fluttering on the breeze.

"It'll be my new fishing gear," Dad said, looking over his shoulder to waggle his eyebrows at me. He loved his fishing almost as much as he loved my mom. His obsession with getting up to go stand on the pier at the crack of dawn every morning drove her crazy, though. She could never see the point in spending hours down there, waiting, wasting time (as she saw it) to catch fish that he couldn't even clean and bring home to eat, since the water wasn't clean enough. It gave Dad an unbelievable amount of pleasure to wind her up by telling he'd bought this new reel, or that new set of floats.

I could hear her swearing under her breath as she retrieved the UPS sticker from the door, scanning the note quickly, all the while threatening physical violence if he'd even dared to fritter away money they didn't have on fishing paraphernalia.

"It's not for you, George. It's for Ophelia," Mom said, holding it up. "Says legal documents in the description."

I'd received a fair number of those in the mail over the past year. My divorce settlement with Will had taken a while to clear—the bastard had tried to wheedle way more money out of me than he was entitled to—and so the paperwork had only recently come through for me to sign and file. I'd thought everything was finished and over with, though. Strange that there would be anything outstanding now that I didn't know about.

"You want me to go and get it?" Mom asked. The guy at the UPS store down the road had been there for years and knew us all by name; it was common for us to pick up mail and packages for each other if we were in the area.

"No, it's fine. I'll walk over there. I think I need to stretch my legs." I'd been on my feet all day, but I didn't feel like going inside just yet. Besides, walking always helped me clear my head.

At the UPS store, Jacob was sitting behind his desk, eating what looked like a pastrami sandwich. He looked up, guilt written all over his face. "Don't tell Bett," he said, grinning sheepishly. "She'll be down here monitoring my calorie intake every afternoon if she knows I'm not eating salad for lunch. My cholesterol's through the roof."

I pretended to zip my lips and throw away the key. "She'll never hear it from me," I told him. "You should probably alternate between the pastrami and the salad, though, Jacob. That uniform's looking a little tight around the midriff these days."

Used to a gentle teasing every once in a while, Jacob just rolled his eyes. "Take it you're here for that envelope I couldn't deliver earlier?"

"Yes, sir."

"Mind my sandwich for a moment while I go get it for you, then. And don't be sneaking a bite." Jacob heaved himself out of his seat and disappeared out back, returning only a few seconds later with the envelope in his hands. It was at least an inch thick, way heftier than I would have imagined any stray divorce documentation to be. "Could kill a man with this if you done drop it on his head," Jacob advised me. "What on earth you got in here, girl?"

"I don't know. I haven't got a clue. I thought it was lawyer stuff from Will, but..." I took the envelope from him, frowning. "I get the feeling it's something else entirely." I signed for the mail and left Jacob in peace, despite the fact that I knew how eager he was to find out what was inside the envelope.

When I got home, both Mom and Dad were in the yard, talking in hushed tones. Dread cycled through me whenever they did that—it meant something bad had happened. Something probably to do with money. Another letter in the mail, maybe. A phone call from a debt collector. Those were the worst. They put everyone in a spin for days, while we all rejigged what little assets we had and tried to find money to pay them off. I left them to it. No sense in making them feel even more awkward than they already did. Instead, I crept up the stairs and closed myself away in my room. I had no idea what was inside the envelope I held tightly in my hands, but I got the feeling that it was nothing good. Tearing back the seal a little at a time, I had to fight to force myself to open it all the way.

Inside: two photographs, a boy and a girl.

Two files in plastic wallets: Connor Fletcher, Age 7. Amie Fletcher, Age 5.

A blue, white and red business envelope, American Airlines. Inside, a business class flight to Knox County Airport, dated for two day's time.

At the bottom, underneath all of this baffling information, one handwritten note.

Ophelia,

I'm sure you've had plenty of time to consider my proposition by now. My children aren't like me. They're young and fragile, and they miss their mother. They need proper mentorship, as well as someone to call their friend. Neither Connor nor Amie have ever been to The Causeway. They know nothing of the world outside of New York and the home they shared here with their mother and me. If you would assist them (and me) during this huge transition stage, I would be eternally grateful.

Yours,
Ronan Fletcher

CHAPTER FIVE

THE CAUSEWAY

Another plane. Another journey. Two days hadn't been nearly close enough to get my affairs in order. I hadn't even had time to rethink my decision to accept the job. Perhaps that had been Ronan's plan all along, to stump me by requesting that I jump on a flight forty-eight hours after offering me the position, so I wouldn't have time to weigh up my options or chicken out. That's what would have happened, I'm sure. Given enough breathing room, I would have talked myself out of it. The Causeway was too far away. What if something happened to Mom or Dad, or with the restaurant?

Mom had burst into tears when I'd told her about the plane ticket and files on the children. She'd been so guilty, didn't want me to leave, didn't want me to feel like I had to. Dad had told me over and over again that we'd figure it out if I didn't want to go, but I could see on his face that he was relieved. If I did this, stuck out six months on a tiny island in the middle of nowhere, I'd come back with enough cash to solve all of the financial problems with the restaurant, and there would probably be enough left over to do a few renovations here and there, spruce the place up a little. If I didn't, the place was going under and that was a fact. Two, maybe three months—that was how long we might have been able to limp along, scraping money together to keep the place open another day.

In the end, the decision had been obvious, though sad.

And so here I was, on another plane. Wheels up. Thirty thousand feet. Another gin and tonic, and another bad airplane meal.

I'd had plenty of time during the seven-hour journey over the country to review the children's files. Connor and Amie. Through the yo-yoing and the indecision of the past few days, I hadn't really considered the small people I was being charged to care for. Normally the children were all I ever considered. From reading the files, both Connor and Amie seemed like your average five and seven-year-olds. Connor loved soccer and apparently wanted to be a zookeeper when he grew up. The first part of his file held records of his favorite food (pasta), his favorite color (orange), his favorite animal (Zebra), and many other small facts that would undoubtedly make it easier to build a bridge with the boy. The later part of his file, however, was way more comprehensive. It contained what turned out to be notes from numerous sessions with a Brooklyn child psychologist by the name of Dr. Hans Fielding.

"Connor demonstrates an unwillingness to comply with authority. Upon speaking with his father, I have confirmed Connor was a happy, lighthearted, fun-loving child before the death of his mother five months ago, but since then has been belligerent and often prone to bouts of anger and depression. This is all to be expected, of course."

And—

"Eight months after his mother's death, and Connor is showing little sign of movement in what might be considered a positive direction. Connor is unfortunately yet to acknowledge the death of his mother. His refusal to believe she is gone denotes an underlying emotional flux within the child, whereby he is not yet emotionally mature enough to handle the deep and painful realities of grief and loss. It is crucial that Connor accepts his mother's death, and soon, otherwise the fantasy in which he maintains she is still alive may become a deep seeded and vital aspect of his personality."

Ten months after Mrs. Fletcher's death, it seemed Connor had a breakthrough, though.

"The time Mr. Fletcher has been spending with Connor has clearly

affected a change in the child. Brighter, more responsive, and generally more positive, Connor appears to have emerged from the fugue of sadness that has gripped him since last May. I'm relieved to hear Connor talk about his mother during our sessions now. Though admitting that she is dead obviously still causes him great distress, Connor frequently mentions her in the past tense. During the joint session where both Connor and his father attend my offices, Connor has expressed a desire to lay flowers at his mother's grave. I encouraged this whole-heartedly. While difficult for Connor, I can only imagine that visiting Mrs. Fletcher's grave would provide a sense of closure for the child. Perhaps even for Mr. Fletcher, too."

My heart ached for the poor kid. The last entry in the notes from Dr. Fielding's office was dated October seventeenth, a month ago, and in his entry Fielding raved about the remarkable progress the boy was making. That made me less anxious to meet him, but still. To lose a parent so young? God, it didn't even bear thinking about.

I was less worried about Amie. She had the same amount of paperwork in her file, the same amount of detail. She wanted to be the tooth fairy when she grew up. Her favorite color was green, and her favorite animal was a dinosaur. She'd clearly spent just as much time with Dr. Fielding as Connor had, too, although his records of their meetings were far less intimidating.

"Amie, like many children her age, has adjusted to this new circumstance very rapidly. Her sadness over her mother's death is something that overcomes her on occasion, however for the most part she remains a calm, happy, bright child. Mr. Fletcher's concern over her is understandable. I have advised him that he should make sure to spend plenty of quality time with her, to ensure she doesn't feel abandoned by both parents. I have urged him to reconsider taking a leave of absence from work, even if only for a short period of time. He has informed me he will do his best to make that happen. In the meantime, I am happy to advise only a biweekly appointment for Amie, unlike Connor, who I would still like to see twice a week."

The photos of the children that had come with the file were rather odd. I'd have thought Fletcher might have sent one of the two of them, smiling and happy, perhaps from before the mysterious tragedy that had claimed their mother. Instead the pictures of Connor and Amie were taken separately, each of them on their own. Connor had a look of his father about him—a halo of dark hair that flicked and curled all over the place, and dark, soulful eyes that stared straight out at me from the image. Both cheeks were heavily dimpled, and must have been even more so when the boy smiled. As it stood, Connor remained stony-faced as he stared down the camera lens, no flicker of emotion caught in the shadows and highlights of his face. He wore a white button-down shirt, done up high under his chin, and a pair of plain khaki shorts that showed off his gangly, skinny legs. It was clear he was going to be tall, just like Ronan.

In Amie's photograph, she was sitting Indian style on an Adirondack chair, propped up with a blue and white striped cushion behind her, and she was looking somewhere off to the left, away from the camera. Just like her brother, she wasn't smiling, though her delicate, incredibly fine features seemed less weighed down than Connor's. If anything she looked impatient, ready for the moment to be over so she could move onto the next.

"Another gin and tonic, Miss?" I hadn't even noticed the stewardess standing next to me in the aisle.

"No. Thank you, though." I wanted to accept the drink, and I wanted to tell her to keep them coming, but the very last thing I needed was a buzzing hangover when I touched down in Knox County.

••••

I'd thought I'd get a fairly decent feel for Maine as I traveled from the airport, north, toward Port Creef, where I would be catching a ferry to The Causeway, however the world was shrouded in darkness when the plane touched down, and the sky remained as black as pitch out of my taxi window until I fell asleep. No town car service for me here. There had been a rather overweight, balding guy with a huge green, waxed canvas coat that came down to his knees waiting for me in arrivals, though. He'd held a piece of paper loosely in one hand, on which my name had been scrawled hastily in black Sharpie. He'd looked like he was about to fall asleep, leaning against the railings, with dark circles under his eyes. Turned out this was Carrick, and he was my cab driver. He was also Irish, and it was next to impossible to understand him.

The first thing he'd said to me was this: "Where's your coat, Miss? Colder than Satan's ball sack out there. You'll catch your death if you step foot outside wearing that flimsy thing." He hadn't seemed all that impressed with the oversized woolen sweater Mom had made me carry on the plane just in case I had gotten cold. I'd been too tired to argue with him, to tell him I was fairly warm blooded and I wasn't going to need a jacket, especially if we were just going from the airport to the car, so I'd just unzipped my luggage and pulled out the thick, hulking coat I'd brought with me. Overkill, I'd thought. Way too much fleece lining, and the hood was just plain ridiculous.

Ridiculous until I'd followed Carrick outside and the frigid wind had tried to suck the air right out of my lungs, that is. How cold had it ever gotten in Manhattan Beach in winter? Fifty-five degrees? Maybe in the forties, though that seemed unlikely. The wind cutting across the concourse at the tiny Knox County Airport could barely have been more than ten degrees. Lower, probably. It stabbed through the swaddling of my jacket like a hot knife through butter, instantly chilling me to the bone. I'd been frozen by the time I'd climbed into the back of the fat, oddly shaped taxi waiting for us a couple of hundred feet away, and Carrick had chuckled under his breath.

Not much passed between us by way of conversation—a fact I was glad of, since I could barely understand a word he was saying. Sleep seemed like the most reasonable course of action.

An indeterminate period of time later, I was shaken awake by rough hands. Carrick shot me a toothy, mirthful smile and said, "We're here, Miss. Don't want to miss this boat now." Out of the window now, weak light was cutting through a swollen bank of dirty gray, weighty-looking clouds—thunderheads, Mom called them. A sure sign of a storm. An age worn coastline stretched out to the left, grass sprouting in between the cracks and crevices of huge tors of stacked rock. Even in the pale, half-hearted dawn, the hills rolling off into the distance looked incredibly green and lush, way brighter, fatter and more vibrant than anything I'd ever seen by the beach. Beautiful. It was truly beautiful.

Carrick had parked the taxi in what appeared to be the parking lot of a dock. The concrete underfoot was cracked and buckled all over the place. Small two-man boats lay on their keels in a makeshift dry dock close by, rusting, sprouting shoots of ryegrass out of their hulls and weatherworn decks.

I'd lived by the beach all my life, and yet I had never smelled anything like this before. The air was filled with salt and brine, raw and powerful at the back of my nose.

"You're on the six-forty crossing. I'll carry your bags down to the boat, Miss. Do you think you'll be fine from there? Better for me to get going back to the city, see."

Thanks to the fresh, snapping breeze that was tearing in over the water, I was wide-awake, but my brain slowed down so rapidly that it felt like it was almost in reverse whenever I tried to understand the words coming out of Carrick's mouth. I nodded, throwing my purse strap over my head. "Of course. Thank you."

The boat service to Causeway Island was more fishing trawler than ferry. Wet plastic seats. Slick deck, with diamond plate panels drilled to the floor for grip. Rusted handrails, painted over so many times that a rainbow of colors were visible in the lengths of steel that had been scraped here and there—festive bruises to the ship's décor that made me smile.

The old guy captaining the ship was surly, toothless and unfriendly. He didn't say a word as I got onto the boat, and he still didn't speak as we sat there, pitching to and fro while he apparently waited for more passengers who never came. It was close to seven o'clock by the time he abandoned his post and gunned the boat's engines, pulling out of the tiny harbor. Port Creef disappeared behind us, to be replaced by a swathe of gunmetal gray water, frosted with white peaks.

The ride was short and choppy. God, I felt so sick. Turned inside out, to the point that I considered leaning over the side of the boat and puking at one point. Wouldn't have gone down well, though. The wiry guy behind the wheel at the front of the boat kept casting shifty glances in my direction, as though he was expecting half as much from me and was prepared and ready to throw me overboard if he needed to.

The Causeway emerged on the horizon, a smudge of color, dark and black. The island wasn't a charming swathe of land that rose gracefully out of the ocean like the arched hump of a whale; it was the angular bunched muscle, tendon and bone of a clenched fist, punching its way toward the sky with a defiance that seemed at odds with the lazy, quiet way the people who occupied its surface generally went about their day (according to Google). The color of the sky was still bleak and promised rain, but in spite of myself I couldn't help but find a savage beauty in the place.

On a shore of ocean-rounded rocks and coarse sand, an old man named Hilary was waiting for me. Dressed in a prim suit with a deep purple tie, there had never been a man so out of place in all the world. He didn't look like he belonged here, in this strange, wild, mystical place, but then again I'm sure I didn't either. "I see you made it safely, then, Miss Lang." He took my huge hard case luggage, packed to the point of bursting with clothes and books, and carried it off easily in the direction of a mud-splattered Land Rover that was parked twenty feet away.

"Looks that way," I agreed. I wasn't too sure if I meant it, though. Part of me felt missing, like I'd carved out a chunk of my heart and forgotten to bring it with me on the flight from California.

"Ronan and the children are already up at the house. If you like, we can drive around the island and I can point out where the amenities are before we head back there. You won't be expected to start work until tomorrow, so today's all yours. You can sleep if you're jetlagged, or you could go for a wander, have an explore or whatever." It sounded like the idea of exploring the island bored the back teeth off him.

I opted for a quick tour and then back to the house. Sleep wasn't on the cards after dozing all the way from the airport in the back of Carrick's taxi, but the effort of being on the road for so long had wiped me out. Lying on my bed, reading and relaxing in the quiet, sounded perfect right now.

Hilary showed me where the local grocery store was, the post office, the bank. He drove me from what he called the Church Quarter all the way across the other end of the island—a grand total of twenty minutes in the car—to a town called Richmond, to show me a beautiful, sweeping lake there. After that, he announced that it was time to go back to The Big House.

"The big house?"

"That's what everyone calls it, the Fletcher's place. It's been in the family for generations. Real old Irish estate money, apparently. A lot of people from the island used to be employed there back in Victorian times. Cooks, service staff, groundsmen, that kind of thing. No one's been living there for a long time now. I think the residents are still in shock when they see the boss tearing around on his motorcycle."

Huh. Ronan was old money. That explained a lot. He exuded an air of entitlement that went beyond his position as director of the Fletcher Corporation. He wasn't New York businessman arrogant, as Mom suspected. He was wealthy third generation Irish landowner arrogant. And where the hell did he even get a motorcycle out here?

I was nervous about seeing him. Nervous in a strange, girly way, which was absolutely crazy. He'd been shitty to me in my interview. He'd managed to strip me down and somehow make me feel less than an inch tall in a period of fifteen minutes, and still his looks and his confidence unsettled me. I shouldn't let it happen, but every time I remembered him entering into his office and sitting down at his desk in front of me, I was helplessly undone. Six months I had to live in the same household as him. Six months was a long time. I was either going to be helplessly in love with the asshole by the time mid-April rolled around, or I was going to hate him more than anyone else on the face of the planet.

When Hilary turned the Land Rover into a long, arrow-straight road and suddenly "The Big House" appeared in front of us, I understood why everyone called it that. The building wasn't a house; it was a mansion. A huge sandstone monstrosity, three stories high, with eight pillars, four on either side of the massive entranceway, propping up a deep lintel that ran from one end of the building to the other. I counted a total of eight windows on each of the floors. How many rooms did that equate to? The place was obscene. It made perfect sense that the Fletcher family, circa 1890, had needed to hire half the island to run the place.

"Seriously?" I couldn't keep the comment in as I sat there, blinking up at the house, which only kept getting bigger and bigger as the Land Rover sped up the driveway. "All this? For Ronan, me, you and two small children? We'll be lost half the time."

Hilary laughed under his breath. "Not for me, actually. I'm heading back to New York tonight. Ronan's asked me to keep an eye on things back in the city for him and report back if anything goes awry."

So, Hilary was more than just a driver. That didn't surprise me. He had a way of holding himself and of speaking that made me think he was highly educated. Weird that he'd been the one to come and collect me from the beach, but then again Ronan Fletcher obviously didn't mind doing things a little differently. "If you need anything, you can always give me a call, though. Here." He reached into his pocket and pulled out a small black leather wallet. "I have some business cards inside. Take one," he said, holding the wallet out to me.

I did so. I flipped the wallet closed and returned it to him once I had the card, but not before noticing the photograph slid into the clear plastic window inside: Hilary and Ronan, both wearing sweat-stained t-shirts, covered in mud, heads tilted back, both laughing raucously at some unknown hilarity that I was never going to be privy to. It was strange to see Ronan laughing; he looked like another man altogether.

No one greeted us inside the house. I didn't know what I'd expected of the interior—maybe something along the lines of a faded, aging manor house, with wingback chairs, chaise longue nestled into the bay windows, heavy, thick curtains with rich brocade, fastened back with gold tassel ties. What I was not expecting was the height of modern luxury. Cool, polished marble floors. Expensive looking flat screen TVs and sectional sofas so big you could fit at least seven or eight people on them at once. Everything smelled new, and looked like it had been shipped out from Pottery Barn or Macy's, from the wildly shaped glass vases to the thick pile rugs underfoot and the fur throw that was arranged neatly over the back of a plush cream armchair.

"Don't worry. It's not real." Ronan Fletcher's voice echoed around the cavernous lounge space, bouncing off the walls so that it took me a moment to figure out his exact location. Standing in a doorway by the window, he was dressed in a simple plain black t-shirt and a pair of black jeans. His feet were bare, which, for some reason made me blush. What the hell was that about?

His dark hair had been slicked back when we met last, full of product, but now it was swept back out of his face in thick waves that any girl would have killed for.

"I'll take your bags up to your room, Miss Lang." Hilary's hand on my shoulder almost made me jump; I'd completely forgotten he was there.

"Oh, don't worry. I can do that." I tried to rescue the handle of my luggage from him, but he was too quick for me.

"It's not a problem. I have to go and pack up myself anyway. And I'm sure Ronan wants to have a quick word with you as well."

"That's right. Thanks, Hilary. Ophelia, come and sit down. Let's go through a few house rules, shall we?" Cool as ever, Ronan sauntered into the room and sat himself down on the sectional, throwing one arm over the back of the sofa. His body wasn't as rigid as it had been back in New York, but there was still a reserved quality to him that made him seem remote and detached from everything around him. I couldn't quite put my finger on it, but that standoff-ish quality was all at once both so overwhelming and so incredibly subtle that it made my head spin.

I went and sat on the other side of the sofa, perching myself on the edge, knees pressed together, hands resting on my thighs, back ramrod straight.

"You look very uncomfortable," he said. "Don't be. This is your home now, Ophelia. For the next six months, anyway. Relax. You'll be miserable here otherwise. And I don't want that."

He was right, but it was going to take me a little longer than five minutes for me to start throwing my feet up on the furniture and lounging around in my sweats. Still, I leaned back into my seat, trying not to be so stiff. "You said there were house rules?"

"Only one or two. Simple, obvious things that don't need saying, I'm sure. For the sake of clarity, however, it'd probably be better to just get them out of the way and then we can both move on. Agreed?" I hadn't noticed the way his cheeks dimpled before. Probably because he hadn't smiled once during our meeting in New York. Now, with the faint suggestion of amusement teasing at the corners of his mouth, they were just about visible. Connor had inherited the feature from his father. It was crazy how alike they were.

"Firstly," he said, holding up his index finger. "I wanted to thank you. I know…I know I'm not an easy person to be around, Ophelia, and I also know that I wasn't very…" He seemed to grope for the remainder of his sentence. It took him a while before he continued. "I wasn't very pleasant at your interview."

"No, you weren't. You were a jerk." The words tumbled out of my mouth before I could stop them. Oh, shit. Where the hell did that come from? Too late to clap my hand over my mouth and shut myself up. Impossible to claw the words back into my mouth where they belonged. What was *wrong* with me? Ronan's eyebrows lifted slowly, his eyes burning a hole in the side of my face. I couldn't look at him. Not directly, anyway. I could only manage a pained sideways glance. He looked a little stunned.

"Wow. No one has been that frank with me since Magda died," he said.

"I'm sorry. That was out of line. I shouldn't have—"

"No, no, please. I *was* a jerk. I behaved in a very jerky manner. For that I apologize. I'm not in the habit of being nice to people anymore. I should probably have had someone else interview you." His voice was rich and smooth, like warm coffee. The accent I'd had such a hard time placing on him when we first met made a little more sense now, here on the island, where it seemed nearly all of the occupants were of Irish descent. It was barely there, but a couple of words he said were faintly tinted with a little brogue. Listening to Ronan speak was an unexpected pleasure that made my toes curl inside my shoes.

"I doubt you would have allowed someone else to make an important decision like that for you," I said. "You don't strike me as the sort of person who would entrust the care of his children with just anyone."

He looked at me for a long time. And then: "You're right. I wouldn't. So here I am, apologizing, and here you are, so far from home. A stranger in a strange land." He turned and looked out of the window beside him, eyes fixed on something in the distance. "I suppose that leads me to the most important rule I'd like you to adhere to. You don't know anyone here on the island. It would be tempting, I suppose, to try and make friends. Guy friends. Maybe someone special to spend time with. Romantically," he added on the end, as if his point wasn't being made quite clearly enough. I was hearing him loud and clear, though, and I was already squirming in my seat.

"Ronan, believe me. I'm not planning on shimmying down a drainpipe to go and hit first base with a local. I'm here to look after the children. That's it. I have no interest whatsoever in meeting people, male or otherwise."

He gave me a tight-lipped, awkward smile. "I'm sure that's true. But like I said. Best to just get these things out in the open and then we can move on. I don't want any guys brought into the house at any point, okay? I definitely don't want you to have guests in your room. I don't ever want there to be a situation where Connor or Amie might find a man they don't know wandering around in his underwear, okay?"

My cheeks were crimson; they had to be. A mixture of outrage and embarrassment fired through me, fizzling just under the surface of my skin. I felt like I was burning up all over. "I'm not that easy," I snapped. "I wouldn't just invite a guy back to my room to hook up, if that's what you're implying."

Ronan shook his head, now looking down into his own lap. "I'm not implying anything. I'm just stating what the rules are. I'm sorry if you find that offensive, Ophelia, but my children are very important to me."

"I know. Of course they are. But—"

"The only other thing I ask of you is that you don't ever let them down onto the beach by themselves. Somehow swimming lessons seemed unnecessary in New York. Stupid, I know. I plan on dealing with the matter, getting them enrolled in classes as soon as possible, but for now if they're outside, don't let either one of them out of your sight. Agreed?"

I wanted to defend myself further—it was insane that he thought I was going to be throwing myself at random men, left, right and center—but I could see backtracking and arguing with him over this wasn't going to serve any greater good. "Yes. I'll be very vigilant of them, you have my word."

"Good. Now, the library on the top floor is at your disposal. There's a home movie theatre in the basement that you can use to watch movies with the kids. You can use that for your own personal use in the evenings as well, once the children have gone to bed, but you should always keep your ear out for them. Amie's usually pretty good at going to bed and staying there, but Connor's a night owl. He'll be up and wandering around in the middle of the night if he can get away with it."

"Yes. Not a problem. I can handle that." My mind was still reeling from the prospect of an entire library upstairs along with a movie theatre downstairs to register much of the other house features that Ronan then explained to me. I did get something about a guest quarters. A lap lane swimming pool, also downstairs, that the children *were* allowed to play in while supervised, since it was only four feet deep.

"The only area of the house that is off limits to you is my study," Ronan said. "I have a lot of sensitive documents in there. I could literally go to prison if unauthorized people caught sight of them. It's really important that Connor and Amie never go in my study, Ophelia. *Never.* Under *any* circumstances. Promise me right now that you'll never let them inside."

An intensity had overtaken Ronan, a fierceness shining in his eyes as he spoke about his office. His tone was sharp, harder than I thought it probably needed to be. So sad that the guy was so desperate to lock himself away in his study away from his children all the time. I knew lots of parents that were like that back in California, though. There were an awful lot of investment bankers and people working in the financial quarter back in Manhattan Beach, and a lot of them had very little time for their sons and daughters. In Ronan's case, the loss of his wife must have had a lot to do with his reluctance to spend quality time with his kids. I hadn't seen a picture of Magda, but it would be strange if her children didn't carry some piece of her in the way they looked, the way their voices sounded, or the things they said. It had to be hard for him to even look at them sometimes, even now.

"I promise I won't let them into your study. Ever," I said. "Over my dead body."

Ronan winced—a flutter of uncharacteristic emotion that made me cringe myself. I should really have learned by now to think before opening my mouth. I had no idea how his wife had died. It could have been an accident. It could have been some awful, fatal mistake that had cost her her life, and here I was making over my dead body jibes. God. Way, way too soon.

"They're very well-behaved most of the time," Ronan said. "If you tell them not to do something, they usually obey. You won't need to reprimand them very often. If you do have to punish them for acting up, I've found the most effective way to do that is to have them sit down and write me a letter, explaining what the problem is and why they're not on best behavior."

Not what I was expecting at all. Most parents confiscate their kids' technology to teach them a lesson these days. It was the most unimaginative way to control the way they conducted themselves, and yet it was also the easiest route. The kids weren't going to kick and scream or create a scene in public if you took their iPads. They were going to be silent as church mice until you gave that shit back. If you threatened to take cell phones away, you could practically work miracles with a child's attitude.

Ronan didn't operate like that, though. He wanted his kids to sit down and reflect on their actions, to process them, and to communicate their feelings as best they could. For Amie, only five, writing down her thoughts was probably still next to impossible, but it was a refreshing ideology, that was for sure.

Ronan got to his feet. "I'm glad we got that ironed out. If you don't have any questions, then I'd say it's time to meet the little hellions, wouldn't you?"

CHAPTER SIX

ANGELS AND DEMONS

Connor and Amie Fletcher were both part angel, part demon. I knew I was going to have fun wrangling them into touch the moment I laid eyes on them. Connor sat across from me in his bedroom, feet hanging off the end of his bed, and he refused to meet my eye. Amie, on the other hand, couldn't stop staring at me, like I was some sort of ghost.

"You don't look like Mommy," she said. Turning to her father, she pouted, staring at him accusingly. "Hilary said she looked like Mommy. I heard."

"No, he said she reminded him of Mommy. That can mean a lot of different things, sweetheart. If someone speaks or acts or talks in a similar way to another person, you can say that they remind you of them. Understand?"

Amie nodded; she looked like she'd just had her heart broken by this news. Two seconds later, she was running around, giggling in a high-pitched voice, playing with a plastic toy Stegosaurus like the disappointment hadn't even occurred. Connor sat quietly, staring at his sneakers, chewing on his bottom lip.

"Connor, please stand up and say hello to Ophelia. She's going to be taking care of you a lot over the next few months. You're going to like her, I promise." *Great.* I really wished he hadn't said that. If kids wanted to be difficult for the hell of it, they'd go against whatever you told them, regardless of whether it made any sense to them. Connor might have thought I was the coolest teacher cum nanny there ever was once he got to know me, but the moment Ronan told him he was going to like me, to get along with me, he pretty much guaranteed that Connor was going to rail against the very idea of me.

"I don't even get why we had to come here," he said under his breath. "I hate this house. None of my friends are here."

"It's okay, bud. School's going to start soon, and you'll make plenty of friends."

"What is she going to be doing with us then?" he asked quietly.

"Ophelia's going to get you up in the morning. She's going to be make your breakfast and take you to school. And when you get back from school, she'll take you for a swim downstairs. She'll play with you. She'll help you with your schoolwork. That will be okay, right?"

So he really had meant it when he said he didn't want to be distracted. According to his list of the duties I was expected to carry out, Ronan wasn't going to have a single interaction with his kids from one day to the next. Didn't even sound like he planned on sticking his head through the door and kissing them goodnight.

The whole thing seemed incredibly strange. Connor slid off the edge of his bed and slumped down onto the floor. He picked up a Lego Star Wars fighter jet and began to dismantle it piece by piece. "It's too cold here," he said. "It's nothing like New York at all."

Ronan shook his head, bending down in front of his son. Connor didn't look up, but it was pretty clear he was waiting with baited breath to see what his father would say. "It's just as cold in New York as it is here," Ronan informed him. "But no, you're right. The island's very different to the city. You've got fresh air here. Places to run and play outside. Doesn't that sound like it would be a fun thing to do? You could even learn how to sail in the summer time. You told me you wanted to do that."

Connor looked up, over Ronan's shoulder, straight at me. Only for a second, but the eye contact was long enough to see the fear in his eyes.

"I don't like new people," he whispered to Ronan.

"It's okay. Ophelia will only feel new for a little while, and then it'll be normal that she's here. Okay?"

Connor didn't look so sure about that. I'd had to win kids over every single time a new school year started, so I wasn't worried about tackling that challenge. If I could find a level to connect with him on, we'd be fine. At least that was how it was with normal seven-year-olds. This was a unique situation, though. Connor had lost his mom, and that turned everything on its head.

Ronan seemed completely in love with his children, and they were equally besotted with him. It was surprising: I'd assumed he'd be awkward and irritable around them considering his desperation to spend the next six months locked away in his study while *I* looked after them, but the opposite was true. He collected Connor up in his arms and sat him in his lap on the floor, chattering and asking him questions about the menagerie of plastic animals he was lining up like they were about to walk two by two into Noah's Arc. Amie eventually went and sat with them too, using her Stegosaurus to attack Connor's lions, giraffes and zebras.

Cold, cold Ronan laughed and played along. It seemed he had a warm heart after all, even if it was reserved for some people over others. I couldn't stop myself from softening to him as I leaned against the wall by the door, watching them quietly play. Then again, I didn't exactly try and stop myself. Ronan, despite our rocky first meeting and his casual way of implying I wanted to sleep my way through the inhabitants of the island, was weirdly growing on me.

"You'll probably want to go and get settled now," he said, catching me off guard when he looked up at me and spoke. "Your room's the one at the very end of the hall on the right. I had one of the cleaning girls fetch some shampoo and soaps. A hairdryer. That kind of thing. I figured you wouldn't have time for grocery shopping for a couple of days. The fridge is fully stocked as well. It'll probably take you the next week to adjust here. After that, I'm sure you'll have found your feet."

"They didn't need to do that. I brought a bunch of stuff with me from home. And don't worry about grocery shopping or anything like that. I can manage. I'm very capable."

Ronan gave me an odd, distracted smile, eyes directed right at my face, though I couldn't help but feel as though he was staring straight through me. "Oh, I know that, Ophelia. That's why I hired you."

CHAPTER SEVEN

THE NOTE

My room was something out of a hotel brochure, all white linens and soft, luxurious throws. A comfortable reading chair was angled by the window to catch the light, and a small desk against the wall was stacked high with books—*Causeway Island Wildlife, A guide to East Coast Islands, Patrick Kavanagh and Other Remarkable Irish Poets of the Twentieth Century*. It seemed Ronan wanted me to fall in love with The Causeway, and had provided with me enough reading material to make it happen.

I didn't join the family for dinner. Ronan wanted to spend time alone with the children before I got to work tomorrow, and to be honest I was relieved. I used the expansive kitchen on the first floor to cook up a fresh fillet of salmon, some greens and carrots, and I camped out in my room, watching unfamiliar TV shows on the huge flat screen TV in my bedroom. At around eight thirty I tiptoed downstairs to make sure everything was okay—the huge, echoing house was full of shrieks and screams, loud enough to wake the dead. When I stuck my head through the door to the lounge, what I saw made me laugh.

A den, colossal in size, configured out of sofas and bookcases, blue and white and pinstripe bed sheets all pegged together to create one vast canopy that draped down over the lumpy construction. Amie was darting in and out of the many openings in the sheets, screaming at the top of her lungs while Connor chased after her, followed by Ronan, who, surprisingly, was wearing a black patch over his left eye and snarling something in a broad, comedic pirate drawl about tossing them both overboard.

Ronan saw me, our eyes making contact, but he didn't really acknowledge my presence. His focus was on the children. I left them to it and went back to bed, and the shrieks continued on for at least another hour before silence claimed the house.

Just after eleven, there was a knock on my bedroom door. I was already in my PJs—just perfect. I needed Ronan to see me in my fluffy white and pink flannel nightwear like I needed a hole in the head. I answered the door, trying to hide as much of myself behind the wood paneling as possible. Thank god I hadn't washed my face and brushed my teeth yet. A ridiculous thought to have, but still...Ronan seeing me without my makeup on? No thanks.

"Hey. Is everything okay?"

He hovered in the hallway, looking far more disheveled than he had earlier. The fire that had possessed him when he was with Connor and Amie seemed to have gone out now, replaced by a general weariness that made him look like he was half asleep on his feet. "Hey, no, everything's fine." He rubbed a hand against his jaw, then his forehead. "I just wanted to check in and make sure you were still okay for getting the kids up in the morning. They need to be up at seven."

"Sure, no worries. I got it."

"Great." And for the first time ever, Ronan Fletcher offered me a smile. It was enough to make me go weak at the knees. His dimples sunk deep in his cheeks, his full lips parting to flash white, almost perfect teeth at me, and my palms broke out in a sweat. "It means a lot to me that you're here, Ophelia. I hope you know that. I'm very, very grateful that you agreed to come out to the island. Connor and Amie are going to rely on you a lot over the next six months. I know you're going to do a great job of taking care of them."

His sudden, earnest way of speaking to me was baffling, but it was a pleasant change, too. This wasn't going to be so bad. I could handle anything and everything that was thrown at me if he was this Ronan, instead of grumpy, distant, kind of rude Ronan.

He opened his mouth, looked like he was about to say something, but then apparently thought better of it. "Anyway. Thank you again, Ophelia. I'll let you get some sleep. Good night." He walked off down the hallway, and I watched him disappear into the darkness, trying not to stare. Mom warned me before I left California that I shouldn't fall in love with the boss. I didn't think for a second I was going to, but that smile was something I could get used to. It would be very nice if I got to see it more often.

••••

5:45 a.m.

I was awake. It was an hour before my alarm was due to go off, and there was nothing to be done about it. Stupid jet lag. My body clock was all over the place, and I'd been lying in bed for what felt like forever, tossing and turning, wrapping myself up in my sheets, fretting. A good start with the kids was what I needed. I'd barely had a chance to speak to them yesterday, and they hadn't seemed all that pleased to see me, an interloper, ruining their private time with Ronan.

Pancakes. The situation called for pancakes. I could easily make them and keep them warm in the oven until it was time to wake up Connor and Amie. And Ronan...Ronan's physique wasn't exactly that of a guy who ate a lot of pancakes in the morning, but the thought of him sitting at the kitchen counter, wavy hair mussed and all over the place, pajama bottoms slung low on his hips, tearing into a breakfast that *I* had made him had me practically tripping over myself to get out of bed.

Downstairs: eggs, milk and flour. Butter in the pan. Kettle on the boil.

I put out four sets of knives and forks on the table, coasters and placemats, and then I panicked, removing one of the settings. *You're not part of the family, O. You're the hired help. Don't go forgetting that.*

Day one and I almost *had* forgotten, though. I was going to have to be really careful to maintain a professional distance from the Fletchers. Every last one of them.

Once the food was made and wrapped in tinfoil, stashed in the warmed oven, I decided to go have a quick shower before getting Connor and Amie out of bed. I was on my way back up the stairs when I noticed the white slip of paper taped to the door of Ronan's study. Was it there before? I couldn't remember seeing it, but then again I'd been concentrating on finding the kitchen so I could easily have missed it.

I wavered. Ronan was so specific about his study that I almost didn't want to go and see what was taped to the door. It was probably a Post-it or something, reminding him to do something when he got up. I left notes for myself like that all the time. They say curiosity killed the cat, though, and it had already damn well near killed me a couple of times. It had certainly ended my marriage. I'd come home early from school one afternoon with a migraine and heard a strange noise upstairs. I'd gone up to our bedroom and found Will in bed with Melissa, and that had been that. So clichéd. If I hadn't gone up there to investigate, there was every chance I would have still been married to Will. He was a coward; he probably would have continued screwing my best friend behind my back, but he would never have had the courage to leave.

Fuck it. I slipped down the hallway and stopped in front of Ronan's study. Confusion swamped me when I saw that it wasn't a Post-it note at all; it was a small, white envelope, and my name was written on it in blocky black biro. Why on earth would Ronan be leaving me notes taped to his study door? Wouldn't he have slipped it under my bedroom door if he needed to leave me a note? Or on the kitchen counter, where I was more likely to find it? The study was tucked away from the rest of the house. You didn't need to pass it on your way to any of the other rooms. It was a miracle I'd even seen the note as I started up the stairs.

I pulled the envelope from the door and opened it.

Ophelia,

Please follow these instructions exactly. Call 825 730 4414 and ask for Robert Linneman. Ask him to come to the house immediately.
Following that, call 911 and ask for the police. Explain that I am dead, and that my body is hanging in the study.

Do not come into the study.
Do not allow the children into the study.

Keep the children calm.
Keep the children safe.

Ronan.

    My heart was a hand grenade in my chest, and I felt like I had just fumbled the pin.
    What?
    I re-read the letter at least three times before I felt bile rising up in the back of my throat, burning there—I was going to be sick. I dropped the note on the floor and knocked on the study door, holding my breath. It wasn't true. It couldn't be fucking true. If this was Ronan's idea of some kind of sick joke, then he was in for the shock of his life when I packed up my shit and left. No way I was hanging around for this sick, twisted kind of a trick.
    "Ronan?"
    Nothing.
    Loud, this time.
    "Mr. Fletcher?"

Still nothing.

Oh, god.

Without thinking, alarm rising through me, coming in crippling waves, I reached out and tried the door handle. The round knob wouldn't even turn; it was clearly locked. "Shit. God*damn* it." I tried rattling it, but the thing was solid, wasn't budging an inch. Could I get into the study through a window outside? I had no idea. It was worth trying. I snatched the letter from the floor and ran back through the house to the front door, flung it open and raced outside. I wasn't wearing shoes. Pain lanced through the soles of my feet as I tore across the gravel driveway. The side of the house was grass, thankfully. No more sharp rocks. Mud spattered up my legs, rank brown water soaking my pajama bottoms. It squelched up between my toes.

The first window was the living room window. The second window was the kitchen. It was the third window around the side of the house that belonged to the study. My palms slapped against the limestone on either side of the huge glass pane and I lurched forward, trying to see in.

I hadn't even noticed that it was still dark. Dawn was moments away, but right now the sky was still a blanket of stars and faint, wispy clouds. There were no lights on inside the study. I had to press my hands against the glass, adjusting my pupils to the darkness before I could make out anything beyond obscure shapes and shadows.

And then I saw.

Bare feet.

The bare feet I'd felt giddy over yesterday. They were spinning very slowly in a counter clockwise motion. Ronan was still wearing the same simple plain black t-shirt and faded out black jeans he'd worn all day yesterday. His body was suspended in mid-air, hands relaxed by his sides. Slowly, slowly, his body spun, and then he was facing me, his head tilted to one side, eyes open and staring into oblivion. He was dead. There was no two ways about it. He was most definitely dead.

"*No!*" I clapped my hands over my mouth, shaking uncontrollably.

What...what the *fuck*? How? How had this happened? Tears of shock sprung to my eyes. I couldn't feel my feet. My legs. I couldn't feel a single part of my body. Everything had gone numb. I braced myself against the wall as I leaned forward and threw up. Ronan's letter was still in my hand. I crushed the paper against the rough stonework as I heaved and I heaved, vomiting onto the wet grass at my feet.

I couldn't bear him staring at me anymore. I ducked away from the window and ran back into the house, my heart slamming in my chest. I was getting mud everywhere, but that seemed the least of my problems. The house phone. Where the fuck was the house phone? I eventually found it in the kitchen, sitting beside the dirty bowl I'd mixed the pancake batter in only twenty minutes ago.

Fuck Robert Linneman. I dialed 911 first. A woman picked up almost immediately.

"911, what's your emergency?"

"Hello? Hello, god, please, I need an ambulance."

"Okay, ma'am. What's your address?"

"I don't...*shit*! I don't know."

"You're not at home, ma'am?"

"No, no. I...I just started a job. I just started a new job here."

"Not a problem. I have an address connected to this phone line. What's happened, ma'am? What's your emergency?"

"My boss...he's hanged himself in his study. The door's locked. I can't...I can't get it open. I saw him through the window."

"Can you break the window, miss?"

I hadn't even thought of that. "Uh, yes, I can. I think...I think he's dead, though."

"Could you see him struggling at all, miss?"

"No. His body was still. His eyes were open."

A long pause followed. "Okay. Someone's already on their way to you now. Won't be a minute. Can you stay on the line with me until help reaches you?"

"Feelya?"

I nearly dropped the phone. Next to me, Amie had appeared out of nowhere and was standing in her tiny little pink nightie covered in fairies, peering through the glass screen into the oven. "Are we having sunshine scramble for breakfast? Daddy always makes us sunshine scramble." Her tiny little face was filled with hope.

"Miss? Miss, can you hear me?"

"I'm sorry, I have to go," I whispered. The phone clattered against the counter as I let go and hurried over to Amie and picked her up in my arms. "Hey, sweetie. You're out of bed early," I told her, tucking her messy hair back behind her ears. Apart from the brief time I'd spent with them when Ronan introduced us yesterday, Amie hadn't had any interaction with me. She looked surprised and uncomfortable at the fact that I'd picked her up and I was mothering her.

"Why have you been crying?" she asked, frowning.

"Oh, I burned my finger on a hot pan, sweetie. It's all better now, though, I promise."

"Your feet are dirty."

"I know, I know, I made a mess, didn't I? I'll be able to clean it all up after breakfast, though. Won't take me long. Why don't you sit down at the table, and I'll get you some of those pancakes, huh?"

Don't let the children see.
Keep the children calm.
Keep the children safe.

Amie seemed appeased by the thought of food. I got her settled at the table and served up two pancakes on a plate for her, hastily cutting them into small pieces and drizzling maple syrup over them. Her eyes lit up when she saw how much food I'd heaped onto her plate. "Stay here for a second okay, honey? I just have to make a quick phone call."

Amie nodded, cheeks bulging.

My fingers were sticky with syrup when I dialed the other number on Ronan's letter. The phone buzzed eight times before a groggy sounding woman picked up. "Hello?"

"Hi. I'm looking for...Robert Linneman," I said, checking the letter. "Ronan Fletcher asked me to call."

"I'm afraid Mr. Linneman's office hours aren't until nine." The woman, who'd sounded half-asleep a second ago, now sounded angry instead. "Mr. Fletcher is really going to have to learn that people aren't at his beck and call twenty-four seven." In the background, I heard a low, deep voice asking who it was. "Someone from Fletcher's office. Damn people need to learn to check the time before they start making calls at the crack of dawn. This isn't New York. We're not all up and working at five in the morning."

"I'm...I'm not in New York. I'm on Causeway Island. I'm afraid there's been some sort of accident over here," I said quietly, shielding the receiver so Amie couldn't hear me. "Ronan left a note and asked that I get Mr. Linneman to come as quickly as possible."

"Oh. I see." Whispering on the other end of the phone, and then the sound of the handset creaking as it was handed over to someone else.

"Hello, this is Robert. You're Ophelia?"

Shock rode over me in another wave. He knew who I was? Well, he was certainly at an advantage because I had no idea who he was. "Yes. There's an ambulance on its way. I was meant to call you first, but..."

"It's okay. I'm on my way. Don't let the police take anything before I get there. Are you listening, girl?"

"Yes. Yes." I nodded, clutching tightly to the phone, as if the receiver were the only thing keeping me upright. "Please. *Hurry.*"

••••

"And what time was it when you came downstairs, Miss Lang? Was the note already there then?"

I'd relocated Amie up to her room when the police had arrived. The red and blue flashing lights of their car had cast long, brilliant shadows across the lawns as it sped toward the house, but the sirens had thankfully been silent. Amie had gone upstairs without a peep, taking her breakfast with her, plate gripped tightly in both hands, before the two uniformed officers had even entered the house.

Now I stood in the hallway outside Ronan's office with the cops, feeling very small and very useless as I tried to answer their questions.

"I don't know. I didn't notice it. I wasn't paying attention."

"Do you have a key to this door?"

I shook my head. "No. He didn't want anyone going in there." I'd already shown them the note.

"We're gonna have to kick it in then. That okay with you?"

I nodded, throat aching and too swollen to speak unless it was absolutely necessary.

"Stand back then." The tallest, broadest guy got the job done in one swift movement, slamming the sole of his boot into the door just below the handle. The door sprang open, hitting the wall with a crash. I didn't look inside the room. I'd seen enough through the window outside; I was going to be dealing with the nightmares for the rest of my life as it was.

I still couldn't wrap my head around what was happening. Less than twenty-four hours inside the house, and the guy who employed me was dead? How did something like this happen? It categorically made no sense whatsoever. It was such a mistake to leave California. I should never have come here.

Both police officers went inside the study. I sat on the bottom step of the staircase and gnawed on my fingernails until they came back out again ten minutes later. "He's been dead for some time. Body's very cold. I'm not a forensics guy, but I'd say he's been there at least six hours, probably."

Six hours? So he'd come up to my room last night and thanked me for coming out here, thanked me from the bottom of his heart for agreeing to come all the way across the other side of the country to take care of his children, and then he'd come straight down here, tied a noose around his neck and stepped off a goddamn chair? That's what it sounded like had happened. God, Ronan had been hanging in there, cold and dead, while I'd been prancing around the kitchen in my PJs, making pancakes, fantasizing about what he might look like all ruffled from sleep, complimenting me on my excellent cooking skills. What a nightmare.

The mud from the lawn had dried on my feet and cracked, turned almost white. My big toenail had been bleeding at some point; I must have caught it on something when I ran outside.

"Did you have any suspicion that Mr. Fletcher was planning something like this?" the second cop asked. He was squat and muscular. A redhead with a smattering of freckles across his face that he probably hated.

"No. No idea whatsoever. Like I said, I barely knew him. He hired me to look after his children. I only arrived on the island yesterday."

Sympathy traveled across the guy's face. "Quite a shock, then," he said, which was possibly the understatement of the century. "Where are the children now?"

"Upstairs. I didn't want them to know anything's going on."

The cop nodded. "Okay. We'll have to call in CPS. They don't have an office here on the island. Can you take care of them until someone can come and get them? Might not be until tomorrow now. There's a storm on its way in."

"Uhhh, yeah. Yeah, sure." Damn. How long was it going to take Child Protective Services to get here? Long enough, I assumed. Long enough that I was going to have to tell Connor and Amie that something had happened to their father.

Officer Hinchliff (his name was stitched onto the breast pocket of his thick, waterproof jacket) was right about the storm. Out of the window in the distance, the sea looked choppy and angry, the faint outline of the mainland six miles away a grim gray streak, hovering above the water. Lightning was striking out over the ocean, tearing across the cloud-heavy sky one second, gone the next, like the tail of a whip.

"You're going to have to come down to the station and make a statement as well, Miss. We won't be able to hand over the documents in Mr. Fletcher's office until we've confirmed that this actually is a suicide."

"I don't think I'll be taking possession of his paperwork," I said, shaking my head. "And what do you mean, confirming that this is a suicide? You can't...you can't think *I* did this."

Of all the ridiculous, moronic things I'd ever heard, that had to be the most astounding. Officer Hinchliffe was quick to shake his head. "No, no. I mean, it looks pretty straightforward in there, but Mr. Fletcher was a very wealthy man. And what with the letter addressed to you in there—"

"What? What letter?"

Officer Hinchliffe frowned at me none too subtly. "So you know nothing about it then? You've never seen it before?"

"I have absolutely no idea what the hell you're talking about!" Losing my temper wasn't a helpful tactic, but my brain wasn't working properly as it was and these vague questions were driving me to distraction. "If there's something in there for me, then you should give it to me, surely?"

Both officers shook their heads in unison. "I'm afraid the room's a crime scene until the body's been cleared of any foul play. The letter inside is evidence. We'll need to read through it thoroughly before we can hand it over."

"Fine. I don't even care right now. Can you just get a hold of CPS? The kids are too young for this kind of trauma, and I don't have a clue how to handle any of it."

"Gentlemen." A cold, flat voice slipped over my head, coming from behind me. The accent was even thicker than the officers', and that was saying something. I turned, and standing in the open doorway of the house was a tall, narrow shouldered man with a pinched face and tufts of gray hair on either side of his otherwise bald head. The coat he was wearing was splattered across the shoulders with droplets of water.

"Mr. Linneman. Surprised it took you so long to get here," Caruthers said, shifting his position, spreading his legs a little wider, blocking off as much of the hallway as he possibly could. "Ronan's dead. Not much counsel you can provide him with now."

"I'm aware of Ronan's condition," the sparrow-like man in the doorway said dryly. He said the word *condition*, as if being dead were something Ronan might recover from. "I'm not here to assist him. I'm here for the girl." His eyes flickered to me, resting somewhere above my head, like he couldn't actually bring himself to make eye contact with me. "Ronan left very specific instructions should he die while Ophelia was at the house. I didn't think I would need to come out here at the crack of dawn to execute his will less than twenty-four hours after she showed up, but there you go. Ronan always was quite...*unpredictable*."

Officer Hinchliffe snorted under his breath, apparently trying to rein in laughter. His cheeks had gone an unfortunate rosy color. "That's one word for it," he said, his voice strained. "Remember that time when he set the McInnes feed store on fire? You could see the smoke from Port Creef."

Caruthers gave him a swift, sharp dig in the ribs. "Yeah, well. He'll not be setting fire to anything now, will he? Come on. Help me take pictures. They'll be here for the body soon." Both police officers vanished back into Ronan's study, closing the door heavily behind them. I remained, frozen to the spot, trying to process, trying to come to terms with the fact that Ronan, who was very much alive and happy enough yesterday evening, had hanged himself and was dead. And moreover, no one seemed all that shocked or bothered by the news.

"Come, girl. I have a number of papers I need you to sign. Ronan left a lot of work for you to do, I'm afraid." Mr. Linneman edged past me down the hallway, into the kitchen, where he placed a very old, worn brown leather briefcase onto the polished marble and snapped the catches open. Looking up at me, he frowned. "I don't suppose you have a pen, do you? I've left mine at home, it seems."

I didn't say anything for a moment. Inside Ronan's study, a loud bang fractured the silence. Sounded like they'd tried to cut him down and dropped his body or something. Linneman flinched but didn't say anything. He was waiting on me to produce something for him to write with.

"Uh, yes. I'm sure...there must be one around here somewhere." Where the hell would Ronan have kept a stash of pens in this barely furnished, unlived in monstrosity? I hurried into the kitchen and began pulling drawers open. Eventually I came across a sleek, heavy, metal ballpoint that had The Fletcher Corporation printed neatly in gold down the side. "Here."

"Wonderful." Linneman began making small scribbles on a stack of papers he pulled out of his briefcase. "If you could please sign everywhere you see a cross, Ophelia, we'll be done in no time."

We wouldn't, though. The sheets of paper were never-ending, as were the efficient little Xs Linneman was dashing everywhere. "What's all this for?" I asked. "I already signed an employment contract before I left California."

"This is so you can assume legal guardianship of the children. Here. This one you have to sign twice, see. One here and one here." He pointed, showing me something, but I wasn't paying attention.

"Excuse me? Legal guardianship? I don't think so."

More bird-like than ever, Linneman's head twisted on his neck so that he was looking at me, his body still facing forward. "Oh, yes. Ronan said he spent a great deal of time selecting you for this purpose. He said you agreed to care for the children for a period no less than six months. Is that not the case?"

"I did, yes, but...but I thought he was going to be *alive* while I was looking after them. He said he was going to be writing a book! I don't...are you saying he *planned* this?"

Linneman shrugged, trickles of water now dripping from the hem of his coat, leaving tiny puddles on the kitchen tiles. "Ronan was a pragmatic guy. He always did consider the future. I suppose that's why he did so well in New York. Never made any brash decisions with his money there, or so I'm led to believe."

"*He just fucking killed himself!* Those cops said he set fire to some feed barn just a minute ago. He clearly wasn't sane. I can't look after his kids!"

"Pssshhh. Ronan was eleven when he set that fire. And there was always speculation that it wasn't even him. A long time's passed since then." He didn't seem to be hearing the part where I told him I couldn't care for Connor and Amie. He held out the pen to me like it was

Excalibur and I was meant to try and yank it out of his hand or something.

"I think given the situation I should probably go back to California," I said, using my most level voice—the one I reserved for unreasonable five-year-olds who wouldn't do as they were told.

"I see." Linneman closed his hand around the pen, dropping his arm to his side. "Well, that *is* a shame. Ronan seemed so sure you'd be able to get everything settled here if he were gone." He paused, and then said, "If you don't mind, I'll leave the papers here for you to look over. If you reconsider, you can always call me on my cell and I can come and pick up the documents tomorrow morning, before the social worker gets here." He said this so breezily, as if it didn't matter either way what I decided. It did, of course. It mattered a great deal. State care was awful—Connor and Amie were in for a rough time. But I was only supposed to be their tutor. Their nanny. I wasn't supposed to be legally responsible for their welfare at all times. It was too much to ask. Way too much to even think about right now.

"You've got my number, of course," Linneman said. "Now, I'm sorry for the flying visit, but I have to get going. There's more paperwork that needs to be signed, and Sully shouldn't hear the news from those two buffoons in there. Better it comes from me." He briskly closed his briefcase, leaving the stack of annotated papers behind on the kitchen counter, then hightailed it off down the hallway again, coat tails flaring out behind him, revealing a dusky gray suit underneath.

"Wait, Mr. Linneman? I'm sorry? Who's Sully?"

Linneman paused, casting a brief glance at me over his shoulder. One of his ruffled, steel gray eyebrows twitched slightly. "You don't know?" He sighed. "No, well, Ronan wasn't likely to mention him to you, I suppose. He wouldn't have brought him up if his life depended on it." He smiled, perhaps a little ironically. "Sully is the benefactor of Ronan's will, Ophelia. Sully Fletcher. He is Ronan's brother."

CHAPTER EIGHT

GHOST

Sully goddamn Fletcher.

If Ronan had a brother here on the island, then why the hell had he asked his lawyer to make *me* the legal guardian of his kids? It made no sense. None whatsoever. And yet I could see his blocky signature, countersigning all of the documents Linneman had left behind, shouting at me like a voice from beyond the grave. *Take them! Take them!* Wherever he was right now, Ronan was probably having the biggest laugh about all of this. I'd barely known him at all, but I could picture *that* just fine.

"The coroner's guys can't get here until tomorrow either now," Officer Hinchliffe said. I hadn't heard him leave the study, and my heart jammed itself as far up my esophagus as it could go as a result of my surprise. "We're going to have to leave him here."

"You aren't leaving him here. You *can't.*"

"I know. Only joking, Miss. We already put him in the car."

I blinked at him. "How? I didn't see you bring him out?" It wasn't that I was desperate to get another look at Ronan, stiff and cold and blue, but it seemed impossible that they could have stretchered him out without me noticing.

"Took him out the window," Hinchliffe said. "Seemed like the best bet. Didn't want Connor or Amie catching sight of him now, did we?"

He gave me a look, like *I* was the inconsiderate one. Winching a dead man out of a window seemed far more insensitive to me, but I wasn't going to argue.

"Where does Sully Fletcher live?" I blurted.

Caruthers appeared through the front door, coughing into the crook of his elbow. "Down Kinkeel way, that one. Proper hermit. Bit of an asshole."

"I should go and see him with Connor and Amie. He should see his niece and nephew. Perhaps he should be the one to talk to the children about Ronan."

Both Caruthers and Hinchliffe began to violently shake their heads. "Not a good idea, Miss Lang. Sully won't be pleased to see them. In fact, he'll probably be crowing from the rooftops when he finds out what Ronan's gone and done." Caruthers got his notebook out and started scribbling in it. "He and Ronan haven't spoken in years. You can bet your bottom dollar he'd rather claw his own eyes out than lay eyes on those children."

Such a brutal thing to say. How could this Sully hate a five and a seven-year-old so badly? By the sounds of things, he'd never even met them. I got the feeling Caruthers was painting the situation a little bleaker than necessary. He tore a piece of paper out of his notebook and handed it to me. "That's Sully's number there. He's the best carpenter on the island. The only carpenter really. Everyone knows his number off the top of their heads. Anyway. Call before you go swanning over there, Miss. He isn't too friendly at the best of times. If he thinks you're connected with Ronan in any way, he'll probably shoot you dead."

"He has a *gun*?"

"Probably. Who knows? Let's get out of here," Caruthers said, kicking at Hinchliffe with his steel toe capped foot. And to me: "We left you the letter after all. No one's second-guessing this one after all, it seems. We did have a read, though, just to make sure there was nothing incriminating inside."

It didn't seem smart to ask if they'd actually found anything. I just wanted them to leave. The longer they stood here, jabbering away, the less time I had to prepare myself for dealing with Connor and Amie. The two of them looked like they'd had enough of poking around in Ronan's stuff, now, anyway.

"We'll be on our way, Miss Lang. If you need anything, you just give us a call at the station, okay?" Hinchliffe tipped his hat to me in a very old fashioned way—was he hitting on me? Oh lord. That was all I needed.

"I'll make sure to do that."

Hinchliffe smiled from ear to ear. "*Grand.*"

••••

"But where did he go?"

Despite all the commotion and the noise downstairs, Connor had still been asleep when I crept into his room. Amie was sitting on the floor, cross-legged, nightie pooled around her as she doggedly chewed on her breakfast. Most of the pancakes were gone, and she was looking a little green. Connor wasn't too happy that Ronan was "out." I didn't know what else to tell him.

"I wanted him to show me the island today. He said I'd like it here, but I hate it. I *hate* it. I want to go home." His heart-shaped face was turning purple with frustration. Almost on the verge of tears, he was fighting not to let them fall. I was in the same boat. I'd been stunned earlier. Shocked. Now that shock was wearing off, and I was on the very brink of breaking down. Ronan had killed himself, and he'd left me to pick up the pieces. How stupid of me last night, lying there in bed, mulling over the possibility that I might allow myself to consider getting close to him. Chances were right at that same moment in time he was tying the noose, lashing it over the ceiling fan in the office, standing on his desk, taking a look around, taking his last breaths. His children were sleeping. He just fucking *left* them.

"It's going to be okay, Connor," I told the little boy, placing a hand on his shoulder. "I can show you the island. We'll have a fun day. You, me and Amie. What do you say?" I wanted to get out of the house anyway. Needed to. I still couldn't shake the image of Ronan hanging from the ceiling. It was torture, being trapped within the same building where he committed such a desperate act. Why the hell had he done it, anyway? The note he left on the door wasn't giving up any clues. The letter addressed to me in his office probably did, but I was too freaked out to go in there and get it.

Connor shrugged away from my touch. "I don't know you. I don't like you. I don't want to go anywhere until Dad gets back."

"I don't feel very well." Amie had been quiet through this whole exchange. Now she was standing up, holding her belly, looking very queasy. The plate at her feet, the one I had stacked so high in my panic to get her out of the way, was empty. "I'm going to be sick," she whispered.

"Okay, baby. It's okay, come with me. Come on." Damn it. I'd already made Connor angry and Amie sick, and we were still technically on day one of me caring for them. *Stellar job, Ophelia. Gangbusters. Seriously.* I hurried to the bathroom with Amie, barely getting her there before she vomited all over the tiled floor. She started crying, shivering, her little body shaking as she retched, bringing up a huge amount of food. Her belly must have been stretched way beyond capacity. What a terrible mother I would have made. I scooped her up and held her to me as she slowly began to settle, the shaking growing less and less until she was just lying still in my arms, looking up at me, strands of her dark hair plastered to her forehead. Her eyes were clear, the lightest of blues, so different to Ronan's. "I feel much better now," she whispered. "I'm sorry I made a mess."

"That's okay, sweetie. It's my fault. I shouldn't have given you so much to eat, should I? What do you say, you hang out with your brother in his room again while I get this cleared up, and then we can maybe watch a movie or something, huh?" Amie, sweet little Amie, nodded, smiling. I already knew I was never going to get the same easy compliance from her brother. No point in even trying.

While I cleaned up the bathroom, I finally allowed myself to break down. I was in way over my head. On the other side of the country, on a tiny island where I didn't know a soul, and my boss had just thrown me in at the deep end in the most profound, irreversible way. So unbelievable of him. So unkind. So fucking cruel. Did he really expect me to just float around The Causeway with his two young children in tow, teaching them and playing with them and pretending like nothing had happened? How delusional could one person be?

The letter downstairs. It would shed more light on the matter. I couldn't face it though. Just couldn't. Instead, I wiped my eyes, finished mopping up the puke from the floor, and I went and got the kids.

"I don't care what you want right now, Connor. You can not like me all you want, but your dad left me in charge, and that means you have to do what I say, okay? And we're going to get dressed and get out of the house. All day. We're going to find somewhere to eat lunch, and we're going to explore down by the beach."

"Yay! The beach!" Amie started dancing around in her camisole and underwear, spinning in a circle with her hands in the air. "I *love* the beach!"

"It's too cold." Connor folded his arms across his chest, chin tilted down, eyes narrowed. He looked like he could have played Damien in the eighties horror movie quite convincingly. "I. Don't. Want. To. Go."

"Well. I'm sorry to hear that, buddy, but you don't have a choice. Now get your shoes on."

••••

Ronan's car keys were in the ignition of the SUV in the garage. There was an orange Post-it note on the middle of the steering wheel that said, USE THE CAR SEATS on it. *Of course I'm going to use the goddamn car seats. Helpful, Ronan. Really fucking helpful. You know what would have been* really *helpful? You not killing yourself, that's what.*

I screwed the Post-it up and quickly threw it into the glove box.

Connor pulled the most dramatic, unhappy face when I opened up the back seat door for him. "Do I have to sit in the back? Dad normally lets me sit up in the front with him."

"Sorry, kiddo. There's a booster back there for you. Amie, look at your car seat. Isn't it cool?" It was red with green dinosaurs all over it. Amie clapped her hands when she saw it; Connor looked like he wanted to set the entire car on fire. Disgust radiated off him in scorching degrees.

"This is bullshit," he mumbled under his breath. His eyes flickered to me, his shoulders stiffening as he waited for my reaction. I gave him none, which, by the looks of things, made him really mad.

I'd dealt with enough kids like him at school though, acting out to get attention. If you gave them nothing, they generally learned it was pointless and stopped after a while. Connor's situation was more complicated, though. He was going to do more than act out when he learned about Ronan. His whole world was going to come crashing down. *Again.* How the hell was *I* qualified to handle *that*?

I didn't know where I was supposed to be going when I drove down the long driveway and out onto the road, but I tried to appear confident, if only for the kids' sake.

The morning slipped by. We drove around the entire island at least twice before I really saw any of it—rolling hills, so green and lush that they almost looked fake; steep, rocky cliff faces that plunged wildly down into white water and the raging sea; tiny little whitewashed houses with peeling green window frames and scruffy dogs tethered to posts out front; so many decrepit looking fishing boats rocking to and fro along the coastline, fraying lines caked in salt crystals threatening to snap under the tension of the boats trying to drift away. It felt like another time, in another world completely.

At around lunch, the storm finally hit. The thunderheads that were lurking out over the ocean finally rolled in, and thunder and lightning crackled overhead. The children weren't scared at all. I parked the car at the side of the winding, narrow road that headed back to the house, and the three of us sat and watched the battle in the heavens commence. We counted the seconds between the lightning flashes and the thunder…

One…two…three…

We didn't make it past three; the fury was right on top of us. It felt safe in the car, even though we probably weren't. For a second, such a brief, unbearably small snatch of time, I didn't think about Ronan swinging from the ceiling fan. I didn't think about CPS coming in the morning to take the children away. I just sat with them in the car and we shrieked and howled every time the ground shook beneath us, and the sky rippled with light, and everything else was just noise.

••••

Negotiating bedtime with Connor was like negotiating peace in the Middle East. It was well after nine by the time he finally agreed to climb into bed, and that was only because his head was nodding and he could barely keep his eyes open any longer. *Jurassic Park* had gone on at seven, and Amie had been so excited within the first twenty minutes that she'd exhausted herself and fallen asleep straight away. I'd carried her up and put her in her tiny single bed in the room next to mine, and she hadn't even stirred. Connor had made it to the last fifteen minutes of the film before he got up off the couch and staggered sleepily off in the direction of his room, silently, unwilling to admit defeat.

Fifteen minutes later, I was on the phone with Mom, balling my eyes out. It took three solid attempts to explain what had happened before she understood what I was saying.

"You aren't *serious*?" she hissed down the phone. "George? George? Where are you? Ophelia's boss *committed suicide!*"

Dad picked up the other line in the den. "*What did you say?*"

I let Mom tell him; I didn't have the energy to get it out all over again. Now that the children were asleep, I finally didn't have to hold myself together anymore. It was a relief, but it was also frightening. I felt out of control, like I was barely retaining my grasp on reality.

"You have got to come home, honey. I knew there was something off about this whole thing. Honest to god, what a terrible thing to do. What a thoughtless bastard. Those poor little mites." Mom was outraged for everyone involved, including me, but the children bore the brunt of her sympathy. Having my mother feel sorry for you was not necessarily a good thing in a situation like this. It tended to make her hysterical. "I mean, really! *Really!*" Her voice was getting higher and higher. "I just can't believe it. How could someone be so self-serving? If you want to kill yourself you wait, until after your children have finished college. It's just not done! I can't believe it. What an asshole. What a complete *asshole*."

"Calm down, Jen. Calm down. We don't know the whole story," Dad said, ever the peacekeeper. "Your mother's right, though, darling. Come home as soon as you've handed the children over tomorrow. That's not a healthy environment for you to be in right now."

I didn't tell them about Mr. Linneman and his paperwork. If they knew Ronan had essentially left his kids to me in his will, they would go ballistic, and I couldn't deal with Mom's voice raising another decibel right now. "I know. I will. I'm going to book a flight as soon as I get off the phone."

The restaurant was going to be shut down. I wasn't going to make the money Ronan promised me if I didn't stay and see out the six months, there was no two ways about that. But maybe, if I was really lucky another job would come up as soon as I landed back in California. There might be enough time to build up a little bit of capital and save the business from going under if I started waiting tables at a second job as well.

"Look, guys, I'm so sorry. I'm beat. I'm going to have to go and sleep. I'll call you as soon as I know what time I'll be getting back, okay?"

My parents both wished me goodnight, and Mom told me to take care of myself about fifteen times. I was headed up to bed, trying not to look in the direction of Ronan's study, when I felt a familiar niggle of doubt shoot through me. Why did he do it? Why? I was never going to know if I didn't read that damned letter. I wanted to go home, yes, but how frustrating would it be to never truly understand what had happened and why? If I didn't go into Ronan's office and get that letter, I was going to be in the dark forever. And he *owed* me, damn it. He owed me an explanation. What he did wasn't fair to me, and it really wasn't fair to his kids.

I halted on the stairs, fear already prickling at my skin. I was going to do it. Being afraid was stupid. Tweedle Dee and Tweedle Dum had taken Ronan's body away hours ago. There was nothing in there now, but the unreasonably superstitious part of me was convinced Ronan's spirit was still lurking in there, poking around in among the books and all of his papers, waiting for someone to come visit him.

Stupid. Really stupid.

I marched down the stairs, across the hallway and straight into the office, holding my breath. Nothing happened. The room was empty. The chair Ronan must have used to climb up onto his desk had been tucked neatly away. All of the sheets of paper on his desk were straight, apart from one small white envelope—the one I had come in here to find. It sat on top of a thick, leather-bound book that looked like it had been carried around by someone for years, all covered in scratch marks, a deep brown oil mark down the spine, probably from extended periods of handling. On top of the envelope and the book, something glinted and shone in the dark—gold and purple. A medal. A purple heart.

"*Shit*," I whispered to myself.

The room, despite the fact that it was full of brand new furniture and still had that universal Ikea smell of flat pack bookcases and fresh woven fabric, was already filled with a sense of emptiness that chilled me inside.

Ronan had claimed the room forever now. No matter what, the space would always carry the history of his actions within its four walls. I picked up the medal first, turning it over in my hand. It looked pristine, brand new, like it had never been handled before. George Washington eyed me balefully from the cast of the metal, stern and cold. I dropped it back on the desk, snatched up the letter, then retreated out of the room at a run, my heart beating out of my chest.

It felt a lot safer sitting at the kitchen counter to read the note. My name was slashed across the envelope like Ronan had been in a terrible hurry when he'd written it.

Inside, the letter:

Ophelia,

We met for the first time today. You weren't impressed with me in your interview, I could tell, but I was impressed by you. You weren't flustered. You were respectful and polite, even when I was rude. You were steady. You were calm. You were exactly what I need you to be now, in this moment, when you're reading this letter.

You probably think I'm a monster, and I suppose I am in a lot of ways. I haven't made this decision lightly. Know I have wrestled endlessly over my decision to take my own life. Not because I wanted to live, but because of the effect it will have on the children. I haven't second-guessed myself. Ever since Magda died, I've wanted to follow after her. My family was fairly religious when I was growing up—Roman Catholic—but I haven't believed in that stuff for a very long time now. I don't think Magda's cancer was a test handed down to her by a higher power. I think more than likely it was a shitty hand dealt to her in a game of poker she didn't even realize she was playing. But if there's a chance there is an afterlife, something more that we go to when we leave this plane of existence, then I have to hope that I'll be joining her soon.

I don't expect you to understand how I can risk my children's happiness on the slim possibility that I might be able to see my wife again. But you see, if I lived my children wouldn't be happy. They would resent me. They would hate me. As the days, the weeks, and the months have passed me by, I have caught a glimmer of the man I am to become if I continue to live and breathe in this skin of mine, and he isn't a good man. Before Magda, I was lost. I was weak. I was broken. I am even worse without her now.

So you see it's better this way. I've amassed a fortune in the past few years. Enough money to make sure Connor and Amie receive the best education money can buy. They'll never have to worry about making their mortgage payments. They'll never have to stress about making ends meet. Their futures lie before them, all the better and brighter for the fact that I won't be in them.

And you...this is where you come in. I'm sorry I lied to you. You're a strong, smart, fiery woman, and in another life I'm sure we would have been great allies. You're like Magda in so many ways that sitting across from you in that interview made me very uncomfortable.

I ask you to please carry out the job I hired you for. I've opened a bank account on the island and left enough money in there for you to be more than fine from now until the summer. Take care of my children. Teach them. Nourish them. Comfort them. If you're too angry to do this for me, then please do it for my wife. Connor and Amie were her sun and moon. She was a sweet, kind, wonderful woman, and no matter how badly I am letting her down right now, I have been determined to make sure someone equally as wonderful as her safeguards the children until their uncle agrees to take them himself.

In case you are still unaware, I have a brother, Sully. Sully and I *haven't spoken in seven years, but the truth of the matter is that he is still my closest friend. He will take the children eventually, Ophelia. He might just need nudging in the right direction. I have every confidence in your ability to make him see sense.*

On my desk, you will find a leather diary along with this letter. Read it. It will explain a lot.

Ronan.

P.s. When he's ready, give Sully the medal.

Great. So not only did Ronan want me to take on the role of mother, father and sometimes teacher to his children, he wanted me to convince his estranged brother to accept the role after me? Ronan and I barely spent any time together whatsoever. How he had figured out I was capable of accomplishing this monumental task in such a short period of time was a mystery. Damn it. Talk about an uphill battle. He must have known it would be too much to ask of one person. He *must* have known.

It was late. I should have been exhausted from getting up so early and the events that occurred shortly afterward, but instead my brain was wired. Too much adrenalin pumping around my body, lighting up my synapses, causing my muscles to jump and twitch of their own accord. I was going to read that damned diary. I was going to read it cover to cover, and if there wasn't something monumentally terrible inside then I was going to curse the name of Ronan Fletcher for what he'd done.

Getting up, I hurried back into his study, moving as quickly as I could—I didn't want to spend a second longer than necessary in that terrible room—but my eyes never landed on the diary. The second I walked through the door, I looked up and saw *him*. Saw him standing there, on the other side of the window. Our eyes met, and I saw the shock on his face. Only a matter of hours ago I'd been outside, feet covered in mud, heart hammering in my chest, watching him swinging back and forth. Now our roles were reversed, him pale, white as a sheet, hair tumbling into his eyes, staring at me through the glass, and me, swaying in the study, barely managing to keep my legs from quitting out from underneath me.

It couldn't be. It just *couldn't* be possible. Ronan was dead. I'd seen him with my own two eyes. The cops had made sure. How the hell could he be watching me from outside if they had taken his lifeless body away to somewhere else on the island? The answer was obvious and yet impossible at the same time: I was looking at a ghost. Ronan's spirit really *had* lingered behind, and he was observing right now me with hard, steely eyes and a firm set to his jaw that told me he wasn't happy with how I was dealing with this situation.

My head spun. I couldn't breathe. A heavy weight pressed down on my chest, constricting my ribcage, preventing me from expanding my lungs properly. My mother had always said ghosts were real. She'd been saying that since I was a kid. I'd never believed her. Never once considered she might not be completely loopy. Until now. The room seemed to be pitching to one side, listing drunkenly. I was about to pass out.

"Ronan?"

The face on the other side of the window—Ronan's face—frowned. My breath shortened even further, coming out in sharp, ineffective pants that felt unwelcome in my body, as if my lungs had hardened, refusing to accommodate the oxygen I was trying to force into my body. I took a step back, my body reacting too slowly. The message my brain was sending to my legs was, *"Run! Run like the fucking wind!"* but they wouldn't cooperate. Instead, I shuffled backward away from the window, hands stiff at my sides, heart beating like a signal drum in my ears, in my temples, everywhere in my body.

The figure on the other side of the window acted as if he were my reflection in a mirror, moving away from the window, vanishing into the blackness beyond. I couldn't take my eyes off him. If I did, he was likely to materialize out of thin air right behind me and kill me somehow.

That's what ghosts did, wasn't it? They wanted to cause harm? They sure as hell didn't show up for a cup of tea and a chat as far as I was aware. My obsession with the TV show Supernatural kicked in, then, and I began frantically trying to remember where the nearest iron poker or piece of rebar might be. It wasn't that kind of house, though. Once upon a time it might have been, but now everything was renovated and brand new. The huge fireplace in the living room was gas powered, and with two small children around it was unlikely anyone had left building materials laying around.

While my brain was thinking these ridiculous thoughts, Ronan was vanishing, disappearing little by little, the shadows eating him, swallowing him, until finally he was gone.

The spell was broken.

I bolted from the study like a shot.

My feet hammered up the stairs; it seemed as though I made enough racket to wake up the children and half of the island, but when I raced along the hallway and dashed into my room, slamming the door closed behind me, I didn't hear another soul stirring in the house. All I could hear was my own labored breathing, and the sound of thunder rumbling off in the distance.

"*Jesus.*" I leaned my back against the door, swallowing hard. *Get yourself together, Lang. Christ, what the hell is wrong with you? It couldn't have been him. It wasn't.*

It took a long time to convince myself of this. I paced my room for fifteen minutes, shaking my head, mind racing. It had been a long day. An awful, heartbreaking day. There was no way Ronan had killed himself, only to come back as a ghost, though. No way in hell. The mind was a powerful thing, and after the day I'd had it was understandable that I would be overly sensitive. Imagining things, seeing things that weren't there.

I was still too freaked to shower. I got changed and climbed into bed with my laptop instead, jumping every time the house creaked or the branches of the trees outside the window shook, casting long shadows on the walls inside my room. Flights. I needed to book my flight home. The sooner I got back to California and away from this god-forsaken place, the better.

I opened up my web browser and had to stop myself from booking the earliest flight available. It would be really crappy of me to leave before the CPS worker came and collected Amie and Connor. I didn't even have anywhere to leave them. Waiting until everything was squared away with them was the right thing to do, even if the prospect of postponing my flight from the island for a few extra hours was enough to make me break out in hives.

Seven thirty in the evening. The flight I booked from Knox County was late enough that I'd have enough time to see the children settled, get my ass across to the mainland, and travel back into the city. I might even have enough time to grab a glass of wine or two in the airport bar—I'd never needed a drink more in my life than I did now. Not even when I found Will in bed with my best friend.

I'd like to say that I fell asleep right away, reassured that I was going to be back on a plane in less than twenty-four hours, winging my way home to my relatively normal life in California, far from the windswept coastline of Causeway Island and the crazy, terrible thing that had happened here. I didn't, though. I lay in bed with the covers pulled up tight underneath my chin, and I stared at the ceiling, chewing on my lip, scared and feeling like a pretty shitty human being.

CHAPTER NINE

UNACCEPTABLE CIRCUMSTANCES

"Feelya. Feelya, wake up. There's a man outside." A tiny hand poked and prodded at my face, patting over my cheeks and forehead. I woke slowly, sluggishly, trying to comprehend my surroundings. It took a second for everything to rush at me—the memory of yesterday and everything that occurred. Amie was standing by my bed, hair snarled into a dark, tangled bird's nest. She had lines on her cheek from her pillow, but other than that she looked like she might have been awake for hours. Her pale blue eyes were bright and alert, crinkled at the corners, and her mouth was drawn into an impish smile. "You were snoring. Really loud," she informed me in a whisper.

"Did you say there was a man outside?" I rubbed a hand over my face, trying to shake the fog from my brain.

Amie nodded. "He's very skinny. He looks like he's very hungry, probably."

A very skinny man outside? Could only be Linneman. I supposed he did have a kind of hungry look about him. "Did you let him inside?" I asked.

"No. Daddy said not to."

"*Daddy?*"

Amie nodded again. "Yes. He always says not to answer the door to anybody."

"Ah, okay. Yes, that's very smart. He's right. You shouldn't." I threw back the covers, now able to hear the polite but insistent rapping on the front door downstairs. The clock on the bedside table read eight forty-five. Jesus, how had I slept so long? Kids get up so early; I should have been out of bed and making them breakfast two hours ago. Typical that I couldn't sleep all night and then I fall face first into unconsciousness around dawn, just in time to make myself late for everything.

Downstairs, Linneman was standing at the front door, small wisps of his gray hair blowing across his face as the wind howled across the huge front lawn. He gave me a tight-lipped smile through the glass as I hurried to the door, unlocked and opened it.

"Morning, Miss Lang. I was beginning to worry that you'd already left. May I?" He gestured past me into the hallway. "It's rather cold out here, and I've been standing here for some time."

"Oh, god, of course. Of course. I'm sorry, I—" I gave up trying to formulate an excuse for the length of time it took me to come to the door. My pajamas and my bedhead were explanation enough. Linneman stalked into the hallway, swinging the same battered leather briefcase at his side that he'd had with him yesterday. His clothing was as official and proper as it had been yesterday, too—dark gray suit this time, that looked like it was in actual fact some kind of tweed, shot through with a fine blue thread, and a severely pressed white button-down, finished off with a blue tie that had been tied so high and tight that it looked like it was strangling him.

"Should we go through to the kitchen?" he asked, casting a cool, businesslike glance over his shoulder.

"Yes. Please. I'll make some coffee."

"Oh, tea, if you have it," he said in answer.

Amie on my heels, holding onto the back of my shirt, was closer than my own shadow. "Amie, sweetheart, where's Connor?" I hissed, hoping Linneman wouldn't hear.

"He's playing Gand feft Auto. He said I wasn't allowed to have a turn." She said this morosely, as if it were the saddest thing in the world, and she had only just remembered to be upset about it now. Her bottom lip jutted out like she was considering crying but wasn't sure if it was worth it yet.

Connor was too young to be playing Grand Theft Auto. Too young by a decade. Ronan must have bought it for him, though, and I was going to be leaving really soon, so there didn't seem any point in racing up there to confiscate the game.

"It's all right, kiddo. How about you sit in front of the fire in the living room and watch Peppa Pig instead, and I'll make you some breakfast? How does that sound?"

Amie perked up immediately at the sound of breakfast. The kid was a bottomless pit. I turned to Linneman, who was setting himself up at the breakfast counter again, laying out paperwork, pens, a check book and a pair of wire framed spectacles neatly in a row. "That's okay, Miss Lang. I shall wait right here for you to return."

And so he did. I positioned Amie in front of the television, turned the gas fire on low to edge the chill out of the air, and made sure the little girl knew not to get too close. There was a glass door on the fire, as well as a huge, sturdy metal grate in between her and the flames, which she wouldn't have been able to move even if she wanted to, but still...I made her promise not to budge an inch.

Back in the kitchen, Linneman was staring at the coffee pot with a very confused look on his face. I got the feeling he'd never operated one before.

"I wanted to come over and discuss Ronan's paperwork with you once more before CPS came for the children," Linneman said, stabbing at a button on the machine. "Now that you've had a little time to consider your options, I was hoping you might have changed your mind?"

He was bound to ask this. He didn't sound like he would be affected either way by my decision, though. He didn't seem like the sort of man to form an emotional attachment of any kind; it was almost surprising that he had a wife. For all I knew (and strongly suspected), he had probably gotten married because it was the pragmatic thing to do. I briefly tried to imagine him swept away in some sordid love affair and couldn't bend my mind around the idea at all.

"I'm sorry, Mr. Linneman. I haven't changed my mind. I booked a flight out of Knox County this evening at seven thirty." I felt awful admitting that the night hadn't brought about some miraculous change in me, but it was the truth. It hadn't. It had scared the living shit out of me, and I couldn't wait to get as far away from this massive, empty house as soon as possible.

"So be it. Then I have the release forms here for you to sign. That means you can go, that you haven't accepted legal guardianship of the children. I'll prepare them for you now." Linneman sat at the kitchen counter while I boiled water for his tea. A rising tide of guilt swelled inside me one minute, receding the next to be replaced with self-righteous indignation.

Ronan really screwed this one up. Yes, it was sad that his wife died, but he shouldn't have done something so terrible and left a near stranger in his place to pick up the pieces. That was just downright shitty of him.

I placed Linneman's tea on the counter, and he placed down three sheets of paper on the marble, and the two of us then sat for a moment and pondered the articles in front of us. Linneman seemed as hesitant and regretful about picking up his mug as I felt about picking up my pen. Still, we both did what we had to do.

I scribbled my name in the spots Linneman had indicated with tiny, colorful tabs, while he gingerly slurped at the pale liquid inside his cup.

"Interesting," he said under his breath, placing the cup down. "Very...*warm*." I'd never made a cup of tea before; I'd clearly messed up some part of the process, but Linneman was too polite to say so.

"If you want to get off the island today, I'd make sure to call Jerry Bucksted and see if he plans on sailing that late. The storm we had yesterday was nothing compared to the one that'll be rolling in around dinnertime. I'd best be off, Miss Lang. It was very nice to meet you, I'm sure."

Another storm? Great. Fantastic. Just what I needed. No way I was missing that flight, though. If I had to bribe Jerry Buckwhatever to get me back to the mainland, then that was fine by me. When I saw Linneman to the door, the thunderheads were back, charging across the horizon toward us like a heard of stampeding horses. Foreboding and black, the clouds did not look promising at all.

• • • •

"You'll be Miss Lang, then?" The CPS representative showed up at eleven o'clock, a little later in the day than I'd anticipated. I thought she'd arrive at the house around nine, but apparently the crossing from Port Creef was already rough, and the boat had to postpone its departure for ninety minutes until a calmer patch of weather presented itself. The woman, Sheryl Lourie, according to the laminated card she showed me on the doorstep, looked so green that I was expecting her to throw up any second. Her shirt was too tight, the material straining to stretch across her considerable chest, and her pencil skirt looked way too constricting and uncomfortable for the morning she must have had, sitting on a boat while the ocean pitched and tossed.

I'd spent the morning playing dinosaurs with Amie and giving Connor some room to brood on the sofa with a book in his hands (something to do with tree houses). They had been asking where Ronan was, and both had looked beyond hopeful when the doorbell rang, immediately shouting out for their dad. Connor looked like he was about to launch his book through a window when he saw it wasn't Ronan.

"Who is *she*?" he hissed at me, as we all went and sat in the living room. "Where's my dad?"

At that, Sheryl spun around, clutching her purse to her chest, eyes wide. "They don't know?" she mouthed.

I shook my head.

I watched as the blood drained out of her face. "I see. Well. Why don't we all sit down and have a little chat, then, huh?" She hadn't been expecting to walk into this situation. No one had let her know I hadn't explained Ronan's death to Amie or Connor. I felt bad for the poor woman. If she'd known, she probably would have had time to acclimatize herself to the idea and figure out the best way to handle the matter. Now she had to think on the fly, and that was no good for her or for the kids.

The coward in me didn't want to stick around for the next part. It would be easy enough to slip out and let Sheryl do the hard stuff. They were going to be leaning on her far more than they would be leaning on me soon anyway. But it wasn't right and I knew it. I sat myself down in between Connor and Amie, taking the little girl's hand in mine. I tried to take Connor's, but he shunted away from me, gripping onto his book, knuckles and nail beds turned white.

"Okay, then." Sheryl tucked her hair behind her ears and got straight to it. I had to commend her—the woman didn't mess around. "Your daddy's been gone for a couple of days, hasn't he?"

Amie nodded. Connor just stared. He had a struck look on his face, his cheeks pale, his dark hair falling in wisps over his forehead and into his eyes. Blinking, he opened his book and started to read, ignoring Sheryl.

"Connor, sweetheart. Put down the book. You have to listen to what Mrs. Lourie is saying now, okay?" I tried to take it gently from him, but he snatched it away, glaring at me.

"It's all right." Sheryl shifted in her seat, clearing her throat. She was uncomfortable, that much was clear. "Maybe Connor can listen while he reads at the same time."

This was a terrible idea, Connor needed to pay attention, to process the information being explained to him, but I couldn't contradict her. Sheryl was in charge. She must have done this before, surely? I tried not to acknowledge the angry look Connor shot my way, and turned my attention to Amie. She was sitting quietly, kicking her heels lightly against the sofa, looking back and forth between Sheryl and me, her tiny eyebrows banked together with concern. She knew something was up, just as Connor did.

"So, you remember how Mommy went away last year?" Sheryl continued hesitantly. Amie sniffed and leaned her head against my arm.

"She went to heaven," the little girl said softly. "She went to be with Oscar."

Sheryl looked up at me sharply. *Oscar?* I shook my head. I had no idea.

"Oscar was our dog," Connor murmured, head still down, eyes on the page in front of him. "He got hit by a car."

"I see," Sheryl said again. "Yes. So your mommy went to be with Oscar. Well, that's where Daddy's gone as well. To be with Mommy and Oscar. Do you know what that means?"

Connor went absolutely still. Amie made a short puffing sound, eyes traveling from me to Sheryl again. "He's not coming back?" she whispered. "Why?"

"Because he's dead," Connor snapped. "He died. He left us, just like *she* left us. I *knew* he wasn't coming back!"

"Your daddy had an accident." Sheryl pressed on, hands clasped in her lap, twisting her wedding ring around and around her finger, nails painted a very outlandish color of burnt orange. "And that means he *can't* come back."

Amie's bottom lip was wobbling. Her eyes were filling with tears of confusion, her little body shaking next to mine. She pressed herself against me, and my heart nearly cracked in two when she looked up at me and a choked sob slipped from her mouth. "I don't want Daddy to go with Mommy," she wailed.

Connor still hadn't moved. "It's tough luck, Amie. We don't get a say in it. We don't get a say in anything. Right?" His eyes flickered up, fixing on Sheryl. She seemed stunned by the blunt, hard words coming out of Connor's mouth. They stunned me, too. No seven-year-old should have had such a stark outlook on life. "I'm afraid not," Sheryl confirmed. "Sometimes these things happen to people, and no one gets a say in the matter. I know it's hard. I know it's sad, but—"

"It's not sad," Connor snarled. "He wanted to go and be with her. I know he did. I heard him say it. He told Dr. Fielding. He didn't want to be with us anymore. He left on purpose. I *hate* him. I hate him!"

Jumping up from the sofa, Connor rocketed out of the room, his book tumbling to the floor. I tried to disentangle myself from Amie, to go after him, but Sheryl reached out and put a hand on my knee.

"Best we give him a moment, I think," she said.

Collecting Amie into my arms, I held her against me, rocking her back and forth while she cried. I wanted to disagree with Sheryl—being alone seemed like the worst possible thing for a grieving child who'd just been told their father was dead—but again, Sheryl knew best. And I couldn't just leave Amie.

"I'm sorry," Sheryl said. "I'd normally take a lot longer over something like this, but time really is of the essence. I can't get stuck on the island, and the man on the boat was rather rude. He said he'd wait an hour for me and no longer. Do you think we could gather up some of the children's things? We can arrange for the rest of their belongings to be sent over to the mainland if and when we find homes for them to go to."

"I'm sorry? Homes? You haven't already found a place for them to go? Together?"

Sheryl inched forward on her chair, pulling her lips into a tight line.

"Mr. Fletcher only…*moved on*…yesterday, Miss Lang. Rehoming children is a process. It's probable that we'll find somewhere for Amie to go in a couple of months. Connor's older, so it might be a little more difficult to place him. Also, his…*behavioral* issues might make it harder to find a family equipped to provide the attention and care he needs."

They weren't going to be kept together? They weren't going to find homes for *months*? I hadn't even considered something like this might happen. God, how could I have been so naïve? I felt sick, all of a sudden. Sicker than I had already been feeling for the past twenty-four hours. "Where will you take them, then? Now? When you get off the boat?"

"To a group home for children. It's a safe place. A wonderful establishment, Miss Lang. I assure you, the children will be taken care of there. The people who run the home are the best at what they do."

A group home for children? I knew what that was. That was basically an orphanage. I could picture the rows and rows of beds, all filled with children crying themselves to sleep. Kids bullying each other, no one around or caring enough to protect them. And I'd heard the stories. The shame-filled confessions of the damaged kids who had been molested by predators in places like the group home Sheryl was championing right now. My arms tightened around Amie.

"I'm sorry, I—" I didn't know what to say next. I didn't have the right words to voice my horror.

"I understand your concern, Miss Lang, I really do. But rest assured, I will be checking in with Amie and Connor *every* week. I'll personally be looking for families to take care of them myself." She said this as though checking in once a week with them was enough, was more than satisfactory, when in actual fact it was disgraceful, and made me want to cry on the spot.

"They definitely won't be kept together?" I said, clutching hold of Amie, who had balled my t-shirt up in her little hands and was clinging onto me as if her life depended on it.

Sheryl's mouth pulled down in a sorry expression. She bore the kind of apologetic look someone might wear if they were informing you they were out of fresh milk at the grocery store, though. It didn't feel all that sincere. It probably wasn't her fault. She was undoubtedly desensitized to situations like this by now. Amie and Connor were just two more unfortunates who'd found their way into the system. They were reference numbers, files on her desk that meant more paperwork and more headaches than she had time for.

"It really is okay," she said. "I've successfully found homes for over sixty-five percent of my kids. That's twelve percent higher than the average case worker," she said, leaning forward to impart the information to me, speaking out of the side of her mouth, as if she didn't want to sound like she was bragging.

Sixty-five percent was meant to be impressive? If she'd said ninety-five percent, it still wouldn't have been good enough. How, in good conscience, could I let Sheryl take the kids, knowing the misery and loneliness they would endure in a group home? *How?* Did Ronan know this would be the case, the consequences for his actions if I refused to be manipulated by him? I was pretty sure he did. I was pretty sure he was still manipulating me now.

I sighed, dreading the next words to come out of my mouth. They had to be said, though. He had won. Ronan, after everything, had won. I was going to have to give him what he wanted, otherwise my guilt was going to consume me for the rest of my damned days. "I'm afraid I can't let you take them, Mrs. Lourie. I'm going to have to keep the children here with me."

She frowned, head tipping to one side. "I'm sorry? I thought you were just the nanny?"

"No. Ronan left the children in my care. He asked me to care for them for the next six months. I had thought they would be better off with another family, someone more qualified to care for them, but in light of this new information..."

Sheryl jerked back in her chair, pulling some paperwork out of her purse. "Well this is highly irregular. No one mentioned Mr. Fletcher had made you the children's guardian in the event that anything happened to him?"

"His will and estate was only recently updated. His lawyer, Mr. Linneman, has the paperwork, I believe." I *seriously* hoped Linneman hadn't destroyed Ronan's guardianship documents. If he had, there probably wasn't much that could be done; Sheryl would be well within her rights to take the children and disappear back to the mainland with them. Where would she even take them, anyway? Back to New York? Doubtful. It would cost money to send them back, and why bother, when they had no family or anything tying them to the area with Ronan gone. They were going to end up in an entirely different state than the one they had been raised in, simply because their father decided to die on a tiny island off the coast of Maine.

"I'm going to have to check into that, Miss Lang." Sheryl was looking severely put out. "I don't think I'll have time on this trip. I really do need to get back to the dock. I should, by rights, take the children with me back to the center while this is all ironed out."

"And if I'd rather they stayed here? With me?"

"It would be remiss of me to leave the children in a situation I thought was unstable."

"Unstable? I'd say the environment is far more stable here, with me, than it would be in a group home."

"Miss Lang…" Sheryl paused, giving her shoes her full attention for a moment while she thought with her mouth open. "Less than five minutes ago, you didn't want these children. You mentioned nothing of the fact that Mr. Fletcher made you guardian over them. You only spoke out when you found out where they were headed, now I don't mean to be rude, but they teach us to look for erratic behavior in people left to care for children at risk, and forgive me for saying so, but your behavior has definitely given me cause for concern. I'm not entirely sure you understand what you'd be taking on here, or that you'd be able to cope along for that matter."

Upstairs, the door to Connor's bedroom slammed hard, the loud shotgun sound ringing out, echoing through the house. *Perfect.* "Look. *Sheryl.* I know this situation isn't perfect. I know there are probably families and homes out there for Connor and Amie that might be perfect for them, but I also know that separating them and keeping them in a group home for weeks on end, potentially months, is not going to benefit them in any way. I have extensive experience with troubled youths. I've worked with children the same ages as Connor and Amie for years. I *will* take care of these children. I *can* do it. I'll fight tooth and nail to make sure they stay with me if it means they can stay together. Now, you can sit here arguing with me about what to do, or you can go and make sure you catch Jerry before he heads back to the mainland. I heard the storm's likely to linger for a couple of days. Unless you want to spend two or three nights shut away in a room above the only bar on the island with no fresh clothes to change into, then I'd be hurrying if I were you."

Playing on her desire to leave The Causeway was a cheap move, but it looked like it had worked. Sheryl shuddered when I mentioned being trapped in the bar. After a long moment where she studied me with watery blue eyes, she said, "All right, Miss Lang. But please bear in mind…I can always come back. It's a hindrance, I'll admit, but I like to take care of my cases. If you realize this task is beyond you, there's no shame in calling and having me come take them. Likewise, if I think they're in harm's way, Ophelia, I'll make sure both Connor and Amie are on that boat back to Maine quicker than you can blink. Do you understand?"

"Yes, ma'am."

"Well, all right, then." Sheryl got to her feet, holding her purse under one arm while she pulled out her cell phone. Sighing dramatically, she tucked the phone away and jerked at her blazer jacket, tugging at it in a ruffled kind of way. "I'll see myself out. No, please don't get up. I'm sure you'll want to go and make sure Connor is all right now, anyway."

It was a none too subtle hint, as if I might not realize that the young boy would need some sort of comfort after finding out his father had died. And after she had told me to give him a moment, too. I gave her a tight smile—one aimed to show civility but not much more in the way of manners.

"Naturally. I'm sure we'll have cause to speak soon," I told her, getting to my feet. Amie was still curled tight against my body, but she was still now, rigid, like a frightened animal.

"Unfortunately, I think that *will* be the case," Sheryl muttered under her breath. I bit my tongue and rushed upstairs before I could say anything I would regret.

CHAPTER TEN

THE MIRROR MAN

Linneman didn't sound all that surprised when I told him I hadn't left. When I asked him to sit on the paperwork I'd signed, releasing the children from my care, he said, "What paperwork?" in the awkward manner of a co-conspirator who was a little too stiff to pull off ignorance convincingly.

My mother, on the other hand, was nearly hysterical.

"What do you mean, *you're not coming back*?"

"I mean, I'm not coming back. Not yet, anyway. The CPS woman was terrifying. And they were going to separate the kids. How could I leave them when—"

"I know you're worried about them, Ophelia, but listen to me for a moment. You're a good, kindhearted girl, but you empathize with other people way too much for your own good. People take advantage of it. This Ronan Fletcher guy knew you were a bleeding heart the moment he laid eyes on you, and then he put you in a position he knew you wouldn't be able to walk away from. How is that fair?"

I sighed. "It's *not* fair. I know that. But I can't just leave them to go off to some gross, unclean, unsafe place, where anything could happen to them, and go merrily on my way now, can I? I'd never get another good night's sleep again."

There was a long pause, and then my mother said something that made me hang up the phone. It went something like this: "Ophelia, this isn't because…you know. Because you can't have children of your own? Amie and Connor…they're in trouble, and they need someone to look after and care for them, but don't get confused, okay, sweetheart? They aren't your responsibility. They're a job and nothing more. Once these six months are up, you're going to have to walk away from them and say goodbye. I don't want to see you getting hurt over something that can easily be av—"

She would have gone on and on for god only knows how long if I'd let her. She probably didn't realize I wasn't on the other end of the line for a solid minute.

I tried not to think about what she'd said. I barely knew the kids; I wasn't living in a make believe land where I'd adopted them as my own and we were all going to live happily ever after. They just needed to be kept safe, and it looked like I was the only way that was going to happen. At least for a little while anyway, until another arrangement could be formulated.

Connor refused to come out of his room. He lay on his bed and stared up at the ceiling, a rainbow striped hat pulled down low on his head, and he didn't even blink. I sat with him for most of the morning while Amie slept in a nest of blankets and pillows on the floor at my feet, sniffling in her dreams. No matter how often I tried to talk to him, Connor wouldn't even acknowledge my presence.

At midday, I left Connor's room to go make some food for them, though I knew neither of them would eat, and I'd made it halfway down the stairs before a figure standing inside the hallway by the front door stopped me dead in my tracks.

Him again.

Ronan.

Leaning against the wall, shoulder butted up against the freshly painted cream plasterwork, dark hair tumbling into his eyes, plaid shirt rumpled and untucked—it was really him. It was Ronan.

I screamed, high and loud, scrambling, trying to run back up the stairs. "Don't! Don't come any closer!"

Ronan didn't even flinch. He studied me with a cold, detached look on his face that made him look more handsome than ever, in a cruel, regal way that sent a shiver through my body. Shouldn't he be more *transparent* or something? I had little to no experience with the recently dead, but I'd read a lot of horror novels as a teenager and ghosts were meant to be pastier and far less flushed in the face.

His cheeks were rosy almost, and his eyes were shining brightly, as deep and dark as ever. I couldn't move my legs. I *had* to move my legs in order to run away from him, but they weren't cooperating in the slightest.

I screamed again, hands grasping at the railing, barely able to keep myself upright.

"Jesus, woman. Hush your mouth." Ronan pushed away from the wall, and then started toward me, anger pulling his eyebrows together into a frown. "You're bellowing loud enough to wake the dead."

He walked to the base of the stairs, shoving his hands in his pockets, and I nearly passed out on the spot. "*Don't*. I mean it. Don't come any closer. I swear, I'll—" I didn't know what I was going to do. There was just no defending yourself against a paranormal force.

Ronan shook his head; for all the world he looked frustrated. His eyes flashed with impatience. "Ophelia. That's your name, isn't it? Look. I already know what you're thinking, and I'm not Ronan. If we could please skip this part and move onto the less ridiculous part of our conversation, that would be awesome."

"You're not...?" He wasn't making any sense. He absolutely *was* Ronan. The hair, the eyes, the savage curl of his lip that made me unreasonably weak at the knees. Admittedly, his hair was all over the place, disheveled compared to the slicked back hipster cut he usually wore, but even so there was no mistaking him. My mouth was hanging open. I knew it was, but I just couldn't seem to do anything about it.

"Sully," Ronan said. "I'm *Sully*, Ronan's brother."

"*What?*"

"*Twin* brother, obviously. We share a passing resemblance, or so I'm told." He was being a jerk, his voice was thick with sarcasm, and I could see why. He bore more than a passing resemblance to Ronan. He was the spitting image of the man. I still wasn't quite sure I believed the words that were coming out of his mouth. Identical twins were very real, of course—there had been two little girls in my class at Saint Augustus's who used to have to wear name badges because they were so hard to tell apart—but this was insane. There was nothing to define the man standing in front of me from Ronan Fletcher. They were the same height, the same build. The way they held themselves when they leaned against a wall was exactly the same; they were carbon copy replicas of one another, not just two people who had happened to share the same embryonic sack.

"Linneman called and told me what happened," Ronan...no, *Sully* said. I had to wrestle to get his name right in my mind. "I came by last night, but you seemed spooked. I thought you'd be less crazy if I came back during daylight hours. Looks as though I was wrong."

Stunned, I took a step down the stairs, eyes locked on him, as though he'd vanish if I looked away. "I'm sure you can understand why..."

"I look like my brother. I've been hearing it my whole life. When I look in the mirror, I get to be reminded of him. *Daily*. So yeah. I understand. Now, like I said. Can we please move on? I've had this conversation more times than I can count, and it gets really fucking old."

Slowly, I descended down the remainder of the stairs, trying to regain some of my dignity. Probably no chance of that happening in Sully's eyes, but still, I had to try.

"Linneman didn't mention that you were coming by," I muttered, rubbing my slick palms against my jeans.

"That's because I didn't tell him. No point. He'd only have tried to talk me out of it, in that round about way of his, and I'd have ended up being rude." Seemed like rude was a predetermined state of being with these Fletcher boys. I'd never have thought it possible, but Sully was even more prickly and unfriendly than his brother. "I don't plan on being here long, either way," he said, angling his jaw upward in a defiant, fuck-you fashion. "I came to tell you not to bother."

"Excuse me?"

"Linneman told me what my brother did. That he wants you to hang around here on the island until I give in and decide to take care of his kids. I came over here to tell you not to bother. I won't be taking them. He was crazy to think I'd ever be able to look after them. So you do what you have to do. I'm staying out of it."

"Daddy?" From upstairs, Amie's high, frightened voice echoed down the hallway. Sully's eyes widened.

"Is that...that's the little girl?" He looked like a rabbit trapped in headlights.

I nodded. Glancing over my shoulder, I tried to catch sight of her, but Amie was still making her way down the corridor, footsteps uncertain and timid. "I get that you're a little freaked out right now. But...maybe you'd like to meet—"

I turned back to Sully, but he wasn't there. The front door was yawning open, and the man was nowhere to be seen. Instead, a short woman in her late twenties, maybe early thirties with bright red hair and a black woolen hat was standing there in his place, an awkward look on her face. She glanced over her shoulder, scowling.

"I see you met Sully, then," she said. Entering the house, she held out her hand, her scowl transforming into a small smile. "Hi, I'm Rose. Ronan hired me to help you take care of the children? Mr. Linneman came to see me yesterday. He told me what happened. I'm sorry I didn't come straight over. To be honest, I was in shock. I've known Ronan all my life. I just...couldn't quite believe what he'd done."

"Tell me about it." I shook her hand, blinking furiously. I must have looked very strange. "I'm sorry, I'm still reeling from..." I pointed out the door after Sully, trying not to look quite so stunned.

"Yeah. He has that affect on people. How about I make you a coffee, and we can go over a schedule or something? I can give you a little more information about the last remaining Fletcher brother while I'm at it."

BETWEEN HERE AND THE HORIZON

••••

Rose was full of freckles. She was also full of hair-raising facts about Ronan and Sully. They'd both been troubled teenagers, both of them prone to fighting and inciting mayhem. In 2004, once they'd completed their degrees, they joined the military together as officers, and that seemed to calm them down a little.

She told me no one really knew what happened, but everyone had been shocked when Sully returned to the island and Ronan married Magda out of the blue. Sully had shut himself away and refused to interact with anyone on The Causeway unless they were ordering furniture from him, and Ronan hadn't been seen again. Not until he'd shown up a week ago with no Magda and two children in tow.

"I used to envy Mags so much," Rose said, taking a sip of her coffee. "She was my best friend in high school, y'know? She was so desperate to get out of here, so desperate to leave. She moved to New York when Sully and Ronan went out there to study, and she just never came back. I visited her once or twice before the whole mess with Ronan."

"I'm sorry? The whole mess with Ronan?"

Rose blanched. "Oh, well, yeah. I mean, Magda didn't start out with Ronan. She was dating *Sully* when they moved out to New York."

Oh. Good. Lord. I supposed that explained a lot.

Rose continued, oblivious of the fact that the information she'd just imparted had blown me away. "Mags tried to get me to move out there with her. I couldn't do it, though. I knew I wanted to teach here on the island. I studied English literature and language at Beal College in Bangor, and then I came right back here and got a job at the school. That was it for me. I still think about it, though. What my life would have been like if I'd upped and left to live in the city with her.

"The local newspaper ran a story on Ronan when he was awarded that medal from the army. That was probably the last time I spoke to Mags on the phone. I'd called her because the article said Ronan hadn't even attended the ceremony to collect the damn thing. That they'd had to send it to him in the mail." Rose shrugged, finishing her coffee. "I wanted to congratulate him, to tell him how proud we were of him here on the island, but he wouldn't even take my call."

CHAPTER ELEVEN

JOURNAL
March 15, 2000

*This journal smells like the tack shop we bought Topper's bridle from. I love it. Dad said it was too boyish for me, but whatever. It's my money. I can buy what I like with it. Sully says he's going to wait until I've filled every single page, and then he's gonna steal it and read it. Such a jerk. He'd better not. Sully James Fletcher, if you're reading this, you're going straight to hell. Do **not** invade my privacy or I'll saw your balls off with a rusty butter knife!*

Should probably make the same threat to Ronan, but why bother? He's too busy plotting out his "Great American Road Trip" to think twice about anything I scribble in here. And good, too! At least I only have to worry myself with one of the Fletcher boys. So...I don't know. I guess I'll only write in here when I have something important to say. The book's too nice to waste, and I'm a sixteen-year-old girl. Seems a shame to cover the pages in shit about boys and high school drama. I want to be able to look back through this book in forty years' time and be proud of the moments I've recorded here.

I hope by then I can say I've lived a life worth writing about. I hope by then Sully and I are married, and we've had kids of our own. I hope we've traveled the world. Seen everything there is to see. I hope we've come back to the island and built a new life for ourselves here, and I can ride every day and Sully can make things in his workshop. That would make me happy. That would make me very happy indeed.

M

M for *Magda*. I'd been mistaken; I'd thought the journal Ronan left for me to read was his, but it wasn't. It was his wife's, and the very first entry on the very first page confirmed all too clearly what Rose had told me: Magda had started out in love with *Sully*. I could have guessed the problem between Ronan and his brother had stemmed from a woman somehow, but I'd had no idea it would be Ronan's dead wife. What strife that must have caused. And how? Magda was sixteen when she wrote on the first page in her diary. Flicking through the occasionally brittle, occasionally damp smelling book, I skipped to the very last entry in the journal, only three quarters of the way through, and noted the date.

April last year. The handwriting had changed from girly, loopy cursive to a more elegant, sprawling text over the years, but the lettering was still unmistakably from the same hand. I avoided the words written onto the paper, not wanting to read them yet. For some reason it felt like skipping to the end of a novel and ruining the story for myself, though in this instance I already knew what happened at the end. Magda was dead, and now so was Ronan. Sully was the last man standing.

After Rose had left, I'd ducked into the office and grabbed the book before I'd had a chance to change my mind. I needed some more background history, and low and behold it looked like I was going to get it in spades. There had to be over a hundred entries in Magda's journal. Some of the pages were rigid and crackled as they were turned. Others were covered with photos. Some bore event tickets, plane tickets...stubs to movies. Closer to the end of the book, I caught sight of a sonogram tacked to a page, and I had to stop myself from investigating closer to see if it was Connor or Amie Magda had commemorated in her book.

Amie sat with me the entire afternoon, dipping in and out of sleep, crying sporadically in quiet, heartbroken jags that made me ache inside for her. Connor remained in his room, rainbow hat jammed onto his head, not moving, not saying a word. He'd lashed out and tried to kick me when I tried to pick him up and take him into my arms, growling fiercely, and so I'd left him alone in the silence of his room, hoping I was doing the right thing.

The rain arrived around four, hammering at the windows, rattling them in their frames, and wind tore at the house, howling through the brickwork in the old pantry, the only part of the house that didn't look like it had been renovated, causing the kitchen door to slam closed behind me every time I went in there to get juice or cookies for Amie.

I couldn't stop thinking about Magda's journal. I couldn't stop thinking about Sully's appearance earlier, either, or the harsh way that he'd spoken. He'd been stark and unwelcoming, but he'd also been afraid, too—when he heard Amie calling out for her father, he'd looked so lost that the transformation had startled me. I needed to know why he'd taken the time to come to the house not once but twice in order to tell me I'd be wasting my time if I tried to fulfill Ronan's wishes. The mystery of it all was killing me.

I flicked through the journal, letting it fall open midway through—a page full of photos. I only knew the images were of Sully because Magda had written underneath each one with a title, time and date.

Sully, Fort Benning, April 2003.
Sully, Times Square, December 2003. Four days until deployment.
Sully, Kabul, May 2004.
Sully, with Daniels and Rogers, Kabul, January 2005.

Underneath this entry, a faded, small photograph was taped to the paper: Sully, in full military uniform, sun blazing, a white hot blister in the background, two tall black guys also in uniform with their arms slung over his shoulders. All three of the men were smiling, teeth showing, sweat on their brows, but there was something a little off about the picture. The smiles seemed edgy, like they'd been painted on. The men stood tall and stiff, as though ready to drop the pretense of happiness at the first sign of trouble in order to pick up the rifles at their feet and start fighting.

None of them looked like they wanted to be there at all.

••••

I didn't see Sully again for a month. Four weeks passed by, and not a peep. Perhaps this wouldn't have been so strange if the island weren't so small, and if everyone didn't keep saying, *oh how funny. You just missed Sully*, to me. It was like he'd tagged me with a GPS tracker somehow, knew my exact location at all times, and was determined to avoid me no matter the cost.

CPS checked in with me, sent Sheryl back to the island to make sure I wasn't neglecting the children (which I wasn't), and they signed off on them staying with me until next spring. Rose's presence was an immeasurable help. I was using some of the allowance Ronan had set aside for me to pay Dr. Fielding for Skype sessions with Connor and Amie. His time with Amie appeared to be helping her a lot, but Connor was proving harder to reach. He often sat in front of the computer screen and refused to speak at all when Fielding asked him questions. If he did speak, then he shouted, screamed and swore until Fielding declared the session counter productive and shut things down. Still, I hoped for a breakthrough. And soon. Really, really soon. My last nerve was frayed down to the quick, but more importantly I felt like I was failing Connor and Ronan at the same time, and that didn't sit well with me at all.

November was frigid and awful. The sky was the color of war—gray and black and grim—and the rain rarely broke. Rose was at home with the children when I finally saw Sully Fletcher again.

"There we go, sweetie. Whew, that's a heavy one. Must have some good stuff in there." Sam, the woman who ran the post office, slid the package I'd come to collect toward me across the counter, smiling. The package was from Mom—probably more winter clothing. She was terrified I was going to freeze to death. Sam glanced over my shoulder, lifting a hand in greeting. "Hi, Sully. You can leave that there if you like? I'll swing by on my way home to pay you."

I spun around so quick I almost lost my balance. Sure enough, Sully was standing in the open doorway of the post office, and in his hands he was holding a huge, beautiful rocking chair. When he saw me, his expression changed from flat disinterest to open horror. "Sure thing, Sam." He put the rocking chair down next to the door, bending at the waist, and I couldn't help but notice how close he'd cropped his hair, or the curls of wood shavings that were stuck to the thick plaid material of his shirt. There was a black smudge on the back of his neck, as if he'd rubbed greasy fingers there and no one had told him about the stain marking his skin. He didn't turn around again or say another word to Sam. He just walked through the door and left.

"I wouldn't do it to myself if I were you."

"Pardon me?" I turned back to find that Sam was giving me a knowing, wary look.

"Sully Fletcher. As handsome as the devil on Sunday. Had every single one of the women on this island in a tizz at some point, but he ain't never looked at a single one of them. Trust me. That one's more trouble than he's worth. You need a cabinet made, or a chair fixed, then Sully's your man. If you're looking for someone with a gentle and tender heart to snuggle up with on the couch when it's raining, then you're better off getting a dog."

"I'm not looking for that. And if I were, I definitely wouldn't be interested in Sully."

"Hmm." From the look on her face, Sam didn't believe me one bit. "All right then. But just so you know, that one didn't come back from the desert the same as when he left, if you get my meaning. Just be careful around him. And don't let those little ones around him too much, either." There wasn't any fear of that happening; Sully had made himself perfectly clear back at the house four weeks ago, and he hadn't changed his mind. I'd heard nothing from him regarding his niece and nephew. I'd heard nothing from him, period.

Outside, I caught him climbing into a beaten truck so covered in mud that I couldn't even make out what color it was. He wanted to throw the car in drive and disappear, I could tell, but I wasn't going to let him. I stepped in front of the vehicle and laid my hands flat against the hood.

Sully leaned out of his window and growled, "What in holy fuck do you think you're doing?" He sounded so similar to Ronan, it was uncanny. I'd never heard Ronan say fuck, but I could imagine it all too well.

"You're avoiding me. And the children. Why?"

"You're insane." Sully looked around the inside of his truck, like he was looking for someone to agree with him. "I'm a busy guy, Miss Ophelia Lang from California. I have work to do. Why would I be playing stupid games and avoiding you?"

"That's what I'd like to know. You didn't even come to Ronan's funeral." The day had been one of the few fine days I'd experienced on The Causeway. The sun had shone for the entire forty minutes I'd stood at Ronan's graveside with the children, the temperature cool but fresh, and the fact that so few people had shown up to say their farewells to Ronan had been heartbreaking. Back in New York, there would have been work associates, friends, neighbors... Here on the island, the only person who I'd known at the tiny Catholic Church had been Rose and that was it.

"Of course I didn't come." Sully turned the key in the ignition; the car's engine roared into life, startling me. "I'm not above running over a girl, you know. I've done it before."

"Where? In Afghanistan?"

Sully sat back in his seat like he'd been slapped. "And what would you know about Afghanistan?"

I'd obviously touched a very, *very* raw nerve. "Nothing."

"That's right. You don't know anything."

"Maybe I should change that. Maybe I should just read Magda's journal, and—"

"What did you just say?" Sully stopped trying to maneuver the car past me and gaped at me out of the window. His anger seemed to have dissipated in a puff of smoke.

"Magda's journal. Ronan told me to read it. To understand what happened between you two better."

"Is that so?" Sully leaned forward, forearms against the steering wheel. With eyebrows so high up his forehead they were almost touching his hairline, he tilted his head to one side. He was angry; I could feel the tension snapping in the air. Given the look in his eyes, I wouldn't be surprised if he *did* run me over. "And what have you learned so far, Lang?" he snapped. He looked suspicious. Almost worried.

"I haven't learned anything. I haven't read it," I snapped back. It was true. I hadn't read a single entry since I'd first picked up the journal after Ronan died. Oh, I'd wanted to for sure. It still sat on my nightstand, and night after night I warred with myself, trying to convince myself of the fact that reading the contents of the journal wasn't invading Sully's privacy. But it was. I knew it was.

"Like I'm gonna believe that," Sully growled.

"You can believe whatever you want. I only know what everyone else on this ridiculously tiny island knows. Ronan came back from deployment, and suddenly..." I didn't feel brave enough to say the rest out loud. Not to his face.

"Suddenly he was marrying my girlfriend and having a baby?" Sully had gone pale. His eyes were filled with a hint of madness that finally, *finally* set him apart from Ronan. What was he going to do next? Scream at me some more? I could take it. I could if it meant that he and I were talking. A month had already gone by, and Sheryl hadn't found anywhere suitable for Connor and Amie. Another five months would easily fly by in the blink of an eye, and then the two children would be shipped off to the group home after all, regardless of what I wanted for them.

I'd come to the conclusion that I needed to complete the task Ronan hired me to do and get Sully to take them, but now that I was standing in front of him and he was acting so unhinged I wasn't so sure that was the best course of action anymore.

"Yes," I answered him. "It wasn't fair. Ronan shouldn't have done it.

But at the end of the day, he couldn't help who he fell in love with either."

Sitting perfectly still, Sully seemed to try and digest these words for a second, which could have explained why he looked like he was about to throw up. And then he said, "He and I shared the same heart. Of course we were bound to fall in love with the same girl." He didn't try and get around me again. Instead, Sully put the car in reverse and gunned the engine, tearing off backwards down the street, a shower of dirt and small rocks kicked up by the tires, raining down on me as he sped away.

CHAPTER TWELVE

HAPPY BIRTHDAY, ROSE

"Did you manage to—god, what have you got all over your face?" Rose met me at the door, Amie hot on her heels, a slab of cake in her tiny hand, chocolate frosting all around her mouth and all over her cheeks. Rose saw the sharp look on my face and had the decency to look apologetic. "Sorry. She didn't touch her lunch. It was this or nothing. Why do you look like you've just been quad biking?"

"*Sully*," I said.

"Ah." Clearly the one-word answer was explanation enough. Rose produced a pack of tissues from her pocket. "I was just about to clean up the chocolate monster, but looks like you might need these more than she does."

"Thanks."

"I could speak to him, y'know? To Sully? He might not be so polite to you, but he wouldn't dare be rude to me. He's coming to my birthday party next week. You'll be there, too. He's going to have to learn how to keep a civil tongue by then, or I'll cut the damn thing right out of his head."

Ah. Rose had mentioned the birthday party a couple of times, but I hadn't had the heart to tell her I wasn't going to be able to come. What was I supposed to do with Connor and Amie? And anyway, now that I'd found out Sully was going to be there, my desire to mingle and be sociable with the inhabitants of the island had strangely disintegrated. The thought of Sully at a party was just so out there that I couldn't help but smile, though. I could just picture the uptight bastard hovering with a plate of cheese in his hand, looking more than a little uncomfortable while a volley of people tried to talk to him about the weather and his carpentry business. I felt manic laughter bubbling up at the back of my throat.

Truth of the matter was, *if* he showed up, he would probably hang around for twenty minutes to fulfill his social obligations, and then he'd make his exit as quickly as possible while no one was looking.

"No, it's okay, Rose. If he doesn't want to be nice, then that's on him. I wouldn't want to submit the kids to his shitty attitude anyway. And I think...it would probably be so confusing for them as well. I mean, he looks just like Ronan. I nearly had a heart attack when I set eyes on him. If *Amie* saw him..." It didn't even bear thinking about.

"Hmm. Perhaps you're right." She didn't say she wouldn't talk to Sully, though. Her mouth had an odd quirk to it. I could tell just by looking at her that she was already planning what she was going to say to him and how she was going to say it, regardless if I begged or pleaded. I didn't waste my breath asking her to keep her mouth shut. If there was one thing I'd learned about Rose in the brief time I had known her, it was that she was extraordinarily stubborn, and when she made up her mind about something, there was no moving her on it.

••••

A week later: a party.

Rose's name had been painted on pieces of paper one letter at a time and pegged to a piece of fishing line that ran from one end of her cramped living room to the other. Good thing she had such a short name. *Happy Bday* was tacked up underneath it, the second word butchered for the sake of convenience. Rose ran around the house, flitting from kitchen, to dining room, to living room, thundering up the stairs to the den she'd set up in her spare room, where a number of children including Connor and Amie were watching Star Wars. In most circumstances, probably not the best choice for a little girl Amie's age, but then again Amie wasn't like most little girls. Her love of dinosaurs also stretched to a love of space ships and aliens, so Star Wars was apparently going down a treat.

Rose's invites, sent to everyone on the island between the ages of twenty and sixty-five, had clearly stated the party started at seven thirty, however people started rolling through the door at five, which seemed completely normal to everyone apart from me. I was dashing about almost as crazily as Rose, pulling finger food out of the oven, chilling as much white wine and beer in the fridge as I could possibly fit in while trying to pin my hair back at the same time and hop into my dress.

Speaking of the dress: tight and black, with a thin cross strap that ran over my shoulder blades. No chance of a bra here. It was so cold even inside the house that Rose's eyes nearly popped out of her head when she saw me wearing it.

"Jesus, O. You do realize Mr. Sweetwater's coming tonight, don't you? The poor bastard had a pacemaker installed a couple of months ago. If he sees your nipples cutting at your dress like that, he'll keel over and die."

"I haven't got anything else to wear." Ronan hadn't exactly made my trip to the island sound like a vacation. I wasn't even going to bring the dress I was wearing, but something had told me I might need it. Admittedly I'd have been better served by something more conservative, but now I just had to work with what I had.

"Here, then," Rose said, grabbing me by the wrist and dragging me into her bedroom. From the top drawer of the chest next to her bed, she pulled out a box of Tit Tape as if by magic. "Tape those puppies up, before you have people talking."

Holly, a fifteen-year-old girl wearing a Slipknot t-shirt, showed up at seven to babysit the children. She smiled, displaying two overly large front teeth when Rose introduced us.

"So nice to meet you," she gushed. "You're from California, aren't you? I've watched every single episode of The O.C. I can't wait to visit there one day. Is it always sunny there?"

"Actually, I guess it kind of is," I told her. I'd taken the balmy West Coast weather for granted up until I stepped foot on The Causeway. Now, the brief snatches of sunshine that infrequently broke their way through the cloud cover were something that people went and stood outside for, craning their necks up at the sky overhead, squinting into the light like it was a goddamn miracle.

Holly beamed. "Do you think you could tell me all about it? Only when you're free, of course. I don't mind watching the children for you in return."

"Of course. You can come over anytime."

By nine, Rose's place was packed and the windows were running with condensation. A huge three-tier cake was broken out, and everyone sang Happy Birthday in a cacophony of drunk, out of tune voices. That's when I noticed Sully, propped up against the wall by the television, holding a beer in one hand and an untouched hot dog in the other. He wasn't paying attention to the food or the drink, or the people singing around him. He was staring straight at me with a dark, brooding look in his eyes that made my heart stop dead in my chest.

God.

Where did he get off, looking at me like that? His expression was confusing; he was either thinking about running his hands over my skin, pressing his teeth into the swell of my cleavage, digging his fingertips into the curvature of my ass, or he was thinking about murdering me where I stood. I couldn't quite decide which was more likely. He blinked when he saw that I'd seen him, but he didn't look away.

Slowly, he raised his beer bottle to his lips and he drank, the muscles in his throat working as he swallowed, his eyes locked onto me, as if he were incapable of looking anywhere else.

Such a strange, uncomfortable sensation, being observed that intensely. Out of the corner of my eye, Rose was blushing furiously, thanking everyone for coming out to celebrate her birthday. She blew out the candles on her cake, and the room was suddenly all long cast shadows and darkness in the corners. Sully's face was transformed, severe, half eaten up by the dark, half highlighted by the light thrown off by a small lamp on top of the TV. He wanted to kill me after all. The savage, hard steel in his eyes told me so. I ducked my head, glancing away. He'd won. The bastard had won. *He* might have been able to stare me down until the sun came up, but I didn't have it in me.

I turned my back on him, and did my best to put him out of my head. I drank more. I danced with old Mr. Sweetwater, who was unable to tear his eyes from my cleavage despite the Tit Tape that was covering my nipples so well. I ate and I laughed, and I made friends.

Everyone wanted to talk to me, to find out who the strange new Californian woman was living up at The Big House with Ronan Fletcher's orphaned children.

No one brought up Sully. No one even seemed to notice he was there.

"So, you're a teacher? You know, the high school on the other side of the island's been looking for someone to teach the rest of the year. Once Connor and Amie are enrolled in the elementary school next month, maybe you should go work over there?" Michael, the stocky blond guy I was talking to, had been talking to for the last thirty minutes, leaned closer and smiled. He wasn't a bad looking guy. He was well built and his button-down shirt strained over his chest, hinting at a wall of muscle underneath the cotton. "It's a well-paid job, y'know? It's hard for the school board to find good teachers who want to stay on the Causeway, so they keep on putting the salary up and up. Teachers here are paid better than anyone else, it seems."

"Oh, I couldn't. No way. I *couldn't* work here fulltime." Slinging back the remainder of my wine, I didn't notice the hurt look Michael was wearing until I'd put my glass down on the table and turned back to him. Perfect. I'd offended him. Shit. "I'm sorry, I didn't mean to be rude. I just meant that I couldn't stay here because I have responsibilities back in California. My parents need me to come back and help out with their restaurant, and—" And I couldn't think of another single reason why I had to go back to L.A. Will was no longer a factor. I didn't exactly have a career I needed to cultivate there. As far as friends were concerned, what few people I still kept in touch with were scattered all over the place—Wisconsin, Oklahoma, Austin, Washington D.C. As soon as college ended, everyone had gone their separate ways, off to work, or get married, or whatever, and I was the only one who'd gone back home.

Kind of pathetic when I thought about it.

"I wouldn't believe a word of it if I were you, Mikey," a clipped, cold voice said over my shoulder. The bare skin across my shoulder blades instantly broke out in goose bumps. I knew without a doubt who it was, and panic sang through my veins. Sully stepped into view, clapping a hand on Michael's shoulder, who looked awkward and edgy all of a sudden. Sully was wearing a plain jet-black shirt, smarter than his usual plaid, though his black jeans were scruffy and worn. A clear foot shorter than him, Michael seemed to shrink even further as Sully massaged his fingers roughly into Michael's shoulder. "This is not the kind of woman that hangs around an island like ours, Mikey," Sully said. His tone was light, though there was an unpleasant edge to it that made me uneasy.

"Ophelia Lang from California is just chasing a pay check. Once her job here is over and my brother's children are packed off back to New York, you won't see her for dust. Trust me. And then, once she's finally left, I might be able to sell that haunted old warehouse she's currently squatting in, and then I'll be able to leave, too."

"What? Sell the house? You can't." Never mind the fact that he was being shitty and spiteful. That was to be expected. But what the hell was he talking about, selling the house?

Sully took a deep swig of his beer, and then arched an eyebrow. "Of course. Ronan left it to me, didn't he? I can do what I want with it once you're gone."

"You grew up in that house, didn't you? It was your parents' house. It's been in the Fletcher family for generations."

"What the hell do *you* care about the Fletcher family home?" Sully asked, cocking his head to one side. "What does that damned pile of bricks and mortar mean to *you*?"

"Not to me," I snapped. "To Connor and Amie. It's their heritage. Their birthright. It's their history."

"Then my brother should have left it to them instead of me, shouldn't he? He knew I was more likely to burn the place to the ground than ever live there, taking care of his kids." Finishing his beer, Sully grabbed a fresh bottle from the box Jerry, the boat skipper, was carrying past us.

Michael winced. He looked like he wanted to back away slowly, one step at a time so as not to be noticed. God knows he couldn't be blamed; I didn't want to be a part of the conversation either.

"You're heartless, you know that?" I shouldn't be doing this. What good was arguing with him? Or name calling? Sully was the kind of guy who lived for bickering and mud slinging. He got off on it. Without a doubt he was far more accomplished at it, and I was only going to lose my temper if I engaged him the way he clearly wanted me to.

"Heartless? Yeah, I guess that's a fairly accurate description. Vile. Repugnant. Selfish. Cruel. The list goes on." He let go of Michael and shoved his hand in his pocket, then. Michael cleared his throat and made his escape.

"Excuse me, Ophelia. It was a pleasure to meet you. I'm sure I'll find you again before Rose drinks too much and kicks everyone out later." He gave me a small smile and hurried off without even casting a look in Sully's direction.

"Why do you have to be so rude?" I hissed.

"To Michael? Psshhhh." Sully knocked back another deep draught of his beer, draining nearly half the bottle. "I wasn't rude to him."

"You were. And you're rude to me. You're rude to everyone. Every time you open your mouth, you can't help yourself. You have to be caustic or unkind to whoever happens to be standing in your direct line of fire."

"Point of fact, that isn't true," Sully said, scowling. "I'm nice to some people."

"*Who?*"

Sully rose up on his tiptoes, scanning the room, and then he pointed. "There. The redhead with the white shirt on? I plan on being *very* nice to her later."

The redhead in question turned just as Sully pointed her out, as though she knew someone was talking about her. She saw Sully looking over and her cheeks flushed bright red. I got the feeling she and Sully had spent a lot of quality time together in the past. "You're a pig. A grade A pig," I informed him.

"Why? Because I plan on showing my girlfriend a good time?"

"She is *not* your girlfriend, Sully Fletcher."

"Oh? And how are you so sure?"

"Because no woman could tolerate your attitude long enough to ever fall into a relationship with you."

"Bullshit. You know she's not my girlfriend because you've asked around."

Now it was my turn for my cheeks to turn crimson. I *had* asked around, subtly or so I'd thought. Cara, Jerry's daughter; Oliver, the guy who brought the papers in the morning; Jillian, Rose's friend, who sometimes dropped her off at the house: I'd asked them all delicate, indirect questions about Sully's personal life that I hadn't thought were all that obvious. I hadn't asked because I was interested. God, no. I'd asked back when I thought the man standing in front of me might be capable of taking care of Amie and Connor. I'd wanted to make sure they were entering a safe and stable environment, the same way Sheryl had with me.

Sully was still looking at me, a lopsided, roguish smile spreading rapidly across his face, and I had the overwhelming urge to scream.

"You're delusional if you think I'm interested in you, Sully James Fletcher. I'd rather become a Carmelite nun and never speak to another soul again for as long as I live than tangle myself up in any of your crap."

Sully's smile evaporated so quickly it almost happened between heartbeats. "Don't do that. Do *not* call me that."

"Call you what?"

"By my full name. You might have read Magda's journal, you might know all of my personal shit, but you don't get to talk to me like you know me. Like you're fucking *scolding* me." He made a guttural, angry sound low in his throat. He went to put his beer bottle down, then changed his mind, gripping onto it tighter. He lifted his free hand and pointed his index finger in my face. "The sooner you leave The Causeway, Lang, the better. For you. For me. For those kids. And when you go, make sure you take that damn journal with you, too. Toss it overboard and let the sea have it. I never want to see it again."

The crowd of people behind Sully parted as if they were used to his stormy exits from conversations and they'd learned a long time ago to get out of the way as quickly as possible. He charged toward the door, shoulders locked and tense, and I caught sight of Rose on the other side of the room, a deflated expression etched into her face. Sully didn't say goodbye to her, or to anyone else for that matter. He disappeared out of the front door, leaving it yawning wide open, and he vanished into the night.

I felt like rushing to the door and screaming after him, telling him I *hadn't* read Magda's journal, had no interest in reading it, but even the thought of expending that much energy on him exhausted me.

"Wow. He's so...*tormented*," a voice next to me sighed. Holly, in her Slipknot t-shirt, looked like she'd just fallen in love, and fallen hard at that. "He's just like Heathcliffe. So romantic."

I gave her a sidelong look, shaking my head. "Have you read Wuthering Heights, Holly? Heathcliffe was a cold, controlling, miserable bastard. There was nothing romantic about him at all."

CHAPTER THIRTEEN

AFGHANISTAN
2009

Sully

"Eight days. We've lost eight of our guys in eight days. That's a guy a day. A guy with a family and loved ones back home. What the fuck are we doing here, man? Why the fuck are we fighting this war? It's none of our damned business, anyway. We should be back at home, taking care of our own. We ain't accomplishin' nothin'. Dirt in our eyes. Dirt in our boots, under our damned fingernails. Nothing but dirt and mayhem all damned day long. Tell me...when is it gonna be done? When will it be *enough*? When the fuck can we go home, that's what *I* want to know." Rogers stabbed the sharp end of his throwing knife into the sole of his boot, squinting at the point where steel met rubber. No one said anything.

It was dark. The night out here in the desert was a lot like it was back on the island—very little light pollution meant stars for days. Stars, thick and clustered, brilliant and white for as far as the eye could see. The black mantle of the sky was different, too. Richer. Deeper somehow, like you could reach your hand into it, feel the texture of it against your fingertips, encompassing you.

Three clicks to the west, or there about, an orange flash popped against the shadow of the horizon, briefly throwing a ragged, broken skyline into view.

BETWEEN HERE AND THE HORIZON

Kandahar.

Over there, in the torn out heart of the city, three of the units from our base were locked in a skirmish with local Taliban fighters. The insurgents had pinned them inside a building and were doggedly trying to get inside, to kill whoever they could find through the sights of the M4s they'd stolen from one of our envoys a little over a month ago.

Sound carried so well out here. A rattle of gunfire echoed over the scrubby plain between the hollow at the base of the hill where we were sitting, awaiting orders, and the outskirts of the city, reminding me of the Chinese firecrackers Ronan and I used to play with when we were kids. He was out there somewhere, on the other side of the city, waiting with his men just like I was, looking up at the same stars, probably bored out of his head. No doubt one of his guys was pissing and moaning, too. There was one in every unit these days, it seemed. Someone who finally wasn't afraid to say what everyone else was thinking: why the fuck were we out here, playing cat and mouse games, theoretically protecting a country of people who didn't even fucking want us here?

"Oil. It's all about the oil," Rogers hissed under his breath.

"Dumbass, it ain't about the oil," Daniels snapped back. "They ain't got no oil in Afghanistan."

"Then why? Why the fuck would the government of the United States of America waste billions of dollars coming out here? Huh? You tell me that, 'cause seems to me like this don't make a lick of sense."

"They sent us out here 'cause these motherfuckers attacked us, you fucking reject. What were they supposed to do? Isn't that why you joined up in the first place?"

Rogers chose not to answer that. We should all have been waiting in silence for our orders to come in over the radio, but there was no point trying to kill this kind of talk once it got started. "S'why I joined up," Daniels continued. "Collins and the captain, too. Ain't that right, Captain?"

Last thing I wanted was to get drawn into the same existential "why are we even here?" argument that had already been the root cause of so many wars and genocides throughout the span of human history. I shifted my weight from one leg to the other, leaning as much as I could against my rifle, stock planted in the ground, trying not to wince as the blood flowed more freely through my stiff joints. When it looked like the men weren't going to continue on their banter without me, I cleared my throat and gave them what they needed to hear.

"Theirs not to reason why. Theirs but to do and die." No one said a word. "You guys never heard of Tennyson?" I asked.

"No, sir,"

"Nope."

"Wa'n't he some kind of Victorian faggot?"

"No, he wasn't *some kind of Victorian faggot*." These guys had my back at every turn. They were my brothers, fierce and loyal to the end, but sometimes I just wanted to strangle them. "He was a *poet*."

"That's what I meant."

I ignored the comment. "Tennyson wrote a poem called 'The Charge of the Light Brigade.' It was about men going into war and dying. And that line, Theirs not to reason why. Theirs but to do and die, basically sums up this whole thing. It's not our job to ask questions. It's not our job to revolt, or doubt the upper chain of command. It's our *job* to do as we're told and do it well. And if that means we go out and we die, a guy every day, five guys every day, ten…then that's what we do. *And we keep our mouths shut.*"

Did I believe this? Absolutely fucking not. But admitting that to the guys would be fatal. They'd lose what little faith they had left in the idea of hierarchy and chaos would ensue.

Three more months. Three more months of this, and I'd be on a plane back to the States. Back to Magda. I'd given enough. Lost enough. Watched enough men die. No more tours for me. Three was plenty; it was time to go home.

More gunfire. More explosions in the distance. The long, whining sound of an RPG missile seeking its target. The men all flinched instinctively when the missile landed. The ground rumbled beneath us. A ball of fire leapt up at the sky, orange and white and angry, and someone sucked in a breath through their teeth.

Our orders finally came in: *Stick to the outskirts of the city. Clear the buildings on the southern side near the markets. Interview everyone. Arrest anyone who looks suspicious. Search for weapons.*

Disappointment ran high.

"Why aren't we coming up behind those bastards? Fucking them hard in the ass?"

"We're the closest unit, Captain. It doesn't make any sense."

I picked up my gun and got to my feet. "Like I said, gentlemen. Ours is not to reason why..."

At least four or five of them finished off the quote for me, groaning out the words, "Ours is but to do and die."

Hours whipped by fast enough for the sun to climb over the lip of the horizon. The ruined city's buildings were a rats' nest of Taliban fighters and families supporting the fighters, hiding them from us, hiding their guns and their food, and any other supplies they could stockpile. We hammered on doors, and kicked over rocks. Anyone who resisted or looked suspicious had their wrists zip tied behind their backs and were escorted back to the base in the back of a Humvee.

The gunfire never ceased. The ground continued to shake.

Must have been sometime after seven when the news was radioed through: the three units stuck inside the old, bombed out hospital were safe. Not a man had been lost. Rogers seemed almost disappointed.

"Captain! Captain Fletcher!" Out of the smoke and the dust choking the early morning air, a young private emerged like a ghost, his rifle, slung over his shoulder, bouncing up and down as he ran through the stacks of rubble and twisted prongs of steel. "Captain Fletcher, sir, you're needed." He was panting, gasping for breath. "It's...it's your brother, sir. The other Captain Fletcher."

A lead weight dropped through me, pulling at my insides, making my head reel. Fuck. Ronan. Ronan was hurt. Ronan was dead. Ronan had been captured, and was about to be executed on national television. A thousand gut-churning possibilities raced through me simultaneously. "What is it? What's happened, Private? Spit it out, for fuck's sake." I was close to slapping him.

"He's sick, sir. Or at least we think he is."

"How? How is he *sick*?"

"He's just sitting on the floor. He won't get up. It's like...like he can't hear us or something. We took the building back. We killed nearly every single one of those bastards. We were celebrating, cheering and whatever, and that's when Simmons saw Captain Fletcher fall. He thought he'd been shot, but...there's nothing wrong with him as far as we can see. He's just...*lying* there."

"Have you radioed it in?"

The private shook his head. "No, sir. We knew you were on mission. We thought we'd better, y'know...come find you first."

"Right. Thank you." Definitely not the protocol Ronan's unit should have followed, but I was glad they hadn't called in medics. The reason they'd held off was obvious; Ronan was in shock. Shock was one of those things. You could snap out of it in a heartbeat, like nothing had ever happened, or it could cripple you for the rest of your life. Either way, there was nothing a medic could do that I couldn't at the moment. "Take me to him." And then, to my own men, I said, "Head back to base. Go eat. I'll be back in a moment. If anyone asks, I came back with you, okay?" As one, the guys all nodded. Even Rogers.

Fifteen minutes later, my shirt pulled up over my mouth to filter out the dust as I ran, the private led me to Ronan. He was sitting up, back leaned against the skeleton of a burned-out Jeep, and his face was splattered with blood. Hands, too. Uniform soaked. It was everywhere. He looked like some crazed serial killer, drunk from the high of the kill.

I sank down into a crouch in front of him, placing my hands on his shoulders. "Jesus, man. You're a mess." I tried to smile, but it felt wrong, like I was probably grimacing instead.

Somewhere, someone said, "Holy shit. I heard he had a twin, but that shit is bonafide crazy."

Ronan blinked; his eyelashes were clumped, dried blood caking them together. "Hey," he said. He was dazed, his pupils unfocused. "Heard you were out tonight, too."

"Yeah, man. Doing clearance. No drama on our end. What's the deal with you, though? You taking a moment to get your shit together?" I laughed, trying to make light of the fact that it looked like Ronan was seriously fucked up.

"Yeah. Yeah, I just need a minute is all. You think…you think you could…?" Glancing around, he gestured toward his men.

"Of course. Of course. You stay here, okay. I'll be right back."

I rallied his guys quickly, ordering them back to base with the few prisoners who remained alive. None of them seemed like they wanted to leave Ronan, but they did as they were told, anyway. We weren't alone. There was still plenty of military personnel knocking around, sifting through the rubble, looking for survivors or escaped fighters. It was safe for the moment, or as safe as Afghanistan ever got, anyway.

"Ronan? Ronan, what happened, man?" I sat down next to my brother, talking quietly. His eyelids flickered, but he kept staring straight ahead, refusing to look at me.

"There was a man," he said slowly. "A *man*. He was trying to take a weapon from one of the dead bodies over there," he said, pointing. It was hard to see the bodies he was talking about amongst all of the debris on the ground, but I nodded. "And I was here," he continued. "There was so much smoke in the air. I couldn't see really well, but I took my gun, and I aimed and fired. I missed twice. He had enough time to free the weapon he was trying to take, and he started firing at me. Screaming. He was screaming so loud. I could hear him, over the other gunfire and everyone else yelling and shouting. This…this high-pitched *wailing* sound. It was awful. I fired again. And again. And again. Eventually he went down. The wailing didn't stop, though. He was still, wasn't moving. I was sure he was dead, but the crying just wouldn't stop. And then the dust cleared a little, and I saw…I *saw*. He wasn't a man. He was a woman. And the crying…"

He trailed off, his words sounding thick and distorted in his throat.

A tear welled up and fell, streaking down his face, cutting a pathway through the blood and dirt and sweat that stained his skin. "The wailing finally stopped. A long, long time, though. It carried on for a long time, Sully."

"It's okay, man. It's okay." I threw an arm around him and pulled him into me, feeling sick. Ronan fought to breathe, panting in short, sharp, shallow blasts that made his ribcage rise and fall erratically.

"You have to go. You have to see," he said. "You have to find out for me."

"No, Ronan. Let's just get you back to base, okay? Get you washed and some caffeine inside you. I think Daniels has some whiskey stashed—"

"Fuck, man, just go and see!" Ronan bucked against me, trying to get to his feet. There was a wild, horrific look in his eye that said he'd go over there and look himself if only he could figure out how to stand up.

"All right. All right." I pushed him back, forcing him to sit. "All right. I'll go, I promise."

The walk over to the woman Ronan had shot was the longest walk of my life. They say time stretched in situations like this, and it really did. I didn't want to see. I didn't want to confirm what Ronan suspected. When I made it to the foot of the stairwell across the other side of the street, a body lay prone on the ground, and I immediately saw the long, messy braid of hair sticking out of the material wrapped around the head. The hands, still gripping hold of the rifle, were small and delicately cut, though incredibly dirty, muck shored up in crescents under the nails.

Stooping, I ripped the Band-Aid off quickly and rolled the body over.

There, just as Ronan expected, was the baby.

Maybe a year old. He'd lost one of his socks, though somehow retained the other. White, dirty, with *Converse* printed along the sole. I didn't even know Converse made socks that small. His skin was pale, his tiny hands clenched into fists. His eyes—pale blue. Striking.

Unusual—were open. Through his left shoulder, a neat hole the size of a dime had ripped through his little t-shirt, and a stream of now black blood had poured free, staining the concrete beneath him.

"Is it dead?" Ronan yelled. "Is…is the baby dead?"

God. How to tell him? I couldn't. I just couldn't.

I closed the baby's eyes.

Gritting my teeth, I stood up, turned around, and walked away. "There was no baby, Ro. It's just a guy. Just a guy with long hair, that's all."

CHAPTER FOURTEEN

CONUNDRUM

The hangover to end all hangovers.
That's what they were going to have to put down on the cause of death section of my death record. Because this hangover wasn't just a hangover. It was brutal. Vicious. Personally wanted me to suffer. And boy, was I suffering.

"Here. Take these." Rose held out two small white pills, and I tossed them back without even asking what they were. She wasn't the type to keep random, unmarked pills in her purse, so I knew they couldn't be too bad. Chugging the glass of water she handed me to wash them down, I felt my gag reflexes stretching their legs again. I'd already thrown up once. I wasn't really looking forward to doing it again. I lay back on the bed, the back of my hand resting against my forehead like some medieval damsel in distress, and Amie snickered under her breath. I cracked an eyelid open.

"What are you giggling at, you little monster?"

She grinned, burying her face into the mattress next to me. She was sprawled out on her front beside me, wearing an oversized t-shirt of Ronan's that scraped the floor whenever she stood up. "You," she informed me. "You're making funny noises."

She was referring to my groaning; every few seconds it felt very necessary to groan as loud and as long as I could manage. "I'm not feeling well. I'm allowed to make funny noises."

"She had too much to drink," Connor added. Slowly, in tiny increments, Connor was coming back to life after Ronan's death. He still played the part of angry little boy very well, but he actually responded when you spoke to him now, and this morning he'd voluntarily followed Amie into my room and parked himself in the chair by the window, book in hand. Rose had stopped by to return some salad bowls I'd loaned her from the house for the party and found me miserably trying to make them breakfast. Packing me back off to bed, she'd fed the kids and brought me some dried toast, though I hadn't touched it. Just the smell was making me feel nauseous.

"Daddy drank too much sometimes," Amie said.

"He'd go running in the park," Connor added. "He said it helped him feel better."

The prospect of walking anywhere, let alone running, made me want to retch. "I think I'll just wait here until the room stops spinning if that's okay with you guys."

Amie patted my hair with a sticky hand. "You want pancakes? Pancakes always make me feel better."

"I don't think pancakes are gonna cut it this time, monster." Amie looked horrified, like she couldn't imagine a reality where this might possibly be true. Rose, on the other hand, looked like she sympathized all too well. I reached out and took her hand in mine. "Thank you. You drank twice as much as me so I have no idea how you're functioning right now, but I'm very grateful."

"You're welcome. What with the crappy weather and the short days, we're all professional drinkers here. Stay too long and your tolerance will go through the roof, trust me." Rose gave my hand a squeeze and smiled. "All right, you two. Let's give Ophelia an hour or so to sleep, and we'll go see if we can find any cool games to play in the cupboards. How about that?"

Amie squealed with excitement. Connor kept quiet, but he got up out of the chair, hugging his book to his chest, and dutifully followed after Rose as she exited the room. He paused in the doorway, looking back at me over his shoulder.

"Dad used to drink coffee with a raw egg in it, too. He always said that helped."

The advice was almost enough to send me rushing to the bathroom, hand clamped over my mouth, but I smiled and thanked him instead. A very short time ago, he would have said something scathing and enjoyed the fact that I was feeling shitty. Deflecting his anger toward Ronan onto me, and anyone else around him, had been a coping mechanism for him for so long. Dr. Fielding had said to give it some time, and there had been days over the past month when I thought he was never going to soften towards me, but gradually, slowly, it looked like Connor might be letting people in again.

Sleep wouldn't come. I tried to get comfortable in the bed, but it was futile. I felt like my bones were locked in their joints, my skin prickly and uncomfortable. After spinning around, getting tangled up in my sheets for what felt like a ridiculously long time, I gave up altogether and reached out for my nightstand—for Magda's journal.

Again, the need to read it was tempting. If I just gave in and read the entries in the journal, I'd have a direct line into the past. I'd know exactly what went down between Ronan, Sully and Magda, and I'd finally know *why*.

But still...

It just felt wrong.

I finally dozed off, holding the journal in my hands. An hour later, Amie screamed with delight downstairs, waking me from fuzzy, uncomfortable dreams, and the guilt began to sink in. I was the shittiest guardian ever. If Sheryl knew I'd gotten drunk while Connor and Amie were being taken care of by a babysitter, she'd have them bundled up and on that boat and back to the mainland in a heartbeat.

Never again. They were my responsibility now. I might not be able to take care of them for longer than six months, and I might not be able to persuade their uncle to take care of them, but I owed it to them to take care of them properly while they were still my wards. No more drinking. No more lying in bed, licking my wounds.

I threw back the covers and proceeded to get dressed, all the while trying to shake off the conundrum that was Sully Fletcher. He was an enigma that I couldn't afford to waste any more time on right now. Or at least for today. However, as I ran down the stairs, feeling marginally better than I did when I woke up, his face was still front and center of my mind.

Escaping him seemed impossible.

CHAPTER FIFTEEN

SEA KING

They say that tragedies come in threes. I'd never been a believer in fate or acts of God, per se, but when I woke up later that night to Connor screaming, voice hoarse, terror echoing through the house like a gunshot, I wasn't shocked. It was almost as if I'd been waiting for something awful to happen, and now that I was going to be hit with the force of yet another disaster, I was already braced and ready for the impact. I scrambled down the hallway and into his room, mentally mapping out what I would do if he was sick or injured in some way. I already had a "go-bag" prepped and ready downstairs. The gas tank of the Land Rover was full. I knew the route to the tiny Causeway medical center like the back of my hand.

I crashed through Connor's door, rushing to his bed, but he wasn't in it.

"Look!" He was standing at the window in just his pajama bottoms, narrow chest bare, ribcage on show. His rainbow-striped hat was missing from his head—probably the first time I'd seen him without it since Ronan had died.

"What's wrong? Are you hurt? Connor, tell me what's wrong!" I ran my hands over his body, looking for something out of place. Looking for blood.

"I'm fine. I'm okay. Look, out there! Can you see?" He handed me his scuffed up binoculars, urging me closer to the window, pressing the palm of his hand against the pane of the glass. "Out there. In the dark. There's a light. There are people in the water."

Outside, the night was black as murder. Black as ink. How he could see anything out there was a mystery. I took the binoculars and looked through them, though, squinting into the dark. Nothing. I couldn't see anything.

"No, not there. Here." Connor grabbed my hand and angled me to the left, huffing impatiently. "We have to do something. They need help!"

Again, nothing. And then…light. A faint flicker of light, yellow and weak, somewhere out at sea. Four miles? Three? It was impossible to judge distance with no frame of reference and no daylight.

"It's just an oil tanker, Connor. Maybe a cruise ship? Come on, let's get you back into bed."

"*No.* Look again. Look harder. It's a boat. A sinking boat."

Sighing, I did as he asked. No way he was getting back into bed without me settling this once and for all. He'd had a bad dream, maybe. He spent so long looking out of these binoculars every day that it wasn't surprising he was having nightmares, imagining all sorts of things happening out there on the water. "Okay, Connor. I can't see anything. I really—"

I stopped. The prow of a ship was breaching out of the water, right there where he'd said it was. My eyes were acclimating to the dark, and I could see more and more with every passing second.

The light was a fire.

The reflection of it shone out over the water, silhouetting the huge rise and swell of the waves—waves that had to be as tall as the house. Each time the water rose, I could see…

My mind went blank.

There was just no real way to comprehend what I was seeing. *People.* People in the water. The ship was much closer than I'd first thought. Not four miles. Not even three. It couldn't have been much more than six or seven hundred feet from the shore.

"Oh god. We have to call somebody." Without thinking I wrapped my arm around Connor and hoisted him onto my hip. He was way too big to be carried far, but I could make it to Amie's room. She was still asleep, and barely roused when I scooped her up from her mattress. "It's okay, sweetie. It's okay. We're going for a little ride. Shhh....go back to sleep."

I took both of them with me back to my room, where I'd left my cell phone on top of Magda's journal. "Who are you going to call?" Connor asked, anxiety causing his voice to squeak.

"911, bud. I'm just gonna call 911. They'll know exactly what to do."

Connor took the binoculars from me and rushed to the other side of the room, ripping open the French doors to the balcony. As soon as it opened, I could hear the wind howling outside like a wounded animal.

"911, what is your emergency?" The monotone voice crackling out of my cell phone startled me. This was the second time I'd had to make a call like this. Never in my life had I needed to call 911, and since I'd stepped foot on this island, I'd had to do it twice.

"A ship's down. Off the coast of The Causeway. People are in the water. It looks like there's some kind of fire."

"The Causeway, ma'am? Causeway Island?"

"Yes."

"Emergency rescue services have already been dispatched to the crippled ship, ma'am. Be advised, the coast guard is already on their way."

"But how long until they get here? It looks bad. I don't know how long they've got before the boat sinks." My words were running together; it was a miracle she could even understand what I was saying.

"Any moment now, ma'am. Remain calm. If you require any further assistance, please call back immediately."

"Thank you." I hung up, not sure what to do next. I placed Amie, still sleeping, onto my bed and I went to find Connor out on the balcony.

"They're going to drown," he said, handing me the binoculars. "The waves are too big." He was shaking, shivering so badly that his whole body was vibrating. "We have to do something." The wind was tearing inland across the water, buffeting the cliffs below the house and racing upward, whipping Connor's words away with them. I could hardly hear what he was saying. He was afraid, though. I could see the fear plainly in his eyes.

"Okay. We *will* do something. Come inside."

Connor followed after me, helping me, leaning his body weight against the French door when I tried to close it. "Go to the cupboard in the hallway. Get all of the blankets you can find and take them downstairs to the front door. Can you do that, Connor?"

He nodded, waited for a second, blinked, and then ran out of the room. I collected Amie, along with the duvet off my bed, and I raced down the hallway after him. A second later, I'd collected a warm sweater for Connor from the chest of drawers in his room, and I was barreling down the stairs after him. "Here, put this on. Find your shoes. Bring Amie's too."

"Okay."

He charged off again to locate his shoes, and I ran to the kitchen, still holding onto Amie for dear life.

Flashlight.

First aid kit from the cabinet above the stove.

Cereal bars.

A bottle of whiskey.

I stowed all of these items into a bag and slung it over my shoulder, then went and found Connor. Moments later, we were speeding out of the driveway in the Land Rover, Amie catatonic in the back seat, Connor with his binoculars pressed against the window up front. The sweater I'd found for him was far too big, like the person who'd bought it for him had accidentally purchased it three sizes too big. The cuffs were hanging down over his hands, and the hem was around his knees.

"Can you see the coast guard?" I asked him.

"No. The light's gone out now."

That wasn't a good sign. If the ship had indeed been on fire, the fire wouldn't just have gone out of its own accord. It would only have gone out if the ship had sunk, which was the worst possible thing that could happen. There was drag to consider. Depending on the size of the boat, and how far the people had managed to swim away from it before it went down, it would pull whatever was floating on the surface down with it.

The clock on the Land Rover's dash read 2:48. Nearly three o'clock in the morning. The island should have been sleeping, but as I tore down the narrow, winding roads and raced toward the dock, lights were flickering on in the houses we passed one by one. Word was spreading. At the dock, a small crowd of people were already gathered, dressing gowns and slippers in some cases, while others had taken time to dress in jeans, shirts and coats before they dashed out of the door.

An ambulance that looked like it had seen better days was parked out on the pier, sirens probing out red and blue into the night, and a guy I hadn't seen before was pacing up and down beside it, head down against the wind, talking into a cell phone that was pressed against his ear. "Stay here for a second, please," I told Connor.

"But, Ophelia!" He looked dismayed.

"I mean it. Stay in the car and make sure Amie doesn't wake up. Can you do that for me, please? Can you look after your sister?"

He was silent for a moment, mouth hanging open, but then he nodded slowly. "Will you come back right away?"

He wasn't upset about missing out on the action. He just didn't want me to leave him on his own. "I will. I promise. I won't be gone for more than five minutes, okay? You see the clock here? It says two fifty-eight? I'll be back before it says three oh-three, I swear."

"All right, then."

I got out of the car and slammed the door shut, hitting the lock button behind me. Scanning the crowd, I saw Michael, the guy I'd met at Rose's party, talking to another guy who looked like he could be his brother. When Michael saw me, he waved, gesturing me over.

"It's the Sea King," he shouted. "Been floundering for the past hour. Storm rolled in from nowhere. A bunch of ships have been smashed against the coastline. Another ship further up the coast, a tanker, was crippled. Guard's out there with them now, trying to prevent a spill."

"But what about these guys?"

"They're gonna get to 'em, they said. But pretty sure it'll be too late by then."

I shook my head, trying to understand what he was saying. "So the tanker takes precedence? How many people are on the other ship?"

Michael shrugged. The other man, about a foot taller than Michael with a gray speckled beard, pulled his jacket tighter around his body. "Usually tankers aren't manned that heavily these days. Everything's automated. Computers run the whole thing. Twenty. Maybe thirty max."

"And the Sea King?"

"Even less. It's just a fishing vessel. Fifteen guys?"

"So the coast guard *is* dealing with the ship with more souls on board." It made sense. And the fact that the tanker's hold was likely full of oil, worth an unimaginable amount of money and liable to cause a natural disaster if not contained, made it a no brainer. Still, it was criminal that the men off shore from the Causeway were being left to drown. "What are we going to do?"

"Nothing we can do from here. Jerry's boat's not built for weather like this. The only other boats on the island are even smaller than his. Tiny three-man fishing craft."

Michael was clenching a bunch of keys in his right hand; it looked like the teeth of the metal was cutting into his fingers. "Fuck." He turned around, eyes roving over the faces of the other worried people out on the dock. "This is crazy. We know those men out there. There has to be a way we can get out there to them." No solution seemed to come to him, or to his friend, though.

"I have the kids in the car. Listen, can you let me know if there's anything I can do to help?" I pointed back to the Land Rover, where I could see Connor's pale, worried face over the dashboard.

Michael sighed, frustrated. "Sure, of course. I think we're all gonna be stuck here like idiots, our hands tied behind our backs, but I'll let you know."

"Thank you."

Back in the car, Amie was snoring and Connor was perched on the edge of his seat, knees up around his chin, sweater pulled down over his legs so they'd disappeared altogether. "What did they say? Is someone going to save them?" he asked.

"Yeah, bud. The coast guard's on their way now. They won't be long at all." The lie was difficult to tell, since it was so big. No one was coming for the poor guys out on the water. No one would be coming until it was far too late. At that point, they'd be retrieving bodies, not survivors, and the inhabitants of the Causeway would have had to watch their friends and loved ones die.

••••

Hours passed. Connor fell asleep against his will, binoculars still clasped loosely in his hand, and Amie continued to snore. I couldn't have slept even if I'd wanted to. More men arrived carrying flashlights. Even more men arrived after that, carrying sea kayaks and what looked like wooden canoes. A couple of them tried to launch into the boiling ocean, but each time anyone tried they were cast back against the shore by the surging waves. At four, or maybe a little later than that, the sun began to rise, casting an eerie gray light across the beach. Even from the car, I could see how tired and hopeless everyone looked, faces pinched, foreheads creased into frowns so deep they looked now permanent.

Connor was covered in one of the blankets he'd brought from the cupboard in the hallway; Amie was tucked up snugly underneath my duvet. Strangely, I wasn't cold, even though clouds of fog billowed out of my mouth every time I exhaled, and my hands had turned blue.

I was considering my options—to go home or to stay—when a rap on my window nearly startled the life out of me; Staring out of the window, straight ahead, out to sea, I hadn't noticed Michael approaching the car, nor the large piping hot flask he was carry in his hands. I buzzed the window down, doing my best to find a smile for him.

"Coffee," he said, as if it were some sort of secret password. "I figured you might need some."

"Thank you."

He handed the flask to me through the window, sighing. "The other ship, the tanker? It went down an hour ago. They only managed to pull two guys out of the water."

"Oh god."

"Yeah." We both remained silent for a moment. And then he said, "It's hard, y'know. It makes you angry. If they hadn't gone to the tanker, if they'd come here instead…"

"No point in *ifs*, Michael." He was right, though. Maybe if the contents of the tanker hadn't been so valuable, the coast guard would have come to the Sea King first. Big oil companies held so much sway with the government. *Owned* half of the government. One word in the right person's ear and all available resources could easily have been diverted to a lost cause, instead of a viable one.

"The sea's calming a little. We're hoping we might be able to get out there soon on some of the smaller boats. Until then, we're just going to have to sit here and wait. Maybe it'd be better for you to get on home. Either way, whatever happens, people have died out there. With the current as strong as it is, the waves pounding the shore, bodies are gonna start washing up soon. The kids…" he said under his breath.

"You're right. I should get them home. I just feel so…*useless*."

Michael couldn't quite look me in the eye. "You, me and everyone else standing on this dock, Ophelia. It means a lot that you came out, though. To the people of the island. Thank you."

"Of course. I haven't been able to do—"

A loud snarl of an engine cut me off, ripping through the air. Over the small rise behind the dock, a black truck appeared, charging toward the shoreline. I thought I recognized the vehicle, and Michael's groan confirmed the identity of the driver.

"*Sully*. Perfect." He clapped his hand against the side of the Land

Rover. "I'd better go try and stop him from doing anything stupid," Michael said. He didn't sound too convinced that he'd be successful in his task, though. "I'll see you later, Ophelia."

From the sounds of it, he expected me to drive off and take the children home, but I didn't. I watched as Sully's truck careened down the slope and skidded to a halt, kicking a spray of sand and tiny pebbles into the air as the tires bit into the beach. He climbed out of the vehicle before it had fully stopped, hair wild, eyes wild, everything about him wild as he stalked toward the ambulance that was still parked on the pier. He broke into a run.

"Oh, *shit.*" Michael took off after him, running flat out, trying to cut Sully off, but it didn't look like he was going to make it. I got out of the car, closing and locking it up behind me, thankful both the children were out cold, and I followed suit, racing toward the pier. Sully reached the ambulance a clear eight seconds before Michael, and he ripped open the driver's door and pulled the guy who had been on his phone earlier out onto the wooden decking in a heap. I could hear Sully yelling long before I reached them.

"Fucking asshole! You're meant to call me. You're meant to fucking—" He stopped shouting to smash his fist into the guy's face. The guy, crumpled in a heap on the floor, didn't stand a chance. Sully landed three more catastrophic blows to his face with one hand, grasping hold of ambulance guy's shirt in the other. The guy went limp, just as Michael barreled into Sully, taking him to the ground.

"Get off me, Michael. *Get. The. Fuck. Off. Me.*" Sully rolled underneath him, wrapping an arm around Michael's throat, wrapping his legs around his waist and locking them out at his ankles. He squeezed, and Michael, still doing his best to try and pin Sully down, began to turn purple.

"Jesus, Sully. Let him go!" I didn't expect my voice to make an ounce of difference to the ex-soldier trying to choke out Michael on the pier, but the moment I shouted his name, Sully froze, his hold falling slack. On his back, panting, he stared up at me like my presence was a complete surprise. Shock was written all over his face. Michael disentangled himself from Sully's arms and staggered to his feet, growling under his breath.

"You're a fucking asshole, Fletcher," he said, spitting onto the decking. "A real fucking asshole."

"Yeah," Sully agreed, still out of breath and still staring at me. "I know." He rose quickly, brushing himself off. The ambulance guy he'd just knocked out wasn't even stirring.

"Why the hell would you do that?" I snapped, pointing at him. "What do you mean, he was supposed to call you?"

"I'm voluntary coast guard," he snarled. "I'm supposed to be out there, saving them."

"You don't have a boat, Sully. How can you be fucking voluntary coast guard without a goddamn boat?" Michael was still red in the face. He wiped his mouth with the back of his hand, scowling.

Sully just shook his head, glaring at the other man. He started striding off back toward his truck.

Michael seemed to take this as a bad sign. "You can't be *serious*, Sully. You're a fucking mad man. You cannot go out on that water with a goddamn Zodiac. It can't handle the swell. You'll drown right along with them if you try."

"Then I'll die out on the water with them, won't I? At least I can say I *did* try."

"You're not in the army anymore, Fletcher. You don't have a team of guys to pull this off. You heading out there isn't noble or admirable. It's *reckless*."

"Go home, Michael."

"Be *reasonable*, Sully."

The people gathered on the dock hadn't chased after Michael and Sully like I had; they'd remained rooted to the spot, watching the scene unfold with a mix of horror and intrigue on their faces. Now, amongst them, I saw Robert Linneman, a head taller than anyone else, his arm around a much shorter, much plumper woman who was standing at his side—his wife, presumably. Linneman broke free and headed for Sully's truck, meeting him there.

"What do you intend to do, Mr. Fletcher?"

"I intend to go out there and get those guys out of the water. If you don't like it, I suggest you get out of the way and let me do what I have to do."

"On the contrary. I was wondering what I could do to help."

I must have heard him wrong. Linneman? Mr. Robert Linneman? The crane-like, stoic, dour man who handled Ronan's affairs, offering to help Sully with what already sounded like a horrible plan that was unlikely to work. I had no idea what a Zodiac was, but it sure as hell hadn't impressed Michael.

Sully opened the back gate of his truck, working quickly, hauling a metal frame down out of the bed. "Best thing you can do to help, Mr. Linneman, is to help keep everybody calm and keep yourself safe on the beach."

"With all due respect, Sully, you're one man, and this doesn't appear to be a job for just one man. My brother-in-law, Ray, was on the Sea King, and I mean to do my best to make sure he finds himself back on dry land as soon as physically possible."

Sully stopped what he was doing and looked at Linneman finally, sizing him up. "All right. But if you go overboard, that's on you. You copy?"

"I do indeed."

"Then help me get this thing inflated and in the water." He began unraveling a huge bundle of gray plastic, unrolling it onto the sand.

I finally understood what he was doing, the kind of craft he was preparing to take out onto the choppy ocean, and my stomach rolled. "Sully? Sully, you're *not* thinking straight." It wasn't my place to tell him what to do. I shouldn't care at all, really, but I couldn't hold my tongue. I'd do the same for anyone. If I thought someone was about to risk their life on a suicide run, then I had to say something. Sully dragged what looked like a small generator out of the back of his truck and put it down in the sand.

"Sully, please, just stop for a second and think—"

He took hold of a twine cord attached to the generator and pulled on it, arm raised high over his head, and the thing roared into life, growling, drowning out my words. Sully looked up at me, defiance and madness in his eyes, daring me to do something. It wasn't like I could tackle him and put an end to his crazy plan; the guy was much taller than me, and his broad frame was packed with muscle. Michael was ripped, and even his attempt to ground him had been rather ridiculous—Sully had looked like he was swatting at a fly.

"Mr. Linneman, please…" I turned to the other man, hoping he'd see sense, but Linneman shrugged helplessly.

"This is probably the most foolhardy thing I'll ever do in my life, Ophelia, I know it, but sometimes you just have to risk all in the face of uncertain odds. People's lives *depend* on us."

I could barely hear him over the roar of the wind, and the choking, coughing, rattle of the generator, but I could see that he'd made up his mind, and there was no point in trying to dissuade him. Out of the corner of my eye, I could see his wife sniffling into a handkerchief, leaning against the shoulder of another middle aged woman in a house coat, who was trying to comfort her.

"Look on the bright side, Lang. If this thing goes down and I die, Ronan's kids will finally get the house. You can stay there and live in it with them forever. That's something to be cheery about, right?" Sully said, grinning.

"You're right. Why don't you do us all a favor and toss yourself overboard then," I snapped. "See if I care. Or anyone else on this island for that matter."

Sully barked out laughter. "Atta girl." He attached a hose from the gray rubber to a small black pump at his feet, and the rubber began to inflate rapidly, expanding and growing quicker and quicker until the items in front of him were no longer bizarre unfamiliar shapes in the darkness, but the counterparts of a small, inflatable boat that simply needed lashing together.

"That'll never hold," I heard someone say behind me. "First wave he tries to bank in that will swallow them whole."

"*Arrogant bastard. Why can't he listen…?*"

"Someone should call the police."

"These Fletchers are all far too ready to die. It's in their bones."

There was no way Sully could have heard them, standing so close to the generator. He didn't even seem to know they were there. He worked quickly, hands lashing and tying, grabbing extra lines of rope from his truck. He pulled a large metal stand from the vehicle and attached it to the front of the boat he'd just put together in less than five minutes, securing a large, high beam lamp to the prow.

"All right, Linneman. Let's get her in the water." The two men picked up the boat via the plastic strapping on the side of the vessel, and then hurried it down to the water. "Lift!" Sully yelled. "Walk her out past the break!"

That made sense. The waves were still high, still rough. If they tried to drive the boat out, they were going to be smashed back time and time again. With the boat hoisted above the water, resting on Sully and Linneman's shoulders, they lifted it every time a wave crashed against the shore, threatening to push them back inland. Soon they were shoulder deep in water, out past the break, and they lowered the boat into the water. Sully vaulted into the boat, holding out his hand to help Linneman in after him.

"Be careful!" Linneman's wife shouted. And then, under her breath, "Lord, please be careful. I don't think I can watch."

Sully levered the boat's small engine down into the water and cranked it; I couldn't decide whether the fact that it started immediately was reassuring, or if it would have been better for the thing to have failed and left them sitting there on top of the water.

Sully was a machine. Efficient. Fearless. Determined. He didn't look back at the shore once. They tore off away from land, the boat bouncing along the water like a skipping stone every time it hit a patch of rough water. Mrs. Linneman started crying.

I ran back to the car as quickly as I could—the children were both still passed out, thank god. I grabbed Connor's old binoculars and then raced back to the shore, frantically scanning through the lenses to find Sully and Linneman, but all I could see was roiling, angry, gray sea, and roiling, angry, gray sky, and my heart wouldn't stop hammering in my chest.

Ten minutes passed. Fifteen. Twenty.

No sign of the boat. No sign of anyone in the water. Michael and his friend were helping Ambulance Guy, who had finally woken up and was swabbing the cuts on his face from a medical bag at his feet. Nausea twisting through me like a snake, I headed down the pier again, counting the steps, trying not to panic.

"How deep is the water?" I demanded. "They're not that far out. Why haven't any of the men been able to swim back to shore yet?"

Michael opened his mouth and then closed it again, apparently frustrated. "It's not that simple, Ophelia."

"The water's very deep," the guy cleaning his cuts said. "The whole island was volcanic. The land falls away straight down underneath the water. Cliffs, dropping for hundreds of feet. And how far can you swim, Miss?"

"I don't know. Over six hundred feet, that's for sure."

"In open water? In a storm? In the freezing cold? And in the dark? I don't think so."

That shut me up pretty quickly. He was right. Maybe in a swimming pool I could swim for six hundred feet. Further. But with conditions the way they were out there…

"If the men went into the water, they probably would have tried to swim into shore, but they never would have made it. The water's too rough, but more importantly it's freezing cold. You can only survive a matter of minutes in water like that." Whoever this guy was, his attitude stank. He barely looked at me as he spoke, dabbing a cotton pad angrily against his lip. He was around my age, late twenties, and his Boston accent told me he wasn't a local.

Michael put a hand on my arm, warning me with his eyes— *probably not a good idea for you to be here right now*. If circumstances were different, I'd give this guy as good as he got, but I was exhausted. And looking for Sully and Linneman was far more pressing a task. I slipped by the men and walked all the way down to the end of the pier, holding each breath for five steps, holding each breath for as long as I could, as if that might somehow help.

I peered through the binoculars, scanning the sea, and I waited. The gray and white and black stretched on forever. Eventually, I saw something moving through the water. A boat? No, a rock. No, definitely…it was the boat. Tearing inland, I couldn't track it well enough at first to see how many men were on board. And then I could make out the shape of one man. Just one. The boat was too far out to tell who it was: Linneman, Sully, or someone else entirely. I took off at a sprint, crashing down the pier, past Michael and the other two guys, back down onto the beach.

The boat was coming in fast. It slowed as it approached the shore and the break, but it was still traveling at a rate of knots. Cutting through the white caps and the rollers, it almost rocketed straight out of the water when it hit land. Linneman was first over the side of the boat.

"Quickly. Get them out," he yelled.

Hands everywhere. Bodies, pushing and shoving. Ice cold water spilling over into my shoes, feet instantly tingling with pain. Water up to my knees, and then up to my waist.

"Ophelia, get back. We can handle it. We've got them. *Please!*" Michael, shoving me back to the shore. I stumbled, fell down in the wash. Hands helping me up, and then bodies being lifted over the side of the boat.

Cold.

So cold.

Soaked.

Lifeless.

"Does anyone know CPR?" Linneman was shouting. "Someone, start checking for pulses."

Then Sully.

He was drenched, hair plastered to his head, breathing hard, his thin white t-shirt stuck to his check, rucked up at the back, exposing two long, bloody scrapes, and a patch of angry red skin. He jumped over the side of the boat, and then somehow managed to lift another man out behind him, throwing him over his shoulder like a sack of wet cement. The moment he saw me, he started to run through the water in my direction.

"Don't just stand there, Lang. Come on. Rally." Grabbing me by the arm with his free hand, he started dragging me out of the water after him. I tripped and stumbled, barely kept up, but then I was on my knees in the sand, ears full of water, and Sully was taking my hands and placing them on the lifeless man he'd laid out in front of me.

"Like this," he said. "Link your hands together and compress. Up and down, up and down. Don't stop until I get back."

I pumped my interlinked hands up and down on the guy's chest like he showed me, stunned, unable to breathe a word, and Sully ran back the way we'd come. His shoes were gone, feet bare. Had he taken them off in the boat? Had he lost them in the ocean? There was blood on my arm. Blood on the sand next to me where he'd just been standing.

One, two, three, four.
One, two, three, four.
One, two, three, four.
One, two, three, four.

I kept up with the compressions, not daring to stop. The roar of the boat's engine shuttered into life again, and when I twisted, looking back over my shoulder, Sully and Linneman were already lifting the boat on their shoulders again, heading back out past the break.

"They're going back out?" I looked around, searching for someone to tell me what the hell was going on, but the people on the beach were frantically running to cars, carrying blankets, carrying bodies, administering CPR like I was, and no one heard me.

One, two, three, four.
One, two, three, four.
One, two, three, four.
One, two, three, four.

I looked down into the man's face lying before me. His lips were blue, parted, showing white teeth. His skin was worn like leather. Late sixties? Early seventies? How many storms had he weathered out on these waters? How many times had he nearly lost his life and won it back?

I fell into a trance. I kept pumping my hands up and down on the stranger's chest until my arms burned and ached, and I felt like I couldn't go on another moment, and then I carried on some more.

Another ambulance arrived, and then a sound, like the beating of a drum, like the racing of my heart, a paddle thumping at the air, everyone looking up, looking relieved. An air ambulance, bright red and white, descending from the heavens like a wrathful archangel. EMTs poured out of the chopper, jump bags over their shoulders, scattering across the beach.

"Ma'am? Ma'am, thank you. If you could step back for a moment, I can take a look at him now." The young guy standing in front of me didn't look old enough to professionally save lives. He seemed to know exactly what he was doing, though, as he dropped to his knees and began checking vitals.

"No pulse. How long have you been administering CPR, ma'am?"

The sky seemed to break open, and a bright, white light lanced down through the grim morning, illuminating the beach briefly before the clouds pressed in again.

"*Ma'am?*"

"Hmm?"

"How long have you been administering CPR for?"

"I'm not sure."

"Was he awake when he was brought out of the water?"

I shook my head.

"I'm sorry, ma'am. This man's dead. Can I check you over? Have you been in the water?"

"No, no, I'm fine. I—" My brain wasn't working. Everything was snapshots, stills, shunting and jumping around, hard to focus on. The EMT wrapped a blanket made of a silver, crinkly material around my shoulders and sat me down on a bench by the pier.

"Stay here, ma'am. Someone will be over to check on you in just a moment, okay?" The young EMT raced off, and I sat, trying to piece together what was happening.

It was a long, long time before the boat came back again.

When it did, I watched as Sully and Linneman dragged another five men from the boat, through the break, and onto the beach.

"I can't fucking believe it," one of the EMTs said. "The guy in the white shirt swam out for all of them. He went in after every single one of them."

"That's Sully Fletcher," another said.

"Ronan Fletcher's brother?"

"S'right."

"Huh. I guess heroics runs in the family."

I didn't hear anything else. I watched as Sully raced back and forth up the beach, trying to coordinate everyone, brushing his wet hair back out of his eyes, ripping his wet shirt off over his head to hold the drenched material to an elderly guy's forehead, applying pressure. I watched him secure the boat, pulling it into shore, the muscles in his back straining and popping as he worked—he was hurt pretty badly, his skin scraped and red and bloody. I watched as he helped lift a guy onto a stretcher, and then I watched as he buckled at the knees and fell to the ground, his eyes rolling back in his head.

CHAPTER SIXTEEN

THE GOOD SAMARITAN

"It's nowhere near as bad as they thought, apparently. Just a simple case of hypothermia. They're bringing him back to the medical center later on tonight."

"God, it's crazy that there isn't a proper hospital on the island. *Crazy*." It had been even crazier watching Sully being choppered off the island with the three surviving crew of the Sea King. In total, Sully had actually dragged eleven men from the water, but eight of them had either been dead already or died on the beach.

Rose was making chicken soup, and I was teaching the children arithmetic and English at the dining room table. Amie was completely oblivious to the events of last night. Connor had slept through Sully's arrival and hadn't woken up until the chopper arrived, so he'd only caught a part of the rescue. He hadn't seen Sully at all, thank god. A guy tearing up and down the beach, the spitting image of Ronan? That would have raised more than a few questions, and I wasn't sure I was ready to handle the monumental task of explaining Ronan's twin brother just yet. Connor kept asking if he could go and look at the wreckage of the Sea King that was still washing up in pieces on the beach. I was too scared to let him. Six men were still missing, presumed dead, and the last thing I needed was to take him down there, only to have a bloated, mangled corpse roll up onto the sand.

"I'm still kicking myself that I didn't come down to the dock," Rose was saying. "I saw all the lights and the cars zipping down the road, but it was just so cold. I couldn't face it. Everyone's still talking about it. Most excitement we've had around here in a very long time." Rose paused, shooting me a sidelong glance that I felt burning into me rather than saw. "I also may have heard that you were quite upset about you know who," she said slyly. We were being careful not to mention Sully's name in front of the children. "Any truth in that?"

"Yeah, sure, I was definitely upset. He'd just risked his life out there in that tiny boat. He'd been in and out of the water so many times. I think everyone was worried about him."

"Hmm. That's not how Michael Gilford said he saw it. *He* said you were hysterical. Started screaming at the EMTs to do their jobs. Running up and down the beach like a woman possessed. He said you looked like you were on the verge of picking up our belligerent friend and carrying him off home yourself."

"Psshh. Ridiculous."

Rose laughed softly under her breath, pinching salt out of her hand and dumping it into the bubbling vat in front of her on the stove. "Poor Michael. Every time a woman steps foot on the island, he takes a shine to her. And then she ends up falling in love with *you know who*, and that's that."

"I am *not* in love with you know who."

Amie's head snapped up, eyes shining, distracted from the piece of paper in front of her, where she had been diligently practicing copying the letters of the alphabet over and over again. "You're in *love*?" she asked, mouth hanging open. "That's really gross, y'know. That means you have to kiss a boy with your mouth open."

"You're right, that does sound gross," I agreed. "But don't worry. Rose is wrong. I'm not in love."

"Good. Because I don't think boys and girls should kiss. I think they shouldn't even hold hands really. It's not hygentics."

"Hygienic?"

Amie shook her head. "*Hygentics*. Big germs grow all over boys.

When you touch them, they get their germs all over you."

"I see."

Rose did her best not to laugh, while Connor rolled his eyes. "Girls have just as many germs as boys, Amie."

She ducked her head, went back to drawing the stalk of a very tall T. "I don't think so. Mommy always smelled nice, like flowers. *Felia* and Rose, too. You smell like dog butts."

"You've never even smelled a dog butt."

"I have. I smelled *you*."

"All right, you two. Why don't you concentrate on your school work, and then you can go play a game or something."

"Outside?" Connor looked way too hopeful. I knew as soon as I let him out the front door, he'd be running to the cliff face with his binoculars to scan the rocks below for debris from the Sea King.

"It's freezing outside, and it's still raining. I'm sorry, sweetheart. Maybe tomorrow, if the weather's a little better." *And they've cleared up the macabre evidence of the accident that took place last night.*

My response didn't make him happy at all. "Whatever. I can't wait until we can go to school properly. At least then we'll get to be outside sometimes."

"Only two more weeks," I agreed. If he wanted me to be offended that he'd rather go to school than stay at home with me, then he was going to be sorely disappointed. I loved teaching them their lessons, but it wasn't good for them to be cooped up around adults all the time. Both of them needed to be around other children, like normal kids. This big old house with its empty bedrooms and winding hallways, though beautifully decorated and comfortable beyond measure, wasn't an appropriate playground for children.

"Will you go and see him?" Rose said out of the blue.

"Who?"

She quirked one eyebrow at me, sighing. "You *know* who."

"Oh, god. No. Why on earth would I do that?"

"Because it might be nice for him to see a friendly, familiar face. I doubt anyone else on the island is going to be stopping by to check on him."

"I doubt he considers my face either friendly or familiar, Rose. We've spoken on a handful of occasions, and every single time he's been an ass, and I've been angry. I'm probably the last person he'd want visiting him while he's recuperating."

"I think you're wrong," she said, stirring the soup faster and faster, as though she wasn't really paying attention to what she was doing. "I think people underestimate him. I think he can be capable of kindness. Then again, I think he also feeds on bickering with people, so he'd probably enjoy a good sniping session with you. It'd have him on his feet in no time."

"Are *you* going to visit him?"

Rose stopped what she was doing and fully turned around to face me, horror on her face. "Hell no. That man's as ornery as a bear with its head stuck in a trap, especially when he's sick. You couldn't pay me to step foot into that medical center."

••••

Call me a glutton for punishment, but later that night I found myself pushing open the medical center doors, trying to figure out if I wanted to bolt and run, or if I really did want to ask the nurse at the reception desk which room Sully was in and pay him a visit.

Rose had stayed with the kids. I was so glad Ronan hadn't really fucked me over and left me to do this entirely on my own. Ronan had been a single father for a little over a year, but he'd had two nannies on rotation at all times, running them around to whatever class or recital they needed to be at, watching over them while he was working, making their meals for them and generally taking care of business. Without Rose's help, I would have been drowning. There were plenty of people out there taking care of their kids all by themselves, and I was sure they were doing a fine job. I admired them, in fact, but I was a firm believer that it took a village to raise children, and I was willing to take all the help I could get.

The medical center was a quiet, sterile place. Single story, the size of a typical outpatient clinic. The walls of the waiting area were plastered with such greats as, *"Causeway General Medical Center is not equipped to deliver babies. At the first signs of labor, please head directly to the mainland to receive medical attention at a suitable facility,"* and *"Chest pains? Our out-of-hours service runs from 6 p.m. to 9 p.m., Monday through Thursday. Please feel free to call for a consultation with a registered nurse."*

There was no mention of how you were supposed to head directly to the mainland if you went into labor in the middle of the night and Jerry wasn't running the boat service. Nor was there any mention of what action should be taken if you were experiencing chest pains on a Friday, Saturday or Sunday any time after nine o'clock, and you actually wanted to see a physical doctor.

"Miss? Excuse me, Miss? Can I help you?"

I turned away from the bizarre wall of printed public service announcements, all of which were in very aggressive capitols, I might add, to find the red-headed woman from Rose's party sitting behind the reception desk. She was wearing a set of dark blue scrubs, pinned to which was an obscenely large name badge that read "Gale." Underneath the name, someone, presumably Gale, had written "Trainee Nurse" in Sharpie. She gave me a bright smile, displaying a wall of cutely jumbled teeth that somehow made her look adorable.

"Ah, yeah. I was—I was looking for Sully Fletcher. I was told he'd been brought back from the mainland this evening."

Gale nodded. "Yeah, that's right! They did bring him here." She seemed way too excited.

"Can you tell me which room he's in? I'd like to visit him."

Her broad smile faded. "Oh. No, I can't." I couldn't tell if she was genuinely upset by the fact that she was unable to do as I'd asked, or if she was managing to pull off a mix of extreme passive aggression, coupled with a liberal side helping of sarcasm.

"What do you mean, you can't?"

"Sully's not here."

"But I thought you just said the EMTs brought him back here earlier on this evening?"

"They did." She nodded again, red curls bouncing everywhere.

"So? Where did he go?"

"Oh, he went *home*. He didn't want to sleep here. He said it smells of death," she said brightly.

"Okay. So...he was well enough to go home by himself?"

Gale popped a pen cap into her mouth and began to chew on it, eyes rolling to the ceiling; she was apparently thinking very, very hard. "No," she said slowly. "I wouldn't say that. I'd say he's still really pretty sick. Colin drove him, though."

"I see. Gale, can I ask you something?"

"Mmmhmm."

"Where are you studying?"

"Studying?"

"Yeah, y'know. To become a nurse." I pointed at her badge.

She looked down at the offending article like it was the first time she'd ever seen the thing. "Oh, that? No, no. You don't need to study to be a nurse. You just kind of learn everything as you go along. It's like being a secretary. Or an inventor."

"I don't think tha—" I stopped talking. Gale was staring at me, hanging on every word coming out of my mouth, and I could clearly see the problem here: the lights were on, but no one was home. How the hell had she managed to score the job at the medical center? *How?* "Can you do me a favor please, Gale? Do you think you might be able to write down Sully's address for me? I'd like to make sure he's okay."

"Oh! If you go over to his house, will you do me a favor? Can you give him these?" She reached under the desk and then dumped a large white paper bag onto the counter, with a script stapled to the front of it. "He forgot his pain meds when he left. He's gonna be miserable without them."

"Yeah, I guess I can give them to him."

"Great." Gale beamed at me like all her problems had been solved. She ripped a piece of paper off a pad by the telephone and scribbled on it for a second. When she handed it over, I was stumped by what she'd written.

The Lighthouse.

That was it.
"I'm sorry? The lighthouse?"
"Uhuh."
"Where is it, though? How will I know how to get there?"
"That part's easy. You just follow the signs. It's the only lighthouse on the island."

••••

Of all the places in the world Sully Fletcher could have lived, a lighthouse actually made some perverse kind of sense. Lighthouse keepers were typically isolated, hermit types, weren't they? With the overwhelming need to shut themselves off from the world? And wasn't it just so Heathcliffe of him to segregate himself on some windswept corner of the island, only venturing out to torment the locals when the wicked mood took him? Maybe Holly had been right when she called him that back at Rose's party.

I drove until I found a sign for "The Lighthouse," and then I drove until I found another and another. Soon, there were no more signs, and I was out of ideas. After a good thirty minutes, navigating the Land Rover down winding dirt tracks and hilly pathways, I gave up and finally asked the first person I saw—an elderly guy in an old wax coat, standing on the side of the road, staring up at the sky like he was waiting for something miraculous to fall from it, and he was determined not to be taken by surprise.

"The lighthouse? Well, you're way off course. Head back to the main road and then take the third right, past the house that's been painted blue. Then all the way to the end of that road. That's where you'll find the lighthouse."

"Thank you. Do you need a ride anywhere?"

He looked startled. "No. I'm fine right here, thank you." There was nothing for miles in either direction, and I could see no real reason for him to be standing out here, staring up at the sky, but I didn't want to offend him so I kept my mouth shut and I left.

Twenty minutes later: a lighthouse perched on the edge of a rocky cliff, cast in broad strokes of burned orange and yellow by the setting sun, like something out of an Afremov painting. As I parked outside, I noted the stack of *"The Lighthouse"* signs stacked up in a pile by a stony pathway leading off toward the cliffs.

The door flew open before I'd even had a chance to climb out of the car, and Sully stood there, one hand resting on his stomach, the other braced against the door jamb, staring at me with the wide-eyed look of someone about to encounter aliens for the first time.

"What the fuck?" he mouthed.

"You tell me," I mouthed back. I didn't want to get out of the car now that I'd seen the shitty expression on his face. His hair was crazy, standing on end, and his jaw was marked with dark stubble that made him look both unkempt and well put together at the same time somehow. He was wearing a tight, gray, long-sleeved shirt, sleeves rolled up to his elbows, and yet another pair of scruffy black jeans. He was pale and there were shadows under his eyes, which made him look haunted.

Slowly, still pressing one hand to his stomach, he hobbled out of the doorway and came and stood in front of the driver's side door, looking at me through the window. When I didn't buzz down the window, he lifted his hand and rapped a knuckle against the glass.

Didn't really seem like I had much of a choice after that. Down the window went. Sully considered me for a moment, considered the car in general, then said, "I don't suppose…that this is a coincidence?"

"You left your meds at the center."

He turned and walked away. "I'm not taking that shit."

"It's pain medication, Sully. They wouldn't have prescribed it to you if they didn't think you needed it."

"I *don't* need it. How do you know they're pain meds anyway?" Slowing, he looked back over his shoulder, frowning. "You been snooping in my shit?"

"I was surprised they weren't anti-psychotics actually," I snapped. "And no, I wasn't *snooping in your shit.* Gale offered up the information before she handed over the bag."

"Ha! *Gale.*"

"Yeah. Your girlfriend isn't the brightest bulb in the box, huh?" I got out of the car and followed after him.

"You know all too well she isn't my girlfriend."

"You implied it."

"Which doesn't mean anything, really, does it?"

"Why are those signs stacked up by the side of the house, Sully?"

"To stop nosy busybodies from showing up at my place, unannounced." Stopping at his front door, he turned and barred the entrance with one arm. "Shame. Didn't seem to work in this particular instance, did it?"

"I'm just trying to do the Good Samaritan bit, you asshole."

"I'm not a Christian."

"What?"

"The Good Samaritan. He was from the bible, right?"

"You don't need to be a Christian to be a good person, Sully."

"I'm sure it helps. Look, it's fucking freezing, and I have four cracked ribs. Can we please do this some other time?"

Over his shoulder, I could see a room in disarray, and a television on a stack of books, its screen turned to static. White noise popped and crackled, rustling low. I should have just left. I shouldn't have come in the first place; as soon as I'd found out he'd refused treatment at the medical center and gone home, I should have left him to his own devices. But he looked terrible. A clammy looking sweat had broken out across his forehead, and his hands were shaking. He hadn't taken any of his damn pain medication, and now he was telling me he had four broken ribs. God, how the hell was I supposed to just drive away now? It would be easy enough to do. It'd feel great slamming the car door and speeding off, leaving him behind in the dust. But I wouldn't get further than a mile before the guilt set in, and I had to turn back.

"Damn it, Sully. Just let me inside so I can fix you up with something to eat and something warm to drink. Set my mind at ease. Then I'll be on my way, I promise."

Sully cocked his head to one side. His breathing was shallow. Shallower than it should have been. "You're quite the little do-gooder, aren't you? What was the chick's name from The Sound of Music again? The nun that wouldn't quit that infernal singing? You know, the one who saved those children from the Nazis? You're just like her. So...*sunny*." He used the word as if it were an insult.

I folded my arms across my chest. "I'm nothing like her. Can we please just go inside? You're right, it is freezing, and I don't feel like catching hypothermia right now."

Both his eyebrows lifted at once. "That's funny."

Okay, so that was a pretty dumb thing to say on my part, but there was no need for him to be such an ass. "Sully. Come on. Please." Lord, I was begging him to let me inside his house so I could take care of him? How had this come about? Really, it categorically, absolutely made zero sense.

He sighed, allowing his arm to fall. "All right. You can come in. On two conditions."

"Which are?"

"If you step foot inside my house, do not even think about trying to tidy anything. Move one book, one plate, one mug, and you'll be back out of the door quicker than you can say *supercalifragilistic-expialidocious*."

He looked so damned pleased with himself that I couldn't help wipe the smile from his face. "That's from Mary Poppins, not The Sound of Music."

"I don't care what it's from. You mess with my shit, you're gone. Copy?"

I held my hands up. "Fine. I won't tidy."

"And the second condition is that there won't be any of that hot tea bullshit. If you're coming in here, you're drinking whiskey."

"What? Why am I drinking whiskey?"

"Because *I'm* drinking whiskey. And that's just the way it is."

"I have to drive."

He shrugged. "Take it or leave it, Lang."

How much would it hurt him if I jabbed him in the ribcage right now? A lot, probably. Enough to make him behave himself? I wasn't going to hold my breath. "Okay. Fine. Whatever. Just let me inside already. My feet are going numb."

••••

The inside of the lighthouse was surreal, like something Escher would have concocted, all weird angles and bizarre staircases that shouldn't have worked but somehow did. I had no idea why he'd forewarned me not to tidy. There were stacks of books all over the place, and clothes, yes, but the clothes were folded into piles, and the books were all lined up neatly. There were no plates or mugs laying around. Not even in the small kitchen he led me to, grumbling under his breath. He took two tumblers from one of the cupboards, and then rummaged around in another cupboard until he found a half full bottle of Dalwhinnie.

"Ice?" he asked over his shoulder.

"I don't know. Sure? I've never had whiskey before."

"You've never—" He couldn't believe it, that much was clear. "You have never had *whiskey*? That might just be the most ridiculous thing you've ever said. I suppose women in SoCal drink Sauvignon Blanc or Pimms or some shit. Mojitos. Cosmopolitans."

"Sometimes. I don't really drink at all."

"Oh, lord save us." Turning around, he handed me a tumbler, three fingers of dark amber liquid sloshing around inside it. "I'd hold your nose and throw it back if I were you. You're not gonna like it."

I accepted the glass. "How do you know?"

"Because I'm a fairly observant human being. Now drink."

I drank. It was foul, awful, evil stuff that burned all the way down my throat and settled in my stomach, a small fire spitting there that wouldn't go out. I'd only had one mouthful. I had at least four or five more to go before I reached the bottom of the glass. I wanted to cough and splutter and pull a face, but then again I didn't want to prove him right.

I managed to hide my disgust, though god knows how. Sully watched me manfully taking gulps of the raw liquor, his expression blank until I tipped the glass up and finally drained it. He gave a small nod, lifting his own glass to me. "Wow." He knocked his back in one, wincing a little as he swallowed.

"Wow?"

"Yeah. I'm impressed. That was three shots right there. And you didn't puke."

"Three shots? Sully, I have to drive back across the island. What the hell?"

He pouted, pouring out more whiskey into the glasses. "I thought you were gonna stick around and 'take care of me'," he said, throwing air quotes onto his last words.

"I am. But I still have to go home and take care of Connor and Amie. Remember? Your niece and nephew?"

"I don't want to talk about them. Or Ronan," he said, holding up his index finger. "If you need a ride later, I can get Jared down the hill to drive you. In the meantime..." He handed me back my glass, which contained a much smaller amount of whiskey in it this time. "Drink up."

I took the tiniest sip of the whiskey, scowling.

"Atta girl." He smiled, but it was a grim, uncomfortable smile that betrayed how much pain he was in. His hand was still pressed against his diaphragm like it was the only thing holding his insides in place.

"You can't take pain meds if you've been drinking," I said quietly.

"I don't plan on it. I told you. I'm not taking that shit."

"Why not? You're obviously suffering."

"Because, little miss know-it-all, I saw enough guys in the military get hurt. They were prescribed morphine and oxy, and I watched them all turn into addicts right before my eyes. It's not worth it. I'd rather take a few shots of the good stuff and grit my teeth if it's all the same to you, thanks very much."

"Oh."

"Yeah. *Oh.*"

He stood there, staring me down, not really breathing, not saying anything, and once again I wanted to leave. I looked away; I wasn't the sort of person to be cowed by anybody. Not even Ronan Fletcher had managed it. But there was something about his brother that Ronan didn't have. Some intense, deep, penetrating quality that made me feel uncomfortable in my own skin.

"I'm going to go sit down now, before I fall down. Please feel free to snoop around and do whatever the hell you like in my absence." Sully left the kitchen and went back through to the living room, his back ramrod straight, his shoulders rigid, and I considered picking up one of the sharp knives from the butcher's block on his counter and seeing how good my aim was.

Instead, I took full advantage of his invitation and began rifling through his cupboards, looking for ingredients so I could cook him something to eat. Surprisingly, there was plenty to choose from. I'd expected a refrigerator full of condiments and a stale, half eaten sandwich; bare shelves, and dust balls in his pantry. But rather his refrigerator was full of vegetables and fruit, along with packs of meat and blocks of cheese, and his cupboards were overflowing with baking products, dried goods, and tins of soup. Staples, nothing fancy, but better than nothing, that was for sure.

I got to work.

Thirty minutes later, I had a beef stew on the stove, biscuits in the oven, and a cup of coffee in my hand for Sully. He'd said no to tea, but a hot, strong cup of Joe might be a different story. When I walked through to the living room—so weird that there were no straight lines in the entire ground floor of the house—Sully was crashed out on the couch, head tipped back, both hands clasped over his stomach now, and he was sleeping.

"Well. *Shit*."

Sully cracked one eyelid open, peering at me. "Mr. Von Trapp would not be impressed by the color of your language."

"Mr. Von Trapp can kiss my ass."

That made him snort. Carefully rolling his head forward, he sighed heavily. "Come on. Let's have it then." He held his hand out, eyeing the steaming cup I was still holding.

I surrendered it to him, thankful he wasn't putting up a fight. "I didn't know if you took sugar."

"I don't."

"Let me guess. You're sweet enough?" My voice dripped with sarcasm.

"No, Lang. I'm *not* sweet. Not even a little. And coffee isn't supposed to be sweet, either. It's meant to taste like battery acid. It's meant to keep you awake, not put you into a sugar coma."

"Duly noted. You're quite blunt, aren't you? Does it entertain you to make people feel uncomfortable all the time?"

Sully sipped his coffee, and then grimaced, clutching at his side. Once the pain had passed, he put down the mug on the small table beside his beaten up leather couch and directed his attention at me in that terrifying way he had perfected. "Does it entertain me to make people uncomfortable?" He thought for a second. "No, it doesn't entertain me. Other people's discomfort is an unfortunate by-product of my 'no bullshit' policy. It has nothing to do with me. It has everything to do with them. They only feel uncomfortable because they're being dishonest, or they're hiding something. I don't like being untrue to myself, and that makes them feel bad because that's all they *ever* are. Their lives are shambolic."

"Shambolic?"

"Mmhmm."

"That seems a little harsh, don't you think?"

"Not at all. I think it's a pretty fair assessment."

"And me? You think my life's a sham?"

He smiled, sharp and wicked, and I knew I wasn't going to like what came out of his mouth next. "Lang, of all the people residing here on this tiny spit of land, your life is the biggest sham of all. You pretend to care about Connor and Amie, when really all you care about it the pay check. And you pretend you came here to be a Good Samaritan, when the truth is that you're attracted to me, and you were worried about me."

The door was only five feet away. Two seconds? Maybe even less. It would take me no time at all to storm out of Sully's lighthouse, get in the Land Rover, drive back to the children and never see this man again. Though it wouldn't be that simple, because on an island as tiny as the Causeway, I was bound to run into him again at some point. He was waiting for me to do it; he was waiting for me to get pissed and leave, I could see it in the hard, dark depths of his eyes.

It was better for me to stay and defy him than to do exactly what he expected me to, if only so I could flip him the bird and prove he didn't know me as well as thought he did after all.

"I don't like lying," Sully said slowly. "I especially hate when people lie to themselves, Lang. It makes society a very dangerous place. If everyone's walking around, choosing to believe they're good people, they're incapable of doing wrong, they don't want things that are bad for them, and that their problems will simply vanish if they ignore them for long enough, then who's going to fix things when they break? Who's going to take responsibility when things go wrong? And who is going to tell the goddamn truth?"

"I don't give a shit what you think, Sully. I always tell the truth."

"Is that so." It wasn't a question. His voice dipped down at the end, telling me he didn't believe me for one split second. "Then tell me. Why did you decide to stay on the island? Was it because Linneman told you there wouldn't be a pay out at the end of your six-month contract if you left? Hmm? I know all about your parents' restaurant back in Cali. How would you have saved the day if you didn't come home with that nice fat check for a hundred grand sitting in your back pocket?"

"You're right. Going home without that check would have been a disaster. But I would have found another job. I would have taken on three extra jobs if I'd had to. I'm not afraid of hard work. I would have figured it out, because that's what I'm good at. Figuring out shitty situations."

"Like the shitty situation with your ex-husband?"

Shock flared through me, sour and unpleasant. "How do you know about Will?"

"Well, you get to know everything about me, Lang. Mags's journal's giving you plenty of insight, I'm sure. So I figured I ought to even the playing field a little. I had a friend spend a couple of hours reviewing your online footprint. He sent me the basics—the details of your divorce. Your parents' business. Your school being closed down. You losing your job. The works."

"You're unbelievable."

Sully sighed. "Do you really care if I know your ex-husband cheated on you? *Really*?"

"Yes!"

"Why?" He was so calm. So reasonable. So *infuriating*. As far as he was concerned, I didn't have a leg to stand on. He was never going to believe I hadn't read that cursed journal. *Never*. My outrage was bubbling over, difficult to tamp down. Sully's smile spread even wider. "How about you quit acting all bent out of shape and admit to me why you're really here right now?"

"I told you—"

"And I told *you* I hate liars. Are you denying you're attracted to me? Even though you know you shouldn't be? Even though you know it's weird because I'm an asshole, and because of Ronan's kids?" He seemed completely unaffected by the words coming out of his own mouth. He didn't seem to care that they were bound to affect me either. He just sat there, watching me, waiting.

He wasn't going to win. Not this time. Even if it meant embarrassing myself by owning something I'd been avoiding acknowledging even to myself. But the things he'd said earlier, about people ignoring their problems, or simply ignoring their feelings in this case...it never helped, and I knew it.

"Fine. You're right. I am attracted to you. It's not something I'm particularly proud of. Not because of Ronan, or because of Amie and Connor, but because you're a spiteful, garbage person who only sees the bad in everything, and caring about a person like you will probably make me a toxic, unhappy person, too. At least Ronan was—"

He heaved himself off the couch way faster than I would have thought him capable of, and stood over me, panting. "Don't do that," he snapped. "Before you even contemplate finishing that sentence, please do *not* compare me to my brother."

"Why not?"

"When you're a twin, when you look so utterly the same as someone else you grow up with, learn with, develop, become a man with, then all people want to do is find the differences between you. He was kinder. You were meaner. He was academic. You were destructive. He was the family man. You were the warmonger. It's fucked. I don't want to hear it. Especially from you—someone who knew Ronan for all of five fucking minutes, and who still doesn't know me at all."

"I would if you damn well let me!"

"I DON'T WANT—" The room erupted with a high-pitched, startling sound, cutting through our argument. Sully almost leapt out of his skin, spinning around, eyes wild and wide, his chest rising and falling rapidly.

"What the hell is that?" I yelled.

He still looked on edge, but a calmness settled over Sully all of a sudden. "Smoke detector," he said, low, so I could hardly hear him over the racket. "You're burning down my kitchen, Lang."

"Oh, shit, the stew!" I dashed into the kitchen. The gas burner underneath the cast iron pot the food had been cooking in was charred, and smoke was curling up from underneath it, thin and black but enough to have set off the alarm. "Fuck." I quickly turned off the burner and moved the pot, checking inside to survey the damage done to the stew. Thankfully it looked fine. It wasn't even burned on the bottom. The base of the pot, however, was ruined. The alarm stopped, leaving my ears ringing.

"I didn't think to ask if you were a decent cook before I let you loose in here," Sully said behind me. "Here, let me see."

I got out of the way, and he poked and prodded at the stovetop. "The element's almost gone," he said, pulling a face. "I've been meaning to replace it for a while. It catches light when the burner gets too hot sometimes."

"So this wasn't my fault?"

"No, this wasn't your fault, Lang. Relax. Go sit down. I'll bring the food through."

I started to argue—he shouldn't be picking up heavy pots, or doling out food. The whole point of me coming here to cook was so that he didn't have to—but then I saw the look on his face and I backed out of the kitchen without another word. He brought in two bowls shortly after, then went back and collected the biscuits I'd made from the oven. We ate in silence, Sully only managing to finish half the bowl he'd served himself before he set it down, groaning.

"Go on. Tell me my food tastes disgusting. I dare you."

"It was great, Lang. But you may have noticed that I'm a little under the weather right now. My appetite isn't what it normally is."

"You should get up to bed. Rest some," I told him.

"Too many fucking flights of stairs in this place. I'm sleeping right here until I've healed up a bit." Lying back, arms wrapped around his torso, he sprawled himself on the three-seater, lifting his legs up onto the cushions, and closed his eyes, breathing heavily. Eating seemed to have taken it out of him. *Really* taken it out of him. His face was even paler than before, and that clammy sweat had returned, beading on his forehead.

"You're looking pretty gray, Sully. Do you think you can be cordial for a couple of minutes while I check your temperature?"

"Sure. As long as you don't try to stick a thermometer up my ass."

"I promise, that's the very last thing I plan on doing." I had no idea where his first aid kit was, and I hadn't brought the one from The Big House with me, so I went old school and used the back of my hand, pressing it against his forehead.

"I'm sure that's really accurate," Sully grumbled.

"Accurate enough to tell me that you're burning up. Jesus, Sully, you should never have left the medical center. What were you thinking?"

"I was thinking I had a better chance of survival at home, where Gale couldn't shoot me up with adrenalin instead of morphine by accident."

"Yeah, well. I suppose that's a good point." Rushing back into the kitchen, I grabbed a clean dishcloth from one of the drawers and ran it under the cold tap before taking it back into the living room with me. Sully's chest was rising up and down so fast, it looked as if he'd just run a full marathon. I held the cool, wet material to his forehead, keeping it in place when he tried to push it out of the way. His arms were made of rubber, though—easy to fend off. He didn't seem to have any strength left in his body at all.

"Can you call Ronan, please? Tell him I need him to come get me? I'm sorry, Mags, I shouldn't have drunk so much." He was slurring like he *had* been drinking. Way more than two glasses of whiskey. More like he'd drunk the whole bottle.

"Sully? Hey, Sully, can you sit up for me?"

"Not really." He tried, though, gave it a valiant attempt. He strained, flexing his abs, rocking forward, and then he howled in pain, eyes shooting open, what little color that was left in his face draining to leave him ghostly white. "Oh, shit," he hissed. "That was dumb." He seemed to have returned to himself, but when he looked up at me, pupils swallowing his irises in the darkening room, he looked like he was vanishing again just as quickly.

Frowning up at me, he reached up with one hand, fingers outstretched. "You...you're not her, are you?"

"I'm Lang." I shook my head, correcting myself. "I'm *Ophelia*. Remember?" He looked hazy, like he couldn't really hear what I was saying properly.

I got my cell phone out of my bag and dialed Rose's number as quickly as I could. She answered on the fourth ring. "Hey, O. Kids are fed and watered. Amie's already passed out, and Connor's reading his book in bed. You on your way back?"

"No, actually, I'm still at Sully's."

"He's not at the medical center?"

"No, he refused to stay there apparently. Long story. Listen, I'm not really sure what to do."

"What do you mean?"

"Well, he was lucid when I got here but he's burning up now, and he's pretty confused. He asked me to call Ronan to come get him and take him home."

"You should call the medical center. Have Collin come get him in the ambulance or something."

"I was going to, but I was there earlier and there were posters everywhere saying out-of-hours treatment was only available Monday through Thursday until nine. And it's Friday."

"Shit, you're right."

"I can't believe you guys don't have a proper emergency room here, Rose. It's so damned dangerous!"

"I know, I know, let me think."

I'd been watching Sully the whole time I was speaking to Rose, but I turned away for a moment now, pinching the bridge of my nose between my thumb and my index finger, so he couldn't see how freaked out I was. He might not know which way was up, but he still didn't need to see me panicking this hard. I was about to ask Rose if there was even a doctor on the Causeway I could drive Sully to, but then I heard a wet, retching sound behind me and I didn't get the chance.

Sully was balled up on his side, curled as small as he could go, and he was throwing up onto his plain cream rug.

"Ahh, Jesus. I have to go Rose. He's puking. I'll call you back in a sec." I hung up, and dropped to my knees, narrowly avoiding the mess he'd made.

"Don't worry, I'm coming," Sully moaned. "Goddamn it, help them. We have to get them out of there!"

"What? Hey, you're okay. Try and lean back a little. Don't worry. I'll clean this up. Just rest a moment. Come on, that's it." I didn't think about what I was doing. I just did it. I slowly brushed my fingers through his hair, *shhh*ing him, trying to make him feel better. "It's okay, just breathe, Sully, just breathe. I got you. I got you."

"It's too hot. The tanks are gonna blow. We have to get them out of there, Crowe. They're all gonna die."

"It's okay, Sully. Shhh, it's all over now. You got to them. You pulled them all out of the water, do you remember?"

"*Water?*"

"Yes. You jumped into the ocean to pull them out. It was stupid and dangerous, but you managed to save three people's lives."

"Three? Only three? Oh. Yeah. That's right."

"Those three men are alive because of you, Sully. I swear, if you hadn't done what you did, they would have drowned like everyone else."

He was shaking his head. Shaking it so violently that his teeth were rattling together inside his head. "No. No, you're wrong. They're trapped inside the truck. They'll burn if we don't get them out there, Crowe."

"Sully! Calm down!" He was flailing, arms everywhere, trying to push me away from him. I lost my balance, fell back and landed on my ass, and Sully managed to sit himself upright.

"Fuck you, Crowe," he spat. "If you don't want to go, then that's on you. I won't live the rest of my life knowing I could have helped and I didn't. I'd rather burn to death along with those poor bastards." He shot to his feet, about to take off, about to do something, to act, to help whoever he imagined was trapped inside a truck somewhere, but he didn't make it more than three feet toward the front door before his knees buckled out from underneath him and that was it. He was out cold.

CHAPTER SEVENTEEN

TAKING LIBERTIES

I stayed the night. I had no other option available to me, unless I was okay with leaving Sully passed out on his living room floor in a pool of his own vomit, which I wasn't. So I stayed. Thankfully Rose was having a grand old time taking care of the children, so that wasn't an issue.

It *was* an issue that Sully kept dipping in and out of consciousness every fifteen or twenty minutes, and he thought I was Magda more often than not. Strangely, he didn't seem all that happy that I (she) was taking care of him.

"*You made your choice, Mags. I told you. I don't want to see you. I don't want to hear from you. I...just leave me the fuck alone, goddamnit!*"

His fever broke at four in the morning. He was running with sweat, his t-shirt soaked, so I ran upstairs to find him something clean to change into, and found myself having a surreal, how-can-this-be-happening? moment standing in his bedroom at the foot of his bed. He didn't have much by way of furniture in his room: a simple twin bed, covers rumpled and turned back (he hadn't been up here since he woke to see the disturbance down by the beach the night of the storm), a chest of drawers, a three tier bookshelf that was overflowing with books, and a huge black, plastic packing box with *Captn. S. Fletcher* stenciled on the side of it in gray paint.

It smelled of him up here. Ronan had smelled of Armani Code, Old Spice deodorant, and laundry detergent. Sully smelled like wood shavings and whiskey, and something I could only hope to describe as specifically *Sully*. There was a pair of socks balled up on top of the chest of drawers, and a book, open and face down on the floorboards beside his bed. "Zen and the Art of Motorcycle Maintenance." He was halfway through.

I found his clean t-shirts folded and stacked methodically by color in the second drawer of his chest of drawers. Grabbing one, I then went on the hunt for a clean pair of shorts for him as well.

Downstairs, Sully was shivering silently on the couch, blanket up around his chin. He glanced up at me standing at the foot of his spiral staircase, blinking with all the solemnity of a pissed off owl. "So you're still here huh, Lang?" His voice was croaky, no doubt from shouting so angrily at Crowe (me) for hours.

"Looks like it, doesn't it?"

Sully glanced around his living room, flinching. "Man. I take it I trashed the place and not you?"

"You were delirious. You refused to keep your ass sitting down, let alone lying down. I think you messed up your ribs pretty good."

"Yeah." Wincing. Pressing fingertips gingerly against his chest over the covers. "I think you're right."

"Are you thirsty? Do you want some water?"

He looked at me uncertainly. "Yeah. If you wouldn't mind, that would be great." His tone was soft and almost...almost *repentant*? Could it possibly be? I never thought I'd see the day when Sully Fletcher might show a little remorse. Or gratitude for that matter.

"No problem. I'll be right back."

I made him some toast, too. He'd thrown up another three times while he was feverish, and he could have probably used some food in his stomach right about now. When I took him the plate I wasn't surprised that he refused it, however.

"Thanks, though. I mean it. I just can't right now."

"Do you want to take something for the pain yet?"

A shadow of anger flickered in his eyes. "I said *no*, Lang. I could be in pieces, bleeding out on the sidewalk, and I would still rather die than take any of that shit. Don't ask me again." Looked like he was feeling well enough to tell me off. That was an improvement. "What time is it, anyway?" he asked, trying to turn to look out of the window behind him. I put a hand on his shoulder, stopping him.

"It's five forty," I said. "Dawn's right around the corner. Been a long time since I pulled an all-nighter twice in one week."

"Such a rebel." He cracked a smile, and two deep, heartbreakingly perfect dimples formed in his cheeks.

"Yeah. If you say so." I smiled, ducking my head. "I have to go, Sully. I can't leave the children for much longer. I was wondering if you'd let me ask you something before I go, though?"

Wariness appeared in the lines of his face. "Sure. Doesn't mean I'll answer if I don't like the question, though."

"Naturally." No lying with Sully. Just the point-blank refusal to hand over the information you'd requested. Sounded about right. "While you were burning up, you kept shouting at someone. Someone called Crowe. I just wanted to know who he was."

Sully went very, very still. For a long moment he held his breath, eyes on me, eyes on the ceiling, and then he sighed, long and heavy. "Crowe was a guy I served with in the army. He was a jerk and a coward. He and I were not friends. That good enough for you, Lang?"

It wasn't. I wanted to know why Sully had been so angry with him earlier, when he'd been screaming and shouting about the men in the truck being in danger, but I knew I was walking on thin ice. He wasn't going to give me any more information. Not today, anyway.

"All right. Well. I'll come back later on to check on you, okay? After Rose is done with work and she can take care of the children again."

"You don't need to do that. I'll be fine now. I think the worst of it has passed."

"Even so. I'll be back around six."

Sully's lips drew into a flat, tight line. He wanted to argue with me, to stand his ground, I knew, but he was a smart guy. He knew he needed the help, even if he didn't want to admit it.

I grabbed my jacket and headed for the door.

"Hey, Lang?"

I turned around.

"Are they...you know. Are they okay? Ronan's kids?"

I pondered on the question for a second, and then answered. "No. No, they're not okay. Their dad just died."

••••

"If you could see your father again, Connor, what would you say to him?"

Connor looked down at his hands, and then out of the window, where a small crane had been erected on the beach to haul the twisted and battered remains of the Sea King up onto the back of a flatbed truck.

"Connor?" Dr. Fielding's voice was crystal clear and perfectly loud through the speakers of the laptop, sitting on the table in front of the little boy, though Connor was diligently pretending not to have heard him.

"Connor, sweetheart. Why don't you answer Dr. Fielding?" I was tired. Beyond tired. I'd already decided the children weren't going to suffer because of the fact that I'd been out all night, tending to their sick, as of yet unknown uncle, however, so I was now on my fourth cup of coffee for the day.

Connor coughed, picking at his fingernails. "I wouldn't say anything to him. He's dead," he said quietly.

"Connor—"

"That's okay, Miss Lang. Perhaps Connor is right. Sometimes, in the early stages of grief, it can be helpful to imagine these dialogues, last words if you will, to bring closure and allow the children to say their goodbyes. In other cases, it can sometimes serve to confuse the situation. Connor, how do you feel about your life on the island? Do you like it there?" With Ophelia?"

Connor looked at me out of the corner of his eye.

"It's okay," I told him. "You can say whatever you like. I'm not going to be mad, I promise."

"I hate it," he blurted. "I hate the island. I hate not going to school. I hate Amie sometimes. She's always too happy."

"And Ophelia? Do you mind that your father left her in charge of looking after you?"

He was quiet for a very long time. I could tell he wanted to look at me again, but he wouldn't let himself. And then, after a few more moments of indecision, he said, "I don't hate Ophelia. I did at first, but now…she's okay. I don't mind that she's in charge. Being here with her is better than being in an orphanage."

"Why do you think Amie is too happy, Connor?"

"Because. She never seems sad. She's always playing and laughing all the time. It's like she doesn't even care."

"Doesn't care that your father is gone?"

Connor looked away again, eyes narrowing out the window.

"You see, the difference between you and Amie, Connor, is that she's much younger than you. While she's very sad that your father is gone, her mind works differently to yours. She doesn't feel the absence of your father quite as much as you do. That doesn't mean that she doesn't care, okay? It just means that she copes a little better with the sadness she feels inside. Does that make any sense?"

"I suppose so."

"So when you see Amie laughing and playing next time, think about this. You're her big brother and she looks up to you and loves you very much. She definitely feels a bit scared sometimes, so maybe it would be nice for you to sit and play with her. Let her know she can count on you to be there if she needs you. Do you think that's a good idea?"

Connor lifted his head, looking directly at Dr. Fielding on the screen for the first time since the session began forty minutes ago. He looked like he had finally heard something that made sense to him. "I guess," he said, his tone changed altogether. "I mean, maybe. If she's not being too annoying."

"That's very kind of you, Connor. That's exactly what a good big brother would do." Fielding was sometimes a little too *softly softly* in his approach for my liking, but then again he was the trained and lauded child psychologist, and I was the out-of-work schoolteacher. He probably had twenty years of experience on me, and the way he'd just handled the situation with Amie actually sounded like it might make a difference around the house. If Connor started interacting with his sister more, instead of snapping at her whenever she was giddy, he might end up lifting himself out of his grief, too. If there was hope of that, then there was hope in general.

"Connor, thank you for spending some time with me today. I've really enjoyed talking to you. I think we've made great progress," Fielding said.

Connor seemed less sure of what might or might not have been accomplished during the session. He arranged his mouth into the tiniest suggestion of a smile, though there was no hint of it anywhere else on his face. He picked up his book and his rainbow striped beanie, and carried both out of the room, closing the door silently behind him. I hated this part. Now was the time when Fielding and I completed our reviews and discussed how best I might handle things with the children over the next week, though most of the time it felt like Fielding was taking the opportunity to poke and prod at the insides of my head, too.

"Well, Ophelia. I have to say, I really do see some progress," he said, as I sat down in the chair Connor just vacated.

"Yes, I agree. He's been a lot more talkative the last couple of days. And he's asked to spend more time outside. Though that was related to an accident that happened during a storm."

"A storm?" He was using his *no-way!* fake-shocked voice he used with Connor, whenever the little boy told him something arbitrary. This wasn't arbitrary, though, so it was kind of frustrating that he was using that tone with me.

"Yes, a storm. A ship was capsized out on the water close to shore.

Not close enough for the ship's crew to swim to shore, though. At last count, thirteen men died."

That seemed to get his attention. "I see. And Connor has been showing increased levels of interest in the accident that seem…out of the ordinary?"

"No. I don't think so. I think he's just curious. He knows people died out there. It was awful."

"Mmm. Yes, I'm sure it was. A terrible thing, by the sounds of it."

Ahh, the soft, coddling tone of a therapist. He managed to sound deeply wounded by the tragedy, and completely insincere at the same time. I wanted to slam the laptop closed and cut him off, but that would have made next week's session really awkward. For Connor's sake, I managed not to snap at him.

"What about you, Ophelia? How did the event affect you? *Mentally?*"

Oh, absolutely not. I wasn't going to be psychoanalyzed by Fielding. No way, no how. It was one thing being here because it was the right thing to do for a child in my care, and another altogether to be stripped down and assessed, to have him making notes about me in his little book.

I gave him my most steely, cold smile. "I'm fine, Doctor. Thank you for your concern."

"You didn't know any of the deceased men that were brought in from the wreckage?"

"No. I didn't. The only person I knew was Sully, and—"

Fielding sat back in his seat, like I'd reached through the computer screen and slapped him across the face. "I'm sorry? Did you just say *Sully?*"

"I did. Is there a problem?" There definitely looked like there was a problem.

"Sully Fletcher? Ronan's brother?"

"Yes."

"Ah. Right. I see."

"What do you see, Dr. Fielding? I'm confused."

"Ronan mentioned his brother many times in his own personal

therapy sessions." He looked uncomfortable, brow furrowed, as if he were hunting for what to say next and coming up short. In the hallway, the clock on the wall started chiming midday. The fifth hour had been struck by the time he continued. "Of course, patient confidentiality is still a legally binding contract, even after a patient's death, Miss Lang, so I'm not obliged to go into any sort of detail about what passed between Ronan and me in our sessions, however I will say this. From what I was lead to believe, Sully is a courageous, very brave man who has suffered through a number of traumatic experiences in his lifetime. And when people experience all the things Sully has experienced, Ophelia, they leave a mark. An indelible one that doesn't rub off too easily. Not without the desire to want to heal, anyway. Ronan told me often about the dangerous stunts his brother would pull. Really reckless, hair-raising stuff. His appetite for throwing himself into the mouth of hell so frequently, while commendable, could also mean that he's putting those around him in danger at the same time. And if he's spending time around you? Around the children?" He fell silent.

"He saved three men. No one got hurt because he reacted in a tough situation. And you speak as though Ronan wasn't the same, Dr. Fielding. He was the one awarded the Purple Heart, remember? I'm sure he didn't get that handing out ice cream at Kabul airport."

"Yes, well. The situation's complicated, whichever way you look at it. I just thought it might be prudent to give you a *heads up*, if you will. A friendly warning from me to you." Here was a man who'd never had cause to use the phrase "heads up" before. He was way too proper, too refined for such things.

"Well, thank you, Doctor, for looking out for me, and for the children, but you really have nothing to worry about, I promise you."

••••

Rose came straight by after work. I'd already given the kids their dinners and both of them were bathed, so all she needed to do was sit with them for a couple of hours, watching Marvel Action Hour reruns (which Amie loved).

I was late arriving to Sully's place. When I let myself into the lighthouse, juggling Tupperware containers of homemade Bolognese sauce and chicken casserole I'd made that afternoon, I stumbled into Sully's living room to find him braced against a wall with a towel wrapped around his waist, water running down his torso, and a look of agony on his face.

"Jesus, Sully, what the hell are you doing?"

"Initially, I was trying to shower," he said through gritted teeth. "Now I'm just trying not to pass out."

"What happened? Damn it, why is there blood all over the floor?" A huge patch of carpet was soaked bright red next to the stairwell, and smaller patches were dotted between there and the point where Sully was now leaning up against the wall.

"I opened up some stitches," he said, wincing. "It's not as bad as it looks."

"Where? And why did you even need stitches in the first place?" I put down the tubs of food I was carrying, wriggled out of my jacket, then hurried to check him over. At first I didn't see the long, jagged slice down his right side, because he was cradling his arms around his body, however the source of the bleeding became all too apparent as I got closer.

"The ship," Sully said. "The rocks out in the bay gutted her. Tore up the underside of the hull. All twisted metal and sharp edges. I saw one of the guys sink below the water, so I dived in to get him. The waves were so big out there. Linneman did his best to keep the Zodiac steady but a big one hit. Nearly took him out. It smashed the Zodiac into the Sea King. I was in between the two at the time. I got pinned. Crushed my ribs. The warped steel from the hull got me pretty good."

"I can see that. God, Sully. Let me take a look." He was shielding his side, body bowed over a little, making it hard for me to survey how bad the damage was.

"It's okay. Lang, seriously. Just sit down and let me catch my breath for a second, damn it."

"Sully, I'm not joking. Move!"

He straightened, sighing in frustration, his arms dropping loose to his sides. The cut was deep and raw, eight inches long, and it looked angry. I lifted Sully's arm out of the way entirely, trying to get a better look, to see if it was infected, which is when I saw the beginnings of the scar. Red, mottled, violent-looking: it started at his hip and run upwards over his side, and then onto his back. I turned him, mouth hanging open, eyes growing wider by the second.

"Turn around," I told him.

"Why?"

"Just do it."

"My back's just fine. There's nothing there you need to concern yourself with," he said in a hard tone.

"Sully. I mean it. Turn around." Lord knows I sounded ready to do him some damage myself. It could have been the determination in my voice, or it could have been the fact that he'd lost a lot of blood and he didn't have the energy to argue, but Sully actually did as I told him, slowly turning to face the wall he'd been leaning against, bracing both hands against the plasterwork so I could see the magnitude of the scar that spread up and onto his back, sweeping up almost to his shoulder. Twisted, puckered skin. Brilliant red and dark pink. It was healed, quite an old injury, but it looked like it had caused him a great deal of pain at one point.

"Pretty, ain't it?" Sully asked. He didn't sound bitter, or angry. He sounded resigned. Empty.

"Damn, Sully. I don't even know what to say."

"Good. Then how about you don't say anything, and we move on."

"How?"

He shrugged. "An accident."

"What kind of an accident?"

Sully leaned forward even further, until his forehead was pressed up against the wall. His eyes closed. He seemed so tired. "One that involved fire, obviously."

"How old were you?"

A long silence. And then, softly: "Old enough to know better."

He clearly didn't want to talk about it anymore, but I couldn't let it go. Not without a proper explanation. Fielding's words were still ringing in my ears, and I couldn't help but panic. Was this a prime example of Sully trying to throw his life away, or was it something else entirely? "Was it your fault?" I asked. "Could you have prevented this, if you'd wanted to?"

Sully looked back at me sharply. He didn't reply straight away. "I might have been able to. But the cost of preventing this injury would have been far greater than a few inches of burned skin."

"It's more than a few inches, Sully. It's your whole side. Nearly all of your back. It would have been—"

"Painful? Yeah, it smarted a little. Right now, I'm far more preoccupied by the pain in my ribcage and the open wound I'm holding together with my bare hands than something that took place years ago, though. Can you go into the kitchen and find me some alcohol?"

"Drinking probably isn't the best option at the moment."

"Not to drink. To sterilize this cut again."

"Ahh, right. Sorry." I rushed into the kitchen and started flinging open cupboard doors, trying to remember where he'd produced the whiskey from last night. It took forever to find the shelf where Sully stashed his booze. Grabbing a small, unopened bottle of vodka, I also snatched up a cloth from under the sink, brand new, straight out of the packaging, and took that with me too.

"Here. Will this do?" I showed him what I'd found.

"Yeah, that's perfect." Taking both items from me, he cracked the cap off the vodka bottle and poured a liberal amount of the alcohol all over the clean cloth. "If I squeal, don't think any less of me," he quipped.

"It's impossible for me to think any less of you than I already do," I informed him, pulling a face.

He pulled one back. The second he planted the alcohol soaked material against his side, his eyes looked like they were about to roll back into his head. "Ah, shit. Goddamn it, that stings."

"Don't be such a wimp. Here, let me do it." I took the cloth from him. Sully grumbled, but he didn't stop me; he placed his hands on the wall again, arching so that his back was curved up toward the ceiling, and he grimaced.

"Make it quick."

"If I were a cold hearted kind of person who enjoyed seeing others suffer, I might take as much time as possible in this situation. Lucky for you I'm more *Maria* than *sadomasochist*, huh?" The sarcasm was thick in my voice as I dabbed efficiently at his bleeding side. Sully closed his eyes and bore it. His body slumped a little, so his head was hanging down in between his arms, but other than that he kept perfectly still while I worked. When I was done, he let go of a shaky, uneven breath and turned to look at me.

"A sadomasochist derives *sexual* pleasure from inflicting pain on others, Lang."

Oh, god. Fire exploded in my cheeks, undoubtedly turning them bright red. *Perfect*. Why was the way he said sexual so, well, *sexual*? It made me feel like I was squirming inside my own skin.

"Good thing this moment couldn't be any *less* sexual, then," I answered. Was I doing a decent job of acting cool? It was highly unlikely, given the burning, hot spots on my cheeks, high up, by my cheekbones.

"It couldn't?" Sully spoke slowly. His head was still hanging low between his braced arms, hands planted high over his head. He was scrutinizing me, cutting a glance at me out of the corner of his eye, and the next few seconds that passed were so intense they damn near sucked the air right out of my lungs. Why was he looking at me like that? And what the hell was he trying to imply? Taking a deep breath, he blinked those long dark eyelashes of his, so fucking perfect, but he didn't avert his gaze. "Because, if you asked me, this moment could definitely be less sexual."

"I have no idea what you're talking about." I balled up the vodka and now blood-soaked cloth into my hand, ready to run away with it into the kitchen, but Sully stood up straight, towering over me with a bemused look on his face.

"Yes, you do. I'm standing here in a towel, covered in water, and you're playing nursemaid, tending to my injuries, your hands on my bare skin… If this were a porno, we'd basically be fucking by now."

"I'm gonna have to take your word for that. I wouldn't know. I've never watched porn."

Amusement flickered across his features, lighting them up in an expected, warm way. "You've *never* watched porn? Not ever?"

"That's what never means."

"Not even when you're turned on?"

"No. Not even when I'm turned on."

"What do you do to take the pressure off, then? Do you just…take care of it all by yourself? No outside input? Just your fingers and your imagination?"

Hot damn. I couldn't maintain eye contact any longer. The words coming out of his mouth were enough to make me avert my eyes to the floor. My cheeks weren't the only things flushed red now. I was the color of a beet from my hairline down.

"I don't think that's any of your business," I said quietly.

"I don't suppose it is. But you can still tell me."

"Just put some clothes on, Sully. God." I tried to slip around him into the kitchen, but the moment I moved Sully was moving too, sliding along the wall to block the entrance to the other room. It was surprising he could move so quickly, given how much pain he was in.

"Remember my no bullshit policy, Lang? Well, I'm calling bullshit. Right now. *On you.*"

"You can't." I tried to duck under his arm, but again he saw where I was headed and blocked my route.

"Why not?" he asked.

"Because. I'm not lying to you, am I? I'm just not giving in to what you want."

He looked up at the ceiling for a second. "I'd call that pretty bullshitty."

"I'd just call it tough luck. Now get your ass out of my way before I knock you down on it."

He grinned—beautiful white teeth, beautiful pout to his lips. "Think you could?"

"Right now I do, yeah. In a couple of weeks maybe not, but you're more fragile than a ninety-year-old man at the moment."

"I could still take you, Lang. Don't tempt me."

The way he said *take you* sent shivers down my spine. I was way out of my depth here. It occurred to me that somehow, out of the blue, Sully and I were flirting, and I was neither equipped nor prepared for such a dangerous undertaking. I backed away, hands held up. "No need. How about I just leave you to your own devices and head on home? You know how to work a microwave, right?"

"I know how to work one, sure. However, I don't *own* one."

"Who the hell doesn't own a microwave?"

"*Who the hell doesn't watch porn?*" He was enjoying this far too much. I never thought I'd see the day Sully Fletcher smiled, and yet here I was, witnessing the miracle with my own two eyes. His whole face changed. The severity lifted from his features, and everything all at once seemed...*light*. It was like looking at another man, a stranger I hadn't met yet.

"Glad to see you're still capable of laughing at my expense, despite the blood loss," I informed him. I was smiling, too, though. Just a little. Just enough to fuel him on.

"I could be laid out on my death bed and I still wouldn't be sick enough to resist taking a pot shot at you, Lang."

"I'm honored. And why does sparring with me bring you such immense joy, I wonder?" I was only half joking when I asked this; his constant need to be baiting me, cajoling me, or just being downright rude to me seemed to be his only goal when we were around one another.

Sully's smile shrank. It went from a blazing level ten, to a much more somber level four. It still lingered at the corners of his mouth and around his eyes, though, like a fire that wouldn't go out. "It *does* bring me immense joy. And you know all too well why I do it, Lang."

"I don't."

"Now that *is* bullshit."

I shook my head, folding my arms across my chest, and Sully sighed. He looked resigned. "Why does any little boy pull a girl's pigtails in the school yard? Why does any teenaged guy with hormones pretend to ignore the prettiest girl in school?"

"You do *not* have a crush on me."

"Sure I do."

"You're playing with me."

"I'm not."

"The way a cat toys with a mouse, you asshole."

"If it's safer for you to believe that, then okay, Lang. I'm playing with you."

"It's not safer. It's the *truth*."

Sully didn't open his mouth again. He simply stared at me with that little half smile on his face, taunting me. Or at least I thought he was. Damn it! Things were crystal clear before—Sully Fletcher hated me—and now they were so muddied, I had no idea what was going on.

Sully smirked, obviously enjoying the fact that I was squirming. "So. Are you gonna stitch me up or what?" he asked.

"Absolutely not. I'm not doing that. Are you crazy?"

"Well, I can't do it myself. I tried to last time, and look how that turned out."

Why was it no surprise that he'd taken a needle and thread to himself? I could almost imagine the conversation he'd had with the doctors on the mainland, when he'd told them all to go to hell.

"I can always superglue myself back together if you're squeamish," he continued. "I have some *Gorilla Glue* around here somewhere."

"You can't!"

"That's how we patch people up out in the field. It's the most effective method there is to prevent blood loss."

I wondered if he realized he wasn't in the field anymore, and that there were other, safer ways of doing things. "How about some food instead?"

He sighed, resigned. "Sure."

He allowed me to pass when I tried to enter the kitchen this time. He didn't follow after me. I put the chicken casserole in the fridge and went about heating up the bolognese sauce, rifling through his cupboards once more, hunting for dried pasta. When I couldn't find any, I stuck my head back into the living room to ask Sully where it was kept and nearly screamed when I found him naked, standing in the middle of the room. Thankfully his back was to me—I got his ass instead of anything more...well, *more*.

Sully didn't turn around, but I could see his shoulders were shaking. He was laughing. The bastard was laughing! "You can help me get dressed if you like?" he offered. "I'm having trouble with the bending part. If you could hold my boxers out, it'd make it a hell of a lot easier to step into them." I saw then that he was holding a clean t-shirt in one hand, a pair of rolled up boxer briefs in the other.

"I think I'll pass. Uhh, where do you keep your pasta?"

Sully must have been all too aware that I was still staring at his ass, because he flexed, making his left cheek jump not once but twice. Slowly, he angled his body, almost turning around, at which point I studiously glared at the kitchen tile at my feet.

"I don't have spaghetti," he said. "There are pasta shells on top of the fridge, though." He was trying not to laugh, but not very hard by the sounds of things.

I disappeared back in the kitchen, shaking my head, trying to dislodge the image of Sully's ass that had burned itself into my retinas. It wasn't all that easy, though. I got the feeling I could bleach my eyeballs and the sight would still be there every time I blinked.

When I took the steaming hot food back into the living room, clattering and banging and making enough noise to wake the dead, just to make sure he heard me coming this time, Sully was sprawled out on the couch, fully dressed (thank god) and he had my cell phone in his hand.

I stopped dead. "What do you think you're doing?"

He tapped something into the phone, and then looked up at me. "Don't panic, Lang. I wasn't reading your texts."

"Then what were you doing?"

"Prank calling myself so I have your number. Next time you bring food over, I want to be able to make requests."

"Who says I'll be bringing anything over ever again?" I placed the plates of food down on the small coffee table in front of him, scowling. "No one ever tell you it's rude to mess with another person's phone?"

"I thought we'd already established that I *am* rude. Aren't you crazy to expect anything else from me? Look, if it's bothering you, here. Have my phone. Do whatever the hell you want with it. Look at my texts. You can go through my photos. Read my email. I don't give a shit." He tossed his cell up in the air, expecting me to catch it, but I let it land on the carpet at my feet with a heavy thud.

"No, thank you."

Sully peered over the edge of the table, presumably to check if his phone was broken. He groaned as he strained his stomach, then sank back into his seat when he saw the iPhone was fine. "Probably for the best. There's some fucked up shit in there. You're quite the conundrum, Lang. Do you know that?"

What did Sully Fletcher consider fucked up shit? I was four parts intrigued and six parts worried. It certainly didn't make me want to search through his cell phone like a crazy jealous girlfriend, though. Even when I suspected something was going on with Will, when he was working late all the time and getting strange texts at two o'clock in the morning, I never stooped that low. I wasn't going to do it now, even with Sully's permission. "I'm hardly a conundrum," I told him, planting a container of Parmesan cheese down in front of him. "I just don't like people taking liberties."

"None taken. Yet," he said, smirking. "But feel free to overstep as many boundaries as you like when you're in bed later, all hot and bothered, staring at my number in your phone, wondering if you should message me."

"You think pretty highly of yourself, don't you?"

He nodded sagely. "I have to. No one else is gonna bother."

That struck me as a sad thought. Rose was right; she'd painted a pretty lonely picture of Sully's personal life in order to get me to go visit him at the medical center, but it had all been true. He really didn't have anybody. His parents were dead. Now his brother. He refused to let anyone else close enough to care about him.

"Don't look too maudlin, Lang," he said, scratching at his throat, still smiling. "Believe me. I prefer it this way."

I did believe him. He'd designed this life for himself, where he didn't have to work with anyone, speak to anyone, see anyone if he didn't want to. The lonely man in the lighthouse. The tormented man living by the sea. It was strange that he would have come back here after leaving the Causeway for so long, training in the military and being deployed. After all of the chaos and madness of Afghanistan, wouldn't he have wanted to live in a big city somewhere? Or at least a little closer to civilization. I'd heard enough about ex-soldiers who'd come back from war, and found "normal" life on the mainland too slow paced. Life, as far as I could tell, had practically ground to a halt on the island.

"Shall we eat?" Sully said, breaking the tension between us. Or at least putting it to one side for a moment. Patting the sofa next to him, he gestured for me to come take a seat. I would have preferred to sit in the armchair, well away from his broad frame and his strangely intoxicating smell, but I knew what would happen if I made a point of sitting anywhere other than beside him now. He would mock me, endlessly, and I didn't know if I could take much more teasing right now. Better just to sit down and deal with the close proximity.

Sully seemed bemused as we started to eat. Minutes passed by while we enjoyed the food without a word spoken between us. His plate was nearly clear when he broke the silence. "I don't hate them, you know. I know they're not to blame for anything that happened between Ronan and me. And *Magda*," he said, in a much smaller voice. I knew precisely who he was talking about. I was just stunned to the core that he'd brought them up. He had made me promise not to discuss them yesterday, and yet he'd been the one to break that rule. Here he was, breaking it again.

When I didn't say anything, he continued. "The thought of even seeing them makes me crazy, though. Magda always told me she didn't want to have kids. And then a handful of years and three ruined lives later, she popped two out, just like that. Like it was nothing. Like she'd been meaning to her whole life."

It made sense that he'd be resentful to the children. When he put it like that, I could understand. It was futile to be holding grudges against minors though. Like he'd said only a moment earlier, it really wasn't their fault.

"I'm sorry, Sully. You must have loved Magda very much. It must hurt like hell to know her children are so close now."

He put down his fork, staring at the mess of sauce and pasta that remained on his plate—I had the sneaking suspicion he'd suddenly lost his appetite. "It doesn't, though. It doesn't hurt at all. I've been numb for a very long time, Lang. Nothing touches me anymore. A nuclear bomb would have to detonate inside my chest cavity to stir even the faintest of responses from the lump of flesh that pumps my blood around my body."

"I sure that's an intentional def—"

"Do *not* say defense mechanism. I'm done defending myself from things. I decided *assault* was the only way forward a long time ago. Facing things head on, tackling the things that scare me without blinking. That's how I've dealt with my problems since Afghanistan."

"I can see that."

"Can you, now?" he looked amused. "Well, there's an interesting thought."

"Why so?"

"Because I work my hide off to make sure no one sees me at all, most days, Miss Ophelia Lang from California. I've been told in the past that trying to get a clear read on me is like trying to see a clear picture through a kaleidoscope. And a fucked up, broken kaleidoscope at that."

I laughed, imagining who might have told him such a thing. Some poor, heartbroken local? Some young, doe-eyed tourist, hoping to turn a holiday romance into something a little more concrete? Sully was the kind of man to ruin a vacation, and all vacations for the rest of time, the moment you laid eyes on him.

"I guess the question is, do you *want* anyone to see you clearly, Sully?" I made sure my tone was light, the question clearly rhetorical. Keeping my head down, I ate while Sully sat next to me, stewing. I could feel him struggling to figure out what he wanted to say. I half expected him to snap and tell me to mind my own damn business, but he didn't. After a long, long dip in the conversation, Sully finally picked up his fork and considered it. Quietly, under his breath, he spoke. "You said just now that I must have loved Magda very much. It took me a long time to realize it, but I never loved her. You can't love something that isn't real. Someone that exists only in your head. She was beautiful, and she was kind in her own way, but she floated along, being whatever she thought everyone else needed her to be. And in the end, she didn't have a personality of her own. She was a mirror, reflecting back at you what you wanted to see. That's it. That's all. An empty, sad shell of a person, waiting to be filled up by someone else. So, no, I didn't love her very much. I loved the idea of her. The reality was grossly underwhelming." He stabbed at his shells, spiking the pasta onto the tines, scooping up the meat, and he ate. He didn't say another word on the matter.

I cleaned up the plates and I left, telling him I'd be back again the same time tomorrow. Hours later, in bed, too tired to sleep and too awake to dream, my cell phone buzzed on my nightstand, lighting up the room.

It was from Sully. Or, as he'd apparently named himself in my phone, the hottest guy in the world.

> **HOTTEST GUY IN THE WORLD...**
>
> Today 8:32 AM
>
> Give it a rest, Lang. I can feel you thinking about me from here.

Such an asshole.

CHAPTER EIGHTEEN

AFGHANISTAN
2009

Sully

The Italians were dropping mortars again. They were meant to send an envoy to the base at least three hours ahead of any assault planned on suburban areas of the city, a common courtesy to let us know as and when we should be relocating our troops away of hot zones, however no one had shown up with intel the last few times, and tensions between camps were running high. Even radioing across would have done the trick, but the Euro guys were all sick of the double standard (we never told them when we were planning a strike, either), and so they'd made it plain they were done playing nicey-nicey with us. Fucking ridiculous that we were all here for the same reason, and we still couldn't get along.

I loved having the Italians around, though. They were the only ones who could sneak hard liquor in-country, and they were always happy to trade for cigarettes and whatever porn files were stored on the unit's shared drive at the time. That was a lot of porn.

I ran across the base, flinching every time the high-pitched whine of a mortar whistled overhead, cursing their names today, however. I ran past one of the first lieutenants from C company heading in the opposite direction, some maverick kid from Alabama who'd probably be running this whole show some day. He slowed, saluting me. "They're buzzing the fences today, Captain. That's a hell of a lot of flack from the hills over there, too. Whitlock's gonna be out, looking to spank some asses tonight!"

I laughed, turning to run backward. "You seen my brother, Lieutenant? Can't seem to find him anywhere."

The lieutenant rocked his head to one side, studying me. "Begging your pardon for asking, sir, but which one are you again? I'll be damned, but I can never tell."

"Sully," I replied, grinning to show there was no harm done.

"Ahh. You got any tips for differentiating you two, huh, Captain? Might make life a little easier for the rest of us out here."

I shrugged. "Sorry, man. There's only one way to tell us apart, and I don't think it's gonna be much help to you."

"Try me."

"Well, my dick is obviously way bigger than his," I said, laughing. "That's how the girls at high school always told us apart, anyway." In truth, Magda was the only girl who'd even seen my dick. And Ronan's was probably exactly the same size as mine, down to the millimeter. Not that we'd compared, of course. That would have been weird. Our hands, our feet, our shoulders, our waists—everything else was exactly the same, though. Why would our cocks be any different?

The first lieutenant laughed. "Well, in any case, the *other* Captain Fletcher just left a briefing with the colonel. I heard Whitlock's intelligence guy complaining about how long their meeting was. Your brother's probably somewhere recovering from the ear chewing he just got served."

Colonel Whitlock wore his eagle with pride. He was a concise, no-nonsense, efficient leader with a shitty attitude, but he got the job done. It wasn't easy overseeing an operation like this, out in the middle of nowhere with limited resources and a whole city full of locals who all wanted you dead. The only time he ever kept the clock running in his office was when he was reprimanding someone. You fucked up and you knew you were spending the better part of a day inside Whitlock's office with your pants around your ankles, receiving the hiding of your life.

"Shit. Okay. Thanks, man." I cut through the base then, skirting around the infirmary and the shipping containers that had been set up as care package general stores, shelves stacked with tubes of toothpaste, toilet paper and Twizzlers, until I reached the other end of the base, where the officers' Alaska tents were pitched. I caught Ronan just as he was about to head inside. He looked relieved when he saw me, though there were dark, ominous circles under his eyes, and he looked like he hadn't been eating properly. If this carried on much longer, it would be all too easy for people to tell us apart. He'd be the one looking like he was about to fall face first into an early grave.

"Hey, man. You were meant to meet me after lunch. They fucked up and gave me your mail again. Whitlock kept you late, huh?" I grimaced, waiting to hear how bad it had been. From the look on Ronan's face, it had been really fucking bad.

He swallowed, looking around, and then urged me inside the tent. Checking first to make sure we were alone, he walked the length of the billet and then back again, his hands clenching into fists and unclenching again every few seconds. He was acting weird, which was how he'd been acting for weeks now, ever since the incident with the woman and the little baby.

He'd seemed relieved when I'd told him he was mistaken, that there was no woman or baby, and yet as the days had passed, he'd started asking questions. What did the guy look like? Was he on any watch lists? What had he been wearing? How old had he looked? Ronan's willingness to believe he was off the hook was obviously wearing off, and it wasn't going to end well.

When he came to a stop in front of me, his shoulders were slumped, his head hanging low. "Whitlock's a cunt, man. He called me in to talk about some missing tires from supply, but that turned out to be bullshit. He really wanted to talk to me about extension."

"*Extension?*" The word was a bullet fired from a high-powered rifle, three miles away. You heard it, knew what was coming, but you didn't feel the impact or the pain of it for a good five or six seconds, until the weight of it had time to sink in. "What the hell are you talking about, *extension*? Our tours are both up in nine weeks. We're headed back to the States."

The muscles in Ronan's jaw tightened. He looked away, brows drawn low. I hadn't seen my brother cry since our parents' funeral, and that was such an old memory that the moths had gotten at it and turned it into dust.

"Doesn't look like home's on the cards for anyone at the base," he told me. "Whitlock says they're keeping all of the officers on as well as the enlisted guys. That's me. That's you. *Everybody*. The whole battalion. Intel projected increased Taliban activity in the area from now until the end of the year. So that's it. All deployments are being extended."

I felt cold, despite the heat. Was he right? No way he was right. They couldn't just spring that kind of shit on us without any warning, especially coming up to two months before we were due to go home. "How long?" I asked. "How long are the extensions?"

Ronan's breath came out shaky. "Six months. He said there was every chance that could be shortened if the intel turned out to be wrong, but he highly doubted that would be the case. He said he appreciated my dedication to the US Army, and that my sacrifice was for the greater good of our fine nation and the protection of her people. Blah, blah, blah. The end."

"What did you say?"

Ronan looked at me sharply. "I said thank you very much, sir, for the opportunity. It's an honor. What else could I say? *Actually, sir, I had plans in April back in Maine, and I don't really feel like cancelling?* Or how about the plain old truth? *Sir, I am done with this bullshit, and I don't think I can take another day of it. I can't sleep, and every second I spend out here is another second I step closer to insanity.* How do you think that conversation would have gone, Sully? He would have had me court marshaled on the spot."

"You can't know that."

"I do. This is Whitlock we're talking about. Then again, if he did court marshal me, at least they'd send me back to a military prison in the States. That would be preferable over another six months in this hellhole. God. What the fuck's happening right now, Sully? The past few years have felt like this one long, unending nightmare that just won't seem to quit. Day after day of humping packs and shooting at civilians, suspicious of everyone and everything, the madness creeping in so gradually that no one seems to notice, until one day the guy standing next to you in line at the chow hall does something so monumentally insane that you suddenly see it, it suddenly clicks, and that's when you realize you're only a heartbeat away from doing the same crazy shit yourself."

He was barely coherent, hands gripping at his khaki t-shirt, sweat beading at his temples. I'd never seen him look like this, and I'd never been so worried for him. People always talked a lot about the bond twins shared. The supernatural link between them. One of them gets hurt, the other feels the pain. One of them is unhappy, the other's down, too. One is in danger, the other is gripped by such an overwhelming sense of foreboding that they have to call and make sure everything is all right.

Ronan and I never experienced such a thing, but I didn't need a made-up psychic link right now to understand how he was feeling. The tension was rolling off him, thick in the air, and his eyes were wild with panic. I stepped forward and wrapped my arms around him, hugging him tight. "Fuck, dude. It's gonna be okay. Six months is nothing. We can do that no problem. Just you wait and see. We'll barely even break a sweat." Ronan buried his face in my shoulder, breathing hard. He was on the verge of breaking down and losing it entirely. Holding onto him as tight as I could, I told him over and over again that it was going to be okay, that another six months wouldn't break us, but this awful notion of dread was coiled in the pit of my stomach like a deadly snake, and it was threatening to strike at any moment. I *didn't* know if he could make another six months out here. I *didn't* know if everything was going to be okay. All I knew was that I had his back, and I was going to do everything and anything in my power to get him through it as best I could.

We stood for a long time in silence while Ronan caught his breath. We would have stood for much longer if one of Ronan's specialists, Crowe, hadn't burst into the tent, yelling out my name.

"Captain Fletcher? Ah, there you are. Sorry, Sully. Colonel Whitlock's looking for you. He asked if you could please head straight to his office. He has some paperwork for you to fill out."

So there it was. Ronan was right; they were extending everybody. Looked like I was up next. My brother stepped back, breathing in deeply, straightening his t-shirt. "Thanks, Sully. I'll see you later, man. Let me know how it goes, huh?" He turned and walked away before I had a chance to reply to him. He obviously didn't want his guy to see he was freaked out, and I didn't want to put him in that position, either.

"All right, Crowe." I turned to the specialist, slapping him on the back. "You lead the way. I'm right behind you."

The entire walk to Whitlock's office, the Italian's mortars continued to rain down on the city four miles away, sending bursts of fire and death into the sky.

CHAPTER NINETEEN

SUNSHINE SCRAMBLE

"Are you ready for this? Are you sure you don't want to wait until after Christmas like we planned?"

Connor was sliding a brand new notebook and a pack of pencils into a dark blue book bag I'd bought for him at the store. Stationary supplies on The Causeway were a little thin on the ground, so I'd had to do the best I could. As a result, Connor had everything he needed for his first day at school, but he was hardly going to be the cool kid in his year. If we were back in New York, I'd have been able to take him all over the city, buying the best shoes, the best clothes, a mountain of different paper, pens, glue sticks etc. He didn't seem to care that he wasn't decked out in brand names, though. He just seemed happy to be getting out of the house.

"Yes, it's fine. I want to go. Really."

Rose had shown up at the house after work the day before, saying wouldn't it be a great idea if the children could make some friends before the holidays, so they'd have people to stop by and visit. She'd already spoken to the principal at the elementary school, who was fine with taking Connor as an early admission. I hadn't had much input in the decision at all—fine with me, because Connor actually appeared to be excited for once, and that was a wonder in itself.

"Do you want me to drive you, or Rose?" I asked him.

He bit his lip and looked at the floor. A second later, with narrowed eyes, he glanced up and said, "You, please."

So I did. When I said goodbye to him at the gate, where other children were filing boisterously into the small, boxy-looking building beyond, Connor turned and hugged me, head pressed into my stomach, arms only just about able to reach my waist, and I felt a stab of anxiety shoot through me. Was he going to be okay? What if he tripped and fell? What if he banged his head? What if some of the other kids started bullying him for no reason? There were endless things that could go wrong on the first day at a new school, and it felt wrong that I was standing around outside the school grounds, watching him run inside, bag bouncing up and down on his back, and I wasn't going inside with him to protect him. I supposed this was how it felt for the parents who used to drop off their kids at Saint Augustus's while I walked inside, too, ready to teach.

The suggestion Michael made at Rose's party came to mind again. There was a position for a full-time teacher open at the school. And it was well paid, too. Once these six months with the children were up, come hell or high water I was finding another job. If I stayed here on The Causeway after the summer, would it be so bad? If the children stayed here somehow, too? I couldn't imagine walking out on them now, or simply handing them over to Sheryl, to be dumped in some awful foster home. And that was after they'd sat for months in a group home, waiting forever to see who would agree to take them. The thought just killed me.

At home, Amie and I made sparkle starfish dinosaurs to put on the fridge, and then we sat and read a book together. Midway through, my cell phone buzzed on the arm of the sofa.

Sully: Macaroni and cheese? Steak?

He'd finished up with a winky face, which made me shake my head.

"What are you smiling at, Feelya?" Amie asked, looking up at me. Her face was so perfect. So sweet and innocent. Her hair was sticking up at the front, floating on a wave of static that prickled between us.

"Nothing at all, little monster. A friend I know just made a joke on my phone."

"Was it a funny joke?"

"Not really. He was being cheeky."

She leaned back, her head resting in the crook of my arm, giggling, teeth on show, and I just wanted to wrap my arms around her and squeeze her tight. She was the most adorable thing. She had the same chin, the same high forehead, and the same dimples as both her father and her uncle. The exact same hair color. The same smile, and the same mischievous glint in her eye. "What did he say?" she asked, still laughing.

"He's sick at the moment, so I've been making his dinner for him and taking it over to his house on the other side of the island. He was just saying that he wanted steak with mac and cheese for dinner, which is really naughty because it's not so easy to make."

Her eyes widened. "I love steaks with mac and cheese."

"Mmm, I know. So do I."

"Can we have it for dinner, too?"

"Oh boy."

So that was it. A quick trip to the store later, and Amie and I were in the kitchen with the necessary ingredients, making the dinner Sully had requested: steak with mac and cheese à la Amie.

Later, when I took over his food, Sully lifted the lid off his dinner and arched an eyebrow so reminiscent of Ronan that it took my breath away.

"Why, may I ask, is the mac and cheese green? And why is the steak...in the shape of a rabbit?"

"It's not a rabbit. It's a Velociraptor. You can't tell because it's not cooked yet. I didn't want it getting tough on the way over here."

Sully frowned some more, staring down at the food. "I'm sensing you had help preparing this meal."

"I did. My sous chef is excellent. Five years old. Loves the color green, and dinosaurs. She's very sorry you're sick, and she hopes you get better soon."

Sully leaned against the counter and sighed heavily, crossing his arms over his chest. "Is this some cheap ploy to get me to fall in love with my niece and nephew via the medium of food? Because it's not going to happen. I'm impervious to cuteness."

"I'm sure you are. I am sure you are, buddy."

Over the next week, that didn't stop me from enlisting Amie's help with the rest of Sully's meals. Monster Brains (clam chowder, with biscuits), Putrid Pot Pie (turkey and sweet corn—Amie didn't like the corn.) Seasick Stew, which, according to Amie was meant to look like vomit. Thankfully, it looked more like another chicken casserole, but Sully still laughed.

My two or three hour-long visits to his place in the evening were becoming less and less stressful and more enjoyable with each passing day. Miracle upon miracle, the edge wore off Sully. It was an interesting thing to watch. He flirted like a fiend, and he was still sharp as a whip with his comebacks, but the hostility was gone. He would text me once or twice a day, and surprisingly I would rarely want to kill him because of the contents. *Rarely.* There were still times when he sent something so barbaric and over-the-line that I considered telling him to go screw himself, but for the most part he was behaving himself.

On Friday, seven days after he came home from the medical center, I let myself into the lighthouse, and Sully handed me a mug of coffee. "Big and black, just how you like it," he said, grinning.

"That doesn't even make sense," I told him, taking the coffee and drinking deep.

Sully smirked, shoving his hands in the pockets of his jeans. "Doesn't it? I'll let you think about that for a while. What terrible creation have we brought over with us today, then?" he asked, waggling his eyebrows at the box I had set down on the coffee table.

"Why don't you come see?" I picked it back up again and went into the kitchen, searching for plates. Sully hobbled after me, still bracing himself, doing his best to minimize the pain from his ribs, which was still constant and grating.

"Damn it, woman. I've already had my workout for the day. I don't need to chase you around the entire house, y'know."

"You call showering and getting dressed a workout?"

"I do. And wiping my own ass. Do you have any idea how painful it is to twist and wipe right now?" He demonstrated for good measure, twisting his torso, and then yelped when his ribcage pinched.

"Serves you right."

"Just open the damn food, Lang," he grumbled, holding his hand to his chest, as if that would stop the pain.

I opened up the Tupperware and showed him what Amie and I had made just before I left the house. "This is her favorite meal," I told him. "She said she wanted to make it for you so that you'd finally get better. I explained that broken ribs took a little longer to mend than a week, but she seemed fairly convinced this was going to do the trick."

Sully considered the meal: pancakes, drowning in maple syrup. Chicken and apple sausages. Eggs, over easy, still hot from the frying pan. He sighed, leaning back against the kitchen counter. "Our mom used to make this for me and Ronan nearly every day whenever we were on vacation," he said quietly. "She called it the sunshine scramble."

I bit my lip, not sure if I should say anything. What the hell, though. It couldn't hurt to tell him the truth. "Amie calls it that, too. Ronan used to make it for her."

Sully stared at the food some more, shifting and twitching like he was extremely uncomfortable.

"Well. Fuck." He ran his hand back through his hair, and left it there at the base of his neck, his lips pressed into a tight white line.

"Let's just eat, Sully. It doesn't have to be a thing."

"No. You're right. It doesn't." He still looked like he'd had the wind knocked out of him, though. We sat and ate in silence. When we were done, Sully did something that surprised the hell out of me. He stood up, and then he reached out and took me by the hand, making me stand up, too. I thought he was going to escort me out of the house or something—he'd been broody and silent ever since I'd shown him the food—but instead he raised his right hand and he brushed my hair back behind my ear, giving me a complicated smile.

"I've never kissed a girl for the first time without being drunk, y'know?" he said.

"What? You're not about to, either." I tried to step back, embarrassed, too shocked to even believe for a second that he was being serious. He slipped an arm around my waist and stopped me, though.

"God, Lang. Not much in my life is easy. Just getting out of bed at the moment is a goddamn uphill struggle. Breathing is far more taxing than it should be most days. Don't go making this difficult, too." He smiled his reckless smile, dimples locked and loaded, ready to kill, and my chest squeezed tightly. He was being perfectly serious, and I had no idea how to react. I just kind of froze, alarmed and unarmed, caught completely off guard.

"I—"

"You don't want me to kiss you?"

Slowly, I nodded my head. "I do. At least, I think I—"

"No more thinking." He rushed me, bending down to meet me, his mouth crashing into mine, stealing what little breath I had right away. If I'd wanted to react in some way, to fend him off or object, I'd never have had the time. He drew me into him, holding me carefully against his body, his chest pressing up against mine, the buckle of his belt flush with my stomach. His hands were firm and persuasive; it seemed as though he wanted to touch me everywhere, to feel the texture of my skin beneath his fingertips, to revel in the sensation of our bodies aligned so perfectly against one another. The kiss was the kind of kiss that made people wolf whistle in the street. It was spectacular—a ground shaking kiss that would send your head spinning and your knees collapsing out from underneath you. I didn't know what to do. I had two options: I could shove him away and slap his face hard enough to knock him into next week, or I could go with it and kiss him back.

I wanted to do both, he had no right to be planting kisses on me out of the blue, slingshotting my sanity into outer space, but then again it really was perfection.

I kissed him back.

Winding my arms around his neck, I popped up onto my tiptoes in order to claim his mouth just as feverishly as he was claiming mine. His tongue flicked quickly at mine, and then Sully was cupping my face in his hand, rubbing the pad of his thumb against the swollen flesh of my lips. He drew back, smiling in the most unimaginably nefarious way, like he was plotting my ruin inside that wicked head of his.

"Your mouth..." he whispered, laughing softly under his breath. "You have no idea how much time I've spent fantasizing about your mouth, Lang."

"You have? Why?" That was an incredibly naïve question. I knew why he'd been daydreaming about my mouth all too well. Sully looked like he was glad I'd asked, though.

"Well," he said, taking a step forward. We were flush up against each other, so I had no choice but to take a small step back at the same time. "Your lips are rather ridiculous. They look so plump and bitable, for fuck's sake. I've imagined trapping them between my teeth more times that I can remember. It's made staying mad at you really fucking difficult. And just so you know, Lang, every time you lick your lips, every time that tongue of yours darts out of your perfectly formed mouth, I love to imagine what it would feel like to have that tongue of yours licking at the head of my dick. It drives me crazy."

I couldn't believe he just came out and said that so easily. Will and I never spoke about sex. We tried talking dirty to each other a couple of times, but he said it made him feel shitty. Disgusting, even. He felt like he was taking advantage of me.

Will was the most vanilla guy, in and out of the bedroom, and I already knew deep in my bones that Sully was the polar opposite. He was mint and strawberry, chocolate and pistachio all rolled into one. Where Will was cool as ice, Sully was blazing fire. Where Will was reserved, always too worried about what the neighbors might think, Sully was fiercely determined to lay claim to whatever he wanted, and screw anybody else of what they thought.

He tangled his fingers up in my hair, twisting it into a messy knot at the nape of my neck, then gently pulling on it, tilting my head back.

"And this?" he said, slowly tracing the index finger of his free hand down the line of my throat. "Your neck, Lang. Fuck. You have the sexiest neck."

"Necks aren't sexy," I countered, trying to ignore the erratic tattoo of my heart as it stumbled all over itself in my chest. Fear was bubbling up inside me. The way Sully was handling me was more than sexual; it was vital. My body was humming at his touch, filled with electricity, and every time he grazed his mouth against mine I felt myself soaring higher and higher away from reality.

I wanted him. He wanted me, too—that was very obvious, given the rock hard erection I could feel pressing into my lower stomach. But this was such a terrible idea. A terrible, terrible idea.

Sully was Connor and Amie's uncle. He was crazy, as far as I could tell, and he wanted nothing to do with his brother's kids. I shouldn't want *him*. I *couldn't*. Pulling myself away, I gasped in a deep breath, already hating myself. I was balancing on a knife edge. The right look from Sully, the right word, and I would be falling back into his arms. Sure enough, when I looked up at him, the dark, brooding expression on his face was like tinder to a flame; I took three giant steps away from him, until my back hit the wall behind me.

"Whew. That was pretty stupid," I said, laughing nervously. "Being locked up in this lighthouse must really be killing you, Sully. If you're willing to make out with me to stem the boredom, then we should probably think about getting you out of the house as soon as possible."

He was walking toward me, chin dipped down, staring at me from under those dark brows of his—Sexy. So goddamn sexy—and I couldn't help it. Adrenalin fired through me like a bullet leaving a gun, tearing everything apart in its wake. "I'm not bored," he said slowly, his voice low. "I haven't been bored for a single second in your company, Lang. From day one, you've intrigued me."

"Harassed you. I've *harassed* you. You said it yourself." I was looking over his shoulder, trying to figure out how to slip by him, across the room and out the front door, but it was as if Sully could sense my thoughts. He sidestepped, shaking his head, tutting. "How long do you have left on the island, Lang?" he asked.

"Three and a half months." I should have stammered. My speech always let me down when I was nervous, and right now I was terrified. I should have been tripping up over my own tongue at every turn, and yet I somehow got the words out in one go.

"Three and a half months. Right. So, do you think we should really be wasting any more of the little time we could be spending together?"

Shock.

I was in shock.

Sully looked serious. The intensity pouring off him had me reaching for the wall behind me, trying to make sure I didn't slide down it and collapse into a pool onto the floor. "You know us spending time together in *that* way isn't a smart move. On my part, or on yours. You're right. Three and a half months is such a short amount of time—"

"It's enough time to get to know each other."

'It's enough time to fall for someone. *Hard*. And then what? I go back to California, without the children, without a job, and with a broken heart?" I shook my head. "No, Sully. This doesn't end well."

"You don't know how it ends," he retorted. "And I can guarantee you, you won't have fallen for me by the time you leave this place. I won't let it happen. I can protect you from it."

"How?"

He closed the gap between us again, moving slowly. "By letting you get to know me. By showing you my true colors." He gently tucked a strand of hair behind my ear, staring at my earlobe like he wanted to feast on it. "And I'll crank up my asshole super powers to the fiendish setting. That ought to do the trick."

I looked up at him defiantly, searching his face. Did he believe his snarky comebacks and his sharp-edged tongue would be enough to hold back the tides of something that already felt unstoppable, like the wave of a tsunami rushing in to shore? I studied his face for a long time, willing myself not to lean into his hand and close my eyes. Sully gave nothing away. His face was blank, his eyes mirrors, only reflecting myself back to me in their dark depths, betraying nothing of him at all. His lips were pressed tightly shut—that was the only thing that gave him away. He was holding his breath.

Pushing away from the wall, I stooped down and grabbed my purse from the floor, then hurried past him before he could stop me. "I'm sorry, Sully. I have to go."

"Lang?"

I didn't turn back.

"Ronan and I fought all the time," he rushed out. "We raged, and we gouged, and we kicked the living shit out of each other, but through it all we always still loved each other. After what he did with Magda, though…there was no coming back from that. It changed me. I'll admit I'm not the man I used to be. But you make me feel…*fuck*." He stopped, growling under his breath. "You make me feel like I might be able to find that man again, the man I was, before Magda and before Afghanistan, and it scares the shit out of me. I don't even know if I want to be him again. So…don't walk away for good. I get it if you have to walk away for now. But make sure you come back, okay? This isn't done yet and you know it."

CHAPTER TWENTY

SNOW ANGELS

Three days. Then a week. Then two.

December arrived, and with it snow. Wet, slushy snow that didn't stick for long and made the roads a nightmare to drive on. Everything felt gray and dismal, especially my mood. Rose commented on my downcast spirit a few times, then gave up trying to figure out what was wrong with me. It was when Amie asked why I was so sad all the time, and was I going to go away like her daddy and her mommy had, that I realized enough was enough. I wasn't alone anymore. I had two little people to consider, and moping around, feeling sorry for myself because I'd been stupid enough to develop a serious attraction to a man who was essentially poisonous, was only going to make them anxious and unhappy.

So I cheered the fuck up.

Connor got a part in the school nativity play. He had two lines, so it didn't matter that he'd joined the cast at short notice. He rocked the part of Shepherd No. 2, and both Rose and I cried a little when he took a bow at the end of the performance, grinning from ear to ear. I'd never seen him smile. Not like that. Not like he was a normal, trouble-free seven-year-old, playing with his friends, looking forward to Christmas.

Another week.

Jerry, the boatman, decided to sail back to the mainland early and didn't tell anyone he wouldn't be coming back until the day after Christmas, so the inhabitants of The Causeway were scrambling through the few small grocery stores that remained open on the island, trying to find last minute presents for each other along with ingredients for their holiday dinners.

Then, Christmas morning. I woke to hear Amie running up and down the hallway outside my room, squealing at the top of her lungs, followed by her brother, who was also yelling and laughing. They burst into my room, giggling like maniacs, half dressed, hair all over the place, both wearing toothy grins and extra cheeky dimples.

Hurtling themselves at my bed, they jumped up on top of me and proceeded to flail and bounce around, hollering at the top of their lungs. "Snow! Snow! Snow!" Amie dropped to her knees, landing right on top of me. "Get up, Feelya. There's so much snow outside. We need to go play in it."

Sure enough, when I allowed them to drag me, groggy and in sore need of caffeine, to the window, the entire view out of the glass was pure white for as far as the eye could see. There must have been a huge storm in the night, and we'd all slept through it.

"Can we?" Connor said, looking hopeful. "We're not even hungry. We don't need breakfast."

"I don't know about skipping breakfast," I said, yawning. "But we can definitely go outside and build a snowman first. How about that?"

They screamed in response. Outside, the world felt fresh and new. It felt like it was holding its breath. Like it was keeping a secret. The huge lawn to the front of the house was a pristine white blanket. Connor and Amie, in pink and green rubber boots, charged at it like wild animals, racing each other, running in circles, pushing each other over, making snow angels on their backs. They dragged me down with them, and I created the most lopsided, shapeless snow angel, which made them both laugh. The three of us lay on our backs in the snow, panting, trying to catch our breath, staring up at the sky, and Connor reached out and took my hand. I'd never forget it. The small, usually unremarkable gesture that had me so close to tears. I squeezed his hand and he pulled away, but he smiled at me as he raced off, whooping and shouting so loud that his voice echoed way off in the distance.

When the cold set in and the glory of charging around in the snow was no longer enough to distract the children from the lure of the presents waiting for them under the Christmas tree, we headed back to the house. On the doorstep, sitting there, stacked one on top of the other, were three presents all wrapped in matching brown paper.

"Look!" Amie ran up the steps and picked up the first present, shaking it in her mittened hand. "Santa brought us extras presents!" She held it up to show me.

"That one's got an O on it." Connor took the present—long and narrow—from her, studying the small gift card that was taped to the top of it. "It doesn't say anything else. I think it's for you." He handed the gift to me, and then picked up the one underneath. "This one has a A on it. And this one has a C." Picking up the largest, bulkiest present from the floor, Connor gave it to his sister, who had to hold it with two hands.

"Whoa! It's heavy! Where did they come from?"

"I don't know, sweetheart. I think Santa maybe *did* just forget to drop these off in the night, so he left them here where he knew we would find them." The presents weren't there when we came outside earlier, I was sure of it. I spun around, scanning the sprawling lawn and the sweeping driveway that stretched on and on for at least a mile back to the main road, and there, in the distance, I saw him—a tall figure dressed in black, so far off he was barely more than a half a centimeter tall, walking away from the house. Black pants. Black jacket. A black hat, or maybe just very, very dark hair. Plumes of smoke rose up on the figure's breath, clouding overhead as he grew smaller and smaller, until I couldn't make him out anymore.

"Who was that?" Connor asked.

"I don't know, buddy. I haven't got a clue. Come on. How about we head inside and have some oatmeal? I think I'm starting to freeze." I *did* know who the mystery figure was, though. It was all too obvious. Sully must have walked right past us playing around on the lawn when he dropped off the presents. He must have slipped by, less than fifty feet away, and none of us had seen him. I slid the small present into my jacket pocket, ushering the children inside, and I couldn't help but ask myself why. Why would he bother sneaking onto the property to bring the children a present? To bring *me* a present. After all he'd said, it made no sense that he would go to such extreme lengths, walking so far in the cold, so early in the morning. Why hadn't he just driven his truck?

I didn't get to spend too long analyzing the man's behavior. Breakfast had to be made, and then the children spent two solid hours ripping open their gifts and playing with their toys. Thankfully I'd had the foresight to order everything for them online weeks earlier, so Jerry's vanishing act hadn't affected me in any way.

Connor and Amie, without meaning to, ended up opening Sully's presents last.

For Connor, a beautiful, small telescope, made of brass and maple wood. As soon as he opened the box and took out the complex looking article inside, I knew Sully had made it. You couldn't buy that kind of craftsmanship anymore. Everything was machine made, but Connor's telescope was unique, the wood hand-turned and sanded, the workings smooth and breathtaking. Connor held it reverently, eyes round and amazed. "It's awesome," he said breathlessly. "So much better than my binoculars. I'll be able to see the stars with this."

"You sure will, buddy."

"Best present ever. I can't wait for it to go dark so I can try it out."

Amie's gift was just as impressive. At first it looked like a box full of random, sanded and varnished pieces of wood. All three of us stood over the open packaging, eyeing the contents with frowns of confusion on our faces until Amie yelped.

"I know what it is! I know! I know!" She dropped down to the floor and began pulling out the pieces and laying them out in front of her, at which point it dawned on me, too: they were bones. Dinosaur bones.

Sully had hand carved her a simplified, to-scale skeleton of what turned out to be (after many hours of playing where-the-heck-does-this-piece-go?) a Velociraptor.

Amie was uncontainable.

Rose showed up in the afternoon, and together we made Christmas dinner. We exchanged gifts—I'd bought her a new Coach purse online. She'd bought me a beautiful cashmere scarf all the way from Scotland—and once we were done with the food and the gifts, and the children were crashed out face first on the sofa, she turned to me and said, "Off you go, then."

"I'm sorry?"

"Don't play coy with me, girl. I may have pretended I didn't know what was going on before, but I've witnessed my fair share of Fletcher-infatuated women to recognize one when I see one now. So go. And tell him Merry Christmas from me, okay? I nailed a sock full of coal to his front door this morning. I'm sure he saw the funny side."

I sat there, debating whether I should stay and argue with her, denying any knowledge of this Fletcher-infatuation she was referring to, or whether I should just gracefully accept defeat and come clean. In the end, there was only one thing for it.

"I'm really sorry," I told her, groaning. "It wasn't meant to happen. He's just...he's so *infuriating*. He gets to you, and then he gets to you some more. Before you know it, he's all you can think about, and you find yourself wishing you'd never laid eyes on him in the first place, but it's too late, and—"

"And he's the one."

"The most inappropriate, unorthodox, unreliable one there ever was."

Rose gave me a pitying look. "Don't we all just know it? Funny how the knowing doesn't change anything, isn't it?"

I hung my head, feeling pretty sorry for myself. "It's the worst."

••••

I hadn't opened Sully's gift. I sat in the car outside the lighthouse, too afraid to get out of the car and go inside, knowing that he must have heard me pull up. I held the small present he'd left for me in my hands, turning it over and over, worrying the corners of the paper under my shaking hands. I was scared. What if it was something and nothing? A pair of socks? A gift certificate to a bookstore? The box was the wrong size and shape to be either of those things, but the thought was still there. What if it was a throw away gift that meant nothing? Was that worse than him giving me something that meant too much? Jewelry? Something personal and handmade like he'd given to the children? Either way, I was screwed.

The passenger door to the car opened all of a sudden, scaring the crap out of me. I'd been staring so intently down at the gift that I hadn't noticed Sully leave the lighthouse and make his way over to the car. His cheeks were flushed red from the cold, and his wavy hair was swept back out of his face. Still the handsomest man I'd ever seen.

He climbed up into the car and made himself comfortable in the passenger seat. Not looking at me, he slammed the door closed and then stared straight ahead out of the windshield. Neither of us said anything at first. And then, "Aren't you going to open it?"

"I've been thinking about it," I admitted. "The children loved their gifts. Thank you."

Sully shrugged, blowing onto his hands. "No big deal." He was trying to pretend that it wasn't, but both he and I knew how much effort he'd put into those gifts. How long they would have taken him to make—hours and hours. Both gifts were labors of love. It really was a big deal. "It smells like Christmas threw up in here," Sully observed.

It really did. I'd set aside a plate of food for him when we'd dished up dinner without really thinking about it. A flask of mulled wine leaked cinnamon and spice smells into the car, which mingled with the scent of turkey, stuffing and gravy to produce an undeniably festive oratory assault.

"If you don't want the food I can always take it home with me."

"Are you kidding? I've been waiting for you for hours. I'm starving."

"How did you know I was coming?"

Sully glanced sideways at me, mouth open in a smile. "There's this part in The Sound of Music, where Maria's trying to deny her true feelings for the stuffy old Von Trapp bastard. He's fallen down some stairs or some shit, and everyone thinks she won't go to him, that she'll let him figure out his shit for himself or whatever because he's been a grade A cunt to her, but then at the end of the film, just as the Nazis are about to cart old Von Trapp off to Auschwitz, Maria shows up with a machine gun and rescues his ass. Well, she *tries* to rescue him and gets herself captured in the process, so he actually has to save her in the end, but it all works out."

I just look at him blankly. "Have you ever actually seen The Sound of Music, Sully?"

"Of course I have. Everyone's seen The Sound of Music."

"I think you might be confusing it with a few other movies."

"Maybe," he agreed, nodding. "There's a very strong possibility that you're right there."

I slapped my hand over my heart, feigning shock. "My god. Did Sully Fletcher just admit I might be right about something?"

He laughed, scathing and amused all at once. "Don't push your luck, Lang. Drive me somewhere, will you? I'm so fucking sick of looking at this lighthouse."

"It's dark."

"I know. That's the best part."

He was a strange, strange man. I drove with the headlights turned off, winding my way down narrow single track roads, curving along the coastline until I reached a wide turnout point at the edge of a cliff face, overlooking the ocean.

"Get out and sit with me," Sully commanded. He reached through to the back seat, pulling a face—his ribs were obviously still a little twingy, despite the four-week period he'd had to recover—and picked up the bag with the food and mulled wine in it. He got out of the car without saying another word and walked off into the dark.

I waited a second. It was freezing cold out there, and he'd only just recovered from a severe bout of hypothermia. The man really was crazy. Certifiable. Still, no point sitting in the car. He seemed pretty determined when he got out and walked off. I had very little choice but to get out and follow after him.

The ocean was roaring, crashing into the cliff face, spitting icy flecks of salt water up at the land. I found Sully leaning against a flat ledge of rock, brushing snow off it with his bare hands.

"Sit down." He pointed at the bare rock, eyes set, firm, daring me to deny him.

I sat. He joined me, leg pressed up against mine, and started handing me things out of the bag I'd packed at home: turkey; potatoes in tin foil; yams; a small container of gravy, lid screwed on tight.

"I didn't bring any paper plates or forks. I assumed we'd be eating at your place. We can't eat out of the tinfoil, Sully."

"Why the hell not?" He picked up a piece of candied yam and dipped it into the tub of gravy, then popped it into his mouth, flashing me a grin.

I rolled my eyes. "You know they're probably gonna find our bodies here in four days' time, frozen to this rock, right?" My ass was already numb.

"Don't be such a baby." He shifted closer to me, though, putting an arm around my shoulders, pulling me into him.

We both ate one-handed, in silence, listening to the ocean beat against the foundations of the island. Out to sea, in the very far distance, the lights of freight ships and tankers winked and flashed red and green, as if marking the holiday.

Once we were finished, Sully cleared away the mess left over from our meal and got out the mulled wine, pouring out a healthy measure into the top of the flask. "We'll share," he said, handing it to me. I held the lid containing the piping hot liquid in my hands until I could feel my fingers again, and then I drank and passed it to him.

"This month has been shit," he said quietly under his breath. "I didn't realize how shit it was going to be. And don't you tell me you've been having a great time, because I know you haven't."

"I *have*."

"I went to Connor's play," he blurted. "I sat at the back. I made sure he didn't see me."

"You *did*?" I couldn't believe it. The presents this morning had thrown me, but this was something else altogether.

Sully nodded, and then drank some of the wine. He seemed lost in thought, eyes shining dimly even though the night was pitch black around us. "I just wanted to see him. See both of them. Everyone on the island is always arguing about who they look like—Ronan or Magda. I guess I wanted to make up my mind for myself."

"Oh." I took the wine from him. "What did you decide?"

"They look like Ronan the most. Which means they also look like me." This thought didn't seem to make him happy. His left hand tightened into a fist in his lap. "I wasn't expecting that. I should have been expecting it, but I wasn't. Goddamnit, Lang, will you open your damn present already? It's making me flip out knowing that we're sitting here with it in your pocket."

I wanted to know more about what he'd seen the night of Connor's play, what he'd been thinking as he watched his brother's son recite his lines, perhaps catching glimpses of Amie and me in the shadowy crowd, but his confession had obviously made him uncomfortable, and he clearly didn't want to talk about it anymore. I took the gift out of my pocket and held it up, studying it with one eye closed.

"Can I shake it?" I asked.

"Sure."

Nothing breakable inside, then. I shook it, and the slender package rattled, many small pieces bouncing around inside. "Hmm." I unwrapped it carefully, and then lifted the lid of the plain blue box underneath, to reveal USB drives. Six, seven, eight of them, each one the same slim, silver design with a small lanyard attached.

"What the hell are these?" I asked, laughing.

Sully picked one up out of the box and held it up, grinning wickedly. "These are the downloaded files from my unit's shared drive when I was deployed, Miss Ophelia Lang from California. Each one is twenty gigs of uncensored hardcore porn, courtesy of Specialist Crowe. Seriously, I hope you understand how honored you should be. These USB sticks are my most prized possessions."

I gaped at the box, horrified. "Are you kidding me? How many...how many hours of porn is that?"

"God knows. At least a hundred." He threw the USB back in the box. "Maybe two."

"Should I be thanking you right now?"

"Only if you mean it," he said, winking.

"Well, I don't. God, what am I supposed to do with two hundred hours of porn, Sully?"

"Watch it. Give yourself carpal tunnel. Make yourself happy, girl."

"I am not...*urgh*!" I thought about dumping the scalding hot wine I was holding down the back of his jacket. I thought about punching him in the balls, too, but I got the feeling he was expecting this reaction and was already preparing to block my attack. "Why do you have to be such a dick, Sully Fletcher?" I growled.

He sighed heavily and threw his arm back around my shoulder, pulling me to him again. "I *told* you. I promised I'd be a super asshole. To protect you."

"Ha! To *protect* me." I squirmed, trying to get up, but he held onto me tight.

"Yeah," he said. "To protect you." And then, much quieter, "And to protect me, too."

I waited a long time, leaning against him, breathing him in, before it felt like the right time to speak. "You know, I have something for you, too, Sully."

"A Christmas gift?"

"Not really. Just...something I thought you should have." I couldn't be sure giving him Magda's journal was the right thing to do—he'd said at Rose's party he never wanted to see it again. I just couldn't shake the fact that *I* certainly didn't have any business keeping it in my possession. I withdrew the hard, leather-bound journal from the inside of my jacket and held onto it with both hands, looking down at it. I gave it to Sully, cringing.

"Jesus," he whispered. "I guess I deserve this after the porn."

"That's not all of it," I told him.

"It gets worse?"

I fished the small piece of ribbon and polished metal out of my pocket, dropping it into Sully's open hand. I closed his fingers around it, sighing. "Ronan may have let you down, Sully, but a medal is a big deal. He earned it. You should have it. You should keep it. One day, you might be able to look at it and be proud of him."

Sully uncurled his fingers one at a time, looking down at the Purple Heart in the palm of his hand. His shoulders rounded in, his posture sagging.

"Thank you, Lang."

"You're not mad?"

"No. I'm not mad, I promise." He slowly got to his feet, holding the journal and the medal stiffly, as if they were live grenades, about to go off any second. I should have known what was coming next. I should have seen it coming. I didn't, though. Sully took two long, purposeful strides toward the edge of the cliff face, and he launched Magda's journal over the side into the roaring dark ocean. Pages exploded everywhere like white birds, diving down into the churning water below.

"Sully! Oh my god!"

He turned and looked at me. "The past is the past, Lang. What's the point in hiding it in a drawer, letting it fester?" He held up the medal, looking at it briefly before drawing back his arm.

"Sully, wait!"

He paused.

"Are you sure? Are you really sure you want to do that?"

He gave me a small, sad mile. "More than anything in the world." The medal rocketed into the night, immediately vanishing from view. I didn't see it hit the water. I didn't hear the splash. It was there one moment, sitting in Sully's hand. The next minute, it was gone.

CHAPTER TWENTY-ONE

THE OBSERVATORY

The light was on at the lighthouse when we got back. A pillar of yellow light blasted out of the round observatory at the top of the building, sweeping slowly back and forth out toward the ocean. "Whoa, I didn't realize this was a working lighthouse. Why didn't I notice that when I pulled up earlier?"

"It's on a timer," Sully said. "I don't have to do anything. It just comes on when it's supposed to. Goes off the same way. I essentially get paid to change the light bulb every once in a while, and that's it."

I knew what was going to happen if we went inside. I went inside anyway. Sully was right. The past month really had been shitty, and today was Christmas Day, damnit. I wasn't going to deny myself anymore. Not for the next twelve hours, anyway. Tomorrow might be a different story, but for now…

"Do you want a drink?" Sully held up a bottle of wine, lifting one eyebrow.

"Whiskey?" I countered.

Sully grinned. "This is why I like you, Lang. You never fail to surprise." He disappeared back into the kitchen; when he came back he was carrying two rocks glasses each containing a good three shots of whiskey and wearing a curious look on his face. "I don't think my friend Jared can drive you home tonight if you drink too much, y'know?" he informed me.

"That's okay. I planned on sleeping in your bed."

"Oh, is that so?" He handed me my glass and took a sip out of his own, smirking down at me. "Let me guess. I'll be sleeping on the couch, then?"

I nodded, trying to hide my own smile. "You should be used to it by now, given how often you've had to sleep down here recently."

Sully stuck his tongue out at me—such a playful, cheeky gesture that I was taken by surprise. "Don't worry, Lang. I've actually been sleeping up in the observatory for the last week anyway, so you can have my bed. I like listening to the sound of the waves up there."

We drank our whiskey and talked. It was strange and comfortable when it should have been anything but. Sully traced the tips of his fingers up and down my arm, barely acknowledging the fact that he was touching me, although I was all too aware of it. My nerve endings were working on overdrive, shiver after shiver traveling through my body.

"So. Do you wanna watch some of that porn or what?" he asked, laughing, face already buried inside his rocks glass as he finished the last of his drink.

I didn't even humor that with a response. Sully laughed openly at the look on my face. "Jesus, Lang. Lighten up. I swear I'm joking."

Three more drinks in, and he leaned in and kissed me. I knew it was coming this time, so I was prepared. He was gentle. No rushing me. No frantic hands running all over my body. It was almost as if he was worried he shouldn't be doing it. Our lips met, and we both stayed as still as possible, both breathing erratically, my pulse thumping all over my body. Slowly, he reached up and pressed the palm of his hand against the side of my face. He made a low humming sound, close to a growl, and kissed me harder, parting my lips so he could slide his tongue into my mouth.

This kiss was a slow burn that sank deep down into my bones and settled there. I felt like I was falling into him. Falling backward. Falling, one way or another, and Sully's arms were around me, holding me tight, ready to catch me. Such a safe feeling, being held in his arms. He was so damned strong. I knew I didn't need to fear anything if he was holding me, and that in itself was a dangerous thought. He wouldn't be holding onto me forever. Soon enough he'd be letting me go, and I'd have to figure out how to do the same. It felt impossible to even consider such a thing right now, though, with him stroking his hands lightly over my hair, his mouth working against mine.

"That feeling," he panted against my mouth. "You know that feeling, where you just can't seem to get close enough to someone? I never really knew what people were talking about until now, Lang. I wanna...I don't even know what I want to do. I just know that I don't want you leaving here tonight. Even if you are sleeping in another room."

"Good. Because I'm not going anywhere."

Our faces were so close, only a few inches apart. Looking into his eyes this closely, it was possible to see all of the details I'd missed before. Caramel and gold flecks rimmed his pupils, lightening his eyes, softening them a little. They were so many different colors, all blended and painted together to create the most beautiful chocolate tone. It was more than that, though. Whenever I'd had reason to spend time with Sully before, his intensity had terrified me, and I'd ended up looking away from him. I'd never spent long enough looking at him to see how the microscopic changes to his expression screamed so loudly of what he was thinking or what he was feeling. Now, I was seeing it all.

He was fearless. He was confident. He was strong, and he was honest. He was also a little broken—a truth that he didn't mind owning. Carefully he ran the tip of his index finger over my forehead, between my eyebrows, down the bridge of my nose. His finger lingered over my lips, and I had to fight the urge to dart my tongue out and lick him. A strange urge to have. I wanted to so badly, but I behaved myself. Over my lips, then, and over my chin, running his finger down the column of my neck to my collarbone. "I'm not used to this," he said softly. "I don't know how to handle you. You seem so...*fragile*."

"I'm stronger than I look," I whispered back.

"I don't doubt it."

"Then you don't need to handle me with kid gloves, Sully. I won't break."

"You don't know how rough I can be," he said, his voice a low rumble that vibrated against my chest. A rush of desire slammed through me, taking me by surprise. I'd never felt anything like it before. My mind was already imagining the places Sully might take me, all the sensations he'd be able to ignite in my body without even trying. I felt drunk on him, my head reeling from the scent and the warmth and the feel of his hard packed chest resting flush against mine.

"You're looking a little red there, Lang. Are you cold?" he asked. There was a wicked glint in his eye, though—he knew I was far too hot if anything.

"No. I'm fine. Just tired. Maybe you could show me where I'll be sleeping?" I'd found his bedroom just fine when I'd needed to get fresh clothes for him a few weeks back. I wanted him to take me upstairs, though. I wanted to enjoy the last remaining hours of Christmas Day wrapped up in him, naked, all pretentions and inhibitions gone. Sully rubbed the pad of his thumb against my bottom lip, staring at it, apparently fascinated.

"Okay," he mouthed. "Then let's go."

My body hummed as he led me upstairs. I was at odds with myself, shaking with nerves and shaking with anticipation, and just shaking for the hell of it. Sully opened the door to his bedroom, and then dipped to kiss me lightly on the lips.

"Goodnight, Lang. If you need anything, I'll just be up one floor in the observatory, okay?"

I didn't know what to say. Dumbly I nodded, trying not to let my confusion show. He wasn't going to sleep with me? We weren't finally going to have sex? Sully kissed my neck, his teeth gently nipping at my flushed skin, and then he backed away. He disappeared up the winding stairs that continued up to the observation deck of the lighthouse, and

I stood by his bedroom door, paralyzed.

What the hell?

Thirty seconds passed, and then another full minute. He didn't want me? That was such bullshit. No. Just *no*. I didn't walk through into his bedroom. That would have been the easy option. Instead I chose the harder, far more embarrassing route. My Christmas Day was not ending like this—alone and confused. I was going to confront him. Ask him what the hell was going on. I took the stairs up to the observatory two at a time, already planning all of the harsh, unkind things I was going to say to him when I reached the top.

"Sully Fletcher, you are *the* most—" My foot hit the top step and I saw him standing there, moonlight pouring in through the bowed windows, casting silver shadows across his perfect skin, and I suddenly forgot what I was going to say. He was naked. And he was waiting for me.

"Took you long enough," he said. "Very brave, though, Lang. Very, *very* brave." He walked slowly toward me, and I felt as though I were about to tumble back down the stairs. He was a work of art. The lines of his shoulders were strong, broad and powerful. His chest was a slab of muscle, forming a perfect vee lower down where his hips dipped into his groin. I couldn't look away. His thighs were muscular and covered in a light smattering of hair. And his cock...

Before I married Will, I'd only slept with one other guy. He'd been smaller than Will, but he'd really known what to do to make a woman come. Will had been considerably bigger, but he'd thought it didn't matter (or maybe just cared less) how he used his size to bring me pleasure.

I already knew Sully possessed both size and expertise, though. One look at the way he moved as he walked toward me told me he was a highly sexual guy. And he was so huge. Almost *frighteningly* so.

I glanced back up and saw that he'd caught me staring. "It's okay, Lang," he said. "Don't hold back on my account. Look as much as you want. *Touch* as much as you want. *Taste* as much as you want. I sure as hell won't be holding back."

"Shit. I think I'm freaking out a little." Admitting that to him was hard. Not as hard as admitting to myself how inexperienced and unworthy I suddenly felt. And vulnerable. God, so, *so* vulnerable. Sully padded barefoot to me and slid his arms around me, lifting me up off the floor, hands moving underneath my thighs as he guided me to wrap my legs around his waist.

"Don't freak out," he commanded. "Relax. Breathe. I'll stop whenever you want me to. Just say the word."

"Okay."

The roof over the observatory was a dome of pure glass. In the center of the room, a huge mirror reflected the light from a surprisingly small bulb behind a wire mesh cage; it swung around to the left, and the brilliant wave of pure white light washed over us, casting a stark silhouette in the beam. Sully wasn't lying when he said he'd been sleeping up here. A low-slung cot was pushed up against one side of the dome, neatly made, his clothes laid out on top of it. He carried me across to it, but he didn't put me down on the mattress. He lowered me back to my feet and pressed me up against the glass, then began kissing my neck, licking and biting at me until it felt like the sea of stars overhead were spinning too brightly and way too fast.

His heart was slamming in his chest beneath my hands, beating just as crazily as my own. I couldn't stop touching him. My hands ran up and down his back, my fingernails digging into his flesh, until the texture of his skin changed, very slick and smooth feeling, and I stopped. It was the scar on his side—the one that run up onto his back. Sully didn't seem to notice me hesitate before I stroked my hand across the scar again, feeling the topography of his body alter as I explored.

He continued to kiss at my neck, but eventually I felt him stiffen a little. "Who's the one wearing kid gloves now, Lang?" he growled under his breath.

"I'm sorry. I don't mean to. It's just—"

"It doesn't hurt. It doesn't bother me. You don't need to tiptoe around it. I have a scar. It's pretty big." He leaned back and gave me a roguish smile. "Now feel free to get over it and pay some attention to the rest of my body. How about...*here*." He took hold of my hand and slid it down, so that I was touching his hard-on.

"God, Sully..." I curled my hand around him, squeezing gently, and his eyelids shuttered, his breath coming out in a short, blunt gasp. Slowly, I worked my hand up the length of him, looking down between our bodies so I could watch what I was doing to him. It was fascinating, seeing him literally grow harder and pulse in my hand as I worked my way up and down his flesh. It was even more fascinating when I glanced up and saw the expression on his face—so much lust and desire, warring with his need for self-control. His bottom lip was fastened between his teeth, and he was biting down. *Hard*. I'd never seen a look so openly sexual and heated on a guy's face before, and it damn near broke me. I wanted to tear my clothes from my body, shove him back on his makeshift bed, and sink myself down on him immediately. I doubted he would try and stop me, but if I did that it would be over too soon. I wanted to savor every last second of this experience. I needed to commit every last second of it to memory, to hold onto each moment we shared as we kissed, and touched and explored each other's bodies.

My senses were overloading, greedily trying to shove each other out of the way so I could focus on how he looked, how he felt, how he smelled and how he tasted all at once. Sully seemed as if he were fighting the exact same battle.

"You're not real," he told me, curling a piece of my hair around his index finger. "How can you be?"

"I'm pretty sure I am," I said breathlessly.

"Then why do I constantly feel like I'm underwater when I'm with you? Dreaming? Imagining every second?" His mouth came down on mine, hungry and demanding. I didn't tell him I felt the same way. He wouldn't give me the breath to do it. He demanded it all from me, demanded everything I had. His hands worked their way underneath my shirt, moving confidently upwards, until he was roughly cupping my breasts. He bit my lip at the same time, tugging on it sharply, growling a little. My head was spinning. The powerful beam of light swept across us again, turning night into day, and Sully took hold of my shirt, pulling it off over my head in one swift movement. My bra didn't last long either. He reached around and unfastened the clasp at the back, then tore the straps from my shoulders, throwing it over his shoulder.

My back arched away from the wall of thick glass behind me so that my chest was offered up to Sully; he took full advantage of the fact and bent over me, taking one of my peaked nipples into his mouth, and then the other. His hands were full of me. My head was full of him.

"Sully. Oh my god, *please*..." What was I begging for? I didn't even know. For him to be inside me? For him to throw me down on his bed and take me? I definitely wanted that, but my plea was asking for more than that. *Please don't hurt me. Please don't ruin this. Please don't let me ruin this. Please don't let me go. Please don't let me love you...*

Begging could only get you so far, though. I was filled with an undeniable, solid awareness of myself, and how little control I had over my own heart. It was a treacherous, cruel thing that kept trying to lead me down a path I didn't want to go down. In reality, I was blundering my way blindly down that path already, lost and so turned around that I didn't know which way was up, and Sully was the only thing I could see anymore.

He smoothed both of his hands over my hair, then down over my shoulders, resting them on my hips. "How stupid are we being, Lang? How much further are we going to let this go?" he asked hoarsely.

"I don't know." My own voice was small. Unsure. Scared. Sully pressed his forehead against mine, breathing out heavily. He closed his eyes, muscles in his jaw jumping, like he was struggling to stop himself from tearing me apart.

"I already told you," he said. He sounded calm, but it was a false calm, too flat and too even to be real. I could still feel how crazed his pulse was beneath my hands, evidence of his true emotional state. "I already told you I wasn't going to hold back."

"Then why are you?"

He laughed softly. "For you. Because I'm thinking of someone else before myself for the first time in a very long time. Frankly, it sucks."

I kissed him. I kissed him long, and I kissed him hard. "Let go of the reins," I said. "Neither of us want to be gripping them so tightly right now."

He opened his eyes. I felt as if I were pinned to the spot, unable to move. "No bullshit?" he asked quietly.

"No bullshit, Sully."

My feet were off the ground. One second I was leaning back against the glass, still stroking my hand slowly up and down his hard cock, and the next I was in his arms. He rushed to the bed, and I waited for the sensation of falling as he lowered me onto the mattress, but it never came. He tore at the sheets and the blanket that were on the bed, throwing them to the floor, and then he was tearing at my jeans, too, ripping them from my body. Dropping to his knees, he planted his hands firmly on my ass cheeks, and he buried his face between my legs, biting at the soft cotton material of my panties, groaning loudly. "*Fuck, Lang!* What the hell have you done to me?"

I was too stunned by the feel of his teeth grazing the sensitive skin of my inner thigh to stutter out a response. He pressed the flat of his tongue against me, pushing my legs open a little wider, and then he was hooking my panties out of the way with his index finger and he was licking me, tracing his tongue torturously slowly over my pussy, teasing at my clitoris, still groaning in that pained way that made me want to scream.

He pushed his fingers inside me as he licked, and my knees buckled out from underneath me. Sully laughed under his breath, guiding me so that I was lying on my back on the welter of sheets he'd just thrown into disarray on the floor.

"Does that feel good?" he asked softly. "Because it feels good to me. And it fucking tastes good, too."

"Shit, yes, it feels good."

"Perfect." He bent down between my legs again, pushing them wide open so he had better access to me. His mouth hovered less than an inch above my pussy. Looking up at me, eyes half closed, lips wet, he said, "Watch me, Lang. Watch me eat your pussy. Keep those eyes on me, beautiful. I want to see your face when you fall apart for me. I want to see your eyes roll back in your head when you come."

I obeyed him without question. He flicked the very tip of his tongue over my clit, pumping his fingers inside me, and it was simply too much to bear. I rocked against his mouth, panting, barely conscious of what was happening anymore. I kept my eyes on him, watching him work his tongue over me, and before long I could feel it rising inside me—that tingling, prickly, delicious, demanding sensation that sank its claws into me, threatening to pull me under.

Sully must have sensed I was close; he started rubbing me with his thumb as well as stroking me with his tongue, and that was it. All I could take. I tumbled, I fell, I screamed and I writhed. Sully grabbed me by the hips and didn't let go. He kept his mouth on me until I was shaking, my heels slipping and sliding on the floor as I kicked, unable to control my legs.

"Shit, shit, shit! Oh god. *Sully!*"

He leaned back, giving me a moment to regain myself. The arrogant wisecrack I was expecting never came. Neither did the smug celebratory pat on the back. I cracked open one eye, and Sully was staring down on me with a look of unmistakable awe on his face. He looked so serious that I felt a flush of heat blossom all over my skin.

"That was incredible," he said, his voice a low whisper. "Fuck, Lang. You're explosive. You're motherfucking dynamite." He was working his cock in his hand, moving swiftly, his grip tight. He wanted me. He wanted me so badly, I could see it plain as day in his eyes. The feeling was mutual. I let my knees drop to either side, and I slowly moved my hand in between my legs, lightly touching my fingertips over my pussy.

"Now," I told him, refusing to break eye contact. "*Please*, Sully. Don't make me wait any longer."

I wasn't ready for what happened next. He looked savage as he fell on me, one hand roughly groping at my breasts, the other supporting his weight as he angled himself between my legs. His hips were pressing against mine, our bodies in alignment, and then he was grinding them upward, thrusting inside me, and I couldn't stop myself from crying out.

Sully immediately went very, very still. His eyes were wide, unblinking, as he hovered over me, his erection buried deep inside me. "Fuck," he whispered. "You feel…" He trailed off, closing his eyes. "Oh my god, Lang. *Shit.*"

His reaction was electric. I was *electric*. I could feel it flowing through me and into him, a relay of intense energy that promised to consume and destroy. Unable to stop myself, I began to rock my hips underneath him, shivering with pleasure at the friction that built up between our bodies.

Sully growled again, snarling almost. He stopped kneading at my breast and moved his hand down between my legs again, rubbing at my clit while he slowly, carefully, began rocking in time with me.

We fit together perfectly. I felt myself melting into him as his movements grew faster, until we were both crazy with the need for each other, clinging onto each other, biting and kissing and digging our nails into each other's skin.

It felt like we both sank beyond ourselves, like we lost track of where we were. The light swung across us again and again, washing over us, casting shadows and highlights across our bodies, but neither of us seemed to notice. The world had shrunk to the smallest of spaces; nothing existed outside of the small observatory where Sully held me against him and thrust himself into me, faster and faster until I was begging him for release.

It came unexpectedly, like a meteor strike, devastating and total. I screamed, clinging to him, head kicked back so far it felt like my neck would snap, and Sully came too, roaring, pressing his forehead against my collarbone, panting, warring for breath as his body shook.

The calm that settled over us after was like a blanket, shielding us, keeping us warm despite the snow and the ice outside. We lay together for a long time, Sully still on top of me, still inside of me, and I drew circles and lines into the hard muscles across his back, down his side, over his scar. We breathed as one, our bodies mirroring each other as we finally came back into ourselves.

"Well," Sully said quietly, after a very long time had passed. "We're well and truly screwed now."

"Why?" I whispered back.

"Because. That was the best sex I've ever had. I'm definitely going to want to do that again, Miss Ophelia Lang from California. I'm going to want to do that again *a lot.*"

CHAPTER TWENTY-TWO

CAPABLE

The rain woke me the next morning, globes of water pattering lightly against the glass dome of the observatory. Sully was still asleep. His feet were sticking out of the bottom of the sheets, still on the floor where we'd collapsed into unconsciousness. His bare ass was sticking out of the covers, too, and I couldn't help myself. I sat up carefully and allowed myself a long moment to admire him in his sleep. He looked less restless than he did when awake, but his brow was still furrowed, as if he were still plagued with the weight of his burdens in his dreams. I lightly stroked my fingers over that creased area between his eyebrows, and they eased, all but disappearing.

"Damn you, Sully Fletcher," I whispered. "Damn you all to hell." Quickly I got up and got dressed, trying not to disturb him. I was fully clothed about to tiptoe my way down the spiral staircase when his voice stopped me.

"Lang, wait."

Crap. I turned, and Sully was sitting up in the confusion of sheets, chest bare, light shining down on him through the huge windows overhead. He had a frown on his face, but his eyes were soft. Not angry. Just slightly disappointed, perhaps. "This isn't going to work for me," he said.

"What isn't?"

"You sneaking off in the early hours of the morning, fully intending not to come back. *Right?*"

I looked down at my feet.

"Lang?" He sighed heavily, rubbing his face in his hands. When he looked up at me, I could see the hard set in his eyes. "I want to meet them," he said. I jerked, not sure I'd heard properly. Did he mean Connor and Amie? He couldn't, surely. Not after being so violently apposed to the idea in the first place. "That's what all this is about, isn't it? You don't want to get too involved with me because of the children?" he continued.

"I don't want to get too involved with you because I have to go soon, and I don't want to be a shell of a person when I get back to L.A., Sully. I thought you wanted to keep this simple, too."

He blew out a frustrated breath, bowing his head. "Maybe that's what I wanted. At first. But now... I don't know. Would it be the worst thing in the world if I wanted more?"

"I didn't think you were capable. That's what you said."

"I don't even know if I am. But I want to find out."

I shook my head slowly. "Sully, I can't risk hurting the children, confusing them, purely so we can figure out if we're meant to be together or not. It wouldn't be fair."

"I don't just want to meet them because of us," he said quickly. "When I saw Connor up on that stage the other night..." He sighed, glancing down at his interlinked hands. "I wanted to come and find you when it was all over then. It was like looking back in time, back to when Ronan and I were little. I couldn't believe it. And Amie. She's so small. So perfect. Seeing *her* actually terrified me. Neither Ronan nor I ever did anything to deserve such a perfect little girl. I felt so protective over both of them that it felt like I'd run head first into a brick wall. I couldn't fucking handle it. But then over the days that followed...I don't know. I couldn't stop thinking about them. So I made them the presents. I saw you guys all playing in the snow yesterday morning, and..." He shook his head, refusing to look at me. "I thought, *I'm meant to be a part of that.* I don't know how I fit into it, but I know that I do somehow." Rubbing the back of his neck with one hand, he looked like he was fighting for the right thing to say and coming up short. "So, it's not just about you, Lang. It's them, too. Do you understand? I'm not promising anything. I'm not saying I'm gonna take them or anything. I just...want to meet them."

I was a lot of things all at once: Excited. Overjoyed. Anxious. *Protective*. Could the children take meeting Sully without being completely overwhelmed? It was a lot to take in. Ronan and Magda had never mentioned Sully to either of the children. They had no idea their father had a twin brother. The resemblance was going to freak them out, especially Connor.

But still. This was what Ronan had wanted. He had wanted Sully to be the children's legal guardian eventually. He certainly would have wanted Connor and Amie to *meet* Sully in any case, despite the fact that *he* never got around to introducing them when he was alive. I squeezed my car keys in my pocket, making up my mind.

"Okay then."

Sully looked up quickly. "*Okay?*"

"Yes. But they're so young, Sully, and they've been through a lot. Don't fuck them over. I swear to god, if you do, I'll castrate you and hang your balls out to dry. Do you copy?"

He flashed his teeth, probably smirking at my use of one of his favorite phrases. "Copy. I promise I won't fuck them over. And Lang? Just so you know, I don't plan on fucking you over, either. I promise that, too."

••••

"So, he looks just like him then? He's exactly the same?" Connor hadn't glanced up from his book since I sat him and his sister down to talk about Sully, but he was clearly paying attention because he was asking a lot of questions. "How come we didn't know about him?"

"Your dad and Sully had a really bad argument, and they weren't friends for a very long time. Your dad came here to make friends with him again, though, and he really wanted you to get to meet Sully."

"I heard Mommy say Sully in her sleep," Amie announced. "She was sad. She was crying in her dreams."

"No, she didn't," Connor snapped. "That never happened."

"That's okay." I put a hand on Connor's shoulder, trying to cut that line of conversation off before he could grow agitated. "All I want to know right now is if you would like to have Sully over to the house?"

Connor closed his book and put it down on the arm of the chair. "What if we don't want him to?" he asked.

"Then that's okay. He doesn't have to come here at all. I think you would like him, though."

"I want him to come," Amie sang. "I want to say thank you for my dinosaur." I'd confessed that Sully was the one who'd sent them the gifts at the beginning of the conversation, and Amie's eyes had lit up. Likely she was planning how to obtain even more dinosaur skeletons from this stranger so she could start up a proper collection.

"What about you, Connor?" He was silent. "Connor?" I went and sat down next to him. "I mean it, you know. It really is okay if you don't want to meet him. I get it."

"Why hasn't he come and seen us before now?" he asked.

"Well." God, this was going to be difficult. "You remember how you felt when your dad died, don't you? Sully felt the same way. He's been very sad. It's taken him a long time to feel better, but now that he does he would really like to see you." It would have been far too complicated to explain it any other way. Connor nodded a little and sniffed.

"Okay. He can come over. But if I don't like him, I'm not going to talk to him."

"That's all right, buddy. It's totally okay if you change your mind."

I could imagine it all too well: Sully showing up and not knowing what to say or how to act. Connor feeling uncomfortable and running for his bedroom. Odds were that was exactly what was going to happen, but it was better than the alternative. It was better than Connor never meeting Sully, and it was better than Sully always wondering.

There was only one way to find out.

••••

"Are you ready?"

"Not really. This is more intimidating than going before a military court."

"You went before a military court?"

"No. Kind of. Not really. Are you sure they're not going to flip out?" Sully clearly didn't want to talk about the military court comment, however I was all too interested. Another time, though. I rubbed my hand across his chest, trying to reassure him.

"They might at first. But it'll be fine, I promise. They're good kids. You might just need to give them a moment to adjust is all."

"*I'm* the one who needs time to adjust," he said. "What if they call me Dad by mistake? I'll lose my fucking shit, Lang. I'm not joking."

"No, you won't. You'll remind them your name is Uncle Sully, and you'll cut them some slack. This is just as hard for them as it is for you. Harder. You knew they existed, after all. You're completely out of the blue to them."

He looked unconvinced. I'd been so sure he was going to call and bail this morning, but when he'd actually shown up at ten o'clock sharp, wearing a smart, ironed shirt and a pair of clean black jeans I'd had to give him credit: he was a man of his word. A terrified man of his word, admittedly, but still.

"Come on," I told him. "They're waiting for you." Leading him through to the kitchen, both Connor and Amie were sitting at the table, gluing down pictures I'd been cutting out of magazines for them all day onto huge pieces of craft paper. Amie was covered in glitter, her fingers absolutely plastered with glue to the point where she couldn't spread them apart anymore. Connor had small, white fragments of paper down the front of his shirt and in his hair, which was curling like crazy all over the place.

When Sully and I walked into the room, the children fell silent, and Sully froze—a rabbit trapped in the headlights. The three of them looked at one another, staring and I began to wonder if this wasn't just a huge mistake. Connor was the first to look away. Slowly, he picked up a cut-out picture of a soccer player and began to rub his glue stick over the back of it; the tips of his ears were practically glowing, but his cheeks were pale, pale, white, like he was in shock.

"Whoa," Amie breathed. She looked at me, sweet little face full of confusion, as if checking in with me—*is this really happening?* "You look just like my daddy," she whispered. I'd warned them both that Sully was more than just a little bit like Ronan, that he was *exactly* like Ronan, but Amie couldn't be blamed for being surprised now. The resemblance was unnatural.

Sully shifted from one foot to another, clearing his throat. I'd never seen him so out of sorts. "Yeah, well. People say that a lot," he replied. "It must be weird for you, huh?"

Amie nodded gravely. "It's *really* weird."

"I get that. I'm sorry...I haven't come to see you before."

Amie nodded. "Feelya said you were sad, so it's okay. Are you still sad now?"

"I think I might be a little bit," he said. "But I'm getting better."

Was he telling the truth? Was he getting better? Did he hate Ronan a little less every day, and miss him a little bit more? It was so hard to tell with him. As soon as anyone mentioned Ronan's name, it was as though a heavy, metal roller shutter was slamming down in front of him. He didn't want to talk about him. He didn't want to reminisce. As far as I could tell, he didn't even want to *think* about the fact that he had a twin a lot of the time, which made it difficult to talk freely about the situation we were in now. Sully glanced around the kitchen awkwardly. I could tell that he didn't really know what to do with himself, which made me unreasonably proud. This was such a huge step for him.

He paced slowly toward the table and stopped in front of Connor. "What are you making, man?" he asked.

"I don't know," Connor replied. "A picture of under the sea?"

Sully tipped his head to the side, trying to take a better look. Connor leaned over his picture, hiding it from view, though. "Hey, that's okay. Artists don't like sharing their work until they're finished, right? I'm sorry. I forgot."

Connor glanced quickly up at him and shrugged. "I'm not an artist. I'm just a kid."

"Well, you're way better at art than I am, either way." Sully shot me an anxious sideways look. He clearly thought he was drowning, making zero headway with the little boy; he didn't realize just how amazing it was that Connor was interacting with him at all, though.

"Are you staying here for lunch with us?" Amie asked, clambering up so that she was standing on the seat of her chair, glue spatula in one hand and a dog-eared picture of Victoria Beckham in the other.

Again, Sully looked at me, worry lines forming on his face. "Ahhh, I'm not sure. I guess I hadn't thought about that."

"Maybe Sully will stay, depending on a few things," I told her.

"What few things?"

"Well, depending on if you guys all like each other and want to hang out, I suppose."

"*I* like him," she said. "*And* I like Connor, and I like you. I think we should spend all day together."

"That's very nice of you, Amie, but we'll just play it by ear, though, okay?"

She accepted this with a tiny frown on her face, and didn't push the matter further. "You can sit here," she said, patting the table across from her. "Would you like some beers?"

Her offer surprised me since we didn't have any beers, and I hadn't had any in front of her. *Ever.* Maybe Ronan used to have a drink or two when he got home from work or something. "That's all right, Amie. It's ten fifteen in the morning. It's a little early to be drinking beer," Sully said, smiling.

"Daddy used to like drinking beers," she replied. "Daddy had beer for breakfast all the time."

Ronan used to drink beer for breakfast? Jeez. He's lost his wife. He'd been fucked up enough to take his own life. The fact that he was knocking back a beer or two before heading out to work was pretty sad, though.

Sully looked like he was about to snatch up his jacket in the hallway and bolt out of the place, never to return, so I grabbed him by the hand and sat down at the table, sealing the deal. No escaping now. Normally Connor would have been surly and snappy if he found himself in a situation he couldn't control. He didn't seem that way today, though. He seemed too stunned to be anything but silent.

"Why don't Sully and I make a picture, too, and you guys can tell us what you think, huh?" I picked up a couple of the magazines in the middle of the table and offered one to Sully. He took it gratefully and began to cut out pictures with the tiny kiddie scissors I'd been using earlier, his hands far too big to wield them efficiently.

An hour later, Rose let herself into the house and came into the kitchen to find Connor and Amie laughing raucously at the picture we'd just completed. We'd turned Lady Gaga into a nun, and some famous-right-now model had been given a makeover, transformed into a vampire, complete with drawn-in fangs and evil laser eyes, courtesy of Sully. In the middle of the page, a huge picture of some English boy band member was riding a stallion that Amie insisted was a unicorn, and the rest of the band members' heads had been cut from their own bodies and glued onto the bodies of cats.

Rose stood in the doorway and took in the scene, her arms filled with groceries, amusement written all over her face. "Looks like I've been missing all the fun, doesn't it?" she said.

"Come and draw with us," Amie squealed. "I made a Triceratops! Look!"

Rose dutifully looked at the mess of images Amie had stuck down on the paper and nodded, telling her what an excellent job she'd done. She then turned to me and said, "O? Think you could help me put these groceries away for a second?"

"Sure."

Sully was so engrossed in his conversation with Connor, debating with him whether or not a skinny bikini clad woman from one of the fashion magazines we'd cut up was actually an alien, poorly disguised as a human, that he didn't even look up when I left the table.

Rose dragged me into the pantry and pulled the door half closed behind us. "What the hell is going on?" she hissed. She was smiling, delighted, but at the same time she seemed concerned, too.

"He asked," I said. "I didn't drug him and bundle him into the trunk in order to get him over here, if that's what you're thinking."

"I wasn't thinking that at all. But now I am!"

"There's nothing to be worried about, Rose, I promise. I explained about Sully to them, and both of them agreed that they wanted to see him. The whole morning's gone really well, actually."

"Hmm. I don't know. I never thought he'd change his mind. He's not the kind of guy to go back on something once he's sworn to it once or twice."

"I know. *I know.*"

"Do you think he's gonna do what Ronan asked and take them, then?"

"I don't think so. I don't know."

"All right, O. But god, just be careful, okay? Sully's a good man, and he's definitely mellowed since he met you, but I wouldn't be surprised if he freaks out on you after this. Just watch for it, honey. I'd really hate to see you or the children get hurt."

••••

Sully stayed for the rest of the afternoon, and it was worrying. Worrying, because I spent the entire time waiting for the other shoe to drop. Amie was giggly and silly with Sully, playing with him and screaming at the top of her lungs when he chased her around the living room. Connor was quiet for a long time, but soon warmed up and joined in the fun. It was surreal. I kept getting hit with the strongest sense of déjà vu, back to the night before Ronan killed himself, when he was charging around the same living room, wearing that pirate patch.

Four o'clock rolled around, and Sully said he needed to leave. Amie looked like she was going to cry. "But I didn't even get to ask for another skeleton," she whispered.

"Well, maybe, if Sully comes back again another day, you can ask him then." She'd spoken loud enough that he heard what she said anyway, and he winked at me. He seemed light. Carefree. Less like the world was weighing down on him from all angles. He'd changed so much over the past couple of weeks that it was almost hard to believe.

"Why don't you go and relax for a little while, too?" Rose said, as I went to see Sully out. "I've got things handled here. If this is what happens to Sully Fletcher when he falls in love, then you two should definitely spend as much time together as possible."

I nearly died. No one mentioned being in love. I hadn't. Sully sure as hell hadn't. Why would she say something like that? It felt like the ground was yawning open and about to swallow me up whole. I glowered at Rose over Sully's shoulder, subtly trying to let her know how mad I was, when I saw Sully's reflection in the mirror on the wall right next to us, along with my own, and realized that he'd seen every single frown and glower I'd sent her way. Perfect.

"I always knew a woman could speak volumes with one look. That was a whole new level, though, Lang."

Embarrassment nearly drowned me. I must have been red. No, scratch that. I must have been *purple* with horror. "Forget the last three minutes," I said, grabbing my purse. "Thanks, Rose. I'll be back later, okay? Goodbye, guys."

Connor and Amie got up from the table and gave me a hug, one at a time. Connor seemed to be growing more and more tactile by the day, so I wasn't all that surprised when he wrapped his arms around my waist and gave me a very brief, tight squeeze. I *was* shocked when he shyly held out his hand for Sully to shake, though. "It was very nice to meet you," he said in a quiet voice.

Sully swallowed, looking down at the little boy. He seemed a little lost for words. "You too, little man. Any time you want to hang out, you just let me know, okay?"

Connor considered this for a moment, and then nodded. "Okay."

CHAPTER TWENTY-THREE

THE LAMEST

Over the following weeks, Sully came to the house more and more. At first it had to be by formal invitation. Would he like to come for dinner? Would he like to come with me to take the children down to the beach? Was he free to come build forts in the library? But then as the days and the weeks passed, he just started showing up. He would come by the house at around ten in the morning, have lunch, come with me to pick Connor up from school, and *he* would be the one to help him with his homework while I cooked dinner with Rose. *He* would be the one to take Amie to bed at seven. *He* would be the one to sit through endless episodes of *Peppa Pig*, and *Marvel Action Hour* re-runs.

The change in him was spectacular. And in amongst the quality time he spent with the children, he was constantly pulling me aside, hands all over me, mouth rough on mine, touching me, caressing and kissing me. Never in front of the children. But when they weren't looking? Boy, that was a different story altogether.

"I just can't believe it," Rose told me, one day toward the end of January. "I swear, I've never seen him like this before. This is…well, it's kind of shocking. I never thought I'd see him smile like that again."

Sully was lying on his back on the living room floor, and Amie was straddling his chest, sitting on his stomach. Her tiny hands were pulling at his cheeks and his forehead, mushing his face into strange expressions. She giggled at the top of her lungs every time he growled or poked his tongue out. Her laughter was infectious. Connor might not have taken to Sully so quickly, but the little boy loved having him around. He sat Indian style on the floor a couple of feet from them, watching, smiling, not saying anything but clearly happy.

I leaned my head against Rose's shoulder, sighing. "I know. I'm scared."

She glanced out me out of the corner of her eye. "I get that. I can see why you might be worried. But *I'm* not anymore. I don't think this is a flash in the pan, O. He didn't have PTSD when he came back from Afghanistan, thank god. He was just...*angry*. He might *still* be angry, but look at him. He's happy now, too. He's found some sort of balance. That's pretty damn special."

She was right about him still being angry. There were days when he was so prickly and unapproachable that I wanted to kick him in the balls. Days when I came so close to doing exactly that. But all it took was calling him out on his crap and he pulled his shit together. It was remarkable that he was able to flip the switch so easily. When I asked him about it, he simply said, "War puts things into perspective, Lang. Sometimes you lose sight of things. Sometimes it takes a riled up SoCal girl to kick you into touch, but nothing is ever as bad as it seems. Feel free to remind me what an ass I am as many times as you like. If I'm too unbearable, then toss my ass out of the house." I hadn't had to do that just yet, but he knew I was prepared and willing. Perhaps that's why he was clearly trying so hard to make this work. Weeks passed. A month. Valentines day arrived, and with it single pink rose and a simple handwritten card on my pillow.

Lang.

You're not as smart as you think you are. I'm impervious to your wicked ways. I am not in love with you. When you leave this island, I won't care.

The world won't stop turning.
I won't feel hollow, or bereft.
I won't look out of the windows of my lighthouse and see only greyness and misery where there was once beauty.
I won't stare at my cell phone, waiting for you to call.
I won't mourn the loss of you.
I won't cry (in a very manly way).
I won't pray your parents decide to close down their restaurant after all and move to the east coast.
I won't watch The Sound of Music over and over again, wishing for my too-good-to-be-true girlfriend to return to me.
Every second.
Every minute.
Every hour.
That would make me the lamest guy in the world.

Yours, temporarily,
Sully Fletcher.

P.S. check your phone.

I picked up my phone from my nightstand, skin prickling all over with hurt, eyes stinging a little too brightly at the words he'd written down on the paper...until I saw the text message waiting for my on the screen.

At some point, Sully had changed his name in my contacts from 'Hottest Guy In The World' to 'Lamest Guy In The World'. The lone message he'd sent to me contained few words, but they hit hard.

BETWEEN HERE AND THE HORIZON

Sully: Don't do it, Lang. Don't go.

I sat up in bed, staring at the note, re-reading it over and over again, knowing now what he was really telling me. He *did* love. He *would* miss me. He didn't want me to go. Later, over dinner at the house, I tried to talk to him about what he'd written, about what he'd asked of me, but it was difficult. The children were too excited, covered in glue and glitter yet again from making love heart and cupid decorations with Rose. And of course Rose was with us, too, and so it was almost midnight by the time we had a second to ourselves.

Sully never stayed at the house. He didn't seem to mind visiting for extended periods of time, but I still caught him every once in a while staring off into the distance, or standing in the doorway of a room with a lost look on his face. It was easy to forget that the house we were living in was the same house where he grew up. Each and every inch of the place was full of memories for him, no matter how expertly it had been renovated. And I just so happened to be sleeping in his parent's old bedroom, which freaked him out endlessly. He never stepped foot upstairs if he could help it.

In light of that, I tended to sleep over at the lighthouse with him whenever we wanted time alone together. More and more often Rose was staying with the children overnight and I was sneaking out of the house under a cloak of darkness, spending the night with Sully, only to drive back home at the crack of dawn before Connor and Amie woke up.

Tonight would be no different. We didn't make it back to the lighthouse, though. Sully drove halfway home, and then peeled off down a narrow track, taking us in the opposite direction. When he stopped his truck, we were in front of what looked like a ruined castle, the roof disappeared, most of the walls tumbled down. The snow covered what little standing stonework remained, obscuring what was left of the structure, so all I could make out were a few odd sections of wall and the very tops of some of the huge foundation stones.

"Why have we stopped here?" I asked.

"Because I'm going to fuck you now, Lang. I couldn't wait until we got back to the lighthouse. This was the closest place I could think of where we wouldn't be seen."

"No way! I'm not having sex with you in your car. It's freezing cold, Sully."

"Pussy." He unfastened his seatbelt, and then he reached across and unclipped mine, too. "Straddle me. Climb up out of your seat and straddle me, before I spank you for being disobedient." He was joking, but there was a scandalous glimmer in his eye that made me blush a little too hotly. Being spanked by Sully wasn't such a horrible prospect. In fact, the idea of his hand tanning my bare behind made me want to press my knees together in the weirdest way.

"We can't be more than ten minutes from your place. Can't we just go back there? Where it's warm?" I tried not to think about being bent over his knee, but the image was well and truly cemented in my brain now.

"I swear to you now, you won't be cold for long, Lang. I'll have you hot and bothered in no time." He buzzed back his seat so that it reclined almost flat, smiling wickedly at me the whole time. "Look," he said, taking hold of my hand. "Feel this." He guided me to his pants, where I instantly felt the huge hard-on he was hiding in his jeans. He was harder than hard. He was rock solid. He closed my hand around him, closing his eyes.

"If I let go of your hand right now, Lang, what are you gonna do? Make me drive you home? Or are you going to let me use this," he squeezed his hand on mine again, emphasizing just how turned on he was, "to make you come?"

When he put it like that, heading straight back to the lighthouse seemed like a hasty option after all. "Hot and bothered, you said?" I asked, lifting an eyebrow.

He opened one eye and peered up at me out of it. "*So* hot. *So* bothered."

"Okay, then. Show me."

"I was hoping you would say that." His calm demeanor a second ago was all an act. The second I green lit his evil plan, he sprang up and had hold of me, pulling me out of my seat toward him. I didn't have time to protest, or even spread my legs in order to sit myself on top of him properly. Sully had everything under control, though. His hands were strong, and my body seemed to melt to his will without any effort on his part. The next thing I knew, my hair was twisted into a knot around Sully's fist, my shirt was hiked up, my bra pulled down and Sully had my left nipple in his mouth. He massaged the swollen bundle of nerves with his tongue, flicking it, pinching it between his teeth, and the sensation was so big and so immediate that I could do nothing but struggle to regain my breath. It wasn't happening, though. My lungs were working at half capacity and couldn't catch up with my body's need for oxygen.

Sully pushed his hips up underneath me, grinding his pelvis against me, and I could feel his cock again, hard and insistent, rubbing up against my pussy through my jeans. "Goddamn it, Lang. Why the hell can't I keep my hands off you? I can't get enough. You're more addictive than any drug. I crave you twenty-four seven."

"Shit, Sully. Ahh!" I bucked against him when he bit me again, squeezing my nipple hard between his teeth. The sensation was electricity and fire all rolled into one. I couldn't take it, couldn't bear it another second longer, and yet the pain and pleasure swirling through me was all I wanted at the same time. I couldn't have told him to stop, even if I'd wanted to.

Sully's hands worked quickly, ripping my shirt off over my head. My bra went next, and then I was half naked and shivering, my skin exploding into goose bumps. Sully growled low in the back of his throat as he studied me for a second. "Fuck, Lang. Look at you. You're perfect. You're the most beautiful girl on this island."

"I'm one of the only women under the age of thirty-five on this island. That's not a very grand compliment, Sully Fletcher."

He laughed. "You're the most beautiful woman I've ever seen, then. How about that?"

"Now you're being ridiculous." My cheeks were warming, though, pride washing over me. Sully stopped smiling and propped himself up on one elbow, head angled back so he was looking up at me. His dark hair was brushed back out of his face, at least three or four days' worth of stubble marking his jaw, eyes dark and simmering with intensity. He told me so easily that he thought I was beautiful. Why was it so hard for me to tell him he was easily the hottest guy I'd ever had the pleasure of meeting, then? "I mean it, Lang," he whispered. Skimming his fingertips over the ends of my hair, brushing them lightly over the bare skin of my chest, he breathed out slowly, his eyes never leaving mine. He looked like he was staring straight inside me, as if he could see through the flesh and bone, straight into my soul. His words echoed that thought when he spoke again. "You're wildfire. You're stubborn, and you don't take any shit. You're *strong*. You won't be talked down to. You're a woman, and you're a warrior all at once. You're brave, and you're kind. And I've learned recently that being kind really does take courage sometimes." He paused, eyes narrowing as he watched me. "Fuck. I've been living in my lighthouse, casting a narrow beam out to sea for a long time, Lang. And then you swept into my life and lit up the dark. That's pretty fucking scary for me. I'm not used to the way you make me feel. I feel like I'm constantly on the back foot with you, one step behind the game."

My heart was in my throat. He was always so closed off, the first to crack a joke or a sharp-edged comeback to avoid being serious, but right now he couldn't have been any more serious. There was a calm resting over him that I'd never experienced before, and it made me want to fold myself into him, to wrap my arms around him and just lie there, our heartbeats syncing and beating together. Who *was* this man? He was so different to the cautious, aggressive, cold guy who'd nearly scared me half to death at the bottom of the stairs all those weeks ago. Here was a man who could love, who had so much love to give if only he just let himself.

"You promised me," I whispered.

"Promised you what?"

"That you wouldn't let me fall."

Sully blinked, remaining absolutely still. "You knew all too well that was going to happen the moment you started showing up on my doorstep with food in your hands, Lang. It was nice to pretend we were gonna be able to prevent it, but we both *knew*…"

"I thought you didn't like people who lied to themselves," I said, giving him a small smile.

"I'm not perfect. I break rules."

"I've noticed."

Sully smirked, taking my hand in his, placing it over his heart. "Let's not hide anymore. Let's just be honest. It's time."

"God, Sully, I just…the situation, it's…"

"Don't," he whispered. "Remember? No bullshit. Tell me. Say it."

"Say what?" It was too late for games now, though. We'd already come too far.

"*Ophelia*." He said my name softly, carefully, so that it carried weight. He said it like it mattered. It was a reprimand, and it was a caress. It was the first time he'd ever called me by my first name, and the way he shaped the word flooded my body with a warm vibration, a deep undercurrent, like a tuning fork that had been struck and would hum on and on forever unless someone closed their hand around it.

"I love you, Sully. I tried not to. I tried really hard. God knows I tried." I wanted to bury my face into his shirt, but he placed his fingers under my chin and lifted my face so that I couldn't.

"Open your eyes," he commanded.

I opened them, but it was so hard to look at him. Impossible, almost. He sighed heavily. "Don't you think," he said softly, "that I feel what you feel? I told you as much in that letter. Don't you think the bravado and the machismo are simply signs that I'm running scared? Because I am, y'know. I have been since the very first moment I saw you. I love you, too, Ophelia. God, loving you is the cruelest, most unkind thing I can do to you, and yet I'm going to do it anyway. Do you know what that means?"

I tried to look away again—I was buried under an avalanche of emotion, and I felt as though I would suffocate from it. Sully wouldn't let me hide from him, though. He ducked down, bending so our eyes were locked once more. "Loving you isn't me telling you something we both already know. It's waking up together every morning. It's making love, and arguing and fighting, and dealing with each other's shit. It's walking across hot coals for you. It's protecting you, and keeping you, and honoring you *always*. There's no half measure in this, okay? So you have to be fucking sure, because once we travel down this road together, there is no turning back. There is no good ol' college try. There's me, and there's you. *Forever.* This will change me, and it'll change you, too. It's a part of us already. Once we let it overtake us, there won't be any turning back. Is that what you want?"

"Is it what *you* want?" I asked in a small voice.

"Don't do that. Own your feelings. You don't need to know what *I* think before you can make up *your* mind."

"I know I don't. I'm just scared to say it."

Sully smiled—big, contagious, unfathomable—and my heart felt like it was going to burst. "You've already done the hard part, Lang. This next part is just the first step."

"Toward what?"

He gave me a chiding look. "You tell me. *Actually* tell me, Lang. Right now."

A cold shiver of panic ran up my spine, but I ignored it. I pushed down my fear, and I plucked up every last scrap of courage I owned. "The rest of our lives," I said firmly. "It's the first step toward the rest of our lives, because that's what I want. I want it all. With you. I can't imagine it any other way."

Sully moved quickly, sitting upright. He grabbed hold of me, his hands fisting my hair, running down my back, groping my ass through my jeans. His mouth found mine, and for a moment the world outside of the truck drifted away. There was no snow falling out of the window. There were no dark, ominous clouds blocking out the moonlight. There was no island, and there was no tomorrow. There was just this moment, *our* moment, and the breath we shared as we kissed.

He was a man possessed. I was a woman lost. Together, we were two halves of something fragile and delicate, beautiful in its complexity.

Sully bit at my lips and my tongue, growling. Placing one hand at the nape of my neck, he kissed me harder, grinding his hips up again; his hard-on was still raging, still made of solid steel. He rocked his hips back and forth, rubbing himself against me, igniting a desperate ache inside me. I needed him. I wanted him more than I'd ever wanted anybody, and I couldn't wait any longer.

I tore at his shirt, wrestling it over his head, and then my hands were frantically pulling at his belt buckle, trying to unfasten it. Sully took over; he made quick work of the belt, ripping it from his belt loops entirely and flinging it over his shoulder onto the back seat. I unbuttoned his pants and shimmied them down his body, trying not to gasp when I tugged his jeans down over his hips and his erection sprang free.

"Damn it," I murmured under my breath.

"What's wrong?" Sully panted.

"I want to ride you so hard, Sully. I need to feel you inside me right now. But I want you in my mouth, too. I want to make you come so hard. I want to taste you. I want to swallow you. But I want to feel you coming inside me as well."

Sully groaned, head falling back against the car seat. "God, I can't even take you talking to me like that. You're gonna kill me, girl."

I flicked the end of my tongue over the tip of his cock, shivering with pleasure. "Which would you prefer?" I asked. My voice was raspy and filled with desire. Sully reached his hand between our bodies, down, in between my legs, and yanked my jeans open. His teeth were bared, his eyes burning, on fire.

"Oh, we're doing both, Lang. We are doing both." He took a handful of my hair and pulled on it—gently enough that it didn't hurt, but hard enough that I knew where he wanted me. He thrust up into my mouth, lowering my head down on him at the same time, and his cock slid all the way to the back of my throat. At the same time, he began working the fingers of his other hand against my pussy, rubbing small circles against my clit through my panties.

"Shit, you're so wet," he panted. "You really want me, don't you? God, I can feel how badly you want me."

I could feel how badly he wanted me, too. He was getting harder and harder by the second. I worked my tongue over him, from the base of his cock to the very tip, and Sully bucked underneath me, his breath quickening until he was almost hyperventilating.

"Fuck, Lang. Oh god. Oh *shit*. I'm gonna come. Baby, I'm gonna—"

Light suddenly shone through the truck window, bouncing around the inside of the vehicle. Sully reacted so quickly, it took a second for me to figure out what was going on. He wasn't coming. He was pushing me off him and grabbing his t-shirt, trying to cover me up with it.

"Sully Fletcher, you dog, you." Someone was standing at the car window on the driver's side, peering in through the glass. They had a flashlight in their hand, and they were pointing it directly at us. "That you, Miss Lang? Good to see you again." I recognized the voice but couldn't place it. I was too busy scrambling, trying to get dressed. Sully was red in the face, yanking his jeans back up his body, swearing under his breath.

In the space of five seconds, we'd gone from on the brink of fucking to Sully kicking the truck door open and jumping out of the vehicle, his chest bare, roaring at the top of his lungs. "Hinchliffe, you motherfucker. What the hell is wrong with you?"

Hinchliffe? *Hinchliffe*. Oh, *no*. The cop that showed up after I reported Ronan's death? Lord have mercy. My own shirt was nowhere to be seen, so I grabbed Sully's and threw it on, quickly climbing out of the car after him. Hinchliffe was in uniform, flashlight still gripped in his hand. Sully had him by the throat, and was about to punch him square in the face.

"Sully! *Stop!*" I ran through the snow, grabbing hold of the arm he had raised and pulled back, ready to strike. The moment I touched him, Sully let go, snarling under his breath.

"What the fuck are you doing, man?" he hissed, shoving Hinchliffe. "You're spying on people making out in cars now?"

Hinchliffe spat on the floor, rubbing at his neck. "I'm a police officer, Sully. Fuck, man, sex in public is an offence. And so is assaulting a cop. I could write you up right now if I wanted."

"You're gonna arrest me?"

"Of course not."

"Then what's the point in writing me up? Fucking pathetic, dude."

"Whatever. You'd better get out of here before I call for backup."

Sully barked out laughter. "Backup? You mean *Caruthers*?"

"Let's just go, Sully." I threaded my fingers through his and squeezed. I knew we were safe from another explosion of rage when he squeezed back. Turning to me, he gave me a small smile, but I could tell he was still fizzing with anger.

His dark gaze remained fixed and locked on me. "All right," he said. "If that's what you want."

"It is."

Hinchliffe grumbled after us as we both got back in the car. Sully climbed into the driver seat, still simmering, and grabbed hold of the steering wheel, gripping it tight. "I'm sorry. Fuck. I shouldn't have lost it like that. I just—the thought of him seeing you naked..."

"I doubt he saw anything at all," I told him. "The windows were too steamed up."

Sully turned to me, face very serious, and his sober expression broke into amusement. His head rocked back, his eyes closed and he laughed. "Jesus, they were pretty fogged up, huh? Damn it. You've turned me into a teenager, Lang." He started the truck, gunning the engine so the tires spun, kicking up snow, and we burned out of there, leaving Hinchliffe on the side of the road.

When we got back to the lighthouse, I fully intended on picking up exactly where we'd left off before we'd been so rudely interrupted. My phone started ringing in my purse before I could even slip out of Sully's t-shirt, though. Once upon a time I might have ignored the call, but not now I was responsible for two children; I couldn't afford to pick and choose which calls I answered and which ones I didn't. I picked up without looking at the caller ID, keen to get the call over so Sully and I could focus on each other again. Sully ran his hands over my shoulders, down my back, kissing at my neck as I spoke into the cell phone.

"Hello?"

"Ophelia? Oh, thank goodness, honey. Where have you been? I've been trying to call you for hours."

It was Mom. Her voice was strained, frantic, and she was running her words together, speaking so fast I could hardly understand her. "I'm sorry, I didn't hear my phone. What is it? What's wrong? Mom? Are you there?"

A choked sob crackled down the line. "Oh, honey. It's your father. I'm sorry, sweetheart, but he's dead."

CHAPTER TWENTY-FOUR

CONSEQUENCES

Heart attack.

He'd gotten up early in the morning and gone down to the pier with his fishing gear. Mom had kissed him on the cheek and told him to be back by midday, which he hadn't done. She'd stewed for most of the afternoon, ready to chew him out when he got home for not coming to help with lunch service at the restaurant, and then by four she'd begun to get worried. He wasn't answering his phone. She'd walked down to the pier, but he was nowhere to be seen.

That's when she'd called the police, and they'd told her what had happened. He'd grabbed at his chest and toppled over the railings into the water at nine in the morning. Two other men had jumped in after him, trying to save him, but he'd disappeared into the water and was nowhere to be found.

At two in the afternoon, his body had washed up onto the shore five hundred feet down the beach, out toward El Segundo. Three skaters found his body first, but they didn't call for help. They went through his pockets, looking for anything of value. A woman walking her dogs on the strand had chased them off and called for the police. Dad's wallet, his wedding ring and the Saint Christopher he always wore around his neck were gone, so the police had no means of identifying him until Mom called the station to report him missing.

"God, I am so sorry, O. Is there anything I can do to help?" Rose was fussing around me in the kitchen, offering to make tea, coffee, sandwiches, anything to try and make me feel better. There was nothing to be done though. I wasn't going to be feeling better any time soon.

"Thanks, Rose. Really, it's okay. I just need to get back home as quickly as I can. Can you watch the children? I don't know how long I'll be gone for." Taking them with me was out of the question. And the thought of leaving Mom when she needed me most was difficult to comprehend, too. Rose rubbed my shoulder reassuringly.

"You don't even need to ask. They'll be just fine here with me. I'm owed about three years' worth of vacation time anyway. You take as long as you need."

It was dawn. The sun was rising up over the lip of the ocean, and I was waiting on the dock for Jerry, the boatman, to arrive when Sully's truck came speeding up over the hill toward the parking lot. He'd driven me back to The Big House last night and kissed me long and hard, telling me to call him in the morning when I knew what was happening. He parked the truck and locked it up, then came running down the boat launch, a bag slung over his shoulder and a grim look on his face.

"You didn't call. You were just going to leave?"

Guilt rocked me. I couldn't stand the hurt look on his face. "I'm sorry, Sully. But what was I supposed to do? I can't just ask you to drop everything and get on a plane with me across the other side of the country."

He shook his head, frowning. "You *are* everything, silly girl. I'm not letting you go through this alone."

I burst into tears. It was the only response I could manage. For the past twelve hours I'd been trying to keep it together, telling myself I could be strong for Mom, that I'd be able to make my way back to California without breaking down in the airport or on the plane, but I wouldn't have been able to. I needed him. I needed Sully so badly, but I'd been too afraid to ask. Now that he was here, scolding me for not leaning on him, the relief I felt was just too much.

He crushed me to him, running his hand over my hair, whispering softly to me, soothing me while I cried. I buried my face into his dark sweater, sobbing, taking comfort in his warmth and the rich smell of him. "Shh, Lang. Don't worry. I'm here. I'm gonna take care of you, baby."

Hearing him say those words was enough. I could get through the next twenty-four hours if he was by my side. And I could get through the following twenty-four hours after that. The days and the months that came next were a mystery, but I got the feeling I'd be okay if Sully was around to strengthen and support me.

Jerry arrived at just after seven. Sully booked an extra plane ticket on his phone as we crossed back to the mainland, and by the time we reached the airport everything was in order. The plane back to L.A. was practically empty, and Sully and I had three seats to ourselves. I lay out with my head in his lap, his hand softly brushing my hair over and over for most of the flight, and I tried to sleep. I couldn't manage it, though.

LAX was just a short car ride from Manhattan Beach and the place where I'd grown up. Where my dad had taught me to drive. To fish. To cook. To become a responsible adult in the world. How could he be gone? How could he be *dead*? My heart was aching so fiercely as we disembarked from the plane that it felt like it would never be whole again.

Sully took my single bag from me and carried it down the concourse, holding me to him tightly. "It's going to be okay, Lang," he said into my hair. "I promise. It may not feel like it right now, but everything is going to be okay."

"Captain Fletcher? Captain Sully Fletcher?"

To our right, a group of men were fast approaching, dressed in full military gear. I was so surprised they knew Sully's name that it took me a long moment to process what happened next. Sully stiffened next to me, coming to a stop as the five men cut us off.

"Yes. I'm Sully Fletcher. Not a captain anymore, though. I've been out of the military for a long time now."

The soldier at the front of the group stepped forward. There was a hard, cold look in his eye that made me instantly nervous, though I couldn't tell why. "You're going to have to come with us, sir," he snapped.

"What for?" Sully's face was devoid of all emotion. He seemed suddenly as though he was made out of stone.

"You're under arrest," the soldier said. "For impersonating a commissioned officer in the U.S. Army." The men gathered around Sully, pulling at him, taking both his bag as well as mine from him, turning him around so they could handcuff him.

"*What*? What the hell is going on, Sully? Tell them! Tell them they've made a mistake!"

Sully didn't say a word, though. He looked stunned, but at the same time there was an air of resignation to him that scared me half to death. "Sully? Sully, tell me what's going on." The soldiers took him by the arms on both sides and began to march him off down the concourse without giving me a second thought.

"Hey! Hey, tell me what the hell is going on!" I grabbed the closest soldier, trying to get him to stop, to explain this madness to me, but he ripped his arm away. Spinning around, he drew himself up to his full height and barked at me.

"Ma'am, I strongly advise you not to touch me again, or there will be *severe* consequences."

"Don't you fucking touch her, asshole," Sully snarled. It was the first time he'd said anything since they'd told him he was under arrest; he went from stony compliance to extreme anger in a flash, struggling to free himself from the soldiers. He twisted, trying to wrestle himself loose, but the men had hold of him tight and it didn't look like they were planning on letting him go. "Get your fucking hands off me, motherfucker!"

"*Sully!*" I tried to get past the huge, towering man in front of me, blocking my path, but he was a wall of muscle, and I had no hope.

"Ma'am? *Ma'am*. Stop. Captain Fletcher is required to come with us.

If you don't calm down, we'll be forced to call for local law enforcement to come and detain you until we are off the property."

"Good. Call the police. You can't just take him like this. He has the right to due process, just like anyone else."

"He does *not*, ma'am. He's still governed by the United States Army, regardless of whether or not he's on active duty. Fletcher's committed a crime. He's under investigation. That's all there is to it."

"But he has the right to a lawyer. He has the right to know why he's being—"

"*Ophelia*." Sully had stopped struggling and was looking at me. "Please. It's okay. Just go and be with your mom, okay? I'll come find you as soon as I can, I swear."

And so that was it. They led Sully away, and he was gone.

CHAPTER TWENTY-FIVE

AFGHANISTAN
2009

Sully

"We can't do this, Sully. There's no way we can pull it off. We're mad to have even considered it."

I straightened Ronan's tie and cuffed him on the shoulder, trying not to let my nerves show. What we were planning on doing was madness indeed, but there was nothing else for it. Ronan couldn't take another day here in-country, let alone another month. Or three. Or five. Or twelve.

Whitlock hadn't called me into his office to tell me my deployment was being extended. In a strange twist of fate, he had called me into his office to thank me for my fine service, and to tell me I was going home. Not only was my deployment over, but my contract with the army, too. I was out. I was done. I was finished. Unless I wanted to re-enlist, of course. I'd stared at Whitlock at first, too stunned to speak or even blink. But then the cogs had started turning.

"*No, sir. I think I've had my fill of Afghanistan. For this lifetime, anyway,*" I'd told him. "*It's high time I went back to New York. I've made my girlfriend wait six years for me already. I should probably marry her before she grows bored and gets hitched to some barista or something.*"

Whitlock had laughed, but I could see it in his eyes—he thought I was less of a man for leaving. "*Well that's settled then. Lucky for me I get to keep hold of at least one of the Fletcher boys for a little longer.*"

As soon as I'd left Whitlock's office, I'd gone to find Ronan, to explain my plan, and that had been it. Ronan had argued at first, told me I couldn't make such a ridiculous sacrifice for him, that I was mad, but in the end he'd given up. He couldn't stay. I could. That was all there was to it.

"If we get caught..." Ronan fidgeted, rubbing his hands over his face.

"We're not going to get caught, asshole. We've been screwing with people our entire lives and no one's ever been able to tell the difference between us. Why would they now? I know your men. We've gone through every single aspect of your past missions. I'm not going to trip up and make a mistake here. It's going to be fine."

"And what am I going to do when I get back to the States? I'm just gonna move in with your girlfriend and pretend to the world like I'm happy and in love? Magda's going to *hate* me for this. Living with her, pretending to be you? That's not just going to affect me. It's going to affect her, too."

He was right on that count. Magda and Ronan had never been all that close. Ronan had constantly told me she wasn't right for me, while on the other hand Mags had always said Ronan was a liar and couldn't be trusted. Now, we were *all* going to be liars. I'd explained to Magda what was going to happen as best I could without directly saying the words, and after a while she'd managed to decipher what I was talking about. She'd been mad. Boy, had she been mad. But she'd agreed to play along for my sake.

"Just make sure she's not too worried," I said, handing Ronan his military bag. The one with *CPTN. S. FLETCHER* stenciled onto its side. "And remind her she can't talk about this to anyone. Not her parents. Not Rose. She can't even write about it in that diary of hers, okay? Hey? Are you listening to me?" I took Ronan's face in my hands, forcing him to meet my eye. "This is so fucking important, man. Tell me you can handle this."

"Running home, hiding from my responsibilities? Oh sure. I can handle that just fine," he said bitterly. "I can't believe you're doing this for me. I'm never going to be able to forgive myself for this."

I shook my head, sighing. "There's nothing to forgive. You'd do this for me if I needed it. I have your back. I always will. Now go, before you miss your damn flight out of this hellhole. And make sure you give my girl a kiss for me, brother."

Behind me, a private I didn't know hurried through the tent flap, saluting us both, eyes frantically flickering between the two of us before landing on me.

"Captain Fletcher, sir. You're needed in Colonel Whitlock's office immediately. He needs you out on night patrol with B company." The private hadn't batted an eyelid. He'd found the letter R on my breast pocket—*Cptn. R. Fletcher*—and he'd believed I was Ronan. I smiled at my brother, and then slapped him on the shoulder: *see?*

"Goodbye, Sully," I said, hugging him hard one last time. It was weird calling him by my name, but it was a good show in front of the private. "Catch you on the flipside, huh?"

Ronan nodded, giving me a tight smile. "Sure thing, brother. *Thank you.*"

••••

Three months passed. Six, and then eight. Whitlock used me for night patrols nearly every single shift, which was fine by me. The city lit up with gunfire after the sun went down. We played cat and mouse through burned-out buildings, hunting down insurgents, disarming bombs, providing backup to Seal teams and support to the marines, and through it all I was confident in the knowledge that Ronan was safe back in the States.

I spoke to him every few days at first, and then once a week. As our communication trailed off, I told myself it was because he felt guilty. We didn't talk about the missions I was going out on, or the danger I faced every day. But I knew it was hard for him—seeing the uniform made him visibly pale and uncomfortable. When Magda started answering her phone less, I figured...I don't know *what* I figured. We went from talking every day, her missing me, her loving me, her crying every time I said goodbye, to her screening my calls and rarely picking up at all.

I knew what was coming deep down in my bones, but I wasn't prepared for it. Exactly nine months after I'd assumed Ronan's identity and sent him back to the States to pretend to be me until my return, I got the call that changed everything. Not a call from Magda or from Ronan, but a call from both of them. I knew the moment I saw them on the laptop screen, sitting at the table together, chairs pushed too close, hands hidden under the table, that they were about to tell me something I didn't want to hear.

"We didn't mean for it to happen," Magda said, tears welling in her eyes. "But living together, spending so much time together, pretending all the time... It was inevitable, Sully. We couldn't help it."

Ronan looked like his shame was eating him alive. "I don't know what to say," he whispered. "You gave me everything, and I took even more. It's unforgiveable."

I stared at the screen, trying to figure out if it was all a huge joke. God, it had to be, right? How could it possibly be true? And then Magda drove the final nail into the coffin. "I'm pregnant, Sully. I'm so, so sorry. We're having a baby."

Baby?

The word rattled around inside my brain, setting off explosions that clean took my breath away.

"I still love you," she whispered. "I love *both* of you. How can I not?"

"So, what?" I choked on my laughter. "I get done out here in a couple of months, come back to New York and then we all live together? One big, happy family? Ronan gets you Monday through Wednesday, I get you Thursday through Saturday, and we take alternating Sundays? *Jesus fucking Christ, Magda.*"

She cried, unbearable, gut-wrenching sobs, hands covering her face, and it was Ronan to put his arm around her and comfort her, not me.

"How long?" I demanded. "How far along are you?"

They were both silent for a moment, and then Ronan gave me an answer that made me want to throw up: "Sixteen weeks."

"Four months? *Four fucking months?*"

"I know, brother. I'm so, so sorry. I know there's nothing I can say to make this right, but—"

"Don't call me that. Don't call me brother. We're done here, Ronan. You're right. This *is* unforgiveable." I slammed the laptop shut, cutting off the connection. It wasn't enough, though. I picked it up and threw it, sending it hurtling across the tent.

It was over. It was all over. The world as I knew it was gone. Magda was having Ronan's baby, and I was still stuck in Afghanistan, pretending to be him. I rushed out of the tent and ran across the base, my head thumping, my heart galloping in my chest. It didn't take me long to find the colonel. He was bending over some intel reports in the comms room, squinting through the wire framed glasses he'd taken to wearing. When he saw me, he drew himself up to his full height and cleared his throat.

"What can I do for you, Captain? Where's the fire?"

"I want to extend again, Colonel."

His frosty expression thawed a little. "That's not possible, Fletcher. Much as I'd like to keep you on out here, you've been in-country too long. The higher-ups will demand you go back to active duty in the States for at least six months before we can have you—"

"With all due respect, Colonel Whitlock, do you think I am unfit for duty?"

"No. I don't think so."

"Do you think I'm mentally competent?"

"Normally, I'd say so, but right now you're looking a little crazed, Ronan. Might I ask what's brought this on?"

"Just the need to serve my country, sir. The need to protect those I love and keep them safe." This was the perfect spiel to reel out to Whitlock. Blind patriotism got him in the feels every single time. He scratched his nose, looking at me, and then gave a perfunctory nod.

"All right, then. I'll have the paperwork drawn up for you to sign in the morning. I'll write a personal letter of recommendation requesting that your application for another extension is granted, but I can't guarantee it'll be accepted."

"Thank you, sir."

"No, thank *you*, Fletcher. Good men are hard to come by out here." He paused for a second, glancing back down at his intel papers. "You know, out of the two of you, I was always sure your brother would be the one to build an exemplary military career for himself, Ronan. Don't get me wrong. You were always an excellent soldier. You'd never have made it to captain otherwise. But when Sully left, you really began to shine. I suppose sometimes a man needs to step out of his brother's shadow in order to show his true colors, hmm?"

Five months later, I was on my back in a desert just outside of Kabul. My body was burned, my lungs raw from smoke inhalation, and Colonel Whitlock was calling me a crazy bastard, ordering men to get me onto a chopper before I bled out and died.

On the other side of the world, Magda was giving birth to my nephew. His name was Connor. On his birth certificate, under the section titled "father," a nurse in bright pink scrubs, exhausted from a fourteen hour shift, wrote the name *Sully James Fletcher* in neat blue ink.

CHAPTER TWENTY-SIX

TRIGGER

The funeral was gray and grim. The sun never seemed to stop shining in California, but somehow the world was a dark, black place, and the cheerful weather couldn't do anything to change that.

Mom hadn't stopped crying. I hadn't stopped either. It was all too much. Dad was gone. Sully had been dragged off by the military police, and no matter how many times I'd called to find out what was happening with him, no one would tell me anything. Eventually I found out that he was being held at Camp Haan Army base in Riverside, and that he was awaiting a hearing. I still couldn't believe any of it.

Impersonating a commissioned officer. That's what the soldier had said when they arrested Sully at the airport. There was no way he had impersonated a commissioned officer. No fucking way.

We held Dad's wake at the restaurant. Half of the neighborhood turned up to bid my father farewell. We drank, we ate, and we told stories. The afternoon was bittersweet—a true homage to a wonderful, kind and generous man who had touched so many people's lives. My aunt, Simone, organized absolutely everything. She was a godsend. She greeted everyone at the church. She coordinated everyone, making sure they knew where and when to show up for the wake. She arranged the flowers. She made sure everyone was comfortable and had enough to eat and drink. She corralled people away from Mom and me whenever it looked like we were on the brink of total breakdown (which was often). Without her we would have been lost.

As the day was winding down, I busied myself collecting plates and glasses from the restaurant, trying to keep my head—it was lovely that so many people had come to show us their love and support, but I really couldn't take another person telling me how sorry they were for my loss. I was carrying a stack of plates through the back into the kitchen when I saw a tall, bird-like figure dressed in black, stood apart to one side.

Robert Linneman.

He gave me a small, sad wave when he saw me. What on earth was he doing here? I put down the load I was carrying and made my way over to him. "Mr. Linneman? You came here for my father's funeral?" Even as I was saying it, I knew it made no sense.

Linneman shook his head slowly. "No, Miss Lang, though I was terribly sorry to hear of your loss. I also have to apologize for showing up here like this, but I came on Mr. Fletcher's request."

"Sully? You've seen him?"

"Yes. I've represented both Sully and Ronan for a very long time now. I represented their father before them, too. Anyway, I was called and informed of Sully's situation. I've been out here trying to resolve the matter for a couple of days now. Sully asked me to bring this letter to you. Against my advice, I might add." He held out a small envelope, which looked like it had once been sealed and then ripped open again.

Linneman sighed when he saw me brush my fingers against the torn edge of the envelope. "Yes, unfortunately the military police did read it before I could take it off the base. I'm afraid the contents of Sully's letter probably haven't done his case any good."

I took out the letter and began to read. It explained everything. As I read, eyes scanning quickly over the pages Sully had written to me, things began to make a lot more sense. At the same time, they were far more confusing, too.

"So...*Sully* was the one who pulled those men out of the wreckage, not Ronan?"

Linneman nodded.

"I don't understand. How did Magda and Ronan explain why they got married, and not Magda and Sully? When did they switch back their identities?" My head was hurting, to the point where every single last scrap of this new information I was being given simply wouldn't make sense.

"Ronan found out when Sully finally came home from deployment. He came back to the island and found him. They agreed then to become themselves again. It was time for them to be who they were meant to be. I oversaw the meeting between them. Ronan was worried that Sully might not exactly be pleased to see him."

"So you *knew* about this? All these years?"

"I did."

"And you didn't think to mention anything about it when Ronan died? You didn't think to explain why it would be so damned hard to get Sully to take Connor and Amie?"

Linneman smoothed down his suit, politely declining a tray of hors d'oeuvres from Aunt Simone. "It wasn't my place. I can only legally discuss the matter with you now because Sully has asked me to."

God, what a mess. It was *all* such a mess. In times like these I would normally have turned to my father for guidance, but that wasn't possible anymore. "How much trouble is he in?" I asked.

"A considerable amount," Linneman said. "It seems he triggered some sort of red flag when his ID was entered into the airline's systems back in Maine. The army has been trying to hunt him down for some time. It seems a number of sensitive files were leaked during the time that Sully was deployed under Colonel Whitlock. A specialist named Crowe was arrested for selling military secrets to outside parties. He'd somehow figured out Sully was pretending to be Ronan back then, and he told the police *Sully* was the one selling the information. That he had taken a number of files when he left the army, and since Crowe didn't have any files on him when he was arrested, it looked like Sully was at least complicit in hiding evidence if not directly involved in the crimes that were committed."

"Espionage? I've never heard anything so stupid in my whole life."

"I know. Sully insists he doesn't have any secret files, but the military aren't likely to believe him since he lied about who he was for so long. Basically, it's not looking good, Miss Lang. It's not looking good at all."

"Haven't they searched his place back on the island?"

"They've torn the place apart. Not a thing was found, but now they're saying he could easily have hidden the files somewhere else. Buried them. Secured them in a safe place. Given them to someone else, perhaps."

This was outrageous. There was just no way Sully would be involved with selling top secret military information to anyone. No way whatsoever. And no way he was involved with this Crowe guy, either. The name was familiar to me, Sully had mentioned him once or twice, but if they were aligned with each other in any illegal activities, surely he wouldn't have mentioned him at all?

Then...

My blood ran cold as I remembered something. Sully, sick with a fever after the Sea King went down, tossing and turning on his couch, yelling out a name. Yelling at a man to help him. He had been yelling at Crowe. When I'd asked him about Crowe later, I recalled the sour look on Sully's face as he'd said he wasn't a friend.

There was another time, too. Another time Sully had mentioned Crowe. I wracked my brain, trying to bring the memory to the surface of my mind, scouring every single moment Sully and I had spent together, trying to scan through conversations and interactions until I came across it.

"Miss Lang? Ophelia, are you quite all right?" Linneman touched my shoulder, a deep frown of concern on his face, but I held up one hand, burying myself deeper in my thoughts.

When? When had it been? God, I had to remember. I *had* to. And then, just as I was about to give up, it came to me in a sudden rush, a revelation that made my head spin. "Shit," I hissed.

"What is it, Ophelia?"

"I know what the files are," I told him, shaking my head. "I know exactly what they are, and I know where to find them, too."

Linneman looked alarmed. "If they can help clear Sully's name, then we need to get them to the police immediately," he said.

"I know. You should call them and tell them they need to go back to the island. The files are a set of USB drives. They're in my underwear drawer. And...well." I cleared my throat. *"They're full of porn."*

••••

The USB drives Sully gave me for Christmas were actually full of tactical operations intel and Taliban profiles. Each and every one of the files was apparently corrupt and the drives had been overwritten with porn, but the information was still there, lurking beneath the surface, waiting for someone to come and find it. Crowe's digital military ID was stamped on the files, showing the times and dates when he had downloaded them from the army's protected servers. Sully's digital military ID was nowhere to be found. A week after the drives were handed over to the military police, Sully was unexpectedly released from Camp Haan. Linneman called me to relay the good news.

"I think you should be the one to go get him," he told me. "He's been pretty wild over the fact that they haven't let him call you. I'm sure he'd appreciate a pick up from his girl over a dusty old man like me."

I drove out to Camp Haan in Mom's 4Runner, the whole way dreading having to face another arrogant man dressed in uniform, but when I got there, a tall, handsome guy dressed in civvies greeted me instead. He came to get me at the gate and walked me inside the building, introducing himself as Sam. He was pretty young, still in his mid twenties, but he walked with an air of importance, and when we passed other soldiers in the hallways of the administration building Sam took me through, they all stopped and saluted him without exception.

He led me to a small, windowless room and gestured for me to sit down at a low table—the only item of furniture inside the room. "Sully will be with you in a second, Miss Lang. If you'd please wait here, I'll be back in a moment too with Sully's release papers." He left, and I sat down at the desk as he'd instructed, trying not to bite my fingernails.

Five minutes later, Sully was escorted into the room by two armed guards. He was dressed in military uniform, and he looked like he hadn't slept in days. There were dark circles under his eyes, but his back was ramrod straight, his chin held high and proud. When he saw me, he rushed into the room and threw his arms around me, sweeping me up off the floor.

"Damn it, Lang," he said through gritted teeth. "I thought you wouldn't come." He rained kissed down onto my face. Putting me down, he cupped my face in his hands, scanning me from head to toe, as if storing every last minute detail of me to memory in case he never saw me again.

"Of course I came," I whispered. "You didn't do anything wrong."

"The U.S. Army doesn't see it that way," he said. "I still fucked up pretty bad. I should never have done what I did."

I leaned my forehead against his chest, closing my eyes, breathing a sigh of relief. "You loved your brother. That's all. And whatever you may have done, it seems like you're in the clear. They told Linneman you were going to be released."

Sully frowned. "They did?"

"Yeah. The officer who came and got me at the gate said he was getting your release paperwork."

At that moment, the door opened again and Sam appeared, hurrying into the room. He gave us both a brief smile, and then held out his hand to Sully. "Second Lieutenant Coleridge. I don't believe we've met."

Sully shook Sam's hand, head tilted ever so slightly to one side. He looked perplexed. "Coleridge?" he repeated.

"That's right, sir. Sam Coleridge. Your brother pulled me out of that burning wreck outside of Kabul. I was only nineteen at the time."

Sully rocked back on his heels, recognition dawning on his face.

"That's right. *Kabul.*"

"We're almost done here, sir. If you'd just sign here, where we've indicated with the red crosses, then we can get you on your way." Sam handed Sully the paperwork in his other hand, smiling wider.

"I don't understand. Ronan wasn't—"

"Don't worry, sir. It's all been taken care of. I personally testified that you weren't the one to pull me out of that wreck. It was definitely Ronan Fletcher, as records of that night confirmed."

"But what about the letter I wrote? I confessed that—"

Sam shook his head. "I'm sorry, sir. I don't know of any letter being held in evidence relating to this matter. As far as we're concerned, Ronan Fletcher served a total of five tours in Afghanistan, saving the lives of well over thirty-eight men during the period of his service. The USB drives that were found in his house were taken by him, under the proviso that they were something else entirely. We believe he had zero knowledge of their hidden contents."

Sully closed his hand around the pen Sam was offering him. "Ah. I see."

"Yes, sir. Luckily for you, this matter was resolved. You'd have been sent to Gitmo for sure, otherwise. Probably wouldn't have stepped foot in the States again." The tone in Sam's voice made things very clear—he knew Sully was the man who saved him. He knew perfectly well that Sully had broken the law, but he was feigning ignorance in order to save *him* now.

"Then I ought to be thanking you," Sully said slowly. He signed the paperwork and handed it back to Sam while I watched on in amazement. Sam took the paperwork and reached into his pocket.

"I always wished I'd seen Ronan again," he said. There was an odd, obvious twist to his voice that made me want to cry. "I've wanted to thank him for a very long time for what he did for me. That wreck was catastrophic. I was badly injured. *Beyond* badly injured. It took me eighteen months to regain full use of my body. It was a long, hard, painful road, but I was grateful that I was alive to take each agonizing step of it. Ronan risked his own life to save me and the two other guys he dragged out of that truck that night. I'll never forget it. Neither will my wife, or my two kids." He opened up his wallet and held it out for Sully to see—inside was a photograph of a beautiful blonde woman, holding onto two tiny little boys who were unmistakably Sam's. "They want to convey their thanks to the man that saved my life just as much as I do, Captain Fletcher. It's a debt that can *never* be repaid."

Sully stood motionless, looking down at the picture. He nodded very slowly, his hands now curled into fists as his sides. "I'm sure my brother would be honored that you'd built such a beautiful life for yourself, Sergeant Coleridge. And he'd want to tell you that saving your life was one of the only things he was proud of accomplishing in *his* life, too."

Sam's eyes shone brightly, filled with tears. "Well. Hoo-rah for second chances, huh, Captain?" he said, his voice choked with emotion. "For me, *and* for you, I think."

EPILOGUE

Dr. Fielding was way taller than I'd assumed in person. His office smelled like worn leather, but not in a manly way. In the kind of way it might smell of worn leather if he'd gone to an interior design store and bought a candle called "Worn Leather" that he burned on a shelf, while he mentally assessed troubled children and their equally troubled parents.

Connor sat on the very edge of his seat, pressing two Legos together and pulling them apart again over and over. Amie was happily entertaining herself on the floor on the other side of the room with another little girl, who seemed perplexed by Amie's disinterest in her Barbie collection.

Fielding, at least six foot four, refused to sit down and was standing by a bookcase, running his fingers absently over the spines of the books displayed there: *Dr. Seuss* mixed in with *From Childhood to Adolescence* and *The Cambridge Anthology of Child Psychiatry*. "So, Connor. Tell me. Are you happy to be back in the city now?" he asked.

Connor stopped pressing the Legos together and pulling them apart. "Yes. I like it here a lot."

"And do you like your new place? Were you sad you weren't moving back into your old apartment? The one you lived in with your mom and dad?"

Connor put down the Legos and raised his head, looking Fielding right in the eye. "No, I'm not sad. I like the new apartment. You can see the park from my bedroom window. And the river, too."

A lot happened after Sully and I left Camp Haan. The restaurant was safe, and Mom was determined to be independent. I'd been worried about telling her I was going to move permanently to New York, but when I'd plucked up the courage and blurted it out, she'd been absolutely thrilled for me. Aunt Simone was moving into a house a couple of doors down the street, and she was going to run the restaurant with Mom. With the extra money left over from the payout Linneman put into my bank account, there was enough cash to rebrand the place and really give it a fresh start. Umberto's was now "George's Place," and I couldn't have been happier.

When I'd gotten off the plane at JFK, Sully was by my side, smiling softly. To me, he hadn't looked anything like his brother in that moment. He was purely Sully—a new man. Tall, dark, devastatingly handsome, and all mine. He'd picked me up and taken me into his arms, holding onto me like he was afraid I was some kind of mirage and I was going to disappear any second, and he'd kissed me hard. The world had stopped. There was no airport. There were no announcers over the tannoy. There were no crowds of people waiting for their loved ones, or hurrying to make their flights. There was only me and him, and our future lying out before us, and it was the most perfect moment.

"Are you ready to go home?" he'd asked.

"God, yes. *So* ready."

And so we'd gotten in a cab, and we'd driven through the traffic and the confusion of New York until we'd reached our new apartment building in Lower Manhattan. After he'd bundled me into the elevator, he proceeded to pinch and roll my nipples beneath my sweater and kiss my neck until I had to slap him and make him stop.

Our apartment was pure perfection: high ceilings, and beautiful architraving. Parquet flooring, and south-facing sunshine all afternoon long. We only had two bedrooms, but that was enough for us. More than enough. Unexpectedly, Rose had moved with us. She'd signed onto a night course at Colombia, and was finishing her bachelor's in

English literature, which meant during the day she got the children up and ran them both to school. Later on, I collected them and brought them back to our building, but instead of taking them to the apartment I shared with Sully, I took them up one extra floor to the much larger, more spacious place the Fletcher Corporation had bought for Connor and Amie: four bedrooms, and a view to die for.

Everyone was happy. Everyone loved the arrangement. We still felt like a family, all living together, sharing the responsibilities and day-to-day pleasures of growing together, but Sully and I got our privacy when we needed it, and so did Rose.

"Do you miss being on the island?" Fielding asked, taking down a book from the shelf.

"I do sometimes," Connor said, which surprised me. He'd been perfectly happy to return to New York—it was all he'd ever known before Ronan had uprooted him and transplanted him to the tiny island off the coast of Maine. "Sometimes I miss the sound of the ocean," he continued. "And the quiet, too. It can be pretty loud here."

Fielding smiled. "It can, can't it? I think you'll get used to it again, though. Then it will feel like you never left in the first place."

"Mmm. I suppose so."

"And what about spending time with Ophelia? And Sully, and Rose? Do you like spending time with all of them at home?"

"Yes. I really like it. I really like them all. Amie does, too." He spoke quickly, as if he were a little panicked. Child Protection Services had conducted a very thorough, terrifying interview with all of us when we explained what we were planning, and ever since then Connor had been worried he and Amie were going to have to go away. As the days passed, he was more and more confident, showing more personality and more attitude than ever before. Still, he knew Fielding had the power to drag CPS back into our lives, and he really didn't want that.

Fielding nodded, smiling in a comforting way that seemed to settle Connor. "That's really wonderful news. I'm so pleased to hear it. Is there anything you'd like to talk to me about today? Are you worried about anything? Is there something maybe you'd like to talk to me about alone?" Fielding shot me a perfunctory glance as he said this, barely acknowledging me, and I wanted to junk punch the man. I got it, though. I understood. Connor's safety was his main priority. If Connor needed to talk with Fielding alone, then of course he could. The implication that I, or Sully, or Rose might have done something wrong was rather grating, though.

Connor declined his offer. "No, thanks. Tomorrow we're going to the Natural History Museum to show Amie the dinosaur skeletons. Real ones! And then we're going to get pancakes for lunch. It's Amie's birthday."

"That sounds like it's going to be a very special day, Connor. I hope you enjoy it."

Later, with Connor holding one hand and Amie holding the other, I managed to flag down a cab and get us across to Tribeca, to Sully's warehouse. He'd set up shop making unique, handcrafted items of furniture for New York's elite. He could easily have retired on the money Ronan had set aside for him in order for him to take care of the children, but he refused to touch a cent of it. It was all for them, he said. He'd made his way in the world just fine despite his brother, and he didn't plan on that changing any time soon.

We found Sully covered in sawdust and smelling like fresh cut pine at the back of his studio. Connor and Amie both whooped and hollered, racing to him and throwing their arms around his body. He held up his arms, looking down on the two little people clinging onto him, and he laughed.

"Wow. Anyone would think you were happy to see me," he said, grinning.

"We are, we are!" Amie told him, giggling. "It's time to go home for dinner!"

"I see." Sully looked up at me, and his smile transformed into something softer. His face was filled with light, where there was once such darkness and anger. It was as though he was a different man entirely. He was still as playfully arrogant as ever, and his comebacks were just as sharp and caustic as they had been when I'd first met him.

But now there was a quiet calm to him that had made me fall even more impossibly in love with him.

We traveled home, Sully in the front seat with the cab driver and me in the back with the children. The entire six miles from the warehouse back to the apartment, Sully had his hand wedged behind him through the gap between his seat and the door, gently stroking my leg, his fingers curled around my ankle, touching me in one way or another.

We ate dinner with Rose and the children, and then stayed to bathe the kids and put them to bed.

"Will you tell us a story, Uncle Sully?" Amie pleaded. "A story about when you and Daddy were little, like me and Connor?" Sully looked uncomfortable for a second, and then he sat down on the end of Amie's bed, folding his arms across his chest.

"All right. But your dad and I used to get into all sorts of trouble together, so you have to promise you won't follow our lead, okay?"

Both Amie and Connor nodded solemnly.

"Right. Well. There was this one time, when Ronan and I were maybe a little bit older than you are now, maybe ten years old, and he and I did something very bad. We burned down the McInnes feed store…"

I backed out of the room, cringing. Trust Sully to tell them something completely inappropriate like that. He'd taken to the children so well, though. He loved being their uncle. Would he have ever gotten to know them if Ronan and Magda were still alive? It was doubtful. Most likely, they would have grown into adulthood and never met him once. Now, despite the fact that their parents were both gone, Connor and Amie had a loving uncle and a loving aunt taking care of them, as well as me. I may not have had a familial title for them to call me, but the way they said my name—with love and buckets of affection—was enough.

An hour later, Sully came down into our apartment, red cheeked and looking very sheepish. "Rose says she needs to vet my bedtime stories from here on out," he told me, huffing as he sank himself down onto the sofa beside me.

"I'm not surprised."

Sully stuck his tongue out at me, reaching up to stroke his index finger down my temple, cheek and underneath my chin. "You look very beautiful right now, Miss Ophelia Lang from California. Did you know that?"

I bit back a smile. It would be no good if he knew how happy his compliments made me; he'd tease me over them without mercy. "Sure I do," I said airily. "You don't look so bad yourself, I suppose."

Sully laughed, rolling his eyes. "Come on. We both know I'm the most attractive man on the planet. Heavy lies the crown and all that." He was joking, but he was also telling the truth—he really was the hottest guy on the planet to me. I leaned over him and planted a kiss square between his eyebrows, and Sully moaned softly under his breath.

"A letter came for you," I whispered to him, face still hovering only an inch above his. "It's from The Causeway."

"Probably from Medical Center Gale, wondering when I'm leaving you and going back to her," he told me, winking. He got up and collected his mail from the table, then opened it, scanning the letter he unfolded in his hands. There were two pieces of paper in the envelope. Sully read one and then the other in silence, then he just stood there staring at them both.

"What is it, Sully?"

He didn't move.

"Sully?"

He folded the papers together and walked slowly back to the sofa, where he handed me both pieces of paper. "A voice from the grave," he said quietly.

The first letter was from Linneman. It was brief and to the point:

Dear Sully,

Before your brother died, he came to see me and he made

significant changes to his last will and testament. As you know, he provided a significant sum of money to you, along with your childhood home to do with as you pleased. He also made sure the children were financially secure for the rest of their lives, thanks to their majority share holding in the Fletcher Corporation. Additionally, Ronan also left me in possession of a letter addressed to you, to be mailed to you wherever you were living as of today's date, being October 19th. As such, please find enclosed his correspondence as per his instructions.

I wish you all the very best in your new life with Ophelia and the children in New York, Sully. I can't say that I will ever forget the drama and the chaos that came with knowing the Fletcher family, but then again I can't say I would want to forget, either.

We may not have been able to save my dear brother-in-law that night we climbed into that boat together and rode into the unknown, my dear friend, but I consider myself lucky to have had the opportunity to weather the storm beside such a man as yourself.

My best regards,

Robert Clyde Linneman.

I unfolded the other piece of paper, holding my breath, not sure if I should even look at Sully to make sure he was okay.

Brother,

It's been my greatest honor to call you this for the past thirty-one years, even if it has been your greatest shame to acknowledge me with the same title.

I can't say I'm sorry anymore. I can't ever mean it enough, and so the word has lost its meaning to me. Instead, I write this letter to you now, knowing the circumstances under which you will receive it, with the greatest of thanks in my heart.

You always were and always will be the better man. I'm so grateful that you will be a father figure to my children. I'm so grateful that you have found happiness, too. The moment I laid eyes on Ophelia, I saw a great and beautiful love story laid out before you. I know this because I know I would have fallen in love with her, too, of course. Wasn't that always the problem? We were doomed to love the same women throughout our lives? Not this time, though. This time the happily ever after belongs to you, dear brother. At least I hope it does, anyway. Good luck to you, and to Ophelia.

Enough time has passed now that I also hope the hurt and suffering I caused you has dulled a little, and that as the coming years pass you by, you may even learn to forgive my weaknesses and my betrayal. Because my love for you is second only to the woman who died in my arms last year, Sully. Please know I would never have risked the precious bond I shared with you for anything less.

Thank you for doing what I could not, Sully.

Thank you for doing the right thing.

Your brother always,
Ronan.

I folded the paper again, taking a long moment to consider Ronan's words. He orchestrated this from the beginning? He knew Sully and I would fall in love? How could he possibly have known such a thing? But then again, perhaps he *could* see it. They had both loved Magda, after all. Perhaps Ronan knew when he met me what would transpire between his brother and I.

"Do you want to talk about it?" I asked quietly.

Sully held out his hand and took Ronan's letter from me. It was already cold in the city—a fire burned and crackled happily in the grate—and I thought for a moment that he was going to cast Ronan's letter into the fire. He didn't, though. He placed it down on the arm of the sofa and looked at it for a very long time, shadows playing and flickering across his face as he thought.

"No. No, I don't want to talk about it," he said all of a sudden, smiling at me. "I just want to feel you in my arms, Lang. That okay?"

I moved over, lying my head on his chest, listening to his heart beat slow and steady beneath my ear for a long time. Sully absentmindedly stroked his hand up and down my arm for a while, before he leaned down and kissed me.

"Are you happy?" he asked me quietly.

"Yes."

"Do you love me?" he asked.

"More than I ever thought possible."

He went quiet for a moment, then he curled his index finger underneath my chin and lifted it, so that I was looking up at him. "Do you want to spend the rest of your life me with, Lang?" His eyes searched mine, looking for something that might or might not be there. My heart slowed, barely beating at all. Was he asking me…was he asking me to *marry* him?

Carefully he reached into his pocket, hunting for something. When he removed his hand from the pocket, he had made a fist, clutching hold of something tightly in the palm of his hand.

"I was going to do this tomorrow," he said. "When we were standing underneath a giant Velociraptor skeleton with both the children watching so you couldn't say no. But I see now how that might be unkind. I don't want you to be swayed by Amie or Connor. Or an eight-billion-year-old dinosaur. I want you to make up your mind on your own, okay? So tell me, Ophelia. I need to know. Would you like to be my wife?"

I couldn't look away from him. So much had happened in the last year. It was crazy to think that Sully was this sure of us this quickly. But then again, was it really? *I* was this sure of *him*. He was all I wanted. All I was ever going to want. I placed my hand on top of his, smiling.

"I would very much like to be your wife, Sully Fletcher. I would very much like that indeed."

A blazing smile lit up Sully's face. "No bullshit?" he asked.

I grinned, incapable of keeping my happiness from my face. "No. No bullshit, Sully. No bullshit."

If you read Between Here and the Horizon and enjoyed it, you might also enjoy VICE!

In war, there are only three rules.

Obey orders.

Protect the guy standing next to you.

Stay alive.

Cade Preston left the military a long time ago, but he has never ceased to live by the laws of combat. As vice president of the Widow Makers Motorcycle club, he's been loyal. He's fought tooth and nail to stay alive. He's shed blood to save the lives of those who matter to him.

And now he's gone and done something he swore he would never do.

He's fallen for the one girl he can't have.

Cortina Villalobos is an untouchable. The daughter of one of Ecuador's most notorious cartel leaders, she is beyond Cade's reach in every way. Fernando Villalobos is a murderer and a madman. He will kill anyone who dares look twice at his daughter, and yet Cade can't walk away.

Will he disobey orders?

Will he abandon his club?

And will taking on the House of Wolves cost him his life?

Vice is a STANDALONE novel, with a complete beginning, middle and end. If you would like to read more about Cade Preston, you can find him featured in both the Blood & Roses series and the Dead Man's Ink series. However, you do NOT need to read those books in order to enjoy this one.

CALLIE'S NEWSLETTER

it's a GIVEAWAY!

As a token of her appreciation for reading and supporting her work, at the end of every month, Callie and her team will be hosting a HUGE giveaway with a mass of goodies up for grabs, including vouchers, e-readers, signed books, signed swag, author event tickets and exclusive paperback copies of stories no one else in the world will have access to!

All you need to do to automatically enter each month is be signed up to her newsletter, which you can do right here: http://eepurl.com/IzhzL

*The monthly giveaway is international. Prizes will be subject to change each month. First draw will be taking place on Nov 30 2015, and continue at the end of each month thereafter!!!

ABOUT THE AUTHOR

Callie Hart is the international bestselling author of the Blood & Roses and Dead Man's Ink series.

If you are yet to dive into either series, book one, **Deviant, is FREE** right now!

If you want to know the second one of Callie's books goes live, all you need to do is **sign up at http://eepurl.com/IzhzL**.

IN THE MEANTIME, CALLIE WANTS TO HEAR FROM YOU!

Visit Callie's website:
http://calliehart.com

Find Callie on her Facebook Page:
http://www.facebook.com/calliehartauthor

or her Facebook Profile:
http://www.facebook.com/callie.hart.777

Blog:
http://calliehart.blogspot.com.au

Twitter:
http://www.twitter.com/_callie_hart

Goodreads:
http://www.goodreads.com/author/show/7771953.Callie_Hart

Sign up for her newsletter:
http://eepurl.com/IzhzL

TELL ME YOUR FAVORITE BITS!

Don't forget! If you purchased BETWEEN HERE AND THE HORIZON and enjoyed it, then please do stop over to your online retailer of choice and let me know which were your favorite parts!

Reading reviews is the highlight of any author's day.

Made in the USA
Columbia, SC
14 February 2018